Ruth Hamilton is the bestselling author of *A Whisper to the Living, With Love From Ma Maguire, Nest of Sorrows, Billy London's Girls, Spinning Jenny, The September Starlings, A Crooked Mile, Paradise Lane, The Bells of Scotland Road, The Dream Sellers, The Corner House, Miss Honoria West, Mulligan's Yard, Saturday's Child* and *Matthew & Son*. She has become one of the north-west of England's most popular writers. Ruth Hamilton was born in Bolton which is the setting for many of her novels, and has spent most of her life in Lancashire. She now lives in Liverpool.

For more information on Ruth Hamilton and her books, see her website at: www.ruthhamilton.co.uk

Also by Ruth Hamilton

A WHISPER TO THE LIVING
WITH LOVE FROM MA MAGUIRE
NEST OF SORROWS
BILLY LONDON'S GIRLS
SPINNING JENNY
THE SEPTEMBER STARLINGS
A CROOKED MILE
PARADISE LANE
THE BELLS OF SCOTLAND ROAD
THE DREAM SELLERS
THE CORNER HOUSE
MISS HONORIA WEST
MULLIGAN'S YARD
SATURDAY'S CHILD
MATTHEW & SON

and published by Corgi Books

CHANDLERS GREEN

Ruth Hamilton

CORGI BOOKS

CHANDLERS GREEN
A CORGI BOOK : 0 552 15033 9

Originally published in Great Britain by Bantam Press,
a division of Transworld Publishers

PRINTING HISTORY
Bantam Press edition published 2003
Corgi edition published 2004

1 3 5 7 9 10 8 6 4 2

Set in 11/12pt Baskerville by
Phoenix Typesetting, Auldgirth, Dumfriesshire.

Corgi Books are published by Transworld Publishers,
61–63 Uxbridge Road, London W5 5SA,
a division of The Random House Group Ltd,
in Australia by Random House Australia (Pty) Ltd,
20 Alfred Street, Milsons Point, Sydney, NSW 2061, Australia,
in New Zealand by Random House New Zealand Ltd,
18 Poland Road, Glenfield, Auckland 10, New Zealand
and in South Africa by Random House (Pty) Ltd,
Endulini, 5a Jubilee Road, Parktown 2193, South Africa.

Printed and bound in Germany by
GGP Media, Poessneck.

Papers used by Transworld Publishers are natural, recyclable products
made from wood grown in sustainable forests. The manufacturing
processes conform to the environmental regulations of the
country of origin.

I dedicate this work to the township of Bolton, chartered in 1253 and celebrating its 750th anniversary in 2003.

Some facts about the town of which I am inordinately proud to be a daughter:

1253 – Bolton established by charter as a free borough.
1256 – Market chartered by Henry III.
1337 – Flemish yarn makers settled.
1631 – Population 500.
1641 – Grammar school founded.
1643 – Civil War – Bolton besieged with much bloodshed.
1651 – James, seventh Earl of Derby, beheaded in Churchgate.
1760 – Arkwright, founder of cotton factory system, kept a barber shop in Bolton.
1763 – Samuel Crompton, inventor of cotton mule, born in Bolton.
1763 – Cotton quilting and muslins first made in Bolton.
1791 – Canal to Bolton opened.
1828 – Bolton's first railway.
1832 – First parliamentary election – population 41,195.
1901 – Population 168,215.
2001 – Population 261,037.

The most beautiful civic buildings oversee an excellent shopping centre. I spend many a day footling about in shops, researching in the library, getting help from the *Bolton Evening News* offices.

Countryside surrounding the town remains exquisite. Visitors should go to Hall i' th' Wood, where Crompton built his mule. This house, together with Rivington Pike and surrounding lands, was bequeathed to the people of the town by Lord Leverhulme, son of a Bolton trader who, after following his father into business, went on to manufacture Sunlight Soap and many other household brands at Port Sunlight on the Wirral.

There are parks, wonderful country pubs and restaurants, there is the best jeweller north of Birmingham, there are villages where weavers' stone cottages stand row upon row with the Pennine foothills visible from their gardens. The Last Drop is a splendid place to the north, where craftsmen show their wares, and a day can be spent at an antique fair or simply wandering through the little lanes.

Sorry to sound like a travelogue – but I want to share my wonderful town with others. Perhaps I am biased, but it remains the best town I know. I have enormous respect for Liverpool, but my aim is to buy one of those weavers' cottages as a second home, because I love two places and I want to own a small slice of both.

Last, never least, I pay homage to the people of Bolton, who fed, educated and clothed me from the civic purse. I can never repay my debt to the town, but I hope the books bring back memories and encourage others to take an interest in this, the largest seat of the Industrial Revolution in the north.

Ruthie

Acknowledgements

I thank:

My family, as always, including Sam, Fudge, Geri (two labradors and one cat), and Jack and Vera, my noisy cockatiels. These are my constant companions when I write. (See – animals first, as ever).
Particular thanks to my son Michael and his partner, Lizzie. These two have borne the brunt of my journey towards correcting diabetes and I could not have managed so well without them. As they venture forward to their own life and their own home, I wish them Godspeed and much happiness together.

My new editor, Linda Evans – hope she can tolerate me as well as Diane did – and everyone at my publishing house – bless you for putting up with me.

Angela Kelly of the *Bolton Evening News* for staunch support and some laughs.

Joanna Frank, my agent.

Dorothy Ramsden, Barbara Kerks, Tess Scott for research support.

Readers, you know how grateful I am. Please continue to visit me at www.ruthhamilton.co.uk

ONE

The house was white and square, three windows across the top, two at the bottom, a large black door in the centre. Its roof was of grey-purple slate and the whole façade was covered in Virginia creeper, so pretty in the autumn, its leaves russet-coloured as they crisped their way towards the year's end.

'It's lovely.' Leena Martindale stepped back to take in the whole view, her heels suspended over the edge of a narrow pavement. 'Eeh, I never thought we'd be living in a place like this, Alf. It's like a dream come true, isn't it? Tell me I'll not wake up in a minute, love. Tell me it's real.' She would surely come to her full senses any second now, would be back in Emblem Street, mills to the left, mills to the right, chimneys belching into the sky for hours each day.

'It's real, Leena. God knows we worked long and hard enough for it. We're as good as any of them round here now, love – even yon pot-bellied bugger up at the grange. Wait till he realizes it's us, eh? That'll take the skin off his rice pudding.' Alf managed, just, not to rub his hands together in glee.

9

He had trounced Chandler for the second time and the feeling was more than good – it was glorious. There would be no beating the first occasion, of course, because that had been a show-stopper . . . No, no, he must not laugh out loud.

Leena walked forward and opened the gate. Unused to movement, the black-painted wood creaked, while its hinges screamed for oil as they dropped flakes of rust onto the weed-covered path. 'It's not been shifted in a while, this gate,' she commented as she led her husband towards their new home. She pointed to a gap in the fence. 'I reckon folk have been coming and going through that hole. Eeh, the whole place looks sad. But I don't care what state it's in, Alf. We're here. We're up on the moors and no bugger can say different.' Here, she could get better; here, her lungs would heal, would learn their full capacity all over again, no smoke, no fumes, no specks of scarlet contained within a white handkerchief.

They had bought the house unseen, had negotiated through agents and solicitors, had mentioned to no-one that they would be moving out of Bolton and up the moorlands to a village so select that it was beyond the reach of most ordinary folk. Aye, well, there'd be a few eyes wiped when the removal van arrived, because Alf and Leena Martindale were not doctors or lawyers, were not any kind of gentry, landed or otherwise; they had made their fortune through collecting rubbish thrown out by rich and poor alike. Alf, the rag-and-bone man, and Leena, the ex-char, had reached for the stars.

Proud of what they had achieved, they were nervous nevertheless, because the move felt like the biggest stride since the Eighth Army had hopped across from North Africa . . . Time froze for several seconds as the pair hovered on the brink of this new horizon, this fresh and much-needed new start.

'They won't like us,' said Leena as Alf broke the moment by turning the key in its aged lock. 'We'll be like sore thumbs.'

Alf laughed. 'He won't like it and that's for certain sure. But he can bloody whistle, because we've bought outright, our money's as good as anybody's and, on top of all that, I can't wait to see his face when he finds out.'

This was Richard Chandler's patch. He acted as lord of the manor, carried on as if he owned everything and everybody for miles around, but he seemed to have forgotten this one empty house at the edge of his principality, the property of an eccentric and housebound spinster who had faded away just weeks earlier. Alf had kept his ear to the ground for ages, had jumped in as soon as the house had become available. And now, here they were, bold as brass and ready to knock the place into shape. 'Hang on,' he said.

Leena giggled like a newly-wed when he lifted her up and carried her over the threshold. After over twenty-five years of marriage, she was not the slender maiden who had stood at the altar of Sts Peter and Paul, was no longer the shy, awkward girl from the bottom of Deane Road. As for Alf, who was nearing fifty, three decades of heavy lifting had taken its toll, so he was glad when Leena was safely deposited in the hall. 'It smells funny,' she remarked.

'Aye, that's what the surveyor said.' Alf regained his breath after a few seconds. 'Give yourself no more second helpings of black pudding in future, lass – I've lifted four-poster bedsteads lighter than you.' He inhaled. 'Dry rot,' was the pronouncement. 'Don't worry, it's all in hand.' This place would be like a little palace once the rough edges had been knocked off. Alf would make it shine, he would, bugger the cost.

At each side of the hall, a door led to twin rooms, both square, both with nice old fireplaces that screamed for a good scrubbing. Behind the room on the left there was another square area, probably the dining room, and on the opposite side a large kitchen led to a back garden of mammoth proportions. 'The jungle was thrown in with the price,' said Alf. 'It'll take an army to shift that lot. Poor old girl depended on her neighbours towards the end, and they couldn't look after her and the garden too. We'll need farm machinery to get through the weeds – we could well find half a dozen bloody lions living out there.'

But Leena was already designing her kitchen, was planning on moving the sink, arranging cupboards and shelves, was wondering whether to have a table and chairs near the window. Aye, once the garden was tidied, there'd be a cracking view from the kitchen – it would be like eating out on the lawn. French windows, perhaps? There was no house behind, just miles of open land, no-one to overlook the cottage. Cottage? Compared to their current home, this was a mansion. She gulped. It was all going to be so different, so splendid. She could see it as it would be after the work was finished, a small mansion, four bedrooms, a proper bathroom, lawns, flower beds.

'Mice,' announced Alf. 'I can smell 'em.'

'At least there's gas and electric now.' Leena was thinking about new pots and pans, nice bright curtains and a great big cooker. 'I could grow my own herbs.' Oh, she would get used to this place, all right. She pictured herself baking, crusty loaves set out on cooling racks, meat-and-potato pies, fancy cakes for the weekends. They could have family and friends round, give them a lovely treat for Christmas, carols by the fire, mince pies, a drop of port. Any minute now, she would die of happiness, because her heart was fit to burst.

They went back to the hall, ascended the stairs gingerly, aware that dry rot might cause the steps to give way at any second. They found four bedrooms and a bathroom that seemed not to have been cleaned for about half a century. The lavatory was a disgrace, filthy enough to make anyone gag, but Alf and Leena took it in their stride – as dealers in scrap and dirt, they were inured to the seamier side of life.

'It's just what I've always wanted.'

Alf agreed. 'Worth all the scrimping and saving, eh? But I still think we should keep it to ourselves. With all that wants doing, we'll not see this straight till Christmas – even then, we'll be lucky. Aye, we shall do it in style, love, no cutting corners. I've at least fifteen years' work left in me, so we'll not go short. And when them policies come in, there'll be enough for a grand retirement.'

Leena's eyes pricked. They'd never been deprived and their children had been adequately provided for, but there was no comparison between Claughton Cottage and the poky little house in Emblem Street, the place that had been their home since just before the war. So, they had

13

reached their goal. The kids were grown and educated, the worst was behind them, the best was here. What was more, this place had come cheap and, once done up, would be a fine legacy for Marie and Colin.

Alf was measuring a wall. He had seen some wardrobes in a house that wanted clearing, big, solid items with fancy handles and mirrored doors. Was there space for a four-poster? 'Yon little bedroom should do for your sewing,' he told her. He was proud of his wife; she did dressmaking, embroidery, water-colours and fancy knitting. Not many men from the bottom end could boast a wife as talented as his Leena was.

'Well, what I thought was—' Leena's words froze in her throat. 'Did you hear that?' she whispered.

'I did.' They both crept to the door. Alf put a finger to his lips. 'Shh,' he whispered.

A voice floated up the stairwell; Leena and Alf stood listening at the bedroom door.

'I've keys to most houses,' said the man. 'Of course, my family can trace its ancestry back to the fourteenth century – we believe that our name was taken from the original art of candle-making, just as Thatchers and Masons got theirs from other crafts. We owned the whole village for hundreds of years. The houses were tenanted, but my father and I sold many of them off – we are firm believers in owner-occupation. One has to move with the times, you see.'

Leena and Alf looked at each other. The enemy was below, was making the noises of battle, would have to be routed, yet Alf was suddenly apprehensive.

14

'Are these floors safe?' asked a female. 'It seems to have been rather neglected.'

'Miss Forrester was not able to look after herself for many years,' the man explained. 'She became very frail and we had to make sure that the whole village pulled its weight in caring for her. There is great camaraderie in Chandlers Green.'

Alf had taken enough and temper began to rise to the surface, bringing with it the pride he had learnt in the army, the pride that had defeated the man who was currently invading his property. Much as he would have preferred his entrance into Chandlers Green to be unannounced, Alf realized that the pair downstairs would want to see the upper floor, too, and that he and Leena would be discovered very shortly. 'Who's there?' he shouted, motioning his wife to remain where she was. He moved to the top of the stairs.

Richard Chandler arrived in the hall. 'Who are you?'

'I asked first,' answered Alf. 'What are you doing in my house?'

'Your house?' The big man's face took on a purplish hue.

'Bought and paid for through Sykes and Moorhead,' answered Alf. 'In cash, deeds in a bank vault, all done, dusted and tied up in pretty red ribbon, Dickie. All right? Is that enough information, or do you want to know what I had for my breakfast?' Mortgage-free, the proud owner of Claughton Cottage bestrode the landing, sturdy legs set wide, arms folding themselves in a gesture of triumph, eyes goading the interloper to make further comment.

Chandler's eyes narrowed. There was something familiar about the intruder's face, yet he could not quite manage to place him. 'I tend to vet the purchasers of property hereabouts,' he blustered. 'I had no idea that anyone had looked at this house—'

'Aye, well, you'd have to be up very early in the morning to beat me to it, Dickie Chandler. You don't remember me, do you? Fusiliers, saved your life, then you tried to get me court-martialled on a trumped-up charge that was overturned? Come on, lad, think back. You left the regiment with your head bowed, didn't you, eh? And I was the one who got the medals.' Momentarily ashamed, Alf wished that he had not bragged about his decorations, but the words were out, had reached the ears of his foe.

Richard Chandler staggered back, his involuntary progress impeded only by a noisy collision with the closed front door.

'Don't be banging into any of Miss Forrester's effects,' said Alf calmly, 'only her nephew sold it all, lock, stock and pepper pot. I shall be having the place gutted, of course. Chandlers Green isn't what it was, is it? Never thought I'd see the day when a lowlife like me could buy into it.' *Go on,* he urged inwardly, *do us all a favour and have the bloody stroke you deserve, you bad bastard.*

Richard Chandler was having trouble with his breathing. His companion, clearly disturbed and embarrassed by the exchange, walked into one of the living rooms and closed the door. Leena, also a reluctant ear-witness, tried not to breathe at all as she stayed well out of view. This was the last thing she had anticipated; oh, it would have happened eventually, but she had wanted the house right and

16

occupied first. This way, she felt that Alf was at a disadvantage, because the house was like the wreck of the *Hesperus* and neither Martindale had got dressed up to visit this dilapidated place.

Good God. Chandler righted himself with difficulty. Here stood his Nemesis, Sergeant Alfred Martindale, the man who had stolen everything from him, who had left him bloody, bowed and disgraced in the eyes of his fellow officers – how the hell had the man managed this coup? 'Sykes and Moorhead should have kept me advised in the matter,' he said. 'I am always informed about what is to happen in this village.'

Alf exhaled slowly before framing his reply. 'Sykes and Moorhead did the best for their client, which is what they get paid for. This is 1960, you know, not the Dark Ages. Life's a free-for-all now, never mind them who thinks they're better than the rest of us. I worked for this place, I earned it. I didn't sit on my arse while my dad paid my bills.' And that was another thing. 'Your father still owns yon land.' Alf jerked a thumb over his shoulder. 'But you keep him locked up, don't you? Aye, we've all heard.'

Richard Chandler shivered involuntarily. With the deeds in the bank, house bought and paid for, what was to be done? 'If it takes me the rest of my life, Martindale, I shall make sure you live to regret this day.' These words were delivered in a tone that was quiet, but menacing.

'Why? Did you feel safe while I was down in Bolton? And are you threatening me? Because I've a witness in a bedroom here, Mr Chandler, a chap measuring up for wardrobes. Shall I get him to write down six feet by four with a tall lid to fit over that

17

paunch of yours? So we can bury you? Full military honours, of course.'

Richard Chandler had taken enough. He fetched his prospective purchaser from the living room and led her outside.

'The key,' called Alf just before the door closed. 'And if owt happens to this place, like spontaneous combustion or flooding, I shall know who to blame.'

The door slammed, then the key clattered through the letter box.

'I'll get the locks changed tomorrow,' Alf told his wife. 'I wouldn't put it past him to have copies of every bloody key in this village. I hope other folk have had the sense to make themselves safe from him. He can't go marching about as if he owns the whole flaming world, Leena.'

Leena sank onto the top stair. 'Have we done right, love?'

'Course we have. It's nice up here, fresh air, lovely views, places where we can walk without ever seeing a factory chimney. All my life, this is what I've wanted.'

'Because of him? Has it all been to get your own back?'

Alf sat beside his wife and placed an arm across her shoulders. 'No, it's been about you, love, especially since you had the TB. Me and our Marie and our Colin – we thought we were losing you when you went up to that open-air hospital. What's the point of them policies, eh? What use would they be if you died from breathing in the filth we get down yon? It's all settled. This is a high-up place in more ways than one, a decent village with good air and a chance for you to grow strong.'

'I am strong. We could have gone to Bromley Cross or Edgworth.'

'This is higher.'

. 'This is where you can rub his nose in his own mess, too.'

He paused before answering. 'Aye, happen there's summat in what you say, Leena. But we've done it now. If you like, I'll smarten the place up and sell it on, then we can get somewhere else nice. Whatever you want, love.'

She pondered for a few seconds. 'I'd like to live in this house. It's as if I can feel her here, as if she wants me to take over.'

'Who?'

'Miss Forrester, you daft lummox. Keep her clock. I feel as though we should start it up again – I'm sure she'd like that.'

'Still a romantic, eh?'

She nudged him with her elbow. 'Take me home, lad. I'm starving – I could do murder twice over for a toasted teacake.'

Number 34 Emblem Street managed to be a cut above its neighbours. There was no undue pride attributed to its occupants, but the Martindales lived well, kept their house in good order and obviously had a few bob tucked away. This situation was accepted with equanimity by the neighbours, because Leena and Alf Martindale had never feared hard work, had not carried on as if they felt better than the rest.

Marie Martindale, a lively and pretty girl in her early twenties, remained at home with her parents. She had her fair share of followers, but no-one had taken her fancy thus far and she often declared herself to be 'on the warpath' whenever she went out with her friends. Educated at the Catholic grammar school, she was a good all-rounder with no particular interest in academia, though she held down a decent job as a legal secretary and was generally considered to be a competent employee.

Her mam and dad were up to something. They had rattled off in the van straight after dinner and Mam's face had been flushed. It hadn't been that TB flush, the horrible harbinger that had appeared a few years ago just before the diagnosis. Oh, no, Leena Martindale was up to something, as was her husband. There'd been a fair amount of electricity in the air for a few weeks; many a time, Marie had felt words hanging in the air, sentences curtailed when she or her visiting brother had entered the room.

She dragged a hasty comb through her dark blond hair and prepared to nip next door. It was time to have a conflab with Mam's best friend, Elsie Ramsden. Elsie was clever enough, but she sometimes let the odd thing slip when her tongue wandered off on its own. Bert Ramsden, husband of the good woman, had been heard to say that Elsie's gob should be kept on a lead and have a licence propped behind the clock, but that was Bert all over.

Marie pushed open the door of number 32. 'Hello?' she called. 'Anybody in?'

'I'm in,' shouted Elsie. 'I'm ironing. I've been ironing since the relief of flaming Mafeking – that's how it feels, any road.'

Marie walked down the narrow hall and entered the kitchen. 'Shall I do a bit for you? Only I've got today off, so I'm at a loose end. Mam and Dad have gone off somewhere secret.'

Elsie pushed a hand through greying brown hair. 'Secret? Alf and Leena don't have secrets. Your mam couldn't keep a secret if you put her behind lock and key and Elastoplasted her gob. Here, love, do this couple of shirts while I make a brew. I'm exhaustificated.'

Marie picked up the iron and tackled a collar. 'They've gone funny,' she said. 'They talk about something, then they stop.'

Elsie paused, two cups in her hands. 'Everybody talks and stops. Even I stop. Mind, Bert says I don't, but I do.' She plonked the cups on the table, found milk and sugar, emptied some biscuits onto a plate. 'She's not ill again, is she?'

'I don't think so. But she's . . . she's concentrating. So's my dad. And she's stopped sewing and she's done no knitting for a while.'

Tea forgotten, Elsie sat down, pulled half a Woodbine from behind an ear and set light to it. 'Happen it's the change of life.'

Marie shook her head. 'She's finished with all that, it stopped all of a sudden when she had the TB. And what about Dad? Men don't get a change of life, do they?'

'Well, I think they do. And if they don't, they should. Aye, I think my Bert's changed, and I'd change him again if I could. Only I wouldn't be able to make me mind up, Marie. I'd change him for Fred Astaire or Gregory Peck – Fred's got the feet and Greg's got the looks and the beef. We need two husbands, really – one for jobs around the house and the other for the dance hall.'

21

Marie laughed.

'But they do go funny, just like women do. They start thinking. You can tell when they're thinking, 'cos there's a funny noise, a bit like an engine what needs oil. They sit in corners and brood. Does your dad do that?'

'No, he does sums on bits of paper.'

'Does he? That sounds a bit dangerous, Marie. He'll be getting his brain all overheated if he does sums. Mind, they're all right working out the horses or the dogs – give them the odds and they'll tell you the exact winnings, plus what colour the animal is and what it's had for its breakfast.'

Marie grinned. Elsie Ramsden had been a part of her existence for ever. Life without Elsie would have been Blackpool without sand, chips with no vinegar, King Lear without his Fool. She turned the shirt and attacked the back. 'Weren't you making tea, Elsie?'

'Ooh, yes. Good job me head's stuck to me body, else I'd be leaving it in the Co-op.' She jumped up and got on with the task of tea-making. As she scalded the pot, she considered what Marie had just said. When she came to think about it, there had been something bubbling next door, a damped-down excitement, a glazed expression on Leena's face when she had been hanging her washing out in the back street.

'Sit down,' she told Marie when the tea was brewed. She poured, added milk, passed the sugar bowl to her young neighbour. 'You still not courting?'

'No.'

'What's the matter with you?'

Marie shrugged. 'I can't be bothered. They either

22

want your knickers off or they're too drunk to remember what knickers are. I still knock about with Josie Maguire and Aggie Turner. They're like me – they're still looking for somebody with brains and looks. Aggie had a fling with a librarian, but she felt as if he wanted to return her within the fortnight, so she gave him up as a bad job before she got stamped and listed as overdue.'

'Shame,' said Elsie before guffawing. 'So, what the hell's your mother up to? Do you want me to ask her? I have a way of making folk talk when I set my mind to it.'

Marie shook her head. 'No. I've a feeling it's one of those things she'll announce all of a sudden when she's ready. I just thought you might have known something, that's all. Best leave them, Elsie, let them play their little games. It's very hard rearing parents in this day and age. Something to do with the war, I'll bet. Their emotional development got arrested by Hitler. I think I'll sue Germany.'

Elsie glanced up at a photograph on the mantelpiece, an enlarged black-and-white picture of a very young man in RAF uniform.

'I'm sorry, Elsie,' said Marie, 'I never thought.'

Elsie bit down on a digestive. She was very proud of their Brian, a grand boy who had gone down in the Battle of Britain, one of many lads from hereabouts who had never returned when the mess had ended. 'It's all right, love. I'm used to it.'

'I wish you hadn't had to get used to it, Elsie.'

'So do I. The worst thing is him not having a grave. When folk go over to cemeteries in Italy and France, when they get the chance to stand there and pray, put flowers on a grave – eeh, I do envy them. Mavis

23

Liptrott from John Street took some soil across and put it on their Ian's plot in Florence – a bit of England. But there were nowt left of our Brian.'

Marie felt like biting off her own tongue. Elsie was supposed to be the one with the runaway mouth, yet this wasn't her fault, it was Marie's doing. She reached across and held Elsie's hand. 'Remember when I used to call you Auntie Elthie? When I had that lithp?'

'Aye, I do.'

'Well, you're thtill my Auntie Elthie. And you alwayth will be.'

'I know, love. Finish them shirts, will you? Me feet feel like they've been in the oven half the morning, nicely risen and ready for butter and jam. Hey, and if you find out what Leena and Alf are up to, give us the nod. It might be a bank job. If it is, make them leave the Trustee alone – my bit of money's in yon.'

Marie finished the ironing while Elsie ran through a list of her husband's escapades on the building site, then she kissed her on the cheek and went home. The house was still empty and Marie remained absolutely certain that her truanting parents were up to no good.

Richard Chandler stamped his way up the path to Chandlers Grange. He felt as if he had been kicked all over, stuffing gone, bones turned to jelly, a headache like a spinning jenny grinding loudly above his eyes. Alfred Martindale, hero, had pulled the rug yet again from beneath the feet of his betters. Well, something had to be done.

He clattered through the vast hallway, threw his walking stick onto a central table and marched up the curving stairway. He couldn't even talk about it, had no wish to remind others of events from more than fifteen years ago. Oh, he had explained it all away, had given an adequate account of himself, but here came the living ghost to haunt him all over again.

In his room, he sank onto a chair in front of his writing bureau, elbows on the blotter, head in hands. He closed his eyes, was back in France, blood and sweat everywhere, that searing pain when the bullet sank its nose into soft flesh, the impact as his body folded to the ground. Along came Alfred Martindale, blood on his own face from a flesh wound—

The bedroom door opened. 'Richard? Would you like—'

'Out!' he roared.

The door closed.

He was carried by Martindale, was left in a bush, lay there with his eyes fixed on his saviour. Martindale abandoned him there and ran off, not towards the sound of battle, but away, back to where he had found Richard. Coward. Bloody yellow-belly, trying to save himself and bugger his fellows.

From his hospital cot, Major Chandler had accused Martindale of desertion. The latter had said nothing in his own defence and had been contained in a prefabricated hut pending hearing.

God. Richard Chandler opened his eyes, saw the scenario, entered it again. Captain George Fenner came into the tent, was sitting in a wheelchair, a medic pushing him along. Captain George Fenner was never to walk again, but he had walked all over Major Richard Chandler. Sergeant Martindale had not deserted; he had gone back for this second wounded officer, had shifted the major first, had assessed that of the two officers Chandler had been

25

the less seriously wounded, so, trained to save the saveable, had rescued him first.

Once Major Chandler had been settled under cover, Alfred Martindale had returned to the scene and had carried the captain's broken body for over half a mile. In a coma for days, Captain Fenner had recovered against all odds and had come forward in great pain to speak the truth.

'Damn him, too,' spat Richard.

Oh, the praise that had been heaped on Sergeant Martindale, such an intelligent soldier, should have a commission, would certainly be awarded medals. Victoria Cross, no less.

'While I got a rollocking.' He leaned back in the chair. The cracks had all been papered over, of course, but the stalwart silence of the accused had stood him in good stead, while Richard Chandler had been avoided after that, had suffered a loss of respect from his fellow officers and from the ranks below him.

The man had saved his life and would never be forgiven for that. If it had been somebody else – anybody else – but no, that cocky-yet-quiet fusilier had taken the curtain call, had been cheered, decorated, had even received the Bar for saving the life of Captain Fenner. An accidental hero, a conscript too sure of himself, Alfred Martindale had now planted himself on land that was sacred to the Chandler clan.

Something had to be done. What, though? If only Miss Forrester's nephew had come to him for advice before putting Claughton Cottage on the market – damn. But the nephew had operated from a distance, did not live in the north, had gone straight to the estate agent.

He looked up at a painting on the wall above his bureau, an oil executed at least three hundred years ago, the stone-built factory in which his ancestors had created candles for churches, for palaces and for ordinary homes. What was left now? Just the grange, a handful of cottages, a few hundred acres of land. And the family. The family? Father, confined to his room due to frailty, had become senile, had developed the unseemly habit of trying to force his feeble flesh on anyone who happened to be female. Richard squirmed when he thought of Father; but the right thing had been done, because the old man could no longer hold the reins – yes, yes, getting rid of Father had been justifiable.

Then the wife, the children – best not to think about them, either. If he thought long and hard enough about Jean, he was likely to run round in circles until he dropped dead. Jean, the fragrant one who had put her head round his door a few minutes ago, Jean the expensive one who spent a fortune on clothes, shoes, jewellery and make-up, Jean whom he disliked to the point where he would have paid somebody to run off with her. Who would want her, though? She had the brains of an oyster, yet sense enough to keep the pearl.

Someone tapped at the door.

'Come,' he bellowed.

And in she came, the blue-eyed girl, yesterday's news, face caked in powder, mouth set in downturned and petulant mode, hair in the daytime ponytail that was far too young for her. She looked at him, was clearly trying to assess his mood, though she had not the brain required. 'An invitation from Dr Beddows,' she said, 'a drinks party on Friday – would you like to go?'

'I shall go,' he replied. 'Anything else?'

She was hovering like a dragonfly, seemed unsure of where to land. 'Are you all right, Richard?'

'I am absolutely spiffing,' he answered, 'never better, in the pink, like a dog with two tails. I am in a state of rapture.'

Jean Chandler frowned. He was being sarcastic again and she had never got used to this mood of his. Why couldn't he answer questions properly, directly and truthfully? She didn't ask him to love her, she had given up on that years ago; but surely he could manage civility? 'Very well, I shall let them know.' No, she didn't want the love of this creature.

'Do that.'

She turned to leave.

'Then get to town and have that ridiculous hair cut. You will never be seventeen again, so try a more dignified look.'

Jean paused in the doorway. The fat pig was mocking her. She wanted to scream, needed to tell him how ugly he was, but she dared not. All the hair-cuts in the world would never improve him, bloated monster that he was becoming. Too fond of his food and drink, he was as hideous as mortal sin. 'I put my hair up in the evenings,' she said sweetly, 'but I shall certainly give some thought to your kind suggestion, Richard.' She closed the door.

Out on the landing, she paused to catch her breath. For the sake of her children and for the sake of the staff, Jean Chandler kept her feelings inside. But they grew like cancer, collected in a solid mass that was becoming difficult to contain. Only one person knew how she truly felt; it was to that person she ran when her breath returned. Nanny Foster would soothe the wounds.

Sally Foster was making cakes. Wrapped in a pristine white apron and with a streak of flour on her right cheek, she pushed the tray into the oven, then set the kettle to boil. It was going to be one of those days; she had heard him coming in, had flinched when his stick had hit the table. The table was worth a small fortune, while he, self-appointed monarch of all he surveyed, was worth nowt a pound.

She picked up mixing bowl and spoons, set them to soak. Mrs Jean, all excited because of an invitation, had gone upstairs to talk to him. Sally judged that her mistress would arrive in the kitchen within the next thirty seconds. There would have been a minute to tell him, a minute of insults, another minute on the landing waiting for the upset to die down. Aye, any second now, Mrs Jean would run into the kitchen.

Sally had been with the Chandlers for many years. Originally nanny to the children, she was now responsible for the running of the household and had grown very close to the mistress of Chandlers Grange. That daft swine upstairs considered his wife to be stupid, but Sally Foster knew differently. Mrs Jean had kept herself out of harm's way by acting in a childlike fashion. In real terms, she owned twice the brainpower of the dolt she had married.

As Sally had predicted, Jean Chandler flounced into the room and threw herself into one of the chairs at the scrubbed table. 'One of his moods,' she said.

'Well, I warned you, Mrs Jean. He came back earlier on in a temper that could have ruptured an artery – banging about like a mad thing, stamping up the stairs – he sounded like an army on his own. All we needed was a couple of drums and a bugle.'

'I hate him.'

'Don't waste your hate on him, Mrs Jean. He's not worth the effort. See, if you let him know he's getting to you, he'll go even worse. All cowards are like that – they're bullies, every one of them. Just stop setting yourself up as a target.'

Jean sniffed. 'Never mind. Let's hope he goes round to Polly Fishwick's house – let her take the brunt of it. At least I have had my bedroom to myself since he started to associate with her. I couldn't bear him to come near me again, Sally. I think I would kill him if he touched me.'

The housekeeper frowned. 'Pol's no fool, you know. If he goes too far with her, she'll likely clout him with the poker. That was why her husband left home – he couldn't manage her temper. Crowned him with her frying pan, she did, hit him so hard that she had to buy a new pan. She's kept the old one, though, has it hung up like an ornament, like a medal she's won.'

Jean felt the bubble rising in her throat. The image of Richard Chandler being assaulted by his very large and extremely energetic mistress proved too much to bear. When her giggles had died down, she spoke again. 'Polly is living there rent-free – she'd be homeless if she attacked him.'

Sally smiled broadly. 'Homeless or a heroine – depends how hard she hits him, eh? She's big enough to bury him, that's for certain sure. Aye, if she did him in, I reckon you'd let her stay there for ever, eh? For services rendered.'

'I'd give her a gold clock, Sally.'

'No, she'd sooner have fish and chips. Come on, cheer up, there's worse things happen at sea. Would you like a cup of Earl Grey and a nice scone? Eh? Or something stronger, a nip of brandy?'

'Just the tea, thanks, Sally. I don't know what I would do without you.'

Sally Foster felt the burden acutely. She was unquestioningly loyal to Mrs Jean, but she wished that others might share the responsibility. The Chandlers enjoyed a large circle of acquaintances, yet no-one save Sally was aware of the state of their marriage. He was seldom pleasant to anyone, so Richard Chandler's attitude towards his wife was never remarked upon. But here, in his own home, his cruelty was such that Sally sometimes worried for the dear woman's sanity. 'I wish you'd leave him,' she whispered.

'Nowhere to go,' came the weary answer, 'nowhere to go, Sally.'

Polly Fishwick, a woman of considerable size, retained much of the prettiness she had displayed in youth. With black hair that now required assistance to retain its raven sheen, she was blue-eyed and even-featured, though her temper did not reflect the regularity of her facial arrangement. Her husband, a woodsman who had been in the employ of Richard Chandler, had abandoned her after a concussion had laid him low for several days.

She was washing dishes at the kitchen sink, a slight smile playing on her lips as she glanced at the pan hanging to the left of her window. Dented to the point of malformation, this was the instrument with which she had inflicted injury on Derek. She kept it as a trophy, was proud of her power, was relieved to have rid herself of the lily-livered man.

The row had been about Chandler, of course. Tired of his insipid wife, he had sought solace in the company of Polly, whose cottage, at the edge of the woods, was isolated. The day of reckoning had arrived, inevitably, and the frying pan had borne the brunt of it. Ah, well, she was comfortable, nothing was expected of her and the job was a doddle. As for the frying pan – that had been easily replaced at the village store.

The back door crashed inward. 'Pol?'

'Hello, Richard. I wasn't expecting you just yet, would have had a bath if I'd known you were coming this afternoon.' She dried her hands. 'Richard?'

'I just want to sit down.' He walked through to the front room and parked himself in an easy chair that was rather less than clean. Pol was a woman with a generous nature, but she did tend to stint on her housework. Still, he could sit here without catching sight of Jean and without coming under the baleful gaze of Sally Foster, the witch who ran the household.

Pol joined him. Sensible enough to know when to keep her mouth shut, she stretched herself out and toasted her toes at the fire. With the big man, it had to be a case of softly, softly, because she depended on him completely for shelter, food and clothing. He was seething. She could tell from his colour and by the expression on his face that something had upset him. In fact, he looked more than upset – the man was clearly furious.

He raised his head and looked at her. 'Sometimes, Pol, life gets too much. Do you know what I mean?'

She didn't. 'Oh, yes, I've been fed up many a time meself. You get so as there's no reason to carry on, don't you?'

'Oh no, not me. I get to the point where I wonder why other people carry on. There are two kinds of people in this world – my kind and the wrong kind.'

'Which am I?'

He raised his eyebrows, studied her for a few beats of time. 'Neither. You just fitted me for a while, Pol, like a jersey I felt comfortable in. But everything has to come to an end.'

She swallowed audibly. Had he found someone else willing to lie beneath that horrible, big belly? Someone else who was content to service him in any way that took his fancy? Richard Chandler enjoyed the unusual, the devious, needed the kind of services that were usually obtainable only from street girls. 'Why?' she managed finally.

'Because you are going to become something else, Pol. For a start, you will be working at the grange – I want you to keep an eye on Sally Foster, because I believe she is leading my wife astray.'

Work? Pol had not worked since girlhood, had been kept by her husband, then by the ugly creature who sat opposite her. She didn't fancy being a servant, didn't like the idea of becoming answerable to Sally Foster or Jean Chandler.

'There's something else,' he said.

Nor did she relish the idea of homelessness . . .

'I want you to befriend somebody. You must be open about your relationship with me, must say that I dropped you then forced you to work as a servant

33

in my house. Call me all the names you like. I shall keep you well provided for. Do you understand me, Polly?'

She nodded.

'Remember Miss Forrester?'

'Yes. Other end of the village, Claughton Cottage – didn't she die?'

'She did. And the house has been bought by somebody I don't like. In a couple of months, they will move into my village – this will be the first time a house has been sold without the involvement and approval of the Chandler family. I want them out within six months.'

Polly frowned. 'But–'

'Don't ask, because I've no idea, no plan just yet. Now, many people know about me and you, so you must make public my ill-treatment of you – tell everyone that I have taken your home away, that I have forced you to live in a garret at the grange. Hate me. Can you do that?'

Again, she nodded mutely.

'That will be useful in both places. Your presence at the grange will confuse my wife, may even unhinge her. Befriend Sally Foster, befriend my wife. Then, when the Martindales come to Chandlers Green, make a play for them, too. Find out everything you can about them, make notes, tell me everything.'

A garret? Polly Fishwick liked her own company, didn't fancy sharing a house, no matter what its size. 'Who are these Martindales?'

'Jumped-up scrap merchants,' he answered snappily. 'They'll tell you soon enough what they think of me, a load of lies and nonsense. Now, look at me.'

She obeyed, just as she always had where the big fellow was concerned.

'You'll have a bank account. I shall open it for you at the Trustee in Bolton and you will keep the book between deposits. Don't tell a soul.'

'All right.'

He sighed, allowed some of the tension to leave his body. 'Right,' he ordered, 'come here, just once more for old times' sake.' His eyes glinted as he ordered her onto her knees. This was a useful woman and he intended to keep her under his control.

TWO

Anna Chandler, seventy-four years old and as thin as a rake, stood at the window of the gatehouse. Here she had moved when life with her nephew had become unbearable; here she lived in solitude save for the company of some two dozen chickens, a few hives of bees and a couple of geese whose temperament was as uncertain as Richard's.

She rolled a cigarette between expert fingers and watched the dolt as he rushed past the gatehouse – bound for that slattern's cottage, no doubt. She lit her hand-rolled indulgence and sank into an old chair. He wanted killing. He wanted a damned good hiding first, then a knife in his heart. 'Bugger,' she whispered. 'Damned cruel, merciless creature.' One day, someone would finish him off. But what could she do about him? Nothing at all. So she had walked away, had left poor Jean, Sally and the three children to endure the unendurable.

There was work to do. Wreathed in smoke, as ever, the spinster sister of Henry Chandler planned her day. The bees, drowsy now at the end of summer, were disappearing fast, would be choosing their queen for next season. But there were chickens to feed, eggs to collect, chores to be done. And there was the book to be finished, too.

The writing of *A History of Candle-Making* had become Anna's reason for living. Oh, the bees and chickens provided an occupation, but her fascination with chandlery was almost an obsession. Apart from the church, this was the old lady's focus, the fulcrum of her existence. But, as she studied today, her eye was drawn continually to the ruined factory behind her little house, that stone-built edifice in which hundreds of people had toiled through the centuries, slaves to wax and tallow, slaves to her own arrogant family. It was crumbling now, was disappearing into the ground from which its components had originally been culled. 'And unto dust thou shalt return,' she whispered.

She tapped her teeth with a pen, finished her smoke and ground its remnants into an ashtray. The reins of the diminishing Chandler fortune now rested in the hands of Richard Chandler. Henry was locked away in an upper room of the grange and no-one was allowed to visit him. Her blundering nephew, currently ensconced with his slovenly mistress in Woodside Cottage, was at the helm. 'God rest all who sail and drown,' muttered Anna. It was no use, she could not work. Sighing deeply, she scribbled a few more hasty notes. Tomorrow. She would start again tomorrow . . .

Life for Meredith, Jeremy and Peter Chandler had been reasonably sweet thus far. With a mother who doted on them and a father who ignored them, this happy band had found themselves free to come and go as they pleased during childhood; little was expected of them and each was surprised when, in their early twenties, they began to examine the fruitlessness of their lives. There were country walks, there was riding and driving, there were dances in Bolton. But they required something more, a sense of direction, a reason to get out of bed in the mornings.

They sat in a barn at the back of the grange, Meredith on a bale, the boys perched on upturned boxes. Meredith, at twenty-three, was the eldest of the batch. An elegant girl with average looks, she was restless and had infected her brothers with her sudden need for fulfilment. Jeremy and Peter, twin boys who were just a year younger than their sister, had always done everything together. Where one went, the other was close behind, and, as both depended greatly on the common sense of their sister, this meeting was important to all.

'What can we do?' asked Meredith. 'We all had a good education, and although none of us fancied university we do have brains. I can't speak for you two, but I am just about sick and tired of this life of idleness.'

The twin boys nodded in unison. Apart from some work around the estate and at a local stables, they had not yet been gainfully employed, because Father had plans for them. No Chandler had yet attended university, and the bee in Father's bonnet was that he would break the mould, would send *his* boys into professions . . .

'We need a project,' declared Meredith, 'a future, something to occupy us. I am fed up with the country set and sick of Father. Mother droops around like a

38

woman in decline, Father treats her like a dog – I can't carry on here, boys. So. Any ideas?'

Jeremy, who had wanted to be a pilot, a train driver, a policeman and a jockey, could think of nothing mundane enough to be realistic. Peter, who had shared the dreams of his sibling, was similarly unaware of anything sufficiently practical to warrant suggestion. Merry would lead the way; Merry had always been the prow of the ship. Both boys stared expectantly at their sister.

'God,' she declared, exasperation clear in her tone, 'has no-one else been blessed with a bit of imagination? Why am I always the one who makes decisions? If I suggested that we all become mountaineers, would you go out and buy boots and ropes?' She jumped to her feet. 'Well, I vote we all go away and think about this. What do we want to do, where and when?'

'We all ride well.' Peter's voice was hesitant; thus far, nothing had ever been expected of him, so he did not value his own notions.

'Good point,' said Meredith, 'that's the sort of thing we want, Peter, ideas, stuff we can kick around. Now, I think that's a good concept, but we could well find ourselves stuck with the country set, crowds of spoilt infants whose mummies want rosettes on the walls at home.'

Peter pretended to shiver. 'Brats,' he declared. 'I remember brats, because I grew up with two.'

'So did I,' chorused the others.

Meredith laughed. 'I thought of an absolute hoot, but I don't know whether we should take it seriously.'

'Go on,' begged Jeremy, 'spit it out.'

Merry grinned broadly, giving birth to a pair of

deep dimples in her cheeks. 'A chandlery,' she said. 'Can't you see it? Chandler's the Chandlers? Only it wouldn't be just your usual ironmonger's shop – it would be fancy goods, too.'

'Mother would die and spin in her grave,' laughed Peter. 'And Father would have a stroke. Still, it would put them both out of their misery. But remember, there's already a general store here. We would be *de trop*, I fear.'

'That's the whole point,' declared Meredith. 'We wouldn't be here, we'd be in the town. Candles are on their way back, you know. People shied away from them until recently, because buying them might have reminded them of the days before electricity. But everyone likes supper by candlelight. We could sell candelabra, too, tableware and so forth.' She warmed to her subject. 'Great-Aunt Anna – look at all she knows. She could advise us. She is an expert in candles.'

The boys laughed mirthlessly. Great-Aunt Anna spoke seldom and was regarded as a total eccentric. Unlike Richard, she did not carry on as if she owned the village – no, the old woman thought she owned the church and any poor incumbent who preached in it. She did the flower-arranging, attended every service, lectured bell-ringers about their timing, mended hymnals, chided choirboys, organized cleaning rotas, but had little to offer in the area of general conversation.

'And what else should we sell in this shop of yours?' Peter asked.

'Everything else – bowls and buckets, teacups and clothes-pegs, bleach and boot polish – an everything shop. That's what chandlers generally do these days.'

Jeremy frowned. 'Mater and Pater would raise Cain – Abel, too. They wouldn't want us in trade, would they? Dad is still trying to guide Peter and me towards university; as for you, Merry, I think you are expected to marry well.' His tone was grim.

She groaned. 'Exactly. The Dark Ages all over again – sell your daughters to the highest bidder. He wants you two to train for something specific and respectable – medicine, architecture, law – but do you have the brains or the inclination? Frankly, you have some of the former and none of the latter. We need to do something, boys. So get the thinking caps on. Come along, now, we have the delightful prospect of lunch in ten minutes.'

The boys sighed. Meals with their parents were like post-funeral wakes, silent except for the sound of cutlery against plates. Dad sat at one end of the table and ate enough for a platoon; Mother occupied the opposite seat and consumed very little. All three offspring had decided some time ago that Mother probably ate in the kitchen with Sally Foster.

They walked reluctantly back to the house, each trying to imagine a future away from Chandlers Grange, each coveting a different way of life. They washed their hands, then went to wait dutifully for their parents, Jeremy and Peter at one side of the dining table, Meredith at the other.

Jean was the first to arrive. She planted a kiss on the forehead of each of her children, then took up her position at the far end of the room. Nothing was said as the family sat and waited for its head of table to put in an appearance. Sally Foster, with the assistance of a village girl, brought in the food and placed it on the white linen cloth.

'Thank you,' said Jean softly.

In came the master, watch in his hand, eyes straying to the mantel clock so that he might synchronize the two pieces. The girl doled out chicken soup, then left the room, closing the door noiselessly in her wake. The younger members of the family began to eat, because there was nothing else to do. Table chatter had ended with their childhood, so eating was an activity that broke the boredom.

Richard cleared his throat. 'Nanny Foster is getting rather old to run a household of this size,' he declared, 'so I have employed a resident maid to assist her.'

Jean's spoon clattered into its dish. He didn't give a damn about Sally, would not have noticed had she been at death's door. And he never spoke at meals except when visitors were present. What was he thinking of now? She shivered as her eyes met his. There was a gleam in his expression, a devilment that made her blood run cold.

Richard enjoyed his moment, made it stretch right through the first course, did not speak again until his spoon rested in its empty soup dish. 'Polly Fishwick will be moving in,' he said. 'With her husband gone, she is in an isolated location. He was a good employee until his accident—'

'She almost killed him,' interjected Meredith. One glance at her father's expression was sufficient to silence her for the moment, though she was sorely tempted to berate him.

Richard continued as if nothing had been said. '— so I have not charged rent since he left her. However, that situation cannot continue, so I intend to reclaim the cottage and install Polly here. She will manage

Father. Having to employ male staff to tend him is a nuisance – Polly will take none of his nonsense.'

Jean lowered her head, raised it again. 'I suggest you make sure that she takes no frying pans into your father's room, dear, or he might well meet his Maker within a very short time.' She rose from her seat. 'If you will excuse me, I find myself without appetite today.' With feet that felt as heavy as lead, she left the room.

Richard Chandler apportioned to himself a huge amount of lunch, attacking it with gusto once his large plate was full. The little scene had made him hungry, had caused the juices to spring into his mouth. Jean was upset and that was a wonderful bonus.

Meredith, furious with her father, angry with her mother for being so easily unseated by this buffoon, took the almost unprecedented decision to speak again. 'We, too, have news, Father.' She averted her gaze from her brothers' faces, could not bear to witness the fear in their eyes. 'We intend to start a business in town,' she said, pleased to note that her father's eating slowed, that he was even chewing the food before gulping it down. She actually managed to smile at him, though her eyes remained cold.

'What?' He dropped his cutlery. 'No chance of that,' he roared. 'These boys want a profession. They have dabbled about for long enough and they need to get off to university.'

'No, they don't.'

Richard's face took on a purple hue that was becoming more familiar with each passing day. Meredith met his angry eyes levelly, wondered idly whether her male parent was heading for a stroke of some kind. 'A shop, we thought. Perhaps

43

a chandlery – it would match the name, after all.'

'Never,' roared Richard Chandler. 'Over my dead body.'

Meredith wondered whether that might be arranged. In this moment, she realized how much she loathed and despised the man who had caused her conception. Her thoughts danced backwards in time to childhood and she remembered how he had played with her and the boys, cricket in the garden, riding begun on small ponies, croquet once the three siblings had grown strong enough to wield a mallet. Now, he was as much fun as a dead fish.

He turned his fury on his sons. 'You will not serve in any shop.'

Peter and Jeremy were frozen, two rabbits caught in the glare of bright light, nowhere to run, no place in which they might conceal themselves.

Meredith forced herself to continue eating, though each morsel dropped into her stomach like a stone hitting concrete. 'We are of age, Father,' she said calmly, 'and we shall do as we please.'

'You will do as you are told!' shouted Richard. 'No son of mine will serve the public. Why do you think I went to the expense of private education? So that my children could sell pots and pans?'

She shrugged lightly. 'It is of no consequence,' she said, 'because we have our own money, the bequest from our grandmother.' Again, Meredith awarded her full attention to her father. 'You will not stop me,' she warned. 'The boys can do as they please, but you will never break me.' There, it was out. The lines of battle had been drawn at last. It had taken many years, but Meredith Chandler had finally managed to speak her mind.

'Leave the table,' ordered Richard.

'Gladly.' She placed her napkin on a side plate, lined up her cutlery next to her unfinished food, then rose very slowly to her feet. It had to be said and it had to come from her, because she was the one who had inherited this man's temper and stubborn nature. 'You have broken our mother,' she said, her tone ominously quiet. 'You are quite the nastiest man I have ever met. I loathe you, absolutely and utterly. But, here's the rub, Father dear. You cannot reach me. You cannot manage me. I am Great-Aunt Anna all over again, because you cannot destroy me as you destroyed Mother. As far as I am concerned, you are a creature of no consequence whatsoever.'

Peter and Jeremy gasped in unison.

The man at the head of the table sat open-mouthed, a spot of gravy dribbling its way down his chin. Had she really said all that? Was his daughter so far beyond redemption that she could attack the hand that had fed, clothed and educated her?

Meredith addressed her brothers. 'I shall not sit at this table again, boys. You may do as you please, but I refuse to break bread with that dreadful man.' On this note of high drama, Meredith Chandler left the room, taking care to close the door quietly; had she slammed it, her father might have experienced a small moment of triumph.

In the hall, she shook and shivered, her hands clammy, her heart pounding in her chest. She had to go, had to get out of here now, today, within the hour.

'Meredith?'

She turned, found her mother standing behind her. 'I heard,' Jean said, 'and I have always known that you would turn out to be the one with the courage.

Yes, there is some of Anna in you. We must talk, dearest girl. Oh, I should like to help you get away from here, though not yet, not until we have thought it through properly. My mother left me some money, too, and you are welcome to take part of it. I dare not hand it all over, because . . . well . . .'

'Because it is your own running-away money.'

Jean nodded mutely.

Meredith grabbed her mother's hands and held them tightly. 'Come with me. I have the energy, we both have some money. Let's do it, Mother.'

'But the boys—'

'The boys are old enough to take care of themselves.'

'And what about Sally?'

'Bring her, too. Let Polly Fishwick look after him. I'm sure she is capable of frying an egg – as long as she has a decent pan to cook it in, that is.'

Jean smiled ruefully. 'He is losing control completely, so I cannot leave your brothers here. They don't have your bravery. Nor do I.'

'Then I shall lend you all some of mine, Mother. It's time to move on. Father is a terrible bully, and even though he is your husband I think you are taking loyalty too far.'

'Loyalty? This is not and never was loyalty. The fact is that he is not a well man. If he dies, we inherit all of this; if I leave, I may have no claim on his estate. It is about keeping my children safe, you see. He is devious enough to alter his will at any time, but if I remain here I shall have grounds to contest. Meredith, do you imagine that I have served all these years for nothing?'

'But the boys and I will inherit whatever happens,

and we shall look after you. Think about it, please. I am going to pack.'

'No, please, not yet.'

Meredith kissed her mother's cheek. 'I must. If I don't get out now, I may never summon the strength again. Leaving you, Nanny Foster and my brothers isn't easy – I am not taking it lightly. But I refuse to live with him and I certainly have no intention of sleeping under the same roof as Polly Fishwick. I should probably kill the pair of them.'

Jean sank into a chair. 'This is all too quick for me. Please let me know where you will be, my lovely girl. I shan't tell your father. But don't disappear from my life – I couldn't bear it.'

The younger woman laughed mirthlessly. 'Tell him – I don't care. I do not intend to lead the quiet life, Mother, so he will hear about me, oh yes.' Meredith's resolve was becoming firmer by the moment. Much as she loved Jean, Jeremy and Peter, she could not continue living at the grange. She kissed her mother again, then bounded up the stairs. She was on her way out of Chandlers Grange and she nursed no intention of returning.

Marie Martindale was slightly shocked, as was her brother Colin. The latter, a teller in a local bank, now had his own little flat in the town centre, but his mother's cooking drew him back to Emblem Street at least three times a week. On this occasion, however, his forkful of Lancashire hotpot was suspended in mid-air as he tried to take in what Dad had just said.

Marie was less surprised. Since she still lived at home, she had been aware for some time that a momentous announcement was on the cards. But Chandlers Green? Nothing happened up there. It was as dead as a dodo – fields and woods, the odd shop, a pub–

'It's lovely,' Leena was saying now. 'So fresh and wild.'

Marie didn't like the sound of fresh and wild and made no bones about the matter. 'It's somewhere to retire, Mam, not to live. You can't have a life up there, not at my age.' She felt like a child who was about to be abandoned at the gates of an orphanage, a poor, unwanted soul with no future.

'I'll drive you to town every day,' promised Alf, 'and, if you don't like it, you'll just have to move in with one of your friends. Remember your mam's TB, love? She was gone for nearly a year and we don't want that happening again, do we? It's crystal clear up yon.'

Colin's fork found its way to his mouth and he chewed the hotpot slowly. Mam and Dad had always been here in Emblem Street; they were part of the scenery. A push-bike was all right for getting him here from the bank or from his flat, but he didn't fancy pedalling all the way up those moors. 'I shall buy a motorbike,' was his contribution to the discussion.

Marie knew that she was being selfish and un-reasonable, yet she was truly frightened by the imminent change. It made her insecure, uncertain. 'I think you'll like it up there, Mam, but I won't.'

Leena had tried to prepare herself for this eventuality. 'It's our choice, Marie, mine and your dad's. Whatever you decide to do will be all right with us. We're not expecting you to uproot if you

48

want to live in town. But you're more than welcome to come with us – either or both of you.'

Marie's appetite had disappeared. Everyone she cared about lived round here in this quadrant between Deane Road and Derby Street. She could enter unannounced any house on Emblem Street, was always sure of a welcome and a sympathetic ear. From here, she had walked daily to Sts Peter and Paul Infant and Junior School, had even hiked up to Mount St Joseph's grammar school except for the odd occasion on which the weather had been too bad.

'You'll be all right, our kid,' said Colin. 'It's not as if they're emigrating to Australia. You can stay with me for a while if you like. The sofa's not too bad if you keep away from the loose spring.'

Marie placed her cutlery on the plate. 'I don't want to live with you, Colin. You'd cramp my style and you wouldn't want my stockings dripping in your bathroom. I'll stay here,' she declared. 'Just put the rent book in my name, then I'll get a lodger and I'll manage.'

A look passed between Leena and Alf. For some reason neither could fathom, they didn't like the idea of leaving her here in this house all by herself. It was a safe street in a friendly area, so that was not the cause of their unease; no, their malaise sprang from a mental picture of Marie standing at this door as they drove off – that would feel like abandonment. It would be better if she, too, moved on to a fresh start, either with them or elsewhere in the town, perhaps with one of her friends.

Alf came up with the solution. 'Tell you what, Marie, we'll hang on to this rent book while we move

– pay the rent for a few more weeks. You come with us up to Chandlers, then, if you don't like it, you can move back here. How's that?'

Well, that would do no harm, she supposed. And it would give her the chance to make sure that Mam and Dad were settled, would allow her to help them to sort out furniture and so forth. 'All right,' she said, 'but don't press me to stay out there in the country, Dad, because I'm sure I'm not made for it. I know writers and poets go on about trees and flowers and birds, but give me an hour in Woolworths any day. Wordsworth's Daffodils? I only read it because it was on the syllabus. Couldn't be bothered with a man who raved on about flowers.'

'They get cuckoos in the woods,' said Leena.

'Good,' replied her daughter. 'Let's hope they stay there, because that one in our clock is enough for me.' She continued with her meal, though she did not enjoy it. Angry with herself for not being more generous, she left the table before emptying her plate.

'She's upset,' said Leena.

'We know,' replied Colin. 'Take no notice, Mam, because she'll get over it. Folk can be spoilt without money, you know. She's had too much of her own way, too much to say for herself – she'll grow out of it.'

Alf looked at his wife's face, could see quite clearly that she was unhappy. He wanted her to live, couldn't bear the thought of her returning to the sanatorium, three walls, freezing cold because the fourth wall was just wide-open windows, those injections of penicillin, X-rays, sputum tests, boredom and fear. He was not a man who gave way easily to anger, but he

50

rose from his seat and followed Marie into the front room.

She was seated by the window and did not turn to look at him.

'I never realized how selfish you are, Marie,' he said.

'Neither did I. But I'm scared and I don't know why. At my age, I should be all right on my own, but I feel . . . frightened.'

'How frightened would you feel if your mother started spitting blood again? Remember? When we thought it was cancer? Remember all those months when you had to look after yourselves, you and our Colin? I am not going to lose my wife, Marie. I've loved that woman since I was a lad and I am not willing to stay here while she breathes in the stink of this town.'

'I know.'

'So you just pull yourself together, Marie Martindale. We've done our best for you, for both of you. Nothing stays the same in this life. Your mam and I are moving to Chandlers Green. Like I said before, I'll hang on to this rent book and you can live where you like. But if you make my wife change her mind about leaving Bolton, I shall never forgive you.'

Marie nodded. 'Don't worry, she's going if I have to drive her up there with a whip, Dad. I just need to get used to it, that's all.'

Without saying another word, Alf left the room.

'How is she?' asked Leena anxiously.

'She's fine,' said Alf. 'She's just sorting it all out in her mind, love.'

Colin patted his stomach. 'Any pudding, Mam?'

'There might be.' Leena got to her feet and walked

to the scullery. She stood at the old sink and looked out into the tiny back yard. Soon, there would be a garden, many different birds, real trees, perhaps the odd squirrel. Marie would be all right. She picked up her sherry trifle and carried it through to the menfolk.

Meredith Chandler was afraid. Anger had sustained her throughout much of the day, but now, having been deposited by a taxi outside the Pack Horse Hotel, she suddenly felt like a child sent away from home during the war, a refugee who was instantly nameless and unimportant. What on earth had she done? How many people in this world enjoyed her privileges, her easy life?

She swallowed painfully, realized that she had never done this sort of thing alone before, was unsure of how to register, how to book a room. Her brothers had disappeared after lunch, were clearly still in awe of their bullying father and would not wish to upset Mother. Mother understood Meredith – even Sally Foster had approved. Knowing that she could never return to her home, Meredith entered the hotel, gave the receptionist her name and followed a porter to her room.

She had done it. The door was closed and she was alone in a place that had nothing of herself in it, no ornament, no memento, no character. Opening her case, she took out Flops, the one-eyed bear who had accompanied her thus far on the journey through life. When the battered teddy was on her pillow, she placed her pyjama case beside him, then arranged some photographs on the dressing table. It was still nothing like home, but there was something of herself on display, at least.

She looked through the window at the education offices, at the cinema, wondered whether to go and sit through a film, decided against it. For want of some better occupation, she picked up her copy of the *Bolton Evening News*, flicked through it, found the businesses-to-let section. How could she start a business all by herself? Where were her brothers when she needed them? All her schoolfriends were settled, some having been to university or teacher-training college, a couple already married, several engaged.

Right, what had she achieved so far, what had she done with her time since school? Seven or eight months at a riding stables, mucking out and mucking about with a handsome stable boy, almost two years as a part-time receptionist for a dentist – a friend of Father's, naturally – then a few months in a florist's shop, nice, dainty, ladylike. What next? Was she supposed to wait at home for a handsome prince on a white charger?

There were probably other girls like herself, people who were dissatisfied with the status quo, who wanted new pastures, challenges, a change. They must be found. She crossed the room to a desk, picked up a pen and a sheet of hotel notepaper. After several crossings-out and much chewing of the pen, she achieved the final product.

YOUNG FEMALE WITH A SENSE OF ADVENTURE, WISHING TO START A NEW LIFE IN COMMERCE, WISHES TO MEET LIKE-MINDED FEMALES WITH A VIEW TO SETTING UP IN BUSINESS. EXPERIENCE AND MONEY WOULD BE WELCOME, BUT ARE NOT PRE-REQUISITES.

She read the piece aloud, was reasonably satisfied

with it. Tomorrow, she would take this round to Tillotson's so that it could go into the evening newspaper. While she stayed at the hotel, she would be able to pick up replies to a box number quite easily. No matter what her father's opinion, she would make something of herself, would show him that women were not the useless creatures he preferred them to be.

Sleep proved elusive. Her mind was filled with ideas: dress shops, a chandlery, a beauty parlour. She would need premises, staff, scaffolding in the form of trustworthy and talented peers. A bank would have to be approached and persuaded to lend money for the project. What about a shop that sold really fancy cakes for special occasions? A restaurant, a coffee bar, a bookshop? There were places in London that catered exclusively for weddings: dresses, flowers, hair, make-up, the provision of cars, the reception. Other companies might join that sort of set-up . . .

What about an agency that could place people in jobs? No, the government attended to that sort of thing – but nannies, babysitters, cleaners, casual workers? Or a firm that could go in and spring-clean a house from top to bottom? It was almost two o'clock and she must sleep. She picked up Flops and cuddled him until drowsiness finally overcame her. She dreamt of home, of Mother and Jeremy, of Peter and Sally. Her father did not enter the picture, because he was no longer a part of her life.

Pol Fishwick was fed up to the back teeth. She didn't want to live in an attic of that huge, draughty house, didn't want to spend time in the company of Mrs Jean Chandler. With her husband gone and the house all

54

to herself, she was happy at Woodside Cottage, was free to come and go as she pleased, with no master save the big fellow – and even his demands had become less urgent of late.

Perhaps that was it. He had found a younger filly and wanted to offload the old stock. Yet he could have waved her off, could have thrown her out. But no, he wanted her help. How the hell was she going to cope? She knew she wouldn't fit in at the grange, was well aware of her own limitations. Small talk was not her forte; nor was she given to bobbing up and down in the presence of her so-called betters. Befriend Jean Chandler? Not flaming likely. And she had caught sight of that miserable-looking house-keeper in the shops, was hardly likely to endear herself to the po-faced woman.

Then there would be the work. Maids in big houses were little better than slaves, bring-me-fetch-me-carry-me, light the fires, sweep the floors, dust the tables, wash the antimacassars, clear the dishes, scrub the pans. So, what was the answer? There wasn't one. She felt like someone condemned to the gallows, no reprieve, no chance that the execution might be stayed. Well, this was to be her last-ditch stand. The master was on his way to finalize arrangements and she would be at her best when he got here.

After emptying the zinc bath outside the back door, she made herself up, donned the pretty night-dress he had provided and planted herself on the sofa in a pose she imagined to be alluring. She had to persuade him, had to win him round. The clock ticked on, the fire wanted stoking, she had begun to sweat because of all the worry, hot one minute, cold the next. Oh, bugger. She applied a liberal amount of talcum powder to her damper parts and reclaimed her place on the sofa.

In the end, she drifted off to sleep, only to be woken by a cold hand on her shoulder. 'What time is it?' she asked drowsily.

'Half past nine,' replied Richard. 'My daughter ran off today, left home and a bloody good riddance.' He placed himself in an armchair. 'There's no gratitude these days. If I had spoken to my father the way she spoke to me – well, I would not have survived to tell the tale.'

She pulled herself together, remembered the matter in hand, tried to smile. 'Richard?'

'You'll have to call me Mr Chandler from now on. Or sir will do.'

'Oh.'

'A bloody good hiding's what she needs,' he said, almost to himself.

'I want to say . . .' She licked her drying lips. 'It's just that I don't want to live at the grange. That house-keeper makes me feel sick every time I see her and I don't think your wife would like me. Can't I stop here?'

'No,' he barked.

'I could come up to the grange every day. Only I'm not cut out for housework, see. It's me knees.'

'You won't be doing housework – well, not much of it. You'll be catering for my father's needs, keeping him happy. He misses the company of a woman and he's becoming a trouble. Dave Armstrong does his best, but he can't be a woman, no matter how hard he tries. My father needs to be comforted.'

'Oh.' The old man was nearing eighty, for good-ness' sake—

'You'll soon find out how to calm him down,' he told her. 'He won't be up to the full job, but you can work out a few ways of keeping him amused. You'll have plenty to eat, money in the bank and a comfortable life. Take it or leave it, Pol.'

So, she was to be a prostitute with just the one client, that client a worn-out bag of bones whose son was demanding that she should pander to the needs of Henry Chandler. 'So will I have to spend all day with your dad?'

He shrugged. 'More or less, though Dave or a lad from the village will stand in when you have the day off. I shall make it worth your while, don't worry.'

It was frying pan time again. In fact, Pol felt like clobbering Chandler with her wash tub, or even with the axe left behind by Derek Fishwick. She didn't mind being used, wasn't afraid to sell her body for the sake of survival. But to be told to lie down with a man who was older than Adam was one bridge too far for Polly Fishwick. In her mind, she picked up the axe and held it poised over the centre of her ex-lover's ugly skull. In reality, she smiled and said, 'All right, Mr Chandler, whatever you say, sir.'

Was she laughing at him? No, her expression was serious enough. Had Richard Chandler been blessed with a scrap of imagination, he might have read past that fixed smile, beyond the glassy expression in those blue eyes.

The axe hovered above his head and would remain in that position for the foreseeable future. Pol was not a clever woman, but she was possessed of that intuitive cunning that belongs to many of her kind. This man had treated her like scum and she would bide her time, would become a double agent, one of that happy band who play both sides of the game. It would not be easy, but life carried few guarantees.

'So we'll move you in as soon as possible,' he said.

She sharpened the blade, saw the edge glinting in readiness. 'Right, Mr Chandler, whatever you say.'

He stood up. 'My father would like to see you in that nightdress,' he said. Yes, she was just right for the job; with luck and a following wind, she could have the old man dead within a fortnight. 'See you soon,' he called on his way out.

When he had left, Pol did something she had not done in years – she wept. But even through her tears, the woodsman's weapon continued to hone itself towards readiness; yes, Mr Richard Chandler had been signatory to his own death warrant.

Peter Chandler sat at the foot of his twin brother's bed. Jeremy, the more decided of the two, was propped on pillows, hands clasped behind his head. The older by half an hour, he was the one who made decisions in the absence of Meredith; and Meredith had gone.

'Do you think she'll come back?' asked Peter. He could not even begin to imagine life without his sister.

'No.' Jeremy placed his arms on the coverlet and leaned back. 'Too much of the old man in her, Pete. If Merry were drowning in quicksand, she wouldn't call for help, not if she'd stepped in deliberately. Mother says she's at the Pack Horse on Bradshaw-gate, but she can't stay there for ever. Granny's few thousand won't last long if there are hotel bills to pay.'

Peter sighed. Father had started his campaign again today, had begun to insist that the brothers take places at universities, that they had been idle long enough, that they had enjoyed a three-year holiday, that they must apply now for the following September. 'What are we going to do?' he asked.

'Not university,' answered Jeremy. 'So, we have to stand up to him just as Merry did.'

'I can't.'

'Well, you have to, there's no choice. There are two of us. Surely, between us, two men can make one Meredith?'

'She's a woman,' said Peter. 'He doesn't hit women.'

'True.' Jeremy stared hard at his brother. Unless a person knew them well, he and Peter were like peas in a pod, just an inch separating them in height, Jeremy owning the slightly sharper nose, while each was endowed with a shock of dark blond hair, hazel eyes and a slender body. 'There are two of us, in case you hadn't noticed. Father might be big, but we are quicker than he is.' He swallowed nervously. 'We fight back.'

Peter managed a nervous laugh. 'He'll kill us.'

'Will he? Well, guess who has the spare key to the gun cabinet?'

'What?'

'We disarm all weapons except for one, then we talk to him at gunpoint. I think, given those circumstances, he may listen to reason.'

'Then what?'

'We leave,' said Jeremy, his calm tone belying fear.

Peter was so terrified that his teeth began to chatter. For the life of him, he could not picture a situation in which he and his brother would point a gun at their father. And what about Mother? What would the brute do to her if his sons got the better of him?

'Stay if you must,' said Jeremy, 'but I am getting out of here. If we simply disappear as Merry did, he will find us, because we are male. Merry does not matter to him, because she had the misfortune to be born female. At this moment, I wish we had been girls, because girls are disposable. But we are men, Peter, and we cannot continue as boys. It will be necessary to make plain to him that we will not go to university, that we will not be bullied and that we intend to join our sister.'

'God help Mother.'

'Yes, I know. She will not leave. She will stay to the bitterest of ends. All we can hope is that the bitter end will be his and not hers. But look, are we going to sit here while he walks all over us? Merry is twice the man that I am, I do know that. I was proud of her today, you know.'

Peter nodded his agreement.

'We have to do it.'

'Yes.'

Jeremy concentrated for a few moments. 'And we must tell Mother first. She deserves a chance to make herself ready. Once his nest is completely empty, she will become his only target.'

'We should force her to come.'

'Mother will not be forced, Pete. She acts silly, but she has a backbone of steel. No, she wants to be here the day he dies, needs to see him defeated. She's waiting for him to suffer a stroke, I think, because she is always mentioning his bad colour and how his temper will be the end of him. She is the audience and she will sit this out until the final curtain.'

Peter left his twin and returned to his own room. The more sensitive of the pair, he could not settle. Pure fear coursed through his veins as he pondered the awesome prospect of facing up to Richard Chandler. All the beatings and humiliations of his younger days flooded his mind, threatening to pour out of his eyes to soak the pillow. But Jeremy was right; they had to leave.

Elsie Ramsden lit another Woodbine. She had taken some knocks in her time, the worst having been the death of her son, Brian, but this was a real shock. Alf and Leena were leaving Emblem Street. Her Bert had just been invited to supervise the renovation of the cottage and they hoped to be gone by Christmas.

'Marie might stay,' said Leena.

'Aye, she's not keen on the countryside,' explained Alf, 'so we'll hang on to the rent book while she makes her mind up.'

Elsie inhaled a huge amount of smoke, coughed, pulled herself together. 'I'll miss you,' she said, her voice clouded by tobacco and emotion.

'Eeh, you'll not get shut of us that easily, will she, Alf?' Leena touched her friend's hand. 'If our Marie stops here, we shall visit her, of course. And even if she doesn't stop, you and Bert can come and stay with us as often as you like. We're moving on, but we're not moving away from you, Elsie.'

Bert, who was seated by the fire, took a swig of beer and cleared his throat. 'Elsie, you have to remember that Leena's chest were bad a long time. She'll get loads of fresh air up yon, so that'll do her good.'

'I know.' Elsie sniffed.

'We're not losing them, love.'

'I know. So why do I feel so terrible? It won't be the same when I'm pegging out on a Monday, no Leena to help me with me sheets. If Marie goes, too, we could get riff-raff.'

'There's talk of a lot of these streets being pulled down,' said Bert. 'All the demolition contractors are queuing up to get the job when it comes. There's new corporation houses getting thrown up all over the place, Else. When that happens, when we get moved, we could finish up at Darcy Lever with Alf and Leena miles away – Doffcocker or Breightmet. It's coming anyway, no matter what. It's got to be faced.'

'I know,' she replied yet again. 'But what I know has nowt to do with what I feel. Leena's nearer to me than any of my brothers and sisters. It means it's all over.' She closed her eyes. 'Remember the war and how we all clung together? Borrowing and lending, swapping coupons, buying half a black-market pig between us? Leena kept me going after that telegram came . . .' She dissolved into tears.

Bert placed his glass on the wrap-around fireguard and walked to his wife's side. 'You can't do this, Else. You can't make things hard for Leena – she's your best pal. It's got to happen one way or the other – we'll all be out of Emblem Street in a few years. This is life, you know. Nothing stands still. They say there'll be men on the moon in ten years.'

Elsie looked up. 'Well, don't go moving there,' she managed, ''cos the buses don't go that far.'

Leena laughed nervously. This was so much harder than she had expected – first Marie, now Elsie. And, according to Richard Chandler, they weren't going to get much of a reception up yonder, either. 'It'd take more than miles to split us up,' she said. 'You're a good friend, always have been, always will be. Tell you what, me and Alf will drive you up to see the house – we can take butties and a couple of flasks. It'll be all right, love. I promise you that.'

'Will it?'

'Course it will.'

But as she walked the few strides between the two houses, Leena Martindale clung to her husband's arm. They might as well have been moving to the moon, because life was going to be so different. The house was detached for a start, no neighbour fastened on, no chattering over a wall. With Alf at work, she would be left to her own devices, just a house to clean and meals to prepare. The first beat of fear hit her heart, making it jump irregularly. She breathed in deeply, tasted soot, knew that she must get out of here. But oh, dear God . . .

He opened the door. 'Come on, Leena, it's near bedtime. Everything'll work out for the best, you'll see.'

'I hope so,' she answered. Nevertheless, she would find her rosary and begin a novena tonight. 'We'll be all right, won't we?'

'Course we will, love, course we will.' He closed his mind against the picture of Richard Chandler's furious face. Leena needed that cottage and Leena was going to have it.

THREE

'I am sick and fed up with smelling of chip fat.' Aggie Turner slammed the thick white coffee cup into its saucer. 'There's bloody dogs following me everywhere. The only reason cats don't follow me is because the dogs chase 'em off. I could be the Pied flaming Piper of Crufts. There's all these Alsatians running about saying, "Here she comes, lads, let's all have a good sniff." Jesus, I'm a dogsbody.' She wiped froth from her upper lip and grinned.

Marie Martindale managed, just about, not to choke on her own bubbly coffee. 'Give over, Aggie,' she begged. 'Why do you always wait until I've got my mouth full before you start clowning? Be grateful. One day, you'll inherit two chip shops and all the mushy peas you can eat.'

'Plus vinegar.' These crowning words arrived from Josie Maguire, the second of Marie's close friends. The tallest of the trio, Josie, dark-haired and with good Irish skin, was training to be a manager at Marks and Spencer, a prospect she viewed with considerable gloom. Her mother worked at Marks and Spencer, as did two of her aunts. The names 'Marks' and 'Spencer' were revered in the Maguire household, since the firm had been its provider for many years. She wondered why her mother had not changed the Catholic blessing, because the Father and the Son should have been followed by M&S, not by the Holy Ghost.

'At least you don't smell of cod,' said Aggie.

'No, but if I see another pair of American Tan fifteen-denier stockings, I'll scream. I've been selling hosiery for about three hundred years. My mother keeps reminding me that we've got our own chiropodist, a nurse on hand, a good canteen. If she mentions my pension one more time, I'll make sure she doesn't live to collect hers. I have to get out of there. I feel like a bird in a cage. Or one of those war prisoners who tried to escape from Colditz.' She shook her head vehemently. 'I have to get out,' she repeated.

Marie pricked up her ears. 'Out of M&S or out of your house?'

'Both,' answered Josie. 'If I leave my job, my mam'll send for the priest to have me exorcized. They'll paint a cross on the door and get the house fumigated. No, if I stay at home, I stay at the shop. If I leave, I leave both places. I can't stand being at home for much longer – we're too old to be living with our parents. I say we emigrate.'

'Same here,' groaned Aggie. 'Australia, here I come. Can you imagine living over a chippy? Drunks singing every Saturday night and throwing up all over the pavement, a back yard full of spuds and dead fish, marrowfat peas soaking in buckets everywhere. If I never see a bag of chips again I'll not be sorry.'

'Well, you can always have steak pudding for a change,' laughed Marie.

Aggie, a short, round girl with a mop of fiery red curls, thumped Marie on the arm. 'It's all right for you, legal eagle, loads of good-looking young men all over the office, a nice clean job with a typewriter. You've got no idea what it's like living with a spud-chipper in one hand and a bowl of batter in the other. You're with decent folk all day, too.'

'You must be joking. They're all dirty old married men. Legal profession? They spend half their time in somebody else's bed, then the other half representing folk who've also been in somebody else's bed. And if one more of them puts a hand on my bum, I'll shove paper clips up his nose.'

'So,' sighed Josie, 'what with cod, nylons and arse-gropers, we're all in a bad way. The bloody circus isn't due for months, so we can't run away, because we haven't the money to get far enough from home.'

Marie leaned back in her chair and eyed a group of likely lads across the Bodega Coffee Bar, gave them the once-over, decided they weren't worth the bother – tattoos, daft haircuts and chewing gum. 'My mam and dad are running away,' she informed her friends, 'but not with the circus. The ringmaster took one look at my dad and said no, they already had one and they were finding it difficult to train. They're moving to a house up in Chandlers Green and I'm not going with them. No, that's not quite true. I will go with them just to help out, then I'm coming back to Emblem Street.'

'On your own?' asked Aggie.

Marie nodded.

Aggie and Josie looked at each other, then eyed

Marie. 'Are you thinking what I'm thinking?' asked Josie.

'Depends,' replied Aggie. 'Were you thinking about Elvis gyrating in his tight jeans?'

'No, I was thinking about Marie needing company in Emblem Street. She doesn't keep fish in her back yard and she doesn't wear American Tan fifteen denier at four and eleven a pair.'

'But I keep vinegar in the kitchen,' said Marie, a bubble of excitement rising in her chest. 'The rent's cheap, especially split three ways. We could have a party – you've got a Dansette, haven't you, Josie?'

'I have indeed, but I'll have to leave Frank Sinatra with my mother, or she'd only pine.'

The three sat in silence for several minutes. The idea of moving away from home was awesome, as each girl realized that she would miss her family. But their friendship had always been close and each knew that she could be happy in the company of the other two. And there came a time when living with family didn't feel right any more, when striking out in a new direction was a necessity.

'I'll still have to fry chips till I find something else,' said Aggie.

'That's all right,' answered Marie, 'we haven't a lot of dogs in our street.'

Josie looked up to the ceiling. 'Well, they won't be pleased, but with you two behind me and without my mother wittering on, I might even leave the hallowed M&S.'

'No,' gasped Aggie, 'you offend St Michael – that'll be sacrilege. You won't even get Purgatory. Your soul will belong to Satan. More coffee, anyone?'

Marie Martindale was delighted. She could keep

her home and she could put Mam out of her misery. To celebrate, she allowed herself extra sugar in her drink and bought everyone a Penguin. She didn't even frown when one of the tattooed gum-chewers gave her a wink. Would Mam leave the beds? How much furniture would she let Marie have? Of course, one of the bedrooms would have to be shared. Oh well, it was a new beginning and she was in a generous mood, so she returned the wink . . .

Richard Chandler was blazing; in fact, his wife would not have been surprised had she seen smoke coming out of his nose. She shuddered to think about his blood pressure, because he was positively scarlet about the cheeks, with some interesting purple patches on the forehead. 'They refuse to go to university,' he yelled. 'How many people would turn their backs on a chance of a proper education? They don't know they're born and that's their trouble. They refuse to work on the estate, too – I could find them something if they insist on working.'

Jean put down her sewing; it had been her experience thus far that her husband reacted badly if he did not have the full attention of his audience. 'They have never wanted university, Richard. They would be quite happy to work their way up through an accountancy firm, or–'

'I told them they could have a couple of years off to decide on which course they wanted. No-one told me that they weren't interested in doing degrees.'

Jean held her tongue; she had heard the boys telling him exactly that, trying to explain that they wanted to work in offices, but he had not heard them, had never listened. Richard was a talker; he pontificated ceaselessly and seldom paused to admit a reply.

'I lay this at your door,' he roared now. 'Namby-pamby lads, the pair of them. No guts and no backbone.'

That was another of his charming traits – he was never to blame for anything, while his wife, who lived life so quietly as to be almost silent, was the cause of all the ills in Chandlers Grange.

'You have spoilt them – all of them. God alone knows where that blasted girl has gone. She could be the ruin of me, might get up to all kinds of mischief. I expect you know where she is, eh? Keeping her safe from her dragon father, are you? Now the twins want to be off. Stood there bold as brass, the pair of them, telling me they plan to leave home.'

Jean swallowed a bubble of grief, but took care to keep her face expressionless. She must not react, must not allow him to catch a glimpse of the fear, the anger and the hatred she felt. There was in her heart a strong urge to rush across the room, pick up the poker and use it as Polly Fishwick had used the frying pan . . . Oh, God, how she wished she dared.

'Nothing bothers you, does it?'

'I try to keep my feelings under control,' she replied carefully.

'I noticed,' he snapped, 'which is why I left you to your virginal bed. You were never a wife to me. Never.'

Her eyebrow raised itself and she wished that she had exercised more control over those small, dis-obedient muscles, but he failed to notice, as he was ranting on again about the boys, about disinheriting

69

his children, about selling up and moving abroad, about ingratitude.

It occurred to Jean – and not for the first time – that there was one murder in every human. This was her murder, her sin not yet committed. Not that she would ever gain the strength or the courage, but yes, she wished him dead, buried and rotted down. The best service Richard could possibly perform for mankind would be as compost, yet she doubted that his heart would return to the soil, because it was as immovable as Mount Sinai.

'There are going to be changes,' he said now. 'I want rid of Nanny Foster for a start. She can have Polly Fishwick's cottage and she can come to work every day – if you insist on continuing to employ the woman.'

Jean's heart stopped, then started up in top gear. This was the moment she had dreaded for years. The room began to darken as he raved on about Sally, about how she was getting on a bit, how she deserved her own home, her own life. Jean Chandler had taken enough; this was the end, the finishing post. With trembling hands, she picked up her sewing and rose from her seat.

'And where do you think you're going?' he roared.

'To pack,' she replied mildly. Yes, she would do as Aunt Anna had done, as Meredith had done, as the boys would surely do soon.

'What? And where will you live? The Salvation Army?'

Unsteady on her feet, she walked to the door. 'I shall move into the cottage with Sally,' she replied eventually. 'There is room enough for two people, as was proved while Polly's husband lived there – until she tried to kill him, of course.'

'Stop!' he shouted.

But she was already closing the door in her wake. Oh, the evil of that man, the sheer badness of him. He knew full well that his wife depended for her sanity on the housekeeper, so he was moving her out, was deliberately taking away the last piece of Jean's very fragile scaffolding.

He stood in the centre of the room, eyes bulging, heart rattling in his chest, mind buzzing like a bee in a jar, his mouth wide open. They were all going. Even she was going, the fragrant one, the saint, the heroine of the piece. He would be left here with Polly Fishwick, with daily servants and with his father, who was as mad as a whole meadow of March hares.

With everyone leaving at once, the village would notice; children maturing and moving on was one thing, but the wife absenting herself simultaneously would surely become the object of huge gossip, especially when said wife was occupying a woodsman's cottage with the ex-housekeeper. Bugger. He would have to lose face, but would it not be preferable to do that inside the house where he could contain it? That would surely be better than becoming the laughing stock of the whole area?

In the hall, Jean placed herself in a chair and wished that her limbs would stop trembling. This was the day she had dreaded, because she was being forced to walk away from all she had endured, so rendering worthless her life thus far. She had tolerated his madness so that her children would be provided for, had stayed in this house, in this marriage, in order to outlive him, to be here on the day of his death, to pick up the money she had earned by tolerating this hateful man. She had even said little when he had locked the old man upstairs, when he had forbidden the family to visit him. Compensation, it should be termed. Yes, they were all due some compensation.

The door opened and he stepped out of the drawing room. 'Forget all that,' he said, his tone gruff. 'Nanny Foster probably feels safer here. The house near the woods is possibly too isolated for her and she may become nervous.'

Something stirred in Jean's breast, not quite fury, but certainly approaching it. She had taken enough of this man. Lifting her head, she looked him full in the face, held his gaze while she rose from the chair. Without a word, she walked past him and up the stairs, her lower limbs gaining strength with every step.

Confused, Richard Chandler dropped into the seat recently vacated by his wife. She had never defied him before, was not the contentious sort. Shy to the point of diffidence, Jean Chandler could not say boo to a goose – in fact, she had been terrified of the creatures when he had kept some behind the house. He recalled how he had laughed while watching her running from the gander, an ill-tempered beast who had taken delight in pecking those who had feared him. For a moment he could not remember what had happened to them – oh yes, Aunt Anna had taken them, hadn't she?

Upstairs, Jean sat at her dressing table and stared at the white face in the mirror. Today, something had finally died in her. Or had she given birth to strength, was she ready to move on? She had no particular talents and could not imagine herself surviving outside the framework that was so familiar. But her children, too, were a part of that structure, and if they were all to leave, then the meaning would be gone.

Meredith was staying at the Pack Horse. She had placed an advertisement in the local press, was looking for other young women who wanted to change their lives. 'You are too old,' Jean informed her reflection. But was she? She was forty-four years of age. Every one of the past twenty-four years had been spent in Richard's company, in this house, with his father. Henry was now virtually locked away, but he remained at the grange, could be heard laughing crazily in the middle of the night, was still feared by women.

So, here was the choice. She could stay with two madmen and a whore, or she could leave in the company of her boys. Perhaps she might even be useful in Meredith's venture, whatever that was going to be. The clock ticked on, each beat measuring another irretrievable second, another slice of life gone for ever. It was probably time to go . . .

Sally Foster put down her dish mop and sat by the kitchen fire. Her head was in a whirl and she did not know where to begin to organize her thoughts. Mrs Jean had told her, calmly, that she was leaving the grange and that Sally, too, should go. There was some vague talk of a business, of a house in town, of Meredith's having plans, but Sally could not take it in. The twins were leaving too, it seemed.

'You won't be here for much longer, anyway,' Mrs Jean had said, 'because Richard wants you out. He knows that you and I are good friends, and he is

73

determined to find a way of punishing me because the children are going.'

Sally, at fifty, felt too old for all this. For twenty-three years, Chandlers Grange had been her home. She had cared for the children, then had taken over the reins of the household, and, in spite of the master's antipathy, she was settled. The routine of the place was printed indelibly into her system; she knew every creak of every floorboard, every crack in the ancient plaster. Had Mrs Jean finally been deprived of her reason?

Sally answered her own unspoken question. No. Jean Chandler was getting out because her children were leaving. The man had ranted and raved once too often, had threatened to move Sally out, was bringing his blowzy mistress into the house. All these factors had weighted the scales so heavily that Mrs Jean could take no more.

The unknown was always frightening and, as the years crept on, security became increasingly important. 'You'll have a much better chance of being cared for if you join the missus,' she told herself in a whisper. The concept of remaining here in the company of two lunatics and a slut was not appealing. It was the end of an era and it had to be faced.

The door opened and Richard Chandler's face insinuated itself into the gap. He never entered the kitchen; it was the province of women and was, therefore, beneath his contempt. He blinked and gazed around the room as if he had not seen it before, then brought the rest of himself into the area. 'Er . . . good afternoon,' he said.

Sally remained seated. 'Did you want something, Mr Chandler?'

He crossed the room and placed himself in the chair opposite hers. 'There's been a misunderstanding,' he began.

'Oh?'

'Yes.' He folded his arms across his very large belly. 'My wife has decided that she must leave, because Meredith has gone and the boys, too, will be moving out soon. She has the notion that she must follow them in order to take care of them. Nonsense, of course.'

She attempted no reply.

'Has she discussed this with you?'

Sally's brain performed a few rapid calculations and decided that this man should know as little as possible. 'No,' she stated.

'Well, I wondered whether you might persuade her to stay.' He hated crawling, but this had to be done.

'I am not sure that I can influence her decision, Mr Chandler. If she has made up her mind, I can't change it for her.'

The man swallowed, imagined that he tasted bile. 'I could make it worth your while,' he said quietly. 'I dare say five hundred pounds might prove useful as a little nest egg? Plus a small increase in salary, sufficient to add to your savings with an eye to retirement?'

He was so ugly. Sally tilted her head to one side and studied him. At over six feet in height, he ought to have carried his weight well, but he did not, because everything had settled around and above his waist, so that he had the overall shape of a very uncomely barrel. Balding and with his eyes set into pockets of fat, he was almost porcine in appearance.

Small, thready veins had exploded beneath the skin of his face, tell-tale testament to a life devoted to food and strong drink. 'No, thank you,' she said at last.

'A thousand?' The eyes seemed to shrink even further as he spoke.

'No.'

'I could throw you out now.' The tone had become menacing.

'Then do it, Mr Chandler. I have many friends in Chandlers Green and they will certainly shelter me when I tell them how I have been mistreated. Just say the word and I shall pack my things.'

He was defeated and he knew it. This was the Sergeant Alfred Martindale scenario all over again, a gross misunderstanding that could alter Richard's life beyond retrieval. 'Then go with her,' he said as he struggled to his feet.

'I shall, Mr Chandler. Anything else?'

'No.' He left the room and slammed the door.

Sally Foster felt sick. It was as if he had contaminated her kitchen and she had a strong urge to throw out everything that had been edible until ten minutes ago. The man was poison. In a few minutes, she would go upstairs to inform Mrs Jean about the attempted bribery. Yes, it was time for both women to leave Chandlers Grange. A smile threatened, but she squashed it before it was born. The concept of Polly Fishwick taking over as housekeeper was hilariously funny, yet terribly sad. The grange was finished, because all sense was about to walk out of its front door within the very near future.

Paul Butlin, vicar of St Augustine's, kept a wary eye on Miss Anna Chandler. To the untrained watcher, she probably looked as she normally did – odd, eccentric, badly dressed – but he saw beyond the immediately visible. Yes, she was a character, and no, he had never met anyone quite like her. He was almost fond of her. In spite of the proprietorial air she wore while organizing his church, this was one good woman. And she was upset. Stiff and straight of back, demeanour almost as usual, yet there was something extra today, something . . . unhappy.

She turned quickly and looked at him, her head seeming to swivel within the hat, as if the hat were a fixture and the skull a mere passing phase. 'Yes?' Her eyebrows raised themselves. Here was the mistress speaking to a mere employee, yet he could not manage to dislike her.

He cleared his throat. 'Miss Chandler?'

'What?' The syllable was delivered crisply. She had been engaged in decorating the altar and was not pleased by the interruption – even men of God should know their place. She laid her basket of leaves on the floor. 'I am busy,' she snapped, 'trying to express the arrival of autumn.'

Paul Butlin sighed. There would be leaves and acorns everywhere, and at the harvest service in a couple of weeks he would be knee-deep in apples and home-made preserves. Anna Chandler did nothing by halves. 'Cup of tea in the vestry?' he suggested.

She nodded. He noticed that her hat wobbled again as she moved. The fedora-style creation was far too big for her, as were most of her clothes. Once a rounded woman, Anna had arrived at old age in a leaner state, yet she refused to spend money on the refurbishment of her wardrobe. A standing joke in the parish was that when Miss Anna looked left or right, the famous hat continued eyes front. Save for the barking of orders, she spoke to few; only the vicar was privy to any of this woman's secrets.

In the vestry, they sat one each side of a tiny table into whose surface were etched initials carved by generations of choirboys. He poured the tea and looked into eyes whose colour, once an impossible shade of green, had been clouded over by the mists of time. 'How are you?' he asked, suddenly aware of his own shortcomings. Her family had built St Augustine's, had maintained it throughout many generations – at least a dozen of the long-deceased were ensconced in the crypt below. She made him feel inadequate, as if she saw straight through him. In fact, this interview was almost like being back at school and in the presence of a teacher whose serious displeasure was about to be made plain.

'I am well,' she replied. She was not well. Her physical self was in a reasonable enough condition for a woman of her age, but her mind was uneasy. She sighed heavily. 'There are goings-on,' she said darkly.

'I see.'

'Do you? Well, I don't. If you see, please explain things to me, Reverend Butlin, because my family is totally beyond my comprehension.' She sipped her tea, then clattered the cup into its saucer. 'Have you tried to see my brother? Have you?'

The vicar bowed his head. 'Yes, I have. And your nephew absolutely forbids me to enter the room in which Henry lives.'

'Exists,' she spat scornfully. 'There is nothing wrong with him, you know. Alcoholism in the male Chandlers is quite normal. My nephew is proof enough of that. He has locked away his own father, yet Richard imbibes daily and in great quantities.' She reached across the table and grasped her companion's hand. 'I think my great-niece has left the grange. It has become too much for her. I shall visit when Richard is out of the way and I shall find out then.' Thin fingers dug into his flesh. 'We must rescue Henry.'

Paul Butlin swallowed. No longer a child in the company of an irate headmistress, he now felt like a peripheral character in one of Enid Blyton's Famous Five books. Was he supposed to round up the rest of the gang, dog included, break into the grange and pick locks with hairpins? 'I have tried to talk to Mrs Chandler,' he offered, 'but she, too, stays away from old Mr Chandler's room. He is reputed to be . . .'

'He grabs women.' Anna spared him the necessity of finishing his sentence and almost crushed his hand. 'It's all a great nonsense, a tale manufactured so that Richard could take the reins. Yes, my brother was disordered at one time, but he must be better by now, especially if he is denied drink. He must have been through hell up there. That was why I left.' She freed the vicar's hand from her vice-like grip.

Paul, glad to regain his fingers, noticed a small bleed where one of her nails had pierced his flesh. 'And you fear that Meredith has gone?'

'Yes, and the boys will follow.' She lowered her voice. 'And that will be when my nephew will finish off my brother.'

Even from Miss Anna Chandler, this was a wild statement. The idea of Richard Chandler murdering his own father was ridiculous. 'Miss Chandler, I–'

'And Jean will not stay here without her children,

no.' To emphasize the statement, she shook her head beneath its unstable fedora. 'No, she has remained here just to guard them, I am sure. Something must be done.'

The something that needed doing lay in regions far beyond the reach of Paul Butlin's imagination. He could not march up the driveway to the grange and beg its master not to commit patricide; nor could he allow himself to be drawn into the other theory expressed by Miss Chandler. 'I cannot . . . er . . . I cannot speak to Mrs Chandler without some facts. It would seem strange if I were to beg her to stay – she has not announced her intention to leave.'

'I know.' She smiled grimly. 'You asked me what was wrong, Reverend Butlin. Yes, it is impossible – I know that only too well. But there is something brewing. I can almost smell it in the air.'

'I am sorry,' he replied lamely.

'And we shall become a great deal sorrier.' With this final statement, the maiden aunt of Richard Chandler left the table and returned to the altar. On the pristine cloth, she spread leaves in shades varying from greens to browns to reds. It was the end of the season. Yes, and it was the beginning of something else . . .

Appointed by the other two as the best writer of letters, Marie Martindale picked up her finished effort and prepared to read it aloud. They were in the front parlour of 34 Emblem Street and, thus far, they had managed to keep secret their intentions. Aggie Turner, stalwart and valued member of a family of fish-fryers, had not told her parents of her plan to leave home, while Josie Maguire had not dared to speak of her desire to move out and, worse still, her need to quit the hallowed firm of Marks and Spencer.

Marie cleared her throat.

'*Dear Miss–*'

'She might be a madam,' said Josie.

'Madams run red-light houses,' Aggie scoffed. 'I read about them in the Sunday papers.'

Marie glowered. 'Will you shut up? If you can do any better, write it yourselves. Now, listen.'

They listened.

'*In response to your advertisement in the local press, we write in the hope that we may be helpful in your search for adventure. There are three of us and we were all educated at grammar school. Miss Agnes Turner helps her parents in the family business, where she has gained experience in the areas of retail and food preparation.*'

'And dogs,' said Josie, 'and vomit and vinegar.'

Marie glared at her. 'Do you plan on living till tomorrow? Because you may need to talk to the undertaker about coffin linings if you carry on.' She turned to Aggie. 'And what the hell are you laughing at?'

'Nothing.' The little red-haired girl organized her features. 'Lead on, Macduff,' she ordered.

'*Miss Josephine Maguire is currently employed at Marks and Spencer, Deansgate, Bolton, where she is being trained for management.* One word about American Tan nylons, Josie Maguire, and you are out on the streets. Right?'

'We do Sandalwood too,' offered Josie. 'And tights before long – they've already got them in America. No suspender belts – imagine that. Don't forget, I shall soon be in tights as well. Do you remember when we did *The Merchant of Venice* in the fifth form and Shylock's pants and tights fell down in the middle of that "pound of flesh" speech? They got more than a pound's worth, didn't they, Ags?'

'They did,' said Aggie, 'they got her daft puffed-out trousers and a bum as big as Manchester. Who played Shylock? Was it Winnie Doodah, her with the teeth? No, she didn't have a big bum. Must have been Cynthia Chorlton . . .' Aggie's voice faded to nothing. 'Go on, Marie.'

'One more interruption and you are both dead.'

'All right.'

'*Miss Marie Martindale is a legal secretary who has been employed by a reputable Bolton firm for the past five years.*' Marie paused, waited for comments about bum-feelers and paper clips, was relieved when none arrived. '*All three of us are looking for a change of direction and an opportunity to be part of a new venture. We have very little money to invest, but we are capable and hard-working women with enthusiasm and a willingness to learn. We remain, Yours faithfully.*'

'Is that all?' asked Josie.

'What did you expect?' replied Marie. '*A Tale of Two* flaming *Cities*? Now, shut up and sign it. Are your hands clean, Aggie?'

'Course they are,' came the swift answer, 'I'm not frying till tonight.'

Each girl applied her signature to the document, after which event the atmosphere became more serious. 'It doesn't mean anything,' volunteered Josie. 'We don't need to do it.'

'No,' agreed Aggie, 'we don't need to take the jobs. Anyway, she might not like us. She might not want a little fat redhead who stinks of chip fat, or a lanky loony who sells stockings. She might not even want a legal secretary who's dangerous with paper clips.'

'And we've no money,' added Marie. 'She could even get some rich people wanting to join her. And, let's face it – we might not like her. But we still have our steady jobs to fall back on if we're not suitable.'

'Just don't fall back into a potato-chipper,' Aggie advised.

'Or into Sandalwood stockings.' Josie's tone was gloomy.

'Don't look at me,' said Marie, 'because I'm saying nothing about falling back into Mr Garswood. He's a bloody pervert, he is, always staring at my chest.'

The other two girls eyed said chest. 'It is big,' said Josie, her tone serious.

'It'd make a good life jacket,' was Aggie's contribution. 'You'd not drown with that lot in front of you, Marie.'

'The chap who designed the Eiffel Tower makes Marie's bras,' offered Josie, 'all scaffolding and whalebone.'

Had the advertiser seen the cushion-fight that followed, she would not have been impressed by these prospective giants of industry . . .

Dave Armstrong was fed up to the back teeth with his job. For six days a week, he was shut in with old Mr Chandler, a shrivelled wreck of a man in his seventy-ninth year. At night, the old reprobate was locked in his room, as he was still able to walk and could cause a fair amount of mayhem around the house, especially when he came into contact with a woman. During the days, however, he needed feeding, changing and keeping calm. Feeding was not easy, changing was difficult, while the word 'calm' was not in the repertoire where Henry Chandler was concerned.

Well, thank God, Polly Fishwick was supposed to be taking over in the near future, because Dave had had enough. At the age of thirty, he was ready to move on, to get an outside job: labouring or farm work, something that did not involve human waste and regurgitated food.

Henry, who was far from happy in his own twilight world, regarded Dave as a challenge. He clawed at him, sank dentures into his flesh, spat in his face and enjoyed the reactions of his victim. The clawing was solved quite easily – Dave waited until Henry was asleep, then trimmed the nails. Dentures proved more difficult, though they were confiscated from time to time, but the spitting was continuous.

Dave, who had just had what he called 'a bugger of a time', made sure that his patient was asleep, turned the key, then went downstairs to speak to the master. He knocked at the study door. 'Come,' called Richard.

The servant entered the room, found Richard Chandler at his desk and in his cups. Oh, no. Richard Chandler sober was abusive; Richard Chandler drunk was abusive *and* unreasonable. Dave cleared his throat. 'I can't manage any more, sir,' he began. 'He's just brought all his breakfast up on purpose and bitten my right hand nearly through to the bones.' He raised the bandaged fingers. 'One day off isn't enough, Mr Chandler. Can you not get that lad to do more days? And when is Polly Fishwick starting?'

Richard drained his glass and refilled it. He was in

a mess. The fragrant one was still here, as was the housekeeper, but either or both could walk out any day now. If he moved Polly in, Jean and Sally Foster would disappear within half an hour; if he didn't move Polly in, Dave Armstrong might give in his notice. Why wouldn't the old man die? 'I'll sort something out,' was his blurred response.

But Dave Armstrong suddenly decided that he was truly at the end of his tether. Working for a drunk was not his idea of a good life; spending his days with a senile old man was equally unsavoury. He steeled himself. 'Sorry, sir, but I want to leave. It's no life for me, this isn't. Your dad is very confused now and I can't manage him. Polly won't manage, either. I think you'd be better putting him in a home, somewhere that has enough staff to cope with him. He's going through two or three sets of bedding a day. He even stands there and pees on the new sheets as soon as I've put them on. It's all a game to him, but I can't see the funny side.'

'Quite.'

'So I want to leave, sir.'

'A week's notice, then?'

Dave Armstrong nodded.

'Very well. You may go now. Just work the rest of the week, then I shall have him moved to a nursing home.'

Shocked, Dave left the room and stood in the hall, his head shaking slowly from side to side. There had been no insult, no threat, no pleading, no bribery. It was almost as if Richard Chandler had changed overnight, because he had behaved like an ordinary, sensible man. That could mean only one thing – the master must be up to something. Oh well, it was no skin off Dave Armstrong's nose. He would be out of here in a week's time, and that was good enough for him.

Inside the office, an inebriated man stared at the spot on which his sons had stood just days earlier. They had explained about not wanting university, had told him that his reaction would be predictable – Jeremy had even mentioned his idea about the gun cabinet. They were definitely leaving, had attended no meals since the day of the announcement. Jean continued to sit in the dining room, the vast space between herself and her husband proving that those final, tenuous links had been severed. No children any more, nothing to hold together the Chandler household.

He drank another double Scotch. He had to go and speak to Polly Fishwick yet again, because the rules were changing all the time. Damn and blast Jean, stupid bitch. She had the upper hand now, didn't she? He had allowed that brainless, gutless woman to get the better of him. No further reference to her plans had been made, so, if he behaved himself, she might stay. He shivered. What a delightful prospect – just himself, Sally Foster and the fragrant one rattling about in this vast house, the only interruptions coming from dailies and tradesmen. Wonderful.

Dad would have to go, of course. That would be yet another expense, payment to a nursing home whose staff would do their best to keep Henry alive, because Henry and others like him were their source of income. 'When am I going to start winning?' he asked the empty glass.

There was no answer; even if this inanimate object

86

had been able to consider the question, the indisputable fact remained that there was never to be a final solution. The old man should be dead. Nanny Foster, too, needed to be history, while Jean Chandler ought to relearn her place in the scheme of things. But the sands of time continued to shift, while Richard Chandler had to walk softly on the surface so as not to disturb his own dubious underpinnings.

Jeremy and Peter were visiting their sister. She was living in a rather grand though characterless room with adequate furniture, its own bathroom and a view of one of the town's squares. She was delighted to see her brothers. 'Good for you,' she exclaimed when they had recounted the tale of the showdown with Father. 'Did he change colour?'

'Puce,' said Jeremy.

'With some magenta,' added Peter. 'And we managed not to use a gun, though Jer did tell him how desperate we are. Then, there's Mother. Have you heard, Merry?'

She nodded. 'Biding her time, I imagine. Mother may act stupid, but she is a planner. I know for a fact that she has sent Nanny Foster to pick up details from estate agents – Nanny called in to see me. It is beginning to look like a mass exodus, isn't it?'

Jeremy agreed. 'None of this suits Father, so he is on his best behaviour. Dave Armstrong is leaving, which means that Grandfather will go into some sort of nursing home – and we have heard nothing more about Polly Fishwick, so goodness knows what will happen on that front. Father is going to be a very lonely man.'

'Shame,' said Meredith. 'But, oh, I am so glad that

you are here. I had some replies to my advertisement, though most went straight into the bin. But there is one here that caught my eye – three girls who told me just about enough to interest me and not enough to bore me. They will be here shortly for interview. Now,' she perched on the end of the bed, 'how does one do an interview?'

'Crikey,' exclaimed Peter, 'God knows. Jer?'

'I'm not God,' answered Jeremy. 'Father would know.'

'Some use you two are.' Meredith laughed nervously. 'Would you like to go home and ask Father? He could give us some hints, perhaps.'

'No.' Jeremy shook his head. 'God would be a better bet.'

'I don't even know what sort of business I am thinking of.' She jumped up and began to pace the room. No matter how long and hard she thought, she still returned to chandlery. 'I should have waited until I had an idea of what I want to do. But I jumped in before I was ready, as always.'

Jeremy smiled. 'Like that time when you were being taught to swim? First lesson and straight in at the deep end, according to Mother. I think you have inherited your jump-now-and-think-later attitude from Father. He is drinking like a fish, by the way, straight in at the deep end of the whisky decanter.'

Meredith stopped in her tracks, nursed another idea for a moment, set off again. Sometimes, she despaired of herself. She knew that she wanted to do something, yet she could not manage to come up with any sensible plans. Chandlery? And now, here she stood – well, walked about – three young women about to arrive, no concept of how to interview, no questions prepared. She did not often feel like running away from life, but her feet were itching to be out of the hotel, out of Bolton and off the planet altogether.

Peter glanced at his brother. 'It may be time to fasten her to a chair.' Meredith had been their victim many times during their childhoods, had allowed herself to be roped as a prisoner while the 'Injuns' had circled her.

She stopped again. 'If you have nothing interesting to say, Peter . . .' Now she was being nasty to her brother. Was she becoming a female version of her father? Was she going to be an abusive, intolerant type of person? Oh, why had she not inherited Mother's patience? 'I'm sorry. I have decided. Well, I think I have decided. Fancy goods and candles. We make our own candles. We open a factory and employ people. We look into the history of candle-making and make a fuss about it. We demonstrate the ancient art. We–'

But the next piece of information remained frozen in her throat when someone tapped at the door.

Meredith looked frantically at her brothers. She had been about to disclose the most exciting piece of information, the suggestion that customers, under supervision, of course, should be allowed to make their own candles. Now she was interrupted and confused . . . and very nervous.

Jeremy opened the door to reveal three very jolly-looking individuals who had obviously dressed specially for the occasion, all of them neat and in muted colours, the tallest of the three an extraordinarily attractive young woman. He pulled himself to his full five feet and eleven inches, hoped that he now matched her for height – she was one of the tallest girls he had ever seen.

'We've come about the advert,' said another girl, green-eyed, also very pretty. The last of the trio was short, rounded, with curly red hair and an amused expression on her face.

'Do come in.' He widened the door, stood back and allowed them to walk inside. He was pleased to see that his sister had seated herself and had managed to assume an air of reasonable calm.

Marie, Josie and Aggie stood before Meredith like three soldiers awaiting inspection. Jeremy winked at his brother, then leaned against the edge of the dressing table.

The interviewer invited the visitors to sit, and they perched on the foot of the bed, putting Jeremy in mind of a row of people in a doctor's waiting room, all anxious, each slightly afraid of diagnosis. The tall one, in the middle, was flanked by a girl of normal height and one who was tiny, so his eyes had to align themselves differently while he studied the inter-viewees. The tall one was a stunner. He wanted her to get the job – whatever the job was – because he liked the look of her. For a few seconds, no-one spoke.

'Nice day,' remarked Peter in an attempt to break the ice.

The middle-sized girl agreed, then went on to introduce her companions. The tall one was Josephine Maguire, the diminutive one was Agnes Turner. 'And I am Marie Martindale – I work in a solicitor's office. Josie is with Marks and Spencer, while Aggie is a–'

'Fish-fryer.' After completing her companion's

sentence, Aggie grinned. 'I do chips, too, and I am a good wrapper-upper. I am the best wrapper-upper of fish and chips in Lancashire, because I have an O level in Latin. If you want anything wrapped up, I am your man.'

Meredith found herself laughing and she watched as each girl relaxed. They already had work, they were unafraid and there was intelligence here. 'I'll be frank,' she began.

Aggie, always incapable of resisting a quip, declared that she had an uncle called Frank and that she hoped Frank Whatever-her-name-was enjoyed good health.

'Meredith Chandler. These are my brothers. The slightly taller one is Jeremy and the shy one is Peter. We have all run away from home.'

'Are you the Chandlers from Chandlers Green?' asked Marie.

Meredith nodded.

'My mam and dad are running away *to* Chandlers Green,' said Marie, 'so you won't be missed, because there'll be only one less. Well, then, are you the people Chandlers Green got its name from?'

'Yes,' answered Meredith.

Marie grinned broadly. 'This is going to be fun,' she remarked, 'because my dad hates your dad with a passion. He's not the sort of bloke who hates people, but he has made an exception.'

'Everyone has made an exception in the case of our beloved papa,' said Jeremy. 'He is a nasty piece of work, so we are not in the least way offended.' His eyes kept straying to Josie and he wished that she would speak, but she seemed to be the quietest of the three.

91

'I shall still be frank,' continued Meredith eventually. 'I am not completely sure of my plans, but I want to work. The three of us have some money – not enough to start up properly; we shall need to borrow – and I am toying with the idea of chandlery – a play on the name, if you like. And, if we start small, the biggest investment will be premises.'

'I have a five-pound note sewn into my vest for emergencies,' announced Josie with great solemnity. 'My mother's motto is "Be prepared", although she did get kicked out of the Scouts for being too aggressive with the boys. So, if you will all close your eyes, I'll see if I can root it out.'

Jeremy was hooked immediately. The girl had beauty and wit and he would ask her out at the earliest opportunity. As he and his brother tended to have similar tastes, he glanced across the room and was pleased to see that Peter's attention rested on Marie, who seemed to be leader of the trio.

Meredith thanked Josie and said that the five pounds might well be needed at some stage, after which statement she became serious. 'You have jobs, so keep them. If you are interested in investing time with me, I shall make sure that you do not lose out – keep those jobs until the very last minute.'

'Great,' muttered Aggie.

'Wonderful,' Josie sighed.

'I don't mind,' added Marie, 'because I've plenty of paper clips.' She could feel Peter's eyes boring into her and was beginning to wonder whether she had lipstick on her teeth . . .

'How would you feel about manufacturing candles?' Meredith was asking now.

'Water off a duck's back to me,' answered Aggie.

'It'll be just like frying tonight, only without the cod and spuds.'

The other two girls indicated that they would not mind being involved in a factory. 'Would there be a shop as well?' asked Marie.

'Yes.' Meredith was warming to her subject. 'At first, I thought my idea too stupid for words, but it kept coming back. No matter what else I thought of, the word "chandlery" had emblazoned itself on the front of my mind, as bright as the Blackpool lights. Well, now, I no longer think it's silly. The Egyptians had candles, the American Indians made them out of fish – and our name is right.'

'Your family made them hundreds of years ago. We did you in local history at junior school,' offered Josie.

'True,' said Meredith. 'Now, we have to find out about the competition and discover how we can be different. Candelabra, candles moulded into decorative shapes, different finishes, a museum of candle-making. I have a notion about allowing customers to design and make their own. Then there would be the shop. I am sure you three young ladies would enjoy working in that.'

Josie and Aggie looked at each other. 'No tights and no chips,' said Josie.

But Meredith rolled on. 'We need to be competitive in the field of church candles and so forth – also those little domestic ones for power cuts.'

Marie nodded thoughtfully. 'The thing is, I am very well paid where I am. We are thinking of moving into my parents' old house – the three of us – and although the rent is low, it will still want paying.'

93

Peter, afraid of losing sight of Marie, allowed himself to speak. 'But you will carry on working in your current posts until we are set up properly.' He blushed. 'Just a thought.'

Aggie smiled inwardly. As ever, no-one was interested in her, but her generous nature prevented her from feeling jealous as the meeting continued. It seemed that both her friends had hooked a fish and that neither catch was struggling to get away. And these fish were certainly an improvement on battered cod, that was certain . . .

FOUR

'It will do.' Jean Chandler placed the estate agent's printed details in her handbag and walked down the path to a green-painted gate. 'Yes, it is adequate for our needs, even if the boys and Meredith move in with us. Jeremy and Peter would have to share a room, but I am sure that they would not object.' The situation at the grange had quietened; it was plain that Richard expected her to stay, and she had allowed him to believe that she would, because she needed peace and quiet while making her decisions.

'Nice house,' replied Sally Foster. It promised to be noisy, though. After the wide-open spaces of Chandlers Green, Crompton Way, a section of Bolton's ring road, seemed as busy as a Saturday market, people coming and going on foot, plus cars, lorries, motorbikes and cycles rushing by. But the house was a bargain. It had a corner plot, so the gardens were large when compared to others nearby, while the neat, red-brick building was detached, at least.

'We'll get used to it,' promised Jean. 'It's just a case

of steeling ourselves for the change. And, let's face it, we have no future at the grange. He is drinking enough now to merit the purchase of his own distillery.'

'He'll not last,' replied Sally.

Jean shook her head. 'Sometimes, the sickest live longest. Never mind, we shall do very well here, I am sure.' Poor Henry. She had not seen the old man for months, but oh, how she dreaded leaving him to the tender mercies of Richard and his minions. 'Please don't worry, Sally. We shall be quite all right here.'

Sally wasn't quite sure. Mrs Jean had no training for work and her dead mother's money would not last for ever. Yet there was a new confidence in the mistress, a sign that her backbone had stiffened, that she was finally adult. She didn't appear to care any more, took her meals in the kitchen, walked past her husband without speaking, without flinching, had planned the purchase of a house, knew which items of furniture she would claim from the grange.

'I shall bring all my mother's things,' she said now, 'and he will still have more than enough. Come along, let's get home – if such it might be termed.'

They climbed back into the taxi and rode in silence up the moors until they reached Chandlers Green. On their way into the village, they passed Claughton Cottage, a sturdy, rather neglected house that had belonged to a Miss Forrester. A builder's van was parked outside; while two men worked on the broken fence, a third was balanced precariously on the roof. 'A facelift at last,' commented Jean. 'That's a pretty house and it deserves some attention.'

On the driveway of Chandlers Grange, they

passed Richard. He was on unsteady feet, was clearly unfit to take his car and had apparently retained sufficient sense to realize that. Jean and Sally glanced at each other, said nothing until the taxi had delivered them to the door.

'Just look at him,' mused Jean.

'Do I have to, Mrs Jean?'

'Can we stop this Mrs Jean, Sally? When old Mrs Chandler was alive, I suppose the Mrs Jean separated me from her – thank God. What a harridan she was. This is to be a fresh start, Sally. Call me Jean, just Jean. Look – he almost fell into that holly bush – the man is heading for an accident. He thinks I have forgotten about moving out. In fact, from the state of him, I wonder whether he remembers my original threat? He has promised to keep you on and to leave Pol Fishwick where she is, so he thinks I am going to remain here.' She sighed. 'He knows my fear, Sally. Moving is something he considers to be beyond me – if he considers anything at all, that is.'

They stood and watched until Richard had managed to negotiate his way towards the gates. Then, both heads shaking in despair, they went inside to enjoy a cup of tea and the freedom his absence brought.

She must have got the heating process wrong again.

Anna Chandler smiled ruefully at the mess on her hands. At great risk to life and limb, she had harvested a small amount of wax from her hives and, after saturating a wick in paraffin, had tried to soften and coil the product of her bees into a simple column by winding the malleable material round and round until a sizeable candle had been achieved. It would be very pretty – as long as she could retain the honey-comb quality produced by those tiny, buzzing workers. Well, that had been the theory. The result was not as pleasing as she had hoped, but there was always tomorrow.

She sat now at her front window and engaged herself in an attempt to remove debris from under the tips of her nails. She was proud of her hands. They managed to remain younger than the rest of her, and the nails were always neat and polished. 'Vanity,' she mumbled under her breath. Yes, she had wonderful skin and hair that had turned silver rather than grey. Her hands bore none of the stains of time, those liver spots which seemed to arrive after the age of seventy. Really, some new clothes might be a good idea, but–

What was that? Ah. She rose and sighed heavily as she saw the taxi returning to the grange, narrowly missing her nephew as it swept past the gatehouse. 'Fool,' she muttered. 'What on earth is he doing?' He could scarcely walk. He was hanging on to a post as if his life depended on its support. She lit a cigarette and continued to watch Richard. He seemed to be struggling with his breathing and, for a moment, she committed the unforgivable sin of praying for his death. But no, he was righting himself, was preparing to move out into a world too innocent to be deserving of his intrusion.

Anna sat down again. The behaviour of Richard Chandler was becoming more bizarre by the day. After removing his own father from society, he was now following a similar crooked path, mind clouded by alcohol, body bloated and weakened by the same substance, his own life floating away on a sea of whisky, brandy and the contents of the grange's cellars. He was forty-five years of age, yet he looked at least sixty.

She rose slowly, then emerged from her house and walked to the gate. 'You are an absolute fool,' she told him.

Richard concentrated, focused, looked at her. Thin as a rake, she was covered in an ugly grey dress that would have fitted a woman twice her size. 'Aunt Anna,' he managed.

'I am ashamed of you,' she advised him. 'You have imprisoned my brother, you refuse to allow him visitors, yet your behaviour is more spectacular than Henry's ever was. If you do not stop drinking, you will be dead within months.'

'Mind your own business.' The words arrived slurred. 'It's none of your concern.' Richard belched loudly before continuing, 'I do what I think best.'

'Think? You can't think. Your brain cells are dying off. Is it true that Meredith has left home?'

'Yes. And you are still smoking like a chimney.'

She nodded. 'Yes, we are a family of addicts, Richard. Fortunately, although tobacco may shorten my stay in this mortal coil, it does not alter my behaviour.' She looked to the heavens, shook her head, then awarded him her full attention again. 'You will bleed to death,' she announced.

'So will you. You'll get a bad cough and I shall have liver trouble – what's the difference?'

Anna inhaled deeply and blew the smoke in his direction. 'The difference is that I lock no-one in a bedroom and I do not inflict damage on my family.'

He grinned. 'I haven't hit anyone.' He was proud of that, at least.

'Your tongue hurts people,' she told him quietly.

'You are detested by everyone for miles around – most particularly by your own household.'

He steadied himself, drew himself up to full height. 'And everybody laughs at you. You're a ridiculous old woman. You carry on as if you own the bloody church – they all talk about you behind your back.'

'I know.'

Richard could think of nothing further to say, so he advised her to bugger off, then stepped out into the lane. She could go to hell; they could all go to hell.

'Hard as bloody nails, stripping the place bare, mending fences. But he'll mend no fences with me, oh no.' Richard Chandler threw himself into Polly Fishwick's greasy armchair. 'Gall of the man, coming to live here in my village. My grandfather would have had him chased out.'

Polly, who was confused to the point of desperation, kept her mouth tightly closed. She could have mentioned that this was no longer his village, that the Chandlers now owned just a few farms, a handful of tied cottages and their own house, but it was pointless. First, he had used her body, then had demanded that she move to the grange in order to care for his father. But all that was forgotten now, because his wife would not tolerate Polly's presence in her home.

'They went out in a taxi,' he slurred.

'Did they?' Polly couldn't have cared less, because he was making very little sense. Was he talking about the Martindales?

'Passed me on the drive, almost ran me over, completely ignored me. It's like living with a coven of witches.'

Ah, his thoughts had returned to his wife and Sally

100

Foster, it seemed. 'There's thirteen in a coven – I read that in the *Reveille*. They meet in woods at night and say the Mass backwards, then they sacrifice things.'

He looked at her. God, what was he doing here? The only person in the world who would listen to him was the abandoned wife of a woodsman. This was all wrong; he had a wife of his own at home and she should offer comfort, she should be the one to soothe away his troubles. 'What use are you going to be now?' he asked.

Polly attempted no reply. Terrified by the threat of homelessness, she sought only not to anger him. He was very drunk, too, so his behaviour promised to be even more erratic than usual. The whites of his eyes were streaked with red, while his face, white at the outer edges, displayed a variety of colours from pink through to blue, the more purple sections on a bulbous, alcohol-damaged nose pitted with open pores. Well, he was no oil painting, that was for sure. Yet she had to be compliant, was forced to listen, to dance to whichever tune he proposed to play.

'You'll stay here till I think of a use for you,' he announced.

'Right.' True hatred burgeoned anew in that moment. She had not liked him for some time, but now, reduced to the status of beggar, one whose body was no longer required, whose person was valued so poorly, she took up the remnants of her pride and gathered them in. Eventually, she would have her revenge against this man.

Unaware of the emotions nursed in the heart of his ex-mistress, Richard Chandler rambled on. 'You will befriend the wife of Alfred Martindale. She will be unknown here, so, as soon as her husband has gone to work, she is going to feel lonely. People in towns are like ants – they live in colonies, help each other, are seldom alone. The country is different.'

'Yes, I know.' A town girl, Polly had missed her roots when she had first come to live in Woodside Cottage. Now, she enjoyed the seclusion and needed to keep her home, because she could not manage to wish herself back in town on a permanent basis. Bolton was for shopping only, and she was glad to be away from it.

'I shall ruin him,' announced Richard, 'just as he tried to ruin me.'

It seemed that she was to be used as a weapon, then, one who would be fired like a cannon at the Martindales. And, although she had wondered about playing both sides, this was the man who was keeping her alive and she had no power to stand up for herself. Not just yet, anyway. 'Will you be putting money in the bank like you promised?'

'Of course. A Chandler's word is his bond.'

'And I don't need to look after your dad?'

'Not for the moment. Dave Armstrong is there for a few days yet, then, who knows? I did manage to persuade Dave to stay a little longer, but I shall probably put the old man away somewhere. He is beyond retrieval now, too senile for most situations. You could have managed him, but my wife will not allow that.'

'I'm not surprised.'

He glared at her. 'Most men in my position do exactly as they please, but Jean has developed notions; she is under the influence of Nanny Foster, as she has not the brains to make any decisions for herself.'

Inwardly, Polly smiled. She felt a grudging admiration for the wife of Richard Chandler, as she seemed to have brought the unbiddable man to heel for the first time in his life. Oh, how Polly wanted him to leave. She fancied soaking her feet in front of the fire, a nice bit of lunch, then a snooze. But she could not see him off, because her home was his property. She was his property.

Richard stumbled to his feet, staggered, righted himself. 'Be ready,' he said before making his way out of the house. He stood at the gate, looked right into woods owned by him, forward into land owned by him, left towards a village that had once been the domain of his family. Here had lived the chandlers, those who had moulded and dipped, who had been grateful for the work provided by the real Chandlers. It was all going, was slipping through his fingers as fast as tallow had dripped its way along wick and into the retrieval bowls beneath.

He forced himself not to roar with rage, then began the walk back into his village. It was a pretty place with rows of terraced houses built in keeping with the rises and pleats of the land, each house constructed from thick, solid stone, their roofs high, then low, depending on the level of the plots on which they stood. There was a public house, named, somewhat predictably, the Chandlers Arms, then a small green-grocery, a post office-cum-general store that sold everything from envelopes to spades. Further on, a few detached homes with gardens announced that the chandlery had housed its management well – these were now the property of educated men, doctors, lawyers, businessfolk.

Except for one. Claughton Cottage, the last house

– or the first, depending on where one entered the village – was not yet occupied. He watched the builders at their tasks, could see that a considerable amount of work was being done. Still fuelled by drink, he secreted himself behind a tree and tried to calculate the cost of Martindale's renovations. It was sickening to think that a man who traded in rubbish was displaying such affluence.

He dared not burn it down, dared not damage the place. What could be done to stop this man arriving here? It would have to be achieved in town, before Martindale and his damned family arrived in Chandlers Green. How? Who? Could he deal with this himself and, if he could not, was there anyone he might appoint to undertake the task for a sum? How was such a man to be punished, stopped, hurt, persuaded . . . killed?

Uncomfortable with his wicked thoughts, Richard slid away onto his own land and strode homeward. At least the fragrant one had stopped threatening to move out. She hadn't the guts to leave, hadn't the guts to decide what day it was. God, he was surrounded by fools. He would get home as soon as possible; another whisky would help him organize his mind.

'Don't be too hasty.' Anna sat with Jean and Sally at the kitchen table. She could not remain long, as her nephew might return and she did not want to fuel his paranoia. 'I must leave soon,' she said, 'as he is already convinced that the world conspires against him.'

'Perhaps it does,' said Jean, 'because he is hated not just by his family. You left, Anna. You know that you

104

could not have borne it a moment longer, so how can you expect the rest of us to stay?'

Wreathed in tobacco smoke, Anna Chandler shook her head as if trying to redistribute its contents into some sort of order. 'Have you seen my brother?'

'No,' answered Jean sadly. 'The excuse is that he is too dangerous and the minders are under Richard's orders to keep everyone out. He has not left his room for many weeks.'

Anna sighed, then took another puff of best Virginia. 'I hear that Dave Armstrong is ready to move on, probably back to farm labouring.'

Jean already knew about that. 'Yes. Richard wanted to install Pol Fishwick as his nurse. That is where I drew the line. I am sorry, Anna, but for my own sake – and for my children and Sally, too – I must get away from here. Please do not make me responsible for my father-in-law. It isn't my fault.' Nevertheless, she managed to feel hugely guilty. What would become of the old man when Armstrong left? Who would tend him? Would Richard be willing to pay for care in an institution of some kind? Or would he have Henry committed to a mental hospital? 'I am sorry,' she repeated.

Anna rose to her feet. 'Yes, it is too much for me to ask and I apologize. Of course you must save yourselves.' She slammed her hat onto her head. 'Thank you for the tea, Sally.'

Jean stood up. 'What are you afraid of, Anna? It is all right – you can speak freely in front of Sally.'

'I know that.' Anna bit hard on her lower lip. 'It's falling apart, Jean – and I don't mean the heap of stones that used to be the factory. The Chandlers remain landowners and Richard cares nothing for his tenants. He is drinking so much that I don't even know whether rents are being collected or whether we can trust those invested with stewardship. On top of that, he is imbibing any profits we might be making. And I fear . . .' Her voice tailed away.

'You fear?' Jean prompted.

'He may kill my brother.'

There, it was out. The worry shared by these three women had finally been given an airing.

'I am going now.' Anna left the house by the rear door.

Jean and Sally remained in the kitchen. 'What shall we do?' asked Jean.

'I have no idea,' replied Sally. And that was another truth aired.

'So, what did you think of her?' Aggie Turner kicked her heels against the wall outside one of her parents' two shops. This was her home, her territory; the second shop was a lock-up in town, but this one, fastened to the Co-op on Tonge Moor Road, was Aggie's stamping ground.

'I thought she was nice.' Marie glanced at Josie's deadpan features.

'They were all nice,' agreed Josie. 'But I don't know whether I would throw my hat into their ring. I'm not sure that they're sure. From the sound of it, they're on the run from their father – and their mother won't be hanging on much longer, either. They're just three runaways and the girl is the one with the ideas.'

'She's bright,' announced Marie, 'but a candle factory? How bright is a candle? Sounds a bit mad to me – I'd sooner have a hundred-watt light bulb any

106

day. I mean, I don't mind getting my hands dirty, but who wants candles these days? We've all got electricity now.'

'They're making a comeback,' explained Josie. 'There are all kinds of new ones – thin, tapering things stuck in special holders that take up to a dozen, then coloured ones for the table. But we have good jobs. To give up a good job, we'd have to be sure.'

Aggie didn't think much of her job. 'I'm wasted,' she moaned. 'Five subjects including Latin, and all I do is sell chips.'

The smell of hot fat floated through the shop's open door and into the noses of the three girls. Aggie was desperate to be out of here, because no matter what she did the aroma clung to her clothes and to every other item behind and above the shop's premises. She had gone through school smelling of lard, often wondered why her parents had sent her to the Catholic grammar when all they had needed was one more fish-fryer. 'You two can please yourselves,' she said after a few minutes' thought, 'but I am leaving this place. Whether I work for Meredith Chandler or not, I am leaving home.'

'So am I,' said Josie, 'because otherwise I'd never hear the last of Marks and Spencer. I am not spending the rest of my life in hosiery.'

'Look on the bright side,' Marie suggested. 'They could move you up to suspender belts and bras.'

'And vests,' added Josie, her tone its usual deliberately grim self. 'Just think, girls, I could be in corsets by Christmas.'

They sighed simultaneously.

A car drew up at the kerb and two men unfolded themselves from its small interior. Marie and Josie organized their features into unimpressed mode, but Aggie, ebullient as ever, could not contain her joy. 'Peter! Jeremy!' she yelled. 'When did you get that?'

'Don't blame me,' Jeremy grumbled. 'Peter was the architect of this little mistake. If you're a very thin dwarf, it's a good car. But if you are any taller than three feet, keep your head between your knees – even when driving.' He grinned at his brother. 'We grew too tall to be jockeys, didn't we, Pete? So now we are training to be racing drivers. The trouble is, this old girl doesn't do more than thirty – even then, she needs a following wind.'

But Aggie thought the Austin was brilliant. 'If we bend Josie in half, we can all get in the back. Come on, girls, let's go for a spin.'

Josie, who was usually good at not blushing, felt the heat in her cheeks. Jeremy Chandler was clearly smitten; he could not take his eyes off her. At the same time, Peter, the more reticent of the two, kept his gaze averted from Marie. It seemed that the boys had made up their minds to set their caps, and poor Aggie was to be left out yet again. Aggie was usually left out, because she was dumpy and her red hair was too curly to be biddable, yet Josie suspected that she was the most valuable of all of them, the brainiest and the most fun.

Aggie, always determined to make the best of everything, continued to enthuse about the car. She knew what was happening, but she realized, too, that no courtship had started; at this point, she would not be *de trop* – in fact, she might even be useful, especially where the shy twin was concerned. 'Are we going?' she asked.

Peter studied his shoes. Aggie was a good sort, but

108

the car was scarcely big enough for four and would certainly acquire sardine-tin status if three were packed into the rear seat. Marie was gorgeous and he dared not look at her. His brother, forever the leader, was more open in his approach, as he neither feared nor expected rejection.

'I suppose we could crowbar you all in,' said Jeremy.

Josie stared straight into his eyes. Underneath all the banter, she remained a good Catholic girl and this Protestant had better keep his distance. She did like him, though . . .

Marie looked at the car, then allowed her gaze to roam over Josie and Aggie. Josie might well need a hole in the roof for her head, while Aggie, rather rounder, required a seat to herself. 'You four go,' she suggested. 'I should get home, really.' At last, she felt Peter Chandler's gaze. He was clearly displeased by her suggestion, yet he made no comment.

'We can squeeze in,' insisted Aggie. 'Come on, Marie, don't be a spoilsport. I'll sit on your knee.'

'No, thanks. I'd rather keep the feeling in my legs if you don't mind.'

Peter's cheeks were suddenly red as he spoke to his brother. 'Erm . . . why don't you take Aggie and Josie? I'll stay here with . . . er . . . with Marie.'

Marie felt a dart of panic shooting through her chest. This was not a familiar reaction and she was uncomfortable with it. Did she like him, dislike him, was she indifferent? Surely indifference would bring no reaction at all? Perhaps she was afraid of the hard work he promised to be, because extracting opinion or comment from such a man would require intervention verging on the surgical.

'What do you say?' Josie asked her friend.

'I don't mind,' replied Marie. She did mind, but could not admit her reluctance in the circumstances, everyone hanging on her words. 'Just don't be long, because I'll need to get home.'

Peter spoke. 'These three can sit here while I drive you home later,' he said. 'That will be fair play. They get the first ride and you get the second.'

Aggie climbed into the rear seat while Josie sat next to Jeremy. In a cloud of greyish-blue smoke, they shuddered off in a northerly direction, leaving Marie to contend with a boy whose shyness might easily have belonged to someone in early puberty. She reclaimed her place on the wall. Peter took a sudden interest in the shop next door, an iron-monger's whose display of tools, firelighters, buckets and mops was not exactly riveting.

Marie studied her nails, wished that they would grow, wondered whether nail polish might hold them together. She had managed, finally, to stop biting them, but they were still flaky.

Eventually, he joined her. 'That's not the sort of chandlery we are thinking of,' he began.

'Oh?'

'No, we want something more exotic. My sister has a flair for the unusual.'

He was talking, expressing a view. Did he thrive only when he stood beyond the range of his twin's shadow? Meredith, too, was rather outgoing, so perhaps this twin needed his own plot of earth where he might prosper without sharing light.

'We don't know what to do – Aggie, Josie and myself, I mean.'

Peter nodded. 'A man I know always says, "If in

110

doubt, do nowt." Sage advice. But I suggest you take an interest, because Merry is going to be a force to contend with. She is the instigator, always was.'

'While you are rather shy.'

He hesitated. 'Yes. And Jeremy is the more amusing. I expect you find me something of a bore – most do. I think a lot and try not to talk rubbish.'

She smiled. 'Rubbish can be fun.'

'Nonsense can be fun,' he argued, 'whereas rubbish belongs in the bin. The knack is to recognize the difference. My life's work will be sorting wheat from chaff.'

Marie decided there and then that she liked Peter Chandler. He was shy in the company of his siblings, that was all. Apart from that, he seemed an intelligent sort of person, probably capable of great wit in the right circumstances. 'I wonder where Jeremy has taken them?' she asked.

It was Peter's turn to smile. 'Who knows? Who cares? At least I got the chance to spend some time with you.'

She thought her heart would be stopped by the shock. Quiet, reserved Peter Chandler had spoken out already. Mind, she had met him only twice, so her original assessment of him might have been hasty. Glancing sideways, she saw that his skin was slightly flushed, though, for the most part, his demeanour remained calm and unhurried. 'That was a nice thing to say,' she told him.

'Best to speak the truth. It cuts out a lot of red tape. I think I have changed in the past few days, since we told Father to take a long walk. What's the point of keeping it all inside, Marie?'

She laughed. 'If you want your old man to take a

long walk, I'll buy a lead for my dad – he'll exercise him for you and drop him off the end of one of Blackpool's piers.'

'I wonder what happened there?' he asked.

'Something in the war.' She tried to remember exactly what she knew, but came up with very little. 'My dad says Richard Chandler is not a man of honour. But he never talks about the details – not in front of me or my brother, anyway.'

'Which means that your father is a man of honour.'

'I think so, Peter, but I may be biased.'

'He is hated universally – my father, I mean. There is a great deal of the bully about him. Bullies have their feet set in cowardice and cowards are afraid of the world.' He took a few paces, circled and stood in front of his companion. 'Are you afraid of the world, Marie?'

'No, but I have always been a bit reckless.'

'My sister is the same,' he told her, 'which is why I think you should keep in touch, maintain an interest in whatever she does. She will fly or she will crash – there will be no middle road. Whichever, the noise will be heard nationwide. Oh, and Mother seems to be intending to buy a house on Crompton Way.'

Marie processed this new information. 'So, your father is to be abandoned to his fate.'

'Yes. Even the housekeeper will leave. Mother will expect the three of us to live with her, of course.'

'And will you?'

'For a while, yes. Mother will need support.'

Yes, he was a decent sort of man, not as giddy as his brother, not as pushy as his sister, yet there was a quiet power in him, an element Marie had not expected to find. Handsome, too, she admitted, of decent height, strong yet slender build, with dark blond hair and hazel eyes. She was interested. He was not a Catholic, but that didn't matter – he would be a pleasant friend. Wouldn't he?

'I just want a job,' he said, placing himself beside her on the wall. 'Father was keen for us to attend university – wants us to be professionals, the sort of sons he could brag about. But neither of us is cut out for that sort of life. You work for solicitors?'

'Yes.'

'But you don't like the job?'

Marie shrugged. 'I don't like dirty old men – or dirty young ones. Lawyers are strange creatures – they go about upholding the rules, then spend their spare time breaking every commandment on Moses' list. I was brought up to keep my distance, Peter, and to respect marriage. The law is the most corrupt body in the world, I'm sure. As for the police – no comment.'

He grinned. Marie would see it and say it, would go through life without compromise, without making room for those she judged to be wrongdoers. She was educated without being threatening, intelligent, yet not superior in her attitude. A 'good egg', according to Meredith, a 'corker', in Jeremy's eyes, though Jeremy seemed more taken with Josie, which pleased Peter enormously.

'What's funny?' she demanded.

'I'll tell you when I know you better.'

He already knew her well, of that she felt certain. She had a distinct feeling that he had been thinking about her . . . And she knew him, too, which was strange, as they had not met until recently. Some of

113

the people from school she had scarcely known at all, even after many years spent in the same classrooms, yet she felt as if she had known Peter Chandler for ever. Perhaps she was growing up at last. 'I think a lot,' she said eventually, needing to respond to his quizzical expression. 'I have a mind that never seems to stop, as if there's a treadmill in there—'

'And you keep striding on?'

'Yes, I suppose so.'

This amused him – the idea of Meredith and Marie coming together was a fascinating one, because neither woman promised to make room for the other. Sparks might fly. Sparks in a candle factory? Danger, indeed . . .

'Right.' There was an edge to her tone. 'Tell me what is so funny.'

'You are.'

'Me?'

'Yes. You and my sister, irresistible force and immovable object.'

'You calling me stubborn?'

He pondered. 'I shall be kind. You are determined – Merry is the stubborn one. I can imagine either or both of you being reckless. My father is very disappointed in his daughter – she will not be moulded.'

'You and Jeremy have let him down, too.'

His smile faded slowly. 'He has let himself down, Marie. I suppose you enjoy a happy family life?'

Marie thought for a moment. 'Yes, I have been happy at home, though we had a bad time when my mother was ill – she had to go into the TB hospital. That's why Dad bought the house up on the moors. Dad works hard – so did Mam until the TB – they deserve to go up in the world. But your father would

114

stop them if he could.' She stared straight into Peter's clear eyes. 'There's hatred there.'

He nodded.

'Why?' she wondered aloud. Peter had already admitted ignorance, while she knew a little, but not enough. 'Dad got medals.'

'They all did. You survived – you got a medal. You died, you got a couple.'

'He got the VC and Bar. Mam says he got them for unusual bravery, but I think it's all tied up with your father.' She grimaced. 'I wonder what my dad would say now if he caught me consorting with the enemy?'

'Ditto,' was the reply.

Marie grinned mischievously. 'We can find out about some of that when you drive me home. Are you brave enough to meet my parents? If they are in, of course.'

'Yes. Yes, I am.' He was brave enough for anything, wasn't he? He was leaving home, was escaping from a life that was no longer palatable, was reasonably certain of his mother's safety, because Nanny Foster would always look after Mother. Becoming an adult was not a smooth process, then, as it involved a great deal more than simply getting through the years. Growing older and wiser seemed to happen in spurts that were triggered by events. 'Into the lions' den?' he asked, his air deliberately innocent.

Marie thought about that one. 'Lions? Mam and Dad are hardly members of the big cat family, though my mother has been known to bite a few heads off from time to time . . . No. The only time I ever saw Mam really lose her rag was when she got short-changed in the Co-op.'

'A true northerner, then.'

She nodded. 'Hearts of gold, both of them. Dad has a good head for business, though he would never cheat anyone, I'm sure. They are just ordinary people.'

'Hardly,' he replied, his voice almost inaudible. He cleared his throat. 'No, you come from no ordinary stock, Marie Martindale.'

And she knew she was hooked, because she was blushing.

'Get yourself outside of that,' commanded Leena. 'That's what I call an apple pasty, but our Marie calls it something foreign. Now, what with us going up in the world to Chandlers Green, I shall have to come over all Cordon Blue.'

'*Bleu*,' said Marie. 'It's French.'

Leena laughed. 'There's nowt French about my flaky pastry – I learnt it from that there Mrs Beeton, her as goes round with umpteen eggs in her basket and feeds the five thousand in every recipe.' She sniffed. 'Take three pounds of strawberries, indeed. I don't know where Mrs Beeton worked, but they never had rationing.'

'She was pre-war,' offered Marie.

'I'm pre-war and all.' Leena stood to attention, saluted and grinned. 'But I never knew anybody as could afford three pounds of bloody strawberries.' She glanced at herself in the overmantel mirror, patted her hair into place. There was gentry at the table, so she wanted to make sure that she looked tidy. And she should stop swearing; she often swore when she was nervous.

'Lovely,' declared Peter Chandler when he had swallowed the first mouthful. 'Hang on to your

116

mother, Marie,' he advised. 'I know people who would pay a lot of money for cooking like this.'

He was doing excellently, Marie decided. And so was Mam, because she hadn't turned a hair when introduced to the son of the enemy. 'When's Dad due in?' she asked now, 'because we've left three people sitting on the chippy wall up Tonge Moor and they need the car.'

'Aggie and Josie?' asked Leena.

'And Jeremy.' Peter brushed a few crumbs off his shirt front. 'It was my turn for the car.'

Leena poured herself a cup of tea, dark brown and strong, just the way she liked it. 'So, you've a brother and a sister?'

He nodded. 'Meredith is the senior citizen – my twin and I are mere apprentices. Merry plans on dragging us all through the mire while she starts up her business empire.' He managed not to flinch when Marie kicked him, the assault concealed beneath a low-hanging tablecloth. Quickly, he realized that the older Martindales knew nothing of the plans to involve their daughter in Meredith's plots. 'She is going to start a business.'

'Oh.' Leena sipped at her strong brew, stopped herself from blowing on the surface in order to cool it. 'What's she going into?'

'Bankruptcy,' replied Peter seriously. 'Or million-airedom – there are no half measures with my sister.'

'I like the sound of her,' mused Leena. 'That's always been my Alf's philosophy – in for a penny, in for a pound, bugger the consequences.'

The front door flew open, banged against the wall.

'There should be a law passed against your father's treatment of doors,' pronounced Leena.

117

Alf's voice floated up the hallway. 'I've shifted more muck today than I've seen in a lifetime. Chorley New Road? You want to see how they live behind them posh bloody bay windows . . .' His words died as he entered the kitchen. 'Hello,' he said.

Peter stood up and held out his right hand. 'Peter Chandler,' he said.

The older man blinked just once. 'Nay, you don't want to be shaking hands with me, lad.'

The women, uncomfortable, seemed to stop breathing. This was Richard Chandler's son – was the situation going to become awkward? Peter's hand remained where it was, steady and outstretched.

'I'm mucky,' explained Alf.

Marie felt her shoulders as they relaxed; her dad had not let her down, would never fail her. 'Peter's not frightened of a bit of dirt, Dad,' she said. 'He's mucked out more stables than we've had hot dinners.'

Alf grinned, wiped his palm against his sleeve, then shook the visitor's hand. 'Horse-muck's nowt,' he insisted. 'It's just processed grass. Look what it does for roses. But where I've been today – well, it was a dump. Doctor's house, too. Nice to meet you, son. Come on, girl, pour me a mug of tea while I wash my hands – and put some water in it.' He smiled at the visitor. 'You want to watch my Leena's tea. Thicker than treacle – I've seen spoons melt in it.'

He went into the scullery, throwing a final remark over his shoulder. 'I smell like a sewer – slipper baths for me tonight, Leena.'

Marie smiled inwardly. She was proud of her mam and dad, because they knew how to behave. They might never have been the smartest dressed or

118

cleverest of folk, but they were sound, reliable and decent.

Alf returned to the table and picked up his cup of weaker tea. 'Right,' he said. 'So you've been driving my daughter round in that ramshackle contraption outside, have you? Has it got brakes?'

Peter put down his apple pasty. 'Is it still there? If it is, then the answer is yes. Well – the handbrake works, at least. But to stop it, Marie and I have to put our feet through the holes in the floor – it comes to a halt eventually.'

Marie watched her father's face, saw his growing affection for Peter Chandler, witnessed the moment of its inception. 'There's a lot to be said for clogs in them circumstances,' announced Alf. 'See, with clogs, you get irons underneath and a good wooden sole. You can't beat a good wooden bottom – can you, Leena?'

'Eeh, I wouldn't know,' said the lady of the house. 'I've never had a wooden bottom.'

'You have. I remember your corsets.'

The four of them dissolved into laughter and Marie, her eyes moving over her companions, realized yet again how fortunate she was. Peter, in company that brought him out of himself, was clearly at ease, while her parents, bless them, were just themselves. As the laughter died, she could not prevent herself. 'I love you two,' she cried, wiping tears of glee from her eyes.

'She only loves me for me pasties,' said Leena. 'And I can't fathom what she sees in her dad – can you, Peter?'

Oh yes, he could see. He saw all the way through town and on his way up Tonge Moor, saw how family life should be. The short visit to Emblem Street had served to underline what he already knew – that he, Meredith and Jeremy had never had a family. Oh, there had been times, years ago, a lifetime ago, when things had ticked over, when parents and children had played together. Then the drinking had begun.

He turned a corner and drove towards the chip shop. Grandfather, too, had been a drinker. Now, his mind addled after years of indulgence, Henry Chandler inhabited a twilight world, a place in which the tormenting of other humans was his sole hobby. And Richard was going the same way. Mother was a good woman whose life had been destroyed by her husband. Meredith had escaped, he and Jeremy would be leaving, as would Mother and Nanny Foster. What a mess.

He pulled in at the kerb and was pounced upon by his twin. 'Where have you been?' asked Jeremy. 'Aggie has been called into the shop and Josie left ages ago – isn't she wonderful? But what kept you?'

When his brother had settled beside him, Peter spoke. 'I have been sitting at a table with three decent people, Jer. I had an apple pasty and tea strong enough to kill every taste bud on my tongue. We talked and laughed. A rented house with a big coal fire and . . . and love.' He turned his head and looked at Jeremy. 'It's all free, doesn't cost a penny, doesn't need a university degree or proof of any kind, because it doesn't need paying for.'

Jeremy noted the expression on Peter's face and bit back a quip that had hovered naughtily on his lips. 'I know,' he said instead.

'I think I'm in love.'

'With Marie, I take it?'

120

Peter shook his head. 'Well – yes and no. The way they live, so warm – and not just because of the fire. Mr Martindale was very funny, as was his wife. They insult one another affectionately. And Marie – well – she was just Marie. It was like . . . it was like going home. I was at home. I fell head over heels for a way of life, wanted to stay there. They have probably scrimped all their lives to buy Claughton Cottage. But I wasn't an outsider. They open their hearts and let you in, wherever they live.'

Jeremy swallowed a lump of emotion for which he could not account. Peter, outwardly the quieter and more sensitive, was airing notions about which Jeremy had always tried not to think. 'We'll be out of there soon.'

Peter nodded slowly. 'What's going to become of Father?'

'I don't know and I don't care,' came the swift reply.

'He's a human being, Jer.'

'Is he? Oh, that escaped my notice. Mother's, too – and Nanny Foster's. You've got to stop worrying about things you can't change.'

'I know. It still sickens me, though.'

Peter drove homeward at a snail's pace, his eyes straying occasionally to light upon terraced houses that contained families, people who lived together, who were interdependent and affectionate. They weren't all like the Martindales, of that he was certain, but he felt drawn to the smaller life, the larger community, the class whose members had been designated a lower rung on the ladder. 'We haven't got a real life,' he said eventually.

'I know.'

'Mother's damaged – do we really want to live with her and Nanny Foster?'

'She will need our support for a while.'

'Yes, I suppose she will.' Peter changed gears. 'The family I visited today is the one Father hates – the one he has been raging on about since they bought Claughton Cottage. Yet they made me welcome in spite of Father's nastiness.' He pulled in to the kerb. 'I don't want to sound dramatic, Jer, but we have to promise ourselves something.'

'OK. But get on with it, because I am starving.'

'We must lead a good life, you and I. We have to, because we have learnt about the alternative. Oh, I don't mean that we've got to end up as saints, but we must make a fresh start, marry decent girls and look after them properly.'

'I'll drink to that.'

'I won't. I don't want to end up like Dad and Grandfather, so my drinking will be minimal. Alcoholism runs in families, you know. It's in the blood.'

Jeremy turned his head and stared through the window, because he could not bear to look at his brother. A single tear had made its way down Peter's face and Jeremy's throat was suddenly occupied by a sob whose birth he forbade. After all, he was the stronger twin, wasn't he?

'We have to do better than our father did, Jer. We have to go out there and find a life that works.' He dashed the wetness from his cheek, hoped that his twin had not noticed it. Why was he weeping, anyway? Was he mourning the loss of the grange, of a way of life he hated? No, change was necessary. This was self-pity, no more and no less, and he despised himself for it. 'Jer?'

'What?'

'Shall we go to the Chandlers Arms for a pie and a pint?'

'I thought you were signing the pledge,' managed Jeremy.

'No. I'm signing nothing until my solicitor has read it.'

Back to normal, Peter drove his brother to the pub and pushed today to the back of his mind. But today was a cornerstone and he would build on it. Oh, and he would marry Marie Martindale – that was the other certainty.

Richard Chandler slammed the receiver into its cradle. God, the prices of these nursing homes. A man would need to be a millionaire to keep an ageing parent in one of those places. And there was something going on around him – he was aware of activity, quiet, surreptitious goings-on. He should stop drinking and concentrate, but drink was all he had. Dave Armstrong had left and Father was currently in the hands of two village boys; Polly would have managed him, but the fragrant one had dug her heels in. Had he brought in Polly, Jean would have left home. As it stood, she and the boys remained at the grange; perhaps the danger had passed. Since the day of their original announcement, neither boy had mentioned the idea of moving out.

He downed another whisky and closed his eyes. There was movement in the house; several times, he had caught Jean wandering about and staring at furniture. Well, if she thought she was going to buy anything new, she could think again, because he wasn't made of money. What to do about Father? If only a visit by the vet had been a possibility, he would have had Henry put out of everybody's misery.

'Bugger,' he cursed quietly. What was she up to? There was someone skulking in the hall. He rose to unsteady feet, staggered to the door and threw it open. The fragrant one was with Sally Foster, heads together, a notebook in the housekeeper's hands. 'What are you two doing?' he shouted, the words emerging crippled.

Jean sighed and pulled herself to full height. He was a vision of ugliness, waistcoat unbuttoned and stained, face darkened by two days' growth of beard, nose shining like a lighthouse beacon. She found it impossible to remember the man she had married, vigorous, full of mischief, sometimes tender. What had happened? she wondered briefly. He was his own father all over again, had inherited the worst of the Chandler traits and none of the old man's humour.

'Well?' he demanded.

Sally placed her hand on Jean's arm, but she was too late, because Jean had already begun to speak. 'I am moving on,' Jean said.

He blinked. 'Moving on? To what?'

'To sanity,' she replied, amazed by her sudden lack of fear. What was he, after all? A drunk, no more and no less, a man whose limbs no longer belonged to him, whose brain was dying, whose liver was probably reduced to nothing. 'I shall leave you to Polly Fishwick – let her become mistress here.'

He stumbled backwards, tried to regain a degree of poise when he managed to prop himself up against a wall. 'But . . . but I thought you'd changed your mind – I said that she could stay.' He waved a

124

hand towards Sally Foster. 'Why are you going?'

'To make a home with my sons. To be near my daughter. To be as far away from you as I can contrive.'

'What?' He stumbled towards the two women. 'What? You can't manage on your own. You spend money as if there's no end to it—'

'No I don't.' Jean stepped forward to meet him. His breath stank and his eyes were half-closed. 'You spend the money, Richard. Have you seen last month's bill from the off-licence? Do you realize how much whisky you are drinking?' God, there was real malevolence here, evil peering out beneath oily flaps of skin that hung like broken blinds over his irises. 'I am leaving,' she whispered. 'Have your castle, Richard. Bring in the slut from Woodside Cottage, let her cook your meals, because Sally is coming with me.'

'Jean,' called Sally. 'Please come away.'

His mouth opened and a huge roar emerged, a sound that did not match his weakened appearance. From the core of his being, he dredged up every ounce of remaining energy and screamed it out into the hall. At the same time, his hands rose as if of their own accord, great, fat fingers grasping at his wife's throat. He squeezed, heard her choking, almost smiled when her hands clawed at him. She could not reach him, had never been able to reach him.

Sally Foster leapt forward and threw herself at him, her hands gouging at his eyes. He released his hold, allowing Jean to fold onto the floor like a rag doll. With blood pouring down his face, the drunken master of Chandlers Grange balled his fist and drove it into the Foster woman's gut, smiling as he watched her collapse. This was his house and he was master.

He staggered back and looked at the results of his labour. He had given them the hiding they needed and they could both go to hell.

FIVE

Peter swung the Austin between the gateposts. It had been a decent evening at the pub, just a couple of pints each and a game of darts in which the twins had been routed by locals, men who had trained themselves to a level that was almost professional. 'Amazing how they can calculate so quickly,' said Jeremy.

'And how well they play when drunk. There they were, almost unfit to stand, but they could hit a double top with no trouble at all. Amazing.'

They had discussed the situation at the grange, had agreed that Father, who was plainly drinking himself to death at a rate of knots, had been lulled into a false sense of security. He probably believed that the twins' threat to leave had been an empty one; that Mother, too, had abandoned her plans. That was if he thought at all, of course, because his consumption of whisky had reached a spectacular level.

They left the car at the front of the house and began to climb the stone steps up to the closed door. But they needed no key, because the door flew open and

Henry Chandler, dressed only in nightshirt and slippers, stood in the doorway. With an alacrity that defied his age, the old man pushed his way past his startled grandsons and headed towards the woods, thin cotton flapping crazily about his spare frame as he headed for a taste of freedom.

Jeremy and Peter were immediately in several minds. The old man must be captured quickly, yet they needed help, because the fury borne of Henry's particular instability lent him the ability to overcome the youth and strength of these two slender young men. 'I'll go in and find help. He needs to be brought in as soon as possible, because autumn is not the season for a man of his age to be outside with hardly any clothes,' said Peter. 'You try to locate him. Don't corner him, though, because he may have his dentures in.'

But Jeremy had progressed by no more than half a dozen strides when he was called back. A thought drifted through his mind as he ground to a halt – Peter was making decisions, was appearing to grow in many ways. 'What?' Jeremy asked. 'Am I coming or going?'

'Coming . . . and hurry,' yelled Peter before dashing into the house.

Inside, they found chaos beyond the understanding of poets. *'Paradise Lost?'* muttered Jeremy. John Milton had described nothing as nasty as this in his lengthy, tedious meanderings. Mother and Nanny Foster were both on the floor. Father sat at the central table, his face streaming with blood drawn by Sally Foster's fingernails. Eddie Barford and Stan Clarke, two very sturdy lads from the village, were staring open-mouthed at the scene.

'He got out,' managed one of the youths. 'We were upstairs looking after the old man, see. There was a noise, a loud scream, like, so we ran downstairs and old Mr Chandler followed us. We weren't quick enough to catch a grip of him.'

Peter took charge once again. 'Go after him,' he advised the boys. 'Get help if you need it.' He continued to survey the dreadful scene, suddenly aware that his twin had deserted him. Mother was breathing, but her eyes were closed; Sally Foster had managed to achieve a sitting position and had propped herself against the bottom step of the staircase. 'Who did this?' he asked as soon as the village boys had left to pursue Henry Chandler.

'Your father.' The housekeeper's voice was weak. 'He did it.'

'Did he hit you?'

She nodded mutely.

'And Mother?'

'Tried to strangle her,' whispered Sally.

Peter knelt on the marble floor and touched his mother's face. The marks of strangulation encircled her neck; she continued to breathe steadily, but her face was pale, as if the blood had been stopped at her throat. Slowly, he rose and faced his father. 'One step too far this time, Richard,' he said grimly, his lips unwilling to frame the word that would announce this awful man's relationship to him. 'I shall get the police now. If you have damaged my mother in the slightest way, my brother and I will have you prosecuted.'

'No police.' The plea was forced between the bluish lips of Jean Chandler. 'Peter, no police.'

Peter returned to the kneeling position; she was

129

going to be all right, it seemed. 'Thank goodness,' whispered her son.

An unmistakable sound reached his ears; it was the noise of a shotgun being clicked into the ready position. 'Jeremy!' he yelled. 'No, for God's sake, no!'

'Not for God's sake,' came the grim reply, 'but for my mother's sake. Someone has to rid the world of pests and vermin – would you rather I sent for the rat-catcher?'

'Don't shoot him,' begged Peter.

'Why not? Look what he has done.' He glanced at Sally Foster. 'Do you need an ambulance?'

She shook her head.

'And Mother?' he asked Peter.

'No,' replied Jean, pulling herself up onto her knees. 'And put down that gun at once.'

But Jeremy was beyond the point where reason could be employed as counsel. 'Take Mother and Nan into the drawing room.' There was ice in his tone. 'Do it, Peter. Now. Do it, or I shall blow his head off.' He waited. 'I mean it, Peter, so help me, I shall kill him.' The finger on the trigger tingled, as if it had intentions of its own. Terrified by his mounting anger, Jeremy tried to relax the disobedient digit – if he were to shoot Richard Chandler, he would do it deliberately, coldly and not by accident.

Peter gathered up his mother and carried her into the drawing room. Sally Foster managed to stand, then she, too, left the scene.

Richard looked into the twin barrels of his own shotgun. This was suddenly funny, extraordinarily amusing. The laughter gave birth to itself, seemed to have a life that was separate from the rest of him; it

130

burst forth just as his earlier scream had emerged, with himself not so much a creator as a mere attachment. His son was standing over him with both barrels loaded, the gun cocked, finger on the trigger. Henry had disappeared via the front door, his behaviour as mad as could possibly be imagined. The wife was indisposed, as was her familiar, she of the grim face. Oh, it was hilarious. 'It's a bit like *Jane Eyre*,' he commented, 'mad person upstairs . . . oh, God.' He wiped his streaming eyes. 'When does the house go up in flames?'

'But this is not fiction, you see. And I am no timid little governess from an orphanage. Why did you hit my mother? Why did you try to strangle her?'

'I . . . er . . . I'm not sure.'

'She annoyed you?'

The older man frowned. He could not remember. Then his mind snagged on something, stumbled over a vital piece of information. 'She's leaving. I thought she wasn't. I thought–'

'Amazing that you can think, because your brain must be shrivelled to the size of a walnut. You are using more whisky in a week than gets drunk in the Chandlers in a month. In fact, killing you might well prove to be a kindness, because sick animals need to be put down.'

Richard blinked. Some of the haze was lifting, though it was still a fair imitation of a 1950s London smog. She was going. She had stopped rattling on about it, as had the twins, but she was leaving. His eyes felt as if they were burning in their sockets, while blood from just beneath those red-streaked orbs was still dripping down his face. 'She has defied me,' he concluded.

Peter returned. 'Mother and Nan are all right,' he offered by way of reassurance. 'Jeremy – don't pull that trigger.'

Jeremy turned to look at his brother. 'Why? Would you like to do it? I am damned sure Meredith would be glad of the chance.'

'She wouldn't. No right-minded person wants to finish up on trial at the Old Bailey. He is not worth it. You know that – we all know it.'

Jeremy lowered the gun slightly, then picked up a rope from a side table. 'I thought this might be useful – take it. Tie him to the chair,' he ordered. 'Just as we used to tie Meredith when we were cowboys and Injuns. If we fasten him down, we can go and look for Grandfather. Are you sure that Mother is all right?'

Peter nodded, picked up the rope, saw sense in the suggestion. Tied to a very substantial chair, Richard would not be able to hurt either of the women. As he secured his father, Peter breathed in the stench of whisky and saw what a mess the man was. 'Mother is as well as can be expected, no thanks to you. Keep still!' he shouted as his father struggled. 'You will be fastened to this chair until we decide what is to be done with you.'

'You couldn't decide to breathe without prompting,' replied Richard. 'Your brother is the only one with a grain of sense – and he is going to shoot me.' He was suddenly sober and in need of further sustenance. 'Whisky,' he snapped.

Jeremy grinned, though there was no humour contained within his expression. 'I shall get your whisky for you.' He waited until the last knot was tied, then he left the hall, returning very quickly without the gun, but bearing a bin that rattled as he progressed towards the table. He pulled out a bottle, removed the cap, then poured the contents into the large metal container.

'Jeremy?' called Jean from a doorway.

But the slightly older twin had his eyes fixed on his father. He continued until all the bottles were empty, his hands slick with Scotch towards the end of the business. 'There you are,' he said, 'rather a large glass, but sufficient to get you through the rest of the night.'

Richard roared again, struggled, found himself to be completely trapped. The fragrant one looked worried, as well she might, because she had raised these boys from hell, creatures who knew nothing of respect and obedience. 'How dare you?' he screamed.

Peter answered for his brother. 'He dares because you are trussed up like a chicken and can do no harm.'

'Peter, please,' Jean pleaded.

Jeremy pondered. 'Mother, are you sure that you are all right?'

'Yes, yes. Sally is recovering, too. Don't anger him any more.'

Peter shook his head in near dismay – the atmosphere at home was never happy, but this was beyond all his experience. 'The two lads are out looking for Grandfather, so one of us should stay here. You go.' He wanted Jeremy out of the way, needed the chance to unload the gun and to hide it. 'Go on – Grandfather can move at a pace when he wants to.'

Jeremy stared at the scene for a moment, lowered his head and shook it in an expression of disbelief. It

was plain that Mother should leave here immediately
. . . though why should she? Richard Chandler was
the one who ought to be removed. The decision
made itself there and then – the rotten apple had to
be taken away. Why should everyone be driven out
while the perpetrator of madness kept his seat? He
smiled wryly. Just now, Father had no choice but to
keep his seat. 'I am not going for Grandfather,' he
replied, 'because Stan and Eddie will find him. There
is a moon and his nightshirt is white – he will be
visible even in the woods. I am going for Dr Beddows
– someone should see what has happened here.
Anyway, Mother and Nan should be examined.'

'But–' The expression on Jeremy's face curtailed
Peter's answer. Argument would be fruitless. 'All
right,' he agreed with reluctance. Jeremy must get out
and away from the gun. 'Whatever you think is best,
then.'

Jean crossed the hall and sank into the chair that
was furthest away from her imprisoned husband.
'Go, Jeremy.' Her voice remained weak, her throat
and neck still sore from Richard's attack. She didn't
care any more. For the sake of her children, the
police must be kept out of all this. But Richard had
to be dealt with.

Henry was cold, but enraptured by the fairyland in
which he found himself. He had been trapped in that
upstairs room for as long as he could remember.
Remembering was becoming difficult, but that lot
indoors hadn't a clue about his real condition. He
refused to suffer in silence and remained as difficult
as he could possibly manage. They believed him to
be insane; there were, indeed, times when he became

134

confused. Yet he was not a lunatic, not by a very long chalk.

But oh, look at those trees, thinned by autumn falls, stroked by the moon, their thinnest traceries plain against a sky of navy blue. They thought he was mad, didn't they? He wasn't. An owl hooted, then rose in a rush of power that rattled the tree in which it had sat. It was a silver-blue world and it was wonderful – except for the temperature.

He sat down for a moment on a stump. His son was a great deal dafter than he was. Henry, who had not been allowed alcohol for many months, was sober at last; he could, if allowed sufficient time, work out most situations and he remained wise enough to know that his containment was unfair. So, he had given them hell. But they would find him soon; he gathered up his remaining energy and ploughed deeper into the trees. The woods were his, the grange was his, several farms were his – oh, yes, he knew his rights, knew also that they had been removed from him, that Richard had taken the reins because of Henry's infirmity. This time, he would give the buggers a real marathon for their money, by God, he would . . .

Polly Fishwick settled herself with the evening newspaper. She had taken enough of the big fellow and his mind-changes; her pride had surfaced – she would find work and Chandler could shove his bank book where the sun would never shine. It needed to be live-in, of course, because she would surely lose Woodside Cottage once Chandler realized that she was finished here. What a dance he had led her – move to the big house, torment his wife and the

135

housekeeper, befriend some unknown woman who was moving to Claughton Cottage. Then, with no warning, all had changed. For now, she had to wait until Chandler came to his senses and he never would, because he was drinking like a whale.

She scanned the jobs pages, saw a couple of possibilities, didn't fancy the cooking and cleaning that went with these residential positions. A move back to town would not be palatable, yet the bullet must be bitten. Bar work might be all right, if she could find a landlord who would give her a room at his pub. She rather fancied herself as a server of drinks, would prefer that to housework.

Her head rose. What was that noise? Oh, it was probably a fox. The creatures were getting cheeky these days, had even started rooting about in the rubbish, but she could not manage to stir herself. The fire crackled, her eyes closed and she nodded towards sleep.

Suddenly, she was fully conscious; a draught of cold air whipped at her ankles, causing her to jump to the edge of her armchair. Picking up a very substantial poker, she made her way to the kitchen. A pale ghost stood in the centre of this small area, white from head to foot, its status made completely animate by the unmistakable sound of chattering teeth. She hesitated for a second or two. 'Mr Chandler?'

'That's me.' He moved towards her. 'Don't worry, now. My reputation for grabbing women is exaggerated. I may be senile, but I have my wits about me most of the time. Attacking people was fighting back. Please, please, don't be afraid of me.'

'Erm . . . come in.' She led him through to her

136

sitting room and he made straight for the fire, his intention clearly being to thaw out bones made frail by age and wear.

'That's better,' he declared.

Taken all round, old Henry had been surprisingly sensible so far, thought Polly as she watched him warming himself. Yet she continued to hold the poker, because this old chap had a name for tremendous ferocity.

'Very cold out there,' he announced.

Polly felt invaded; this chap's family owned her house, but it was her home, her private place. 'They say you are mad,' she stated boldly.

'I am. I'm as mad as two frogs in a bucket, but not all the time.' He glanced round the untidy area. 'I shall stay here.'

She swallowed. 'Here?' The word emerged high-pitched. 'They'll find you.' How the hell could he stay here? She must remain calm at all costs; if he fell asleep, she could make her escape and find some help. 'You can't stop here. Who'll look after you?'

'You will.' He sat down. 'Where's that husband of yours?'

'Gone. He left me.'

'Ah.' He stared into the fire, seemed mesmerized by the flames. 'I had a wife. She died. Best thing she ever did for me. Any chance of a drink?'

Like everyone else in the area, Polly knew full well that Henry Chandler was a notorious alcoholic, that his confinement to the upper storey of the grange had been implemented so that he would be away from all possible sources of booze. And here he sat, demanding a drink.

'Cocoa will do nicely.' He smiled sheepishly.

137

'Dried out, you see. After a few months, it gets easier.'

'Tell your son that,' she advised, 'because he carries drink very badly. Just lately, he has started going overboard – not sober very often.' The old chap seemed to have a full set of chairs at home, she thought. Bearing in mind her own long-dead grandad, Polly understood senility, was even possessed of insight, because she had adored her mother's father. 'Richard's a mess,' she added.

'I know. He called me mad. And when I still had the whisky in my system, I really was mad, you know. Now, I give them hell, because hell is what they deserve. But I am not completely insane.'

She placed the poker on the hearth. 'All right. So, why did you keep grabbing girls, then? If you're not crazy, you could be arrested for that.' She found herself unable to work out how his mind functioned. There was sense in him, that was certain, so why had he advertised himself as insane? According to Dave Armstrong, some of this man's habits were positively revolting.

'I haven't the brain I used to have,' he admitted. 'But if you put an animal in a cage, it loses its wits. It gets angry, too. I fought my jailers, sometimes because I was raging, sometimes because I could not quite work out what was going on around me. At first, the drink was still in me, so I was seeing things, hearing things. That was when they decided that I was past saving.'

Polly poured milk into a pan, stirred cocoa, cold milk and sugar into a paste, waited for the pan to boil on the fire. What on earth did the old man expect of her? Shrivelled by age, he remained strong enough to require watching by grown men, angry enough to be out of his head from time to time.

'I want you to fetch the doctor tomorrow,' he said. 'I have to make sure of some things. He hasn't seen me for months, so he probably thinks I am still crazy.' He paused, held his hands out to the fire. 'I want my proper status returned to me. The grange is my house, not Richard's. He has stepped in, and from what I have heard he is drinking so heavily that he could not tell the difference between tripe and treacle. That milk's coming to the boil.'

Polly rescued her pan, made his drink. The difference between tripe and treacle? That was the line which finally convinced her. Henry Chandler was bruised, but sane. He was even amusing in a sense, was quite a pleasant old man. She had heard about delirium tremens, about the nightmares that needed to be overcome before sense returned. 'So there was nothing wrong with you apart from the drink?'

He grabbed the mug of cocoa and wrapped thin, almost transparent fingers around its heat. 'I think age has caught up with me. But I have made up my mind—' He took a gulp of cocoa. 'Tell me your name again? Wasn't your husband the woodsman?'

'I'm Polly Fishwick, usually called Pol. Derek was the woodsman, till I half-killed him. He's gone off now, Chorley, I believe, working in some sort of factory. He found out that—' Should she? Should she tell him? 'I was going with your son, Mr Chandler.'

Henry nodded thoughtfully. 'I see. Well, you weren't the first and you're not going to be the last. He's beaten up his wife, you know. I almost stayed behind, because she was on the floor – so was that housekeeper of hers. But I didn't. I like Jean – she's been a good mother to my grandchildren. They wouldn't have let me stay downstairs – the two thugs were right behind me. My bodyguards. I am a prisoner and I don't deserve to be, because there are times when my mind is clear. It's clear now and they can all bugger off, because I am not going to be trapped in my own house. It's not right. I am digging in my heels.'

That was yet another long speech for a supposedly disordered old man. Polly sipped at her own cocoa. She still had no idea of what to do. Here he sat in his nightshirt, mug of cocoa in his hand, a very old man on a very cold night, and she needed her bed. He was showing no sign of moving, looked as if he might be preparing to dig in for the whole night. 'You can sleep on the sofa, then.' Her eyebrows lifted of their own accord, because the words had emerged on their own, with no help at all from their speaker.

'Thanks.'

'More cocoa, then? Bit of toast?'

He grinned, displaying dentures whose edges had inflicted many wounds on the persons of Dave Armstrong and others who had been elected to mind him. 'Thank you. We shall do very well, you and I, Pol. Yes, we shall do very well indeed . . .'

Anna Chandler, her dark coat wrapped tightly about her frame, stood in the garden of Woodside Cottage. Through a small gap in the curtains, she watched the scene, her brother and Pol Fishwick sharing cocoa, the poker returned to its holder, the occupants of the room relaxing in each other's company. She had tried to stop him, had wanted to catch him, to guide him to the gatehouse and safety, but did she need to?

Through the frail glass, she caught snatches of their

140

conversation and decided to leave well alone. Pol was displaying a level of understanding that belied her reputation. So, what had happened, then? How on earth had Henry managed to escape from confinement? Anna had seen him dashing past her house and towards the woods, had grabbed her coat, had followed him here. Would others be in pursuit?

He must not be found. As soon as she was satisfied that her brother was safe, Anna walked back into the woods. Here she had played as a child and, with the moon full, she had no trouble in negotiating her way homeward. Her steps quickened; yes, she must get back, must be there when the questions were asked, because there would be questions . . .

Some fifteen minutes later, as she entered her own home by the back door, she heard them knocking at the front. Quickly, she threw off her coat and hat, then ran to the door and opened it. Two louts stood on her doorstep. 'Yes?' she snapped.

'We're looking for Mr Henry,' said one.

'Asleep in bed,' she replied. 'One foot over this doorstep and you shall know the meaning of trouble. Do you understand?'

Eddie Barford and Stan Clarke looked at each other. Was she telling the truth? Gossip hereabouts said that she had left home because of her brother's containment upstairs – so – was the old man here? Or was she just playing for time? 'We've to take him home,' said Stan. 'They want him back at the grange before he catches his death of cold.'

'He is home,' she replied in a no-nonsense tone. 'Now, leave my property before I fetch the shotgun. This is Henry's place of residence now.' They could have overcome her quite easily and she knew it; she

141

also knew that they dared not touch her. 'Go,' she shouted, 'get away from here and do not come back.'

They stepped away and Anna, pleased, slammed the door home. A bad attitude was useful at times, she told herself as she prepared for bed. They would not return, because Miss Anna Chandler was feared easily as much as the fiercest headmistress. Smiling to herself, she lit her last cigarette of the day and ascended the steep and narrow staircase. Tomorrow promised to be interesting . . . exceedingly so.

Dr Michael Beddows placed his bag on the table and surveyed the scene. Had it not been tragic, the situation might even have been described as funny, because here sat a man with a huge ego, a man who acted as if he owned the village and all its residents – and that man was trussed up like a Saturday afternoon matinee cowboy at the mercy of redskins.

'Untie me,' roared the trapped man. 'Doctor, they held me at gunpoint and–' A sudden eruption of vomit cut off the remainder of Richard Chandler's diatribe.

'Nan and my mother are in there,' said Jeremy, plainly unmoved by his father's distress. 'I think they are all right, but he tried to strangle Mother and he punched Nan Foster very hard in her stomach. Will you look at them, please, Dr Beddows? They deserve attention.' He cast a withering glance in the direction of the drunk who was secured to an Edwardian carver. 'His illness is self-induced. Oh, by the way, Grandfather is missing. His two guards are out looking for him.'

Peter blinked away the wetness from his eyes,

found himself thinking of a fireside in Bolton, of a man and a woman who clearly belonged together, of laughter and friendly insults and apple pasty with love baked into it. Was this self-pity? Was he wishing that he had been born poor, that he had grown up in the shadows cast by chimneys, in air polluted by fumes and smoke? Father was in a dreadful state. Covered in vomit, face purple and stained with dried blood, the man looked like a tramp, a vagrant. Oh, God, yes – anything at all rather than this . . .

Mike Beddows picked up his bag and went to look at the women. Anger simmered, but he sat on it, was determinedly professional as he examined two decent people who had deserved none of this. And had Richard learnt nothing from the behaviour of his own father, an old man who was now locked away for most of the time? So, he was on the loose, too . . . Oh, this threatened to be a very long night.

He returned to the scene of Chandler's crimes. 'They will be sore for a few days,' he advised the sons of the family, 'but there is no permanent damage. They have refused X-rays and do not wish to involve the police. So . . .' He sat down and stared at Richard. 'So, that leaves this fellow. Not a pretty sight.'

Richard's breathing was erratic; his stomach heaved again, but delivered nothing. The edge was wearing off now; the cloak of drunkenness no longer embraced him, was refusing to protect him from reality. He was tied to a chair, to his own chair in his own house. And his own sons had placed him here, had confined him, had even poured away his whisky.

The doctor was staring at the bin. 'That's quite a blend,' he commented.

'At least three brands,' replied Jeremy, 'one of them a twelve-year-old single malt. Better in there than in his stomach.'

Mike Beddows considered the problem. Two women had been attacked, an old man had escaped and Richard Chandler was magnificently drunk. He had attended the women, could do nothing immediate about Henry. Now he had to decide the fate of Richard.

The latter raised his head and glared at the twins, eyes sliding from one to the other, cracked lips parting as he gasped against the urge to vomit. 'I'll kill the pair of you,' he threatened.

Dr Beddows made his decision. The man was clearly dehydrated, was mad enough to renew his attack once given water and released from bondage, seemed capable of threatening lives all over again. 'I shall get an ambulance,' the doctor announced. 'Your father is in need of treatment. I shall also need the signature of a second doctor – your father may need to be forcibly removed, so I shall need a colleague.'

Peter's shoulders sagged with relief.

'Yes, it's rather a case of removing the rotten fruit to save the good.' There was sarcasm etched into Jeremy's statement.

They sat and waited for the vehicle that would remove Richard Chandler from Chandlers Green, near Bolton, Lancashire.

'Where are you sending him?' Jean's voice came from the drawing-room doorway. Her hair was a mess, lipstick smudged, eyes red with weeping.

144

'He will go into a nursing home that deals with such . . . such cases. He will be treated for whatever ails him.'

Jean approached the central table, Sally Foster hot on her heels. 'Can he be cured?'

'Not unless he wants to be,' replied the doctor, 'and he is probably unaware of his dependency – or unwilling to face it. He will be weaned off the drink. We can only try.'

Jean Chandler placed a hand at her throat. It was as if his tightened fingers were still there and she wondered how near she had come to being dead. Placing herself in the one remaining chair, she shivered involuntarily. 'My father-in-law must be found,' she croaked. 'He is too old to be out in weather such as this.' A huge sigh escaped from her lips. 'So, now we house two alcoholics.'

The doctor made no reply. He realized that Jean Chandler's verdict was correct, yet he remained unwilling to discuss tomorrow until tonight had been tidied away. The man in the chair needed fluids; he was possibly suffering from alcohol poisoning – and suffering was his duty, was the price that must be paid. And the other good people in the household owed nothing; therefore, removal of Richard Chandler was the only sane option.

A second doctor entered the house and agreed with Dr Beddows' diagnosis. Papers were signed and placed in an envelope. The ambulance arrived and Mike Beddows went out to talk to its crew, returning quickly with two white-coated men and a straitjacket. He glanced at Jean, at Peter, at Jeremy, then, finally, he spoke to Sally Foster. 'Take them all into the drawing room and close the door.' The tone of the doctor's voice made clear the fact that he would brook no argument.

The four residents of Chandlers Grange sat and listened while the supposed head of this disordered household was restrained by professionals. His objections to the process were loud; Jeremy sat on a sofa, one arm clutching at his mother. Peter held the shaking hand of Nanny Foster while all hell broke loose on the other side of the door.

Finally, Mike Beddows entered the drawing room. 'Two things,' he announced. 'The boys who were caring for old Mr Chandler have arrived; your aunt pretended to be sheltering him, but they were not satisfied by her explanation, so they carried on the search. He is in the woodsman's cottage.'

He smiled wryly. There were two women round here with whom he would prefer not to tangle – one was Anna Chandler and the other was Pol Fishwick; those two boys had faced both within minutes. But the old man was safe, at least. As long as Pol Fishwick did not arm herself against him, that was.

'Pol Fishwick?' croaked Jean. 'He is with . . . that woman?'

The doctor nodded. 'Apparently, he is in Polly Fishwick's cottage and he has fallen asleep on her sofa. According to Polly, he is perfectly lucid and has eaten with her. Secondly, your husband is about to be removed, Jean. I cannot help him – he needs specialist treatment.' He looked at the huddled forms and cursed inwardly. 'The demon drink makes some lives hell.' Shaking his head, he left the arena with the colleague who had helped him certify Richard Chandler as insane.

Jean rose to her feet. 'We should all sleep,' she advised her companions. 'Grandfather is safe and we can do nothing tonight.' She glanced at Jeremy. 'Tomorrow, you and the village boys must bring him home. For the moment, we have all had more than enough.'

'I don't know whether I am coming or going.' This statement was delivered by Leena Martindale who, under the watchful eye of her daughter, was supposed to be selecting furniture for her new home in Chandlers Green. 'I've had enough.' She sat down abruptly, an elbow leaning on the wrap-around fire-guard. 'I've got your father running round talking about damp courses and four-poster beds, then there's you.'

Marie raised an eyebrow. 'Me? What about me?'

Leena motored on. 'On top of all that, there's the dry rot, the wet rot, the roof and the guttering – it's like a war all over again up yon. Last time we went, there were four men on the roof and they'd lost the fifth bloke – he was last seen in the back garden and they were talking about sending for tracker dogs.'

Marie tried not to smile. 'What about me?'

'You could lose a platoon in that jungle. Any road, he was at the shop getting baccy and a paper– What do you mean, what about you?'

'You said there was me.'

'And I don't like the colour they've painted the house, I'd sooner have blue. A nice Wedgwood–'

'Mother?'

'What?'

'Me? About me?'

Leena relaxed and stretched out her legs. 'Well, I

can't take it off you, can I? That's the trouble with being a mother. Now, I don't know whether I'm coming or going–'

'You already said that.'

'I know I have, so shut up. Like I said, I don't know whether I'm coming or going, and you don't know whether you're coming or stopping. If you're coming, I can take some of this stuff with me. If you're stopping, I won't take it. But if I don't take it and buy new, then if you decide you are coming after all, I'll have new stuff and old stuff and I don't know what I'm talking about.'

They both dissolved into tears of laughter. These roundabout conversations were becoming a part of daily life now that work on Claughton Cottage was under way. To add to the troubles, Alf and Bert spent almost every evening in this very room, plans spread all over the table, arguments burgeoning while the beer jug emptied, both men hot under the collar as they discussed the merits of pebble-dash versus the virtues of cement rendering, whether to have a green-house, which roof tiles to use, whose turn it was to go up to the off-licence for a refill.

'Mam?'

'What?'

'I won't stay up there. I'll visit a lot, but I shan't want to live there. It is lovely, really. I'm sure I'll enjoy the break when I get there, a bit of peace and quiet, but that's all.'

Leena hooted again. 'Peace and quiet? You must be joking. Did I tell you about the owls? Night birds? Tell the feathered beggars that, because they come and go in daylight, too. And what about them cows as got in from the back field? They left deposits

148

everywhere. Now, as well as all that, there's the pub. Your dad has become attached to it. They have fights there, because they take their darts and their cards very serious. You could get hanged for cheating.'

Marie settled back. Mam was going to leave her most of the furniture, Josie and Aggie would be moving in, she had met a very charming young man and she might stand half a chance of getting out of that flaming job. If she wasn't very careful, Marie Martindale was in danger of becoming extremely happy.

Alf came in. He was grumbling under his breath. Hot on his heels, Bert Ramsden was in argumentative mode. 'You can't beat slate. I've been in this here business for donkey's years and I have a lot of faith in slate.'

'Who's paying for these alterations, eh?' replied Alf. 'Me, that's who. And that small bedroom needs a new window frame – I don't care what you say about splicing wood in where the rot is.' He stopped, realized that his wife and daughter were both staring at him. 'What?' he demanded. 'What?'

Leena stood up. 'Me and our Marie are going to bed. Your supper's in the oven and I am beginning to wish we'd never bought that house. More trouble than enough, is Claughton Cottage.'

Alf blinked. He and Bert had taken a couple of pints in the Chandlers Arms, because it was becoming plain that Leena was sick unto death of plans and building talk every night. 'Course, everyone in the Chandlers is an expert when it comes to renovations.'

'Then you'll be in good company.' Leena glanced at the clock. 'It's ten past ten and you've got an early start. And I don't like that green, I want Wedgwood blue.'

Alf and Bert looked at each other, sat at the table and waited for the women to leave. They had some calculations to do and there was no fire in the front room and no big table, either, so they had to stay here and—

'Who the hell's that at this time?' Leena asked when someone tapped at the door. 'It can't be Elsie – she'd have walked straight in.' She stalked out to admit whichever creature had no respect for those who needed sleep. A minute later, she re-entered, Peter Chandler following her into the kitchen.

Marie felt her cheeks as they flushed to advertise her awareness of him. He looked upset. She did not like the idea of his being in distress.

'Hello,' said the newcomer. 'I know it's late, but . . . I don't know why I'm here.'

'Don't worry yourself, lad.' Alf's tone was warm. 'Our Leena hasn't known why she's been anywhere in ages. She stood in Woolworths for half an hour last week before remembering why she was there.' He looked at his wife. 'Why were you there?'

'I can't remember,' was the quick response. 'I'll let you do the remembering for me, same as you remembered Wedgwood blue and brass handles in me kitchen.'

Peter felt his shoulders as they sagged towards relief and relaxation. This was a safe place. This was a place in which each man and woman had full permission to be him or herself, where discussions about handles and paint were declarations of affection, where everyone cared. 'I had to get out of the house,' he said. 'And I finished up here after driving

150

round for ages.' He blinked as if waking from sleep.
'It's terrible.'

Bert took the hint and rose from his seat. 'You were
in the pub up yon earlier,' he said to Peter. 'Thanks
for not interfering – every other bugger was full of
advice about pointing and bloody plastering.
Anyway, I'd best get going before my Elsie separates
me from my future.' He smiled at the company and
left the scene.

'Sit down, son,' said Alf kindly. 'Do you want a
cuppa?'

Peter sat. 'No, thanks. I shouldn't be here at this
hour.'

'Course you should,' Leena protested. 'Shall we
leave you with our Marie? Happen you'd be easier
talking to somebody nearer your own age.'

'No.' Peter drew a hand across his forehead. And
everything spilled from him, words pouring from his
mouth, tears clouding voice and vision, knuckles
tightening as he relived recent hours. 'So, my father
is in a straitjacket, my mother is hurt, Nan is hurt,
Grandfather is sleeping on Pol Fishwick's sofa–'

'And you are hurt too,' Marie concluded for him.

He let out a huge sigh. 'We are all damaged,
Marie.'

Leena tutted. 'Drink can be a bugger,' she
achieved eventually. 'Your grandad was a drinker,
too, or so I've heard.'

'Yes. He is supposed to be locked away upstairs.
He got out and we are told that he is safe, but he is in
a cottage inhabited by a woman who is not quite the
lady . . . well . . . she has a way of dealing with difficult men. And my grandfather falls into that category
– except when he is asleep.' He dried his eyes and

151

made an attempt to smile. 'Mr Martindale, please tell me what happened between you and my father during the war.'

Alf shook his head. 'No, son. Sorry, but I can't do that. It was another time and another place – it has nowt to do with life these days. Things were very different then, you know. People acted . . . well . . . differently.'

'I need to know.'

'No, you don't. What happened between me and your dad is between me and your dad.'

'And the regiment,' said Peter. 'I shall find out. I know people who can get the truth for me.'

Alf sighed deeply. 'Up to you, son, but you'll not get it from me. Even Leena doesn't know all of it. I made a pledge to myself, Peter; to me, not to the country or the bloody army.'

Peter lowered his head.

'Is your mother all right now?' asked Marie.

He looked at her. 'I honestly don't know. As soon as everyone had gone upstairs, I got out. I had to. Thank God Meredith wasn't there – she would have killed him. She has his temperament, but I hope she doesn't follow him into drink.'

'She won't.' Leena sounded confident. 'She's a woman, so she has the edge. See, women don't mither like men do, inside themselves, like. Women let it out—'

'So I've noticed,' Alf interspersed in an attempt to lighten the atmosphere, 'specially when it come to paint and brass handles. Look,' he invited the visitor, 'see how she's giving me the witch's eye?' Imitating a child in the nursery class, he placed a finger on his lips.

'Right, where was I?' Leena asked.

'Letting it all out,' answered Marie.

'Oh, aye. Men locks it up inside theirselves and it can come out in drink.' She nodded wisely. 'I've seen it all before, Peter. They'd be best off with a dolly-tub and a posser to worry about. That'd soon put them straight, oh, no mistake about it. While you're hanging washing out, you get talking. And it all comes out.'

Peter smiled faintly. 'I can't imagine Meredith hanging out washing. Or my father chatting with his neighbours.'

Leena paused. She had become distracted for the moment, because she suddenly found herself worrying all over again about who was going to help her up at the cottage. How would she let everything out? There would be no Elsie, no safety valve, no release. Cows and owls were not going to take the place of neighbours, were they?

Marie rose to her feet. 'Come on, Peter,' she said, 'let's go for a drive.'

'Bit late for that, isn't it?' asked Alf.

But Leena, who knew more than enough about life, shook her head. 'No, love,' she told her daughter, 'it's not too late at all.'

They sat at the base of Rivington Pike, looked at a sky that was almost purple, faraway suns spread across its incomprehensible endlessness. 'Like sequins on velvet,' commented Marie. She didn't know him, but she wanted to hold him, to comfort him, to say the words that would show her support, yet she could not, because she did not trust herself. The feelings she harboured were silly and without foundation. She had known him for such a short span – this was only the third time they had met.

'I'm afraid,' he said. To how many girls might he have admitted that?

'I know.'

And how many would have understood? 'Such a mess,' he continued. 'Mother is buying a house on Crompton Way. Now, with Father gone – and we have no way of knowing when his treatment will end – she will be able to stay at the grange. Meredith is in a hotel, her head full of nonsense. My grandfather – oh, I don't want to think about him–'

'Then don't.' She steeled herself and took his hand. His fingers were slender, tense, cold. Her hand, warmer and certainly more relaxed, closed around his. 'You know where we are, me, Mam and Dad. We're not much, but we see life as it is.'

'You mean a great deal to me,' he answered carefully, 'as do your parents. It's so warm there, so pleasant. Your parents love each other.'

Marie realized then how much she had taken for granted. Of course her parents loved each other – they were married. Elsie and Bert loved each other, too. They moaned and they called each other names, but they were solid, had always been rocks strong enough to withstand any storm – and she had never even thought about it. 'I'm lucky,' she said now.

'You have a decent family, Marie. I haven't. Luck of the draw.'

Was it the luck of the draw? she wondered. Children could not choose their parents, but parents could choose to work at marriage, to make sure that it stayed whole and wholesome. 'It may be money that spoils things,' she said quietly.

154

'Privilege,' he replied. 'Privilege without responsibility is a poor foundation. Yes, my family is comparatively rich, but it's the attitude, Marie. He has always been the big man, the squire. I think he half expects the villagers to bend a knee or doff caps at him. He takes a mistress as if he has *droit de seigneur*, as if the chosen one should be grateful.'

Her grip tightened. 'It must be hard, hating your father.'

'It is. Because from him came the seed that is me.' Peter turned and looked at his companion. 'You really are a stunner, you know.'

Her heart fluttered, but she forced herself not to react. This young man was too injured, too needful. To encourage him now would be more than foolish – it might even be dangerous, because his pain was too big and lay not quite within the scope of her comprehension. 'Thanks,' she said.

'You are welcome.'

They sat in silence for a few more minutes, then he retrieved his hand and drove back to Bolton. The past hour or so had given him strength, and he had sense enough to know that he should not be led by his heart while there was no order in his existence.

'Good night.' She pecked him on the cheek, opened her door and dashed into the house before he could leave the driver's seat. Had she waited, he would have played the gentleman, would have walked round and helped her from the car. Sometimes, a person needed to think by herself for a while . . .

Marie Martindale leaned against the closed front door of 34, Emblem Street. He was not a Catholic; he was from the wrong social class; he was from a family so disordered that *Wuthering Heights* seemed almost believable.

'Marie?' called Leena from the kitchen.

'I'm just hanging my coat up, Mam.' She listened as he drove away in his ramshackle Austin; and she knew that a part of her heart had gone with him.

SIX

It was like going back in time. Pol Fishwick dragged open the curtains, turned, looked at the old man. He had cast aside his teeth; they were lying on the hearthrug, tossed away at some point during the night. Before even considering what she was doing, she found herself at the kitchen sink with the tap running, nail brush scrubbing back and forth against porcelain dentures. Grandad. Yes, this was like Grandad all over again. And the man on the sofa looked so frail in sleep, so small and harmless, just an old person who was on the brink of a second childhood. This was a very cruel world.

There was no real harm in Henry Chandler – that much had been plain last night. He had chosen his reputation, had invested in it, had made a career out of it, she supposed. His brain was not as it had been, but he knew that; he had simply screamed and fought, a trapped animal who had needed alcohol, who had been dried out in the cruellest way. How could his own son have done such a thing?

She wiped her hands – aye, this was the doing of

Richard Chandler, a man who wanted his own way, who needed to tidy out of sight all that offended his eye. Well, he had better look into a mirror, because his own image was rather less than perfect. Angrily, Pol cut slices of bread for toast, set out two mugs for tea and went to rouse her unexpected guest. It was a shame to wake him, but she had promised that she would. 'Mr Chandler?'

He grumbled, opened one rheumy eye and glared at her. Who was this? She was big enough, that was certain, but why had they suddenly decided to appoint a woman as zookeeper? Women were afraid of him, weren't they? He had developed an attitude towards them, they were a part of his scheme, his plan to make life as difficult as possible for all who had allowed him to be imprisoned like a criminal—

'Mr Chandler?'

Mr Chandler. Mr Richard Chandler. He was the real criminal. Henry relaxed slightly, remembered where he was. 'You're the woodsman's wife and you got rid of your husband.' He smiled, displaying pale gums and a tongue that looked dry.

'I am that very person and yes, I did. Call me Pol. Here's your teeth. I scrubbed them as best I could – you threw them out in the night.'

Henry planted the dentures in their proper place of residence and grinned broadly. He had escaped, was free, was out of the house and . . . and was wearing a nightshirt. What chance had he of being declared sane while he was dressed like this? Another problem to be considered by a head already full of clutter. 'Did your husband leave any clothes?'

Pol looked him up and down. He had been quite tall, but life had shortened him and he was shrivelled, curled like an October leaf, all the sap gone, dry, withered. 'He was broader than you.'

'And younger. Everyone is younger. I have to get some clothes. But first, a bit of breakfast would be good. And where's the lavatory?'

'Out there.' She waved a hand towards the kitchen. 'It's that little shed in the back garden. And if you want a bath, that's hung on a nail near the door. I'll sort it out for you if you like, get some water heated.'

He gathered around his shoulders the blanket under which he had slept, rose from the sofa and pushed his feet into the slippers. It was a cold day, he needed clothes and he wanted the doctor. In the doorway, he turned. 'They'll come for me today.' His voice was hollow.

'They came for you last night, but I wouldn't let them in.'

He was pleased. 'Thank you. But today they will bring reinforcements. I have no money and can get none, can't buy clothes. I don't know how that damned son of mine did it, but, from what I have overheard while supposedly sleeping, he had me judged unfit to manage my affairs so that he could get his hands on everything. I was never insane; I was drunk, then furious.'

'I know,' she answered. 'And now *he's* the drunk.'

Henry sighed, nodded and went on his way, throwing over his shoulder the opinion that lunacy ran in the family, that every Chandler since time began had been a daft good-for-nothing type, spineless, stupid, all the same, never knew when to stop . . .

Pol smiled to herself as Henry Chandler's voice faded with the rest of him into the back garden. She spread butter on the toast, made a new tablecloth out

159

of a more recent newspaper, threw away the old one. Never the housewife, she suddenly began to realize how shabby her environment was. There was dust everywhere, springs in the furniture were acting as Henry had acted – making a break for freedom. The fireplace wanted a good scrubbing, as did the windows and the paintwork – oh, she couldn't be bothered with any of it.

She sat down to tea and toast, then offered him a smile when he returned and rinsed his hands under the single cold-water tap. 'I did you a bit of toast with plenty of strawberry jam – you'll be needing the sugar today.' And so would she, thought Pol grimly.

He attacked the food with gusto, loose dentures snapping and clicking as he made his way through two doorsteps spread liberally with butter and jam. This freedom hurt, because he understood how tenuous it was, knew that time was slipping through his fingers as quickly and as easily as this surfeit of butter. 'What can I do?' he asked when he had drained his mug for the second time.

Pol had no idea and she said so. Yet there was fight in her, anger that stemmed now not just from her own fury with this man's son, but also from the old chap's sorry situation. 'You don't need to be dressed to see a doctor,' she opined, 'because I can fetch him here if that's what you want.'

'Clothes are armour,' he answered, 'and if ever a man needed chain mail, then I am that man.' He glanced down at a cocoa stain on his nightshirt. Cocoa stains were particularly revolting, as they resembled something far less palatable. 'I look as if I have had a very bad stomach complaint,' he moaned. 'Dr Beddows will think I am still worth nothing.'

160

'And you could shelter from rain under that moustache. I'll tidy it for you in a minute – I've got nail scissors somewhere.'

He sat back and studied her, wondered how a woman as strong as Pol had managed to become involved with Richard. It would have been for security, he decided. This tied cottage was her home; it was also a dump that needed some work to make it fit to live in. Henry framed the question. 'How did you come to be knotted up with that son of mine? Worthless swine, he is. He never treated his wife properly, forbade her to come near me. In fact, I think he convinced her of my madness.'

She shook her head. 'No, you did that, according to Dave Armstrong – he said you carried on something terrible. I'll bet you were mad at the beginning, after all those years of drinking. Alcoholics need the stuff if they want to carry on looking normal.'

'Yes, drunk was normal. So, answer my question. Why Richard?'

Pol gave him the truth. 'I was bored and he had money.'

'And now?'

She raised beefy shoulders in a shrug. 'He doesn't need me any more. There was talk of . . . of him finding something for me to do in the village, but I've had enough of him. He uses people, carries on as if he owns them. So I've got to move on.'

Henry found himself wishing that this relative stranger would not move on. He liked her. Also, should he be recaptured, here sat a woman on the outside who could vouch for his sanity. And he would be found; any moment now, his guards would force their way into Pol's kitchen, would grab him

161

and take him back to a place that really did make him insane. 'I want you to help me,' he said. 'When they come for me, tell them that you believe I am held prisoner in my own home. Please.'

'I will,' she replied, 'but they won't listen to me, Mr Chandler.' She had no value in this community, was judged worthless by her so-called betters. How could she help poor old Henry?

'Call me Henry – or Hal. When I was young, my mother called me Hal.' He closed his eyes. 'She was fragrant, very correct and Victorian, starched collars and stiff lace at her throat, corsets so tight that she could scarcely breathe. Tiny feet. I remember her shoes. My father, on the other hand, was a pig from hell. A buffoon.' Eyelids raised themselves slowly, blinds at windows that did not want to allow in the sun. 'History repeats,' he added. Which of his grandsons would succumb? he wondered.

'It doesn't have to,' said Pol. 'People can change things if they try. We don't need to follow our fathers, even if it is bred into us. I was lucky, I had a good grandad. He looked after me. Mam and Dad were always working, but he made time for me.'

'And you looked after him in return.'

She nodded. 'Died in my arms in the middle of a game of Ludo. Things were never the same after that.'

They sat in companionable silence for a while, each looking back to years that had been different, sometimes better. Pol smiled inwardly. Had she taken the job of looking after Henry, she would have been happy. But Jean Chandler would not have been. 'More tea?' she asked.

He suddenly felt weary. How could he fight them

now? Yes, he had deliberately made himself certifiable, had fought like a geriatric tiger against those who would constrain him. 'No tea. Just tidy me up as best you can.' An amusing thought struck. 'If we had a wig, you could shave the moustache and put me in a frock. I could be your long-lost grandmother.'

Pol looked at the sad, isolated figure who was true owner of the estate, whose son she now hated; the anger rose in her chest. She would fight on Henry Chandler's behalf right to the last ditch. For the first time in many, many years, Pol Fishwick had a goal that was outside her own self-interest. She would do her best to protect this vulnerable man.

She trimmed his moustache, standing so close to him that she could feel, see and almost smell his fear, his near-paralysis. And with every snip, her determination grew; if it was the last thing she ever achieved, she would free this man from solitary confinement.

Jean's neck was very sore. Swallowing was hard, as was speaking, so she sat quietly at the breakfast table and pondered the next step. She must speak, though, had to deal with this new day.

Her husband had been taken away in a straitjacket and she was neither sorry nor surprised. Meredith was living in a hotel. An empty house on Crompton Way was being purchased; everyone and everything was in a state of flux. Then there was Henry, the old man who had drunk himself to the point of no return. What was the next step? And in which direction should she move?

Jeremy and Peter were eating eggs and toast; they noticed, but did not remark upon, the silk scarf round their mother's neck. It was blue and white and it hid

163

their father's crime. For a reason that lay beyond the bounds of explanation, the two boys felt guilty. Peter had a vague notion that simply being male made him answerable; Jeremy, angrier than his twin, was guilty because he had not saved his mother. He should have seen it coming, should have realized that his father had taken that last stride into the special lunacy that was dipsomania.

'We shall have to get your grandfather back.' Jean's voice was croaky, as if it needed oiling. 'We cannot leave him with Mrs Fishwick.'

Peter stirred his tea absently. 'We can find help and drive round the woods to the cottage. Don't worry about it, Mother, because Jeremy and I will organize all that.'

She raised her head. 'You are good boys. Please, I beg you, curtail your drinking. Look what it has done to your father and grandfather. Until recently, I remained unconvinced, but now I edge nearer to the belief that drink plagues generations. So take care.'

Peter nodded. 'We shall.'

Sally Foster wandered in with a fresh pot of tea. 'Here you are.' She was determinedly bright, though her abdomen was not yet at peace.

'Sit with us,' said Jean. 'The rules – his rules – are suspended for now. We have to get Henry back. I know that Mrs Fishwick has a reputation for guarding herself well, but–'

The front doorbell sounded. Sally Foster, who had not had time to sit down, went to answer it. Less than thirty seconds later, she returned. 'It's Pol Fishwick,' she said. 'I've left her in the hall.'

Jean, too weary for proprieties, nodded just once. Everyone in this room had been involved in the Chandler family's exhibition of dirty washing, so one more short step would not cause matters to deteriorate. 'Bring her in, please.'

Polly, standing in an area that was bigger than her whole house, was suddenly nervous. What the hell was she doing here? She had begun her journey in righteous indignation, but now her battlements were crumbling. Generations of Chandlers stared down from the walls, not one of them to mend another for looks. Ugly bastards, the lot of them. There was an overwhelming smell of drink and Mansion Furniture Wax. She was scared.

'Follow me,' said the po-faced housekeeper.

Oh, what had happened to temper? Pol wondered as she travelled on reluctant feet towards the next big event. What could she say? Was she prepared to face Richard Chandler? More to the point, would she cope with his wife and his children? She had to, she had to.

He was not there. Pol's shoulders almost sagged with relief while she counted the occupants of the dining room. Then trepidation returned as she found herself in the company of Jean Chandler and her twin sons. 'I . . . er . . . sorry if I'm disturbing you, like. Shall I wait in the hall while you have your breakfast?'

Jean shook her head. 'We are late today, Mrs Fishwick. Sit down, please. Would you like tea?'

Pol sat on the edge of a dining chair while the lady of the manor poured tea. This room was big enough for a barn dance. Its walls, half-panelled in oak, bore more paintings. The fireplace was enormous, the curtains were of weighted velvet. She was out of place.

'There.' Jean set the cup down in front of her blowzy guest.

Pol took a sip, allowed the cup to shiver its way back into its saucer. 'I . . . I've got Mr Henry in my house.'

'We know,' answered Jean.

The visitor inhaled deeply. 'I am on a message from him,' she said carefully. 'There's nowt wrong with him, you see.' There, it was out. 'So he wants clothes and shoes, then the doctor. He's a bit forgetful, like, but he isn't crackers, Mrs Chandler. In fact, he's a long way from that.'

Jeremy raised a corner of his upper lip. Of course Grandfather was crazy. The old man had been raving for months.

'How do you know that?' asked Jean, the words fighting for survival as they journeyed past damaged vocal cords.

'I'm experienced. I've seen it all before with my grandad.' There was something very wrong here. Henry had mentioned a big argument, had said that these two women had seemed hurt, but Pol had wondered whether that might have been a small corner of senility showing through. 'Excuse me for asking, Mrs Chandler, but are you all right?'

'She is not all right.' These hard-edged words came from the mouth of Jeremy. 'Your fancy man made sure of that.'

An ormolu clock on the mantel chimed the half-hour, its pretty song inappropriate in an atmosphere so tense. Pol turned her head slowly until she achieved perfect eye-contact with the author of the latest statement. 'There's nowt fancy about your dad,' she said, 'so I am going to speak as I find, because it's

166

too late to be nice. Your dad is one bastard. Right. Would you like me to go? Because I've an old man at home what needs me. If I can't get clothes here, I shall try and borrow. I'm used to making do and mending. Us tenants get by, you know, because we have to. And I had to put up with your bloody dad.' Good, she was angry again.

Jeremy could not maintain his stance. There was something powerful, almost forbidding, about the intruder. She was nervous, that was plain, yet she retained a kind of dignity that did not match her clothing, her dyed hair and over-bright red lipstick. She was standing by what she said, was strong in mind and in limb. In fact, she reminded him of Great-Aunt Anna, though that seemed ridiculous, because Anna Chandler was a clean-living woman.

Pol threw caution to the wind. 'Mr Henry is sane. He has acted daft because he was daft at the start, but getting shoved upstairs made him go through hell. He needed the whisky and it got stopped just like that.' She snapped her fingers. 'Then he started to fight. He knew that his chances of getting out alive were thin, so he clobbered everybody who came near. I know he's old, but he's no dafter than the next eighty-year-old.'

'He's seventy-eight,' offered Sally Foster.

Pol gave her full attention to Jean. 'He wants to come back here of his own accord and as master. He is master – you all know that. I don't know how Rich– how his son managed it, but he stole that old man's rights. To get his mind and his rights back, Mr Henry needs clothes and shoes. Oh, and his shaving tackle. That's why I am here.'

Jean nodded and the scarf slipped.

Pol saw the weal and lost her thread for the moment. So, the scene described by Henry was not borne of imagination or senility. 'Where's Mr Chandler?' she asked boldly. Had the bad bugger done that to his wife?

'In hospital,' answered Jean.

Pol gulped a mouthful of tea, wished that it could have been gin. 'Right.' She placed the almost empty cup in the saucer. 'I don't know what's happened here and I don't need to know. I've got no right to know. But there's one thing I'm sure of. Unless Mr Henry is proved to be crackers, he will not come back to this house until he has his own key. So, do I get the clothes?'

Jean nodded again, the movement almost imperceptible, her eyes straying towards Sally Foster. The latter turned and left the room.

Peter spoke. 'We have been kept away from our grandfather, Mrs Fishwick. I do know that he supposedly passed everything on to my father.'

Pol put her head to one side. 'I doubt the old man signed anything. We talked before I set out for here and he can't remember any of that. But I'm sure of this much.' Before continuing, she invested in a huge intake of oxygen. 'Your dad is capable of forgery.'

No-one replied.

'I'm sorry,' Pol went on, 'but Mr Chandler – Mr Richard Chandler – is drinking so heavy now that he is the crazy one.' The silence remained painful and Pol struggled against the need to fill it; if she said too much, she might let old Henry down. She sat perfectly still while the two boys excused themselves and left the arena.

'Very well,' croaked Jean. 'As you have no doubt

168

noticed, we are in some disarray. Thank you for caring for my father-in-law. I shall visit him as soon as my health is improved.'

'He won't hurt you. But if he gets locked up again, it will kill him.'

'I understand.'

Sally Foster brought a small suitcase and handed it to Pol. The latter stood up, took the case and stared at the mistress of Chandlers Grange. 'He wants hanging for that.' She used her free hand to point towards Jean's neck. 'And if I get to him first, I shall be needing something to calm me down.'

'There are many people in the queue,' replied Jean.

Pol sniffed. 'Yes, but I'm the one with the frying pan. And I'm not frightened of using it, neither.'

A slight smile visited Jean's lips. 'So I have heard from several sources.'

'Aye, well, now you can believe the gossip, can't you? Thanks for his clothes. I'll get the doctor out to him once I've got him dressed.' She marched off, her grip on the suitcase firm. It all wanted sorting out, and Pol knew that she was definitely the right man for the job.

Outside, in air that was cleaner and fresher, she gathered herself together. Yes, she had been right to come here. Now she stood a chance of helping Henry to put things right. There was also a distinct possibility that Richard Chandler might be ousted for ever.

She dragged herself to her full height and made for the woods. First, the old man needed a bath and a shave. After that, she would fetch the doctor; if necessary, she would fetch several, because Henry

169

Chandler was as sane as was possible in a man of his age. But his son was not. Hospital? He wanted locking up in prison and the key throwing away. He wanted a better hiding than Derek had received, that was certain.

Pol sneered as she entered the woods. Richard had cleared the last fence, had attacked his own household, was probably raging in a corner of some private nursing home. Well, he could stay there until hell's flames claimed him. Consigning him to her past, Pol Fishwick strode towards a future that was unsure, yet safer without him in it.

'I'm calling that part of it Times Square.' Meredith used her spoon to chase a stubborn lump of demerara into the depths of her coffee.

Josie, eternally humorous and lugubrious, snorted. 'Times Square? In the middle of Bolton? Bolton is not exactly in the lead when it comes to decor. In fact, there are households up Deane Road still using donkey-stones. If you're up to Red Cardinal polish on your doorstep, you are at the forefront of modernity. So how do we drag them into the twentieth century? Sell red doorstep paint?'

'No.' Meredith lifted the thick cup and sipped coffee through half an inch of froth. 'We are paying for air,' she grumbled. 'I shall have non-frothy next time. Marie? Are you with us?'

Marie, who had arrived late, was not attending to business; she was elsewhere, her gaze fastened to the window. She turned and looked at her three lunchtime companions. 'Josie, can you and Aggie go outside for a minute? I have to talk to Meredith on her own. It's all right, I won't tell her you're a serial axe-murderer, Aggie. She'll find that out for herself when your case comes up.'

Aggie saw the expression of pain in Marie's eyes and dragged Josie to the door. 'Don't drink my coffee,' she threw over her shoulder as she stepped onto the pavement.

Meredith raised a quizzical eyebrow. 'Well?'

Marie, uncomfortable with her burden, had not known whether to say anything. But it was clear that this young woman knew nothing of her family's recent problems. 'Peter came to see us,' she said carefully. 'He has taken a shine to my family and—'

'And particularly to you,' Meredith quipped. 'Sorry. Please go on.'

Marie hesitated. 'It isn't nice, but I shall just come out with it. You haven't heard from your mother?'

'Er . . . she phoned me yesterday. Why?' Alarm bells sounded and Meredith's pulse quickened. 'Yes, spit it out.'

Marie told the sorry tale as quickly as she could, leaving out the ride to Rivington. 'I think Peter likes my mam and dad and that he wanted to talk to them. Meredith? Are you all right?'

The fury was huge. 'Why didn't he come to me?'

'He did, but you had gone out and he didn't want to leave a note. He felt it best that you learnt about this while you were with someone who could offer comfort. I know he would have preferred to tell you himself, but I couldn't just sit here and talk about lighting shops and candle factories, could I? It didn't seem right.' Marie stretched a hand across the table and held the tense fingers of this new and valued friend. 'If you need anything or anyone, come to my house. It's number thirty-four Emblem Street and I

171

come home from work at about half past five. You'll like Mam and Dad.'

'Thank you. I must go.'

Marie glanced at her watch. 'Yes, and I have to get back to work – so does Josie. Aggie will go with you if you like – she is doing an evening shift today.'

Meredith retrieved her hand and stood up. 'Thank you. I shall go alone. But tell the other two. If we are to work together, they need to know about these things.'

'All right. I am so sorry.' Marie sat and watched as Meredith left, waited for the other two girls, then went through the whole sorry business again. Sadder than she had ever been before, Marie Martindale returned to work. If any of these bloody lawyers got fresh today, she would be ready for them . . .

No-one listened. They took his pulse, stared at him, scribbled notes on a sheet attached to the foot of the bed, forced him to drink endless glasses of water, changed the bed when it was wet with sweat and urine, stood and whispered in the doorway. He was not ill.

'I am NOT ILL!' he screamed endlessly, but these folk were selectively deaf, were not interested in his suffering. He was alone for much of the time, confined to a white cell, his only ornaments a picture of the Sacred Heart and a crucifix, its impaled figure bleeding red paint from hands, feet, head and side. She had put him with bloody papists, had done that deliberately, because she knew the contempt he felt for those millions of sad sheep who followed Rome blindly wherever it went.

Then there was the food. Mashed potato in nasty

172

brown gravy, bread with margarine wiped thinly over its surface, porridge, milk, soup. This was hell. She had consigned him to hell.

'Hello, Richard.'

Ah, here stood Beddows, he who had plotted with the fragrant one. 'Bugger off.'

Dr Beddows sat in the single, hard-backed chair. 'How are you feeling?'

How was he feeling? 'How would you feel if your wife locked you up in a convent? I feel wonderful.'

'She did not lock you up. I and my colleague did. This is a place where alcoholism is dealt with. I chose it. Your sons wanted the police – and you deserved the police – but Jean disagreed. Had your children had their way, you would be in a prison cell. She saved you, so remember that.'

Richard tried to sit up, failed, fell against the pillows, every cell in his body either burning or numb. He should not be here, should not be confined against his will. 'I shall sue,' he muttered.

'You are certified,' replied Michael Beddows. 'Two doctors declared you unfit to be allowed out into the community. Your case will be under review in four weeks, so co-operate.'

Four weeks? Four weeks in the company of rosary-rattling virgins and a priest who prayed over him? A whole month of water and lumpy mash? 'When I get out of here, you will be dealt with. How dare you do this? Eh? Answer me.'

'Because you are ill. And because, if you do not behave yourself, you will be dead within months. Most of all, because I have seen the results of your violence. Would you rather be tried for injuring Sally Foster? Do you want to go to jail as a sane man, sane

173

but locked up? Better to grin and bear this, I assure you. With effort and a good following wind, you should be out of here in time for Christmas.'

Richard seethed. It seemed that the whole of his circle had conspired against him – his wife, his children, the housekeeper, this bloody doctor. Men drank. That was a well-known fact – everybody drank. Even women drank these days. The fragrant one was not averse to a glass of wine. 'You drink,' he told the doctor. 'When we come for bridge, you have a drink.'

'Yes, but I can stop.'

'So can I.'

Michael Beddows nodded. 'Yes, you stop when you are asleep. Well, one assumes that you do. Richard, your father was a drinker. Although I have not seen him in months, I do know what his problem is. So, you locked him upstairs, didn't you? And, although I asked to see him, I was not allowed. Why is he up there? To keep him away from the very substance that you now abuse.'

'He refused to see you.'

'Did he? Well, I am summoned by him now. He is with Polly Fishwick in Woodside Cottage and I am due to visit him after I leave here. So he wants to see me now. What have you to say about that?'

There was nothing to say. Richard Chandler turned his back on the visitor and waited for the door to swing shut after him. He would bide his time. He had no option but to bide his time . . .

Mike Beddows drove round the edge of Chandlers Copse. The leaves had started to fall, and as he parked his car outside Woodside Cottage he heard

174

autumn crackling beneath his wheels. He seemed to have spent his whole time lately with the Chandler family – the fracas last night, the certification of Richard; now Henry had been added to the cast of players. The whole business had lasted just a matter of hours so far, yet it felt like a lifetime.

Stepping out, he felt that satisfying crunch as his shoes flattened more of nature's debris. Childhood had been so simple – conkers, apple-stealing, pennies paid by farmers to the young who had helped at harvest time. Now, life was rather complicated, and the next complication stood falsely straight and tall in Polly Fishwick's open doorway, navy-blue suit that was rather too large at the shoulders, a gleaming white shirt, tie, shining shoes.

'Good afternoon, Dr Beddows,' said Henry. 'Do come in. Pol has made tea for us all.'

Mike followed the old man into squalor that showed signs of an attempt at tidiness – newspapers and magazines piled in a corner, small bundles of clutter not quite hidden under chairs dirty enough to warrant a health warning. 'And what can I do for you?' he asked Henry Chandler.

Pol, in a cleanish apron, placed a plate of biscuits on an upturned orange box covered by a rather garish scarf in red and white. There was a paper doily under the offerings and it was curling at the edges, probably as old as the house.

'No, thanks, I have eaten.' Mike could not manage to trust Pol's cups, either. He sat down, glad that he was wearing dark clothes. 'Mr Chandler?'

'I want you to take my name off that list,' said Henry.

'Which list is that?'

'The loony list, of course. I am not insane – am I, Pol?'

'But you were never on any list, Mr Chandler,' the doctor replied. 'Had you been declared insane, I would have known. As far as I understood, you had taken yourself upstairs and you were behaving badly, but you were never on any kind of list.'

Henry swallowed, Adam's apple mobile beneath age-thinned skin. 'But he took over – Richard took over. How did he do that if I was still master of my house?'

Pol sniffed. 'Forgery. You don't need the doc, Hal, you need your lawyer.'

'Oh, well.' Henry stood up. 'You might as well give me the once-over while you're here. And I understand you've carted my son off.'

'He's away, yes,' replied Mike.

The old man was in remarkable health, pulse steady, blood pressure just about right. But with his shirt open, Henry seemed alarmingly thin and Mike wondered whether he had been fed adequately. This had never been an unpleasant drunk. Married to a harridan of a woman, Henry had drowned himself in alcohol, had followed the Chandler tradition of hard living, hard drinking and the various illnesses resulting from those activities.

'You don't drink any more?'

Henry shook his head. 'No, I don't.'

Mike Beddows smiled as he put away the tools of his profession. 'Well, you've a few years left yet. Eat well, walk as far as you can and stay away from fast women. As for the rest of it – the bank accounts and so forth, that is for your lawyer, as Mrs Fishwick says.'

'Thanks.' Henry struggled to fasten his shirt and

176

tie, was pleased when Pol did it for him. 'Why is Richard in hospital?' he asked. 'Is it because of what he did to Jean?'

Mike paused on his way out. 'I cannot tell you – part of my job is to keep my mouth shut. But go home, Mr Chandler.'

'See? I told you it was safe.' Pol turned from the old man and spoke to the medic. 'His grandsons came for him, but I told them to come back later, after you had been. And I told him that his son had gone, but he got it into his head that he was going to be locked up again. He does get a bit confused.'

The doctor almost growled. 'So would we if we got kept upstairs. Get that lawyer. Goodbye, Mrs Fishwick. Would you like a lift?' he asked the old man.

'No, thanks. I want to talk to Pol.' Henry sank into a lumpy armchair as soon as the doctor had left. 'I've things to do, Pol – do you think Jean will help me?'

With her eyes clouded by tears for which she could not account, Pol nodded. For a few hours, she had enjoyed the company of Grandad all over again. She was going to miss him. He had been good company, had relished fried egg and chips at lunchtime, had played draughts with her. There was no side to old Hal, no bluster. Oh, he had led a rum life, but he was all right now and she wanted him to stay.

'You understand me,' she heard him say. 'When I can't remember everything, you help. You showed me how to play draughts again. I can remember when you are here.'

Pol swallowed a sob.

'Come with me,' he begged.

Pol, the tough woman who had clobbered her spineless husband with a frying pan, who had

177

tolerated Richard Chandler's behaviour, who didn't care about anyone, threw her pinafore over her head. She could not bear this.

He struggled to his feet and put a thin arm round her plump shoulders. 'What is it? What's upset you?'

'Your son wanted that. Wanted me to come and keep you quiet.' She allowed him to see her tears. 'But the missus wouldn't have me there.'

'It's my house,' he answered. 'And I decide what happens there. Jean's all right, you know. Once she gets used to you—'

'No. I'm a whore, Hal. That's all I am as far as she's concerned. And you can't blame her. I mean, she was fine with me this morning, but she's not well, because he tried to strangle her. And as for that Mrs Whatsername – her with the face – well, she'd leave for a start.'

'Foster. They call her Mrs because she's the house-keeper, but she never married. That saved a good man, eh? And she's all right, too. Come on, Pol, help me to get straight.'

She smiled weakly. 'You go home first. When you want me, send for me. But I've been there once today, Hal, and once was more than enough for me. One of your grandsons – well, if looks could have killed, I would have come out of there in a box with brass handles.'

He sat down again and watched her as she dried swollen eyes. This was a good woman, a fine woman. She should not be living here in a place with a leaky roof and rotted window frames. Pol had embodied his final rebellion, had encouraged him to seek medical and legal advice, was the salt of the earth. He wanted to keep her by him, because she appreciated

178

him, even seemed to care about him. After just a few hours, she had become a firm friend. 'Right, have it your way,' he said as his grandsons' car drew to a halt outside. 'But don't disappear. I need you – you're the bookmark in my memory. You understand me, Pol. I seem to work better when you're around.' He tapped his forehead. 'There's a few spaces in there, you know, and I need somebody who will keep putting the jigsaw together for me. Don't let me down, Pol. Never let me down.'

'I'll try,' she managed, the syllables fractured by emotion.

He disappeared. Polly sat and listened as the sound of the car engine faded. Never in her life had she felt so isolated.

When Meredith arrived, Jeremy and Peter were nowhere to be seen. She found Sally Foster and learned that the boys had gone to fetch Grandfather. 'But he bites,' she said when given this information.

'Apparently not,' answered Sally. 'It seems that your father had his reasons for keeping us away from Mr Henry. A lot of his behaviour came from the drink, and then, when he improved, he decided to fight back.' Sally paused, a hand pressed to her side. 'Well, I can see from your face that you know about your father. Your mother has gone up to change.'

Meredith made off upstairs and found Jean seated in front of her dressing table. Unaware of her daughter's presence, she was examining the mark on her throat. Realizing that she was not alone, she flung the scarf round her neck and turned. 'Meredith – I am so glad to see you.'

But the younger woman remained where she was.

How could her father have done that? And to Jean, who was an excellent wife, no moaning and groaning, no complaining when her husband came and went, when he visited his mistress, when he was too drunk to stand? 'Mother, I am so sorry.'

'This is not your fault.'

'I could have stopped him. I could have–'

'Exactly what your brothers said, my dear. Well, your father is away and we have the time now to work out what must be done.'

Meredith perched on the edge of the bed. Her strong young legs were suddenly incapable of supporting her; she wanted to run to Mother, to hold her and comfort her, but her knees were on strike. Oh, that dreadful purple mark – what a mess. Hidden now, it remained vivid in Meredith's mind, the evidence of her father's badness. She hated him. Why wouldn't he die? And it was wrong to feel like this about a parent . . .

'Sally is not well,' said Jean.

'He hit her, too, or so I understand.'

Jean nodded. 'He did. And now he is declared unfit in his mind.'

'Rubbish. He is a drunk, that's all.'

Jean stood up, walked across the room and sat next to her daughter. 'I could not phone you – my voice was affected. And Peter tried to visit you last night, but you were out. Anyway, here we all are, quite safe, danger over and gone.'

Meredith fiddled with her hair. This habit had pursued her from infancy and she indulged it whenever she was nervous. 'So, what about the house? Do you stay here, do you move – which? Oh, what a mess.'

Jean took hold of her child's hand. 'The mess was always there, sweetheart, but there was a thin coating of icing over it. At least we all know where we stand now.'

'Until he comes out of hospital.'

A huge sigh fought its way past Jean Chandler's sore throat. The immediate future promised to be interesting, to say the least. It seemed that her father-in-law might not be as crazy as had been supposed. And Henry could well be the key to longer-term plans. 'Wait and see,' she whispered.

The front door slammed. 'Your brothers and your grandfather,' said Jean. 'Come along, let's see what is what, shall we? Smile. You are so pretty when you smile.'

Meredith managed a slight stretch of her lips. 'Pretty? Wait until you see Peter's conquest. She is a stunner. I shall never be as pretty as Marie. He will tell you about her himself, I am sure. And Jeremy is smitten, too, but he has not the same serious nature as Peter.' And Josie would suffer no fools, Meredith pondered absently. She tapped the side of her nose. 'Keep quiet about it – I am speaking out of turn.'

They walked downstairs together and found the twins in the drawing room with Henry. The latter had claimed the winged chair: the master's chair, the seat usually occupied by his son. Jean walked to his side. 'Pa?'

He stared at her. 'Why didn't you rescue me?'

'We were not allowed near.'

Henry tutted, his dentures clicking as he moved his tongue. 'Well, I want a cup of tea and my solicitor – in that order. And a biscuit wouldn't go amiss.'

Meredith felt her shoulders melt towards

relaxation. There was, after all, a senior male figure at Chandlers Grange. 'It's lovely to see you,' she told the old man. Then she sat at his feet and her heart broke.

Henry put a withered hand on the soft hair of his sobbing granddaughter. He might not have been quite the full shilling, but he would pull himself together, by goodness, he would. This girl deserved better – they all did. 'Get some tea,' he told Jeremy, 'and you,' he pointed at Peter, 'you can phone Chapman. Tell him to get here quick smart, I've a few words to say to him and some of them will not be pleasant. Lawyers – huh!'

Jeremy went into the kitchen to find Sally, but returned immediately, face pale, his expression one of bewilderment. 'Nan's unconscious on the floor,' he gabbled. 'And sweating. She looks odd. Peter, leave the solicitor for now – go and fetch Dr Beddows. Mother – come and look.'

Peter dashed to the telephone as Jeremy and Jean ran into the hall. Meredith pulled herself together and followed them, while Henry, exhausted after his adventures, remained where he was. He had to remember things. Who was on the floor? Oh, he needed Pol.

Jean mopped her housekeeper's face with a flannel. Meredith and Jeremy, helpless and surplus to requirements, could only watch and wait. Nan Foster's breathing was shallow and her face was the colour of parchment. The clock ticked endlessly slow seconds – when would the doctor come?

Michael Beddows, who seemed condemned to keep repeating this journey, entered the grange once

182

more. Crouching beside the supine form, he assessed the situation and came up with the only answer. 'Ambulance,' he snapped at Meredith. The woman was bleeding internally. Clearly in shock, she required surgery immediately. 'Hurry,' he shouted in Meredith's direction.

Peter spoke up. 'Wouldn't the car be quicker?'

The doctor shook his head. 'She needs a stretcher. I shall go with her.' He opened the motionless woman's mouth and searched for obstruction. 'She is in for a hard time,' he informed the gathering. If she made it, she would be lucky, he told himself. Like everyone else in the room, he suffered a pang of hatred that was dedicated solely to the author of this piece, that disordered and vicious fool who was currently where he belonged.

As they waited for help, each person present stared at the woman on the floor, wondering why on earth this had happened, willing her to breathe, hoping that she would survive the journey. When the ambulance finally arrived, they followed the attendants to the vehicle. Jean made a decision. 'I shall come, too,' she said. 'This is my closest friend and we are all she has in the world. I shall go with her to the hospital.'

The three children of Richard Chandler stood on the gravel path while the ambulance pulled away. Once it hit traffic, it would be blue lights and bells, but for now it moved in relative quiet, though swiftly. 'We had better look after Grandfather,' said Meredith once the vehicle had disappeared.

'If she dies . . .' Jeremy shook his head and went inside.

Peter took hold of his sister's hand. 'Come on, old

fruit, we've a thirsty old man in there – thank goodness he wants just tea and not whisky.'

'I'm afraid,' she whispered.

'So am I,' replied Peter. 'It's a good thing that we go through life blinkered against tomorrow, isn't it?'

'I don't know,' she replied. 'If we could see things coming, we could perhaps stop them.'

'Could we?' he asked, his hand tightening on hers. 'Could anyone stop Father? I suspect not. Grandfather was a drinker, but I am sure he never hit anyone until he got locked away.'

She bit her lip hard. 'We have a wicked father,' she said, her voice still low. 'God forbid that any of us should follow in his footsteps.'

They went inside to reacquaint themselves with a grandfather who had been stolen, and had now returned. And the clock continued to mark each slow, painful second.

Anna stood outside her little home and watched as the ambulance pulled away. What the devil was going on now? That was the second emergency vehicle within a matter of hours and she wondered who was ill this time. The news that her nephew had been taken away was the sole topic of conversation in the village shop – its occupants had clamped their loose tongues as soon as Anna had entered to make her purchases. God, what a mess. She would have to go up to the grange again, because her whole family seemed to be falling apart.

She fed Pierrot and Columbine, scarcely noticing when the geese snapped at her fingers. The chickens were already settled with food, so she pulled on the dark coat and slammed the fedora onto her head, tilting it slightly backwards in an effort to keep the damned thing still. Ah, there was a wind. Practical as ever, she strapped the hat down by wrapping a scarf across its top and under her chin. It was time to face her grand-niece and -nephews and whatever else awaited in the big house. Meredith was there – she had passed Anna's window less than an hour ago.

She entered by the rear door, found a silent and empty kitchen, walked through to the drawing room. 'Henry,' she cried when she found her brother in his wing chair. 'There you are.'

'Don't pretend to care,' he snapped. 'That Pol woman looked after me.'

'Yes, I know.'

'Woodsman's wife.'

'Yes.' She peered into the hallway. 'Where is everyone?'

The old man scratched his balding pate. He needed to sort things out in his head and there was no Pol to prompt him. 'Hang on,' he said. 'I shall get there in a minute.'

Anna sat opposite him and waited.

'The girl and the boys are upstairs . . . er . . . Meredith, Jeremy – stupid names – and the other one.'

'Peter,' she prompted.

'Yes, yes, I'm not daft – I was getting there. My son, damn him, has been locked up somewhere because he took a swipe at . . . at Jean and the nanny. And . . .' Telephone. Solicitor. No, it had been the doctor. 'And the ambulance came and took the nanny and Jean away, because the nanny collapsed.' Triumph wreathed his features. 'See? I remembered all of it.'

'Yes, you did.'

185

He stared at her hard. 'Why did you let him do it? Why was he allowed to shut me away like that? Does no-one care?'

Anna, who was not given to displays of emotion, bit her lower lip. 'I argued with him endlessly, but there was nothing I could do. So I went to live in the gatehouse. It was the talk of the village for a while, crazy Anna Chandler living in a two up and two down with geese, chickens and bees.'

He cackled. 'And crazy Henry in prison here, eh? We were always the talk of the village, weren't we? One way or another, we caused some ructions in our time.'

'We did. And Mother was thoroughly ashamed of us, wasn't she?'

'She was.' His eyes closed and he pictured his mother, long hair confined in a bun, waist nipped in by tight corsetry, eyes dancing as she tried to look stern. 'She would not let us play barefoot like the other children,' he said eventually. 'But we used to hide our shoes when we got outside – remember?'

'I remember.'

'And they got stolen. The Barnes children were the best shod for miles around after they found our good boots. We got the strap from Father.' He opened his eyes. 'I can remember then so well. I can see it all – the factory, the people who worked there. It's yesterday that's hard, Anna. Yesterday and today.'

'I know.'

'I've lost a lot of recent yesterdays,' he told her now. 'Richard stole them from me, but he did me a favour in a sense, because he separated me from the bottle.' Henry sighed heavily. 'Where does it all go? You start school, leave, do a job of work,

186

then – poof – you're old. I am too young to be old.'

'Maypole dancing,' she said thoughtfully.

'Empire Days.' His face lit up, as if someone had switched on a lamp behind the eyes. 'Union flags, bright faces, toffee apples, the races and the Punch and Judy man–'

'That chap with the roundabout,' she put in. 'Remember? It got pulled along by an extremely large horse and was parked out there on the lawn. Mama served cream teas, because none of the servants worked on Empire Day. Then the singing. Remember the singing?'

He nodded excitedly. 'Treacle cake and coconut shies and tugs of war – oh, men were men in those days. Now they have tractors, so there's no muscle left.'

After a small pause, Anna spoke. 'Yes, they were men, Henry.'

He gazed at her, his eyes suddenly filled with tears. 'It's different now, you know. Things have changed. There isn't the same division.'

'I realize that.' Her voice was a mere whisper.

'You could have married him if we had been born in a different time.'

'Yes.'

'Charlie Shorrocks. He was a man, he was, he was. And he loved you, Anna, loved you so much that he moved all the way to Kent when the trouble started. He went to save you any further pain. They should have let you be. They should have let me be. I didn't marry Ellen, I married her father's acreage.' He cleared his throat. 'You should have followed Charlie to Kent, Anna.'

'I should have done many things, Henry, but

moving to Kent was not one of them. I am a northerner through and through, as are you – I didn't want hop fields.' She nodded thoughtfully. 'He wrote for a while – the postmaster kept the letters for me so that Father wouldn't see them. Then he stopped. I expect he married some Kentish girl and forgot all about me.'

He wiped an escaping tear from his face. Anna had been a beautiful girl in her time, but life had conspired to keep her lonely. Young people were so lucky these days, all that freedom, all that education. 'What happened to us?' he asked, expecting no answer.

'Life,' she whispered.

In the hallway, two brothers and a sister stood in silence. Grandfather and Great-Aunt Anna had not always been old. Meredith dried her eyes and decided that they should make their presence known. They had listened to memories and to dreams and it had felt like stealing.

She cleared her throat and led her brothers into the drawing room where sat two children whose boots had been stolen, whose infancy had been sunny, whose old age must be made as comfortable as possible.

SEVEN

The hospital was several miles away in the township of Bolton, and by the time the ambulance pulled up at the front of the huge building Sally was not making sense. Her skin, never very colourful, was almost grey, while her forehead and upper lip were covered in beads of sweat. Her breathing was rapid and shallow, her eyes seemed to have sunk and she was babbling.

Terrified, Jean stood to one side while her friend was trolleyed through reception. She didn't know where to go, had no idea of procedure, but a young nurse, noticing her confusion, came to her side and guided her through ten minutes of slow but necessary torture. Jean had to remember Sally's middle name, her date and place of birth, was asked when the symptoms had started to display themselves. 'Earlier today,' she replied to the last question.

'What happened?'

'Well, she went quiet, had pain in her stomach and in her left shoulder, complained about her neck, too – then, of course, she collapsed and–'

The girl interrupted. 'Has she had an accident?'

Jean felt the blood draining from her own face. 'She . . . she fell. Yes, she was hurt last night. Why? Why?' But the girl was disappearing fast in the direction taken by Sally's trolley. Jean found her strength and tried to follow the nurse, but was held back by one of the porters.

'You can't go in there, missus. Them's the examination rooms.'

'But I'm all she has.'

He tutted kindly and led her to a chair. 'Are you on your own, love?'

'Yes.'

Squatting on his haunches, he took her hand. 'Family?' he asked.

'Two sons and a daughter – they're at home looking after their grandfather. He has just . . .' Her words died. She could not explain to this stranger that her father-in-law had recently escaped confinement. 'He hasn't been well.'

'And are they grown up, these kids of yours?'

She nodded mutely.

The man thrust a pen and a small notepad into her hands. 'Give us your phone number if you have one. Let's get somebody to keep you company.'

She scribbled the digits and stared blankly at the floor while the porter walked away. Why had the nurse asked all those questions and what had alarmed her? Slowly, Jean raised her head and looked at the scene around her. There were people with bandages, with plastered limbs, with patches over eyes. A child in a wheelchair moaned as his mother read a magazine; two tramps staggered in and were immediately shown the door by a nurse.

Phones rang, doctors drifted past, someone at the desk called out a name. The child in the wheelchair was pushed by his mother towards the area into which Sally had vanished.

A hand was suddenly placed on Jean's shoulder. Although the touch was light, she flinched and turned to see the nurse to whom she had given Sally's details.

'Mrs Chandler?'

'Yes?'

The girl placed herself in the next chair. 'My, you are in a state. I'll get one of the orderlies to fetch you a cup of tea in a minute. Try to relax. You'll be fit for nothing if you go to pieces, eh? Come on, do your best.'

The porter returned. 'Your daughter and one of your sons had already left when I phoned – they'll be here soon,' he said before walking off towards his next task.

Jean looked into the eyes of the nurse. 'What is the matter with Sally? She is like family – closer than family, except for my children. She has been with us for so long.'

'I'm Helen,' the girl continued. 'Really, I'm Nurse Hayes, but who's counting? Now, the doctor thinks Miss Foster's spleen is ruptured, so she is probably bleeding internally – that's why she has been in so much pain. They're wheeling her up to theatre now.'

'An operation?'

'Yes, they'll have to take her spleen away. And she will probably be wanting blood transfusions, but the surgeon will work out what she needs.'

Jean put a hand to her mouth for a second. 'She can have my blood,' she whispered through her fingers.

'It has to be matched. She is lucky – we have plenty of her type. I just wanted you to know what was happening. Now, who is her next of kin?'

This was all too much for Jean. Underneath the carefully placed scarf, her own neck stung where her husband's fingers had crushed flesh and cartilage. She could not manage without Sally, would never understand a world that did not contain her close friend and sole confidante. Her mouth opened wide and the grief and fear simply bubbled out in a long howl. 'No, no,' she screamed, 'it can't happen, it can't. These things don't . . .' But she could speak no more, because her body was racked with sobs.

Immediately, several nurses appeared as if from nowhere and Jean was bundled into a small room where padded chairs were arranged. This was a bad room. This was where people were told of death and disaster, she could feel it, could taste it . . . 'No, no,' she shouted.

Forced into a seat, she found herself confronted by Helen Hayes, who brought a similar chair and sat right in front of her, so close that their knees touched. Other members of staff faded away, the last closing the door softly as she left.

Jean fought the hysteria. 'I am sorry.'

'It's all right.'

When a huge, shivering sigh had left her body, Jean struggled on. 'There is no next of kin. Sally was raised in an orphanage, then she trained to be a nanny. She has been with us for well over twenty years, because . . .'

'Take your time.'

'Because she stayed on to keep house for us. She is a sister to me and an aunt to my sons and my

192

daughter. I would trust her with my life and with any secret. There is no-one. Just myself and my family. I am probably the only person who knows her date of birth and where she was born. Her mother died in childbirth and there was no father named. I am the only living soul who knows all that.'

The tea arrived. When the door had closed yet again, Nurse Hayes placed the cup and saucer in Jean's hands. 'Drink it. You may not like sugar, but it's full of it because you need that. Now, did somebody say your family was coming?'

The cup rattled against its saucer. It was an ugly, green thing, thick and heavy. The tea, horribly sweet, seemed to help, but it did not remove from Jean the weighty burden she was shouldering. A fall? It had been no fall. He had done this. Sally Foster was in an operating theatre because of him. She placed the cup on a small table. 'What makes a spleen rupture?' she asked, though she already knew the answer.

Helen organized her thoughts, tried to remember passages from the many books she had been forced to study. 'It can be caused by some diseases,' she said, 'but usually, it's the result of a trauma. It happens to sportsmen, especially rugby players – they take some knocks.'

Some knocks? Oh, the psychological damage had been bad enough – but this? 'I wish it had been me,' the grief-stricken woman whispered. 'Why her? She is just about the best person I have ever known. She isn't even married to him. It should have been me.'

Helen bided her time.

'He calls me the fragrant one, but he says it nastily,

193

keeps telling me I'm a fool and ordering me to get my hair cut.' She smiled grimly. 'Helen?'

'Yes?'

'I would love to have my hair cut, I really would. But I won't, because he would think I had done it for him.' She paused. 'You won't say anything about this, will you? I must get my head in a straight line and I need to talk to my children before I decide what to do.'

'I won't say a word, I promise. Now, will you be all right here until your people come? Because I have some patients waiting for me. If you are afraid, go to the desk and talk to the older lady – tell her to come and find me.'

Jean nodded. 'And you will let me know about Sally?'

'Of course.'

Alone in the bare room, Jean was suddenly overwhelmed by tiredness. She rose unsteadily and dragged three of the armless, padded chairs together, then she lay down across them, closed her eyes and fell asleep almost immediately. Just before oblivion claimed her, she realized that she had not slept at all the night before, the night on which her evil husband had attacked her. And Sally. As she drifted off, she mouthed a prayer and put her trust in God.

Jean Chandler woke to find a familiar face hovering above her.

Where was she? How had she managed to sleep with all those bright lights burning? 'Hello, Dr Beddows,' she managed.

He helped her up and separated the chairs, placing himself next to her when the room had been set to rights. 'Peter and Meredith have gone for a breath of air,' he told her, 'and Jeremy stayed at the grange with your father-in-law.'

He didn't need to say anything else. Jean simply looked into those gentle eyes and knew. She was alone. Yes, she had her children, and yes, her husband was locked safely away for now, but her best friend, her only true friend, had lost the battle. 'When did she die?' she asked.

Mike turned away for a second. The fury in his chest should not have been allowed a seat, not in the heart of a medical man. 'About half an hour ago,' he replied, still unable to look at her suffering. 'It was quick – a blood clot. She never regained consciousness.'

Jean stared at a poster that advertised the dangers of food poisoning. 'He killed her.'

'I know.' The doctor took one of her hands and held it firmly. 'It is manslaughter, at least – possibly murder.' What would she do? he wondered. Frail on the outside, presenting as a mere leaf that was pushed along by the winds of fate, Jean Chandler was possessed of sense, of that he was certain. Her children had gone outside to weep, but Jean's eyes were dry.

'There will be questions,' he said now. 'And a post-mortem for the inquest.'

'I expect so.'

'And your husband cannot be certified indefinitely. I have no doubt that he will buck up and behave himself and that he will be home within the month.'

Jean shivered. 'You were not a witness.' She spoke softly, as if imparting this information to herself alone. 'I was. There was just myself and Sally.' Sally,

195

oh, dear God. 'By the time Henry's minders arrived in the hall, the damage had been done. Now, there is just . . . I alone saw what happened.'

'Yes.'

'What time is it?' she asked.

'It's just after eight o'clock.'

'My children know what happened at home, as do Henry's minders, but I remain the only true witness.' She raised her chin. 'Sally saved my life. She ripped into his face, got him away from me – and he killed her.'

Mike Beddows nodded. The false calm in her voice screamed of shock – he had seen this behaviour before, many times. 'Try not to think about that just now.'

But Jean's mind was gathering momentum and nothing on God's earth could have stayed its wayward course. There would be no move to Crompton Way, not without Sally. Could a wife testify against her husband? Could she drag her poor children through the shame of having a father on trial for murder? Sally's room would have to be emptied. Henry seemed to be in better health. There was Aunt Anna – could she be used as a shield? Geese. If Anna came back to the grange, the geese would come, too. There was some cold pork in the refrigerator . . .

'Jean?'

She did not react, gave no reply. If she went now, directly from the hospital to the police station, if she showed them the marks on her neck . . . According to Meredith, Peter and Jeremy had met two nice girls. A trial? A murder trial? Which nice girls would want to associate with the sons of a killer? This was such a drab room . . .

'Jean?'

The laundry was done by village girls, sometimes on a Monday, sometimes on Tuesdays – it depended on the weather. Sally had baked some scones again yesterday. The pantry was filled with preserves, each label neatly handwritten in Sally's careful script. He was in an institution for alcoholics. He was shut away, just as poor Henry had been.

'You must eat and drink,' advised Mike Beddows.

'I shall,' she replied at last. 'I have much to decide.'

The door opened and Peter walked in, Meredith behind him. At last, Jean awarded full attention to current circumstance. She rose and drew her children in to herself, listened while they sobbed, patted their backs, dried their eyes. 'I know,' she muttered repeatedly. 'I know, I know.'

Meredith was the first to step back. 'We must tell the police,' she announced.

Jean lowered her head and thought about Meredith's statement. 'No,' she answered softly.

'But you have to,' cried her daughter.

Mike Beddows said his piece. 'Not now, Meredith – your mother is in shock. You all need to take in what has happened here.'

The older woman shook her head thoughtfully. 'We know what has happened, Doctor. Sally fell downstairs and collided with the hallstand.'

Meredith gasped – even Peter stopped sobbing. 'What?' shouted the furious girl. 'What? How can you say that?'

'You were not there,' said Jean.

'But your neck – the marks . . .'

'I have many scarves.'

The young man and his older sister stood open-mouthed while their mother lied. Was she going to protect their father? After his crime, after murder, would Jean Chandler be standing by her husband? It defied reason.

Meredith noticed the set of her mother's mouth, a new expression in the eyes. There was weariness and sadness, but there was something else. 'Mother? What are you thinking of?'

'Justice,' she replied, 'real justice. Leave me be, Meredith, for I am in no frame of mind for discussion. But heed this – I forbid you, absolutely, to discuss what happened at the grange. No-one must hear of it. Do I make myself plain?'

Peter was mystified. 'For justice, Mother, you need the police, the courts, lawyers, a jury. If you leave this as it is, how can there be justice?'

Jean studied her hands for a moment. 'Do not confuse the two, Peter. There is the process of law and there is justice. These elements do not always coincide. Now, I am going to say goodbye to a treasured friend. You may come along if you wish.' She left the room and the other three followed at a slower pace.

An attendant peeled the cloth away from Sally Foster's face. Meredith and Peter, who had never seen anyone dead before, remained in the doorway while Jean made her farewell. The doctor stood beside Jean and heard her words. 'You look so young,' she began, smoothing a thread of hair into place. 'I thank you for years of loyal friendship and for all you have done for my family.'

Mike Beddows brushed a tear from his face.

Jean bent forward and kissed the forehead of her dead friend. 'He will pay, my dear. Oh yes, he will pay.' She straightened, turned on her heel and walked to the door.

Mike paused before following her. Had he heard correctly? Was Jean Chandler intending to take the law into her own hands? Surely not. This was a God-fearing woman of principle, one whose backbone had, of necessity, strengthened in recent days. Was she going to kill her husband? As he looked down into Sally Foster's face, he felt a bubble of fear rising in himself. These two women had been close, had been driven closer to each other by the machinations of Richard Chandler.

'Are you coming, Dr Beddows?' called Jean. 'We must get back home – there are things to be done.'

He sighed and took one last look at Sally. Things to be done? Jean Chandler was speaking like a house-wife whose chores awaited her return; she was too cool for his comfort. It was as if today's events had reached some rock bottom in Jean, because there was determination behind the shock. Yes, she was bruised right down to her foundations, and the doctor dreaded the outcome. In his area of work, he dealt with the sick, the dying and the furious. He had met anger in its many forms and he would have preferred to bear the brunt of a strong man's ire than to share space with the cold fury of a woman who had seen the edge.

Mike Beddows followed the Chandler family along the green-floored corridor, breathed in the stench of disinfectants, a smell with which he had become familiar during his student days. Jean led the

199

way, was the first to reach reception, the first outside, the first to arrive at her son's car. As he climbed into his own vehicle, Mike Beddows tutted under his breath. This had been a nasty day; and judging from the expression on the face of Jean Chandler, there would be more unpleasantness ahead.

Jeremy took the news reasonably well, mostly because he was too exhausted to feel anything at all. The hours during which his mother, Meredith and Peter had been absent had all melted into a blur of activity. Henry Chandler had vowed never to set foot upstairs in the grange again, with the result that his grandson and a handful of village boys had been employed in the business of furniture removal.

'Where is your grandfather?' Jean asked.

Jeremy ran a hand through tangled hair. 'He is in the small drawing room with a wardrobe and a load of other stuff. He will use the downstairs facilities and intends to have a small bathroom built on to his quarters. He is the lucky one, because he is asleep.' He sank into the wing chair. 'Poor Nanny Foster.'

'And Aunt Anna?'

'Cooking,' warned Jeremy.

Normally, someone would have made a remark about Anna's cooking, as she was famous for culinary disasters, but both breath and energy seemed to have been removed from members of the Chandler clan. The three young ones remained in the drawing room while Jean, after dredging up the necessary energy, went to impart the bad news yet one more time.

Anna, battling furiously with a paring knife and a potato, placed both on the table when Jean arrived. 'Well?'

'She died.'

The old woman swallowed noisily. 'Did she die because of my nephew's actions?' she asked after a silence of several seconds.

Jean nodded.

'Then what is to be done? He cannot be excused, Jean. He must pay the price for his crime.'

Jean sat down. Everyone 'knew' what needed to be done. The doctor, Meredith, Peter, even herself – yes, she was well aware of the facts. But her mind, as clear now as the proverbial bell, had needed no engine to drive it to its own conclusion. 'Anna, he has been certified insane because his behaviour was so bad when he was taken away. There is a possibility that the killing of Sally might be judged a mere aberration, something he did while in his cups – an accident, even.'

'I see.'

Did Anna see? Did she really? 'He could be confined to a hospital, but I want . . .' The words died.

'You want?'

Jean inhaled; something in the oven was burning – she would have to tell Sally. Oh, Sally. 'I want him here, Aunt Anna. I want him punished properly. The law is often blindfold and labours under too many restrictions.'

A wall clock in the hallway outside chimed the hour, the aged mechanism seeming to cough its way towards nine. The two women stared at each other and, in that fraction of time, they achieved full contact. Jean breathed again, wondered what Anna had managed to destroy this time. The something in the oven continued to burn – where was Sally? No, no – why would her soul not accept the truth? The clock finished its job, whirred a sigh of relief and gave itself a rest that would last for another quarter-hour. Jean could not tell Sally about the burning. There was a will in a bureau in Sally's room; Sally no longer needed a room. Sally's preferred method of self-disposal had been announced years ago – she wanted cremation. 'You must move back into the grange.' Jean's voice was damped down to a near-whisper. The meat in the oven was being cremated.

Anna took a less than clean handkerchief from a sleeve and wiped her face. She had not wept, but beads of perspiration ran down her forehead – the room was far too warm for her liking. She longed for a cigarette, but Jean was staring at her so hard that she felt almost riveted in her current position.

'There is some cold pork,' Jean informed her husband's aunt.

Anna remained motionless. It had taken a lifetime for Jean Chandler to reach the uncomfortable place in which her psyche now resided. The silence continued, each woman maintaining full eye-contact with her companion. They hated him and that hatred filled the room, mixing with a thread of pale blue smoke that had begun to emerge from the oven.

'Cold pork,' said Anna eventually, 'and yes, I shall be here in residence when the damned fellow returns, though I wish to keep the gatehouse. My independence is precious to me.'

'Of course.'

And it was as simple as that; at nine o'clock on an autumn evening, two women reached a decision too awesome for words. The bitterness left unexpressed was easily as acrid as the room's atmosphere.

When all unspoken business was concluded, the

pair worked in tandem, Anna frying chips, Jean dividing up yesterday's pork and some small tomatoes. Sally had cooked the pork and there would be Sally's scones with butter and strawberry jam. 'I don't think I can eat,' announced Jean when the meal had been thrown together.

'Of course you can,' chided Anna. 'You will eat to remain strong for your family; you will eat to remain strong for yourself. Most of all, you will eat because I order you to. We shall have much to face, you and I. By the way – what is the official explanation for Sally Foster's death?'

'A fall downstairs and a collision with the hall-stand.'

'And the doctor will say nothing?'

Jean thought about that. 'He is a doctor, so he keeps secrets. Also, I am the only witness.'

'Very well.' Anna clattered a tangle of cutlery into the centre of the large table. 'We shall eat in here. Sit,' she snapped. 'I will call Meredith and the boys. And, by the way, my brother, who is now ensconced in your sitting room, has spoken with the lawyers. He is back in command.'

Jean felt a slight smile threatening to emerge onto lips that were parched and stiff. 'Really? That will upset someone, I suppose.'

'It will indeed. My goodness, the apple-cart promises to be truly upended. Tell me – how do you feel about Polly Fishwick?'

Jean pondered. 'I have no feelings about her.'

'Good, because she will become one of our soldiers – I believe Henry will insist upon her immediate enlistment.'

While waiting for her children to arrive at the

table, Jean entertained a thought that might have been amusing under different circumstances. Richard Chandler would return home to his reinstated father, his aunt and, quite possibly, his mistress. Polly didn't like him either. In spite of everything, Jean managed two slices of pork and a few chips. Yes, she needed to keep up her strength . . .

Sally Foster had always been neat. A place for everything and everything in its place had been the good woman's motto. Now, her place would be in a coffin and the funeral director would be responsible for that final tidiness.

Jean opened the little bureau and picked out the will. Underneath the large envelope lay a smaller one, Jean's name executed on the front in the dark blue ink so favoured by her friend. She opened the latter item first; it had been written yesterday, the very evening on which Sally had been attacked. She read the date, then placed the page on a bedside table; her eyes had clouded over and she could not see well enough to read.

Even through the fog caused by grief, Jean could pick out the room's familiar objects. How many times had she cried in here? How many times had this sweet woman comforted her? There was little of Sally here. Photographs of the three children decorated the mantelpiece, various stages of their lives portrayed and kept in order of age. Order. Yes, this had been an ordered adulthood, had been about controlling the immediate environment, because Sally Foster's youth had been chaotic. Passed from one family to another, back and forth to various orphanages – how apt her surname had been. And then Sally had fostered the

Chandler family and had made a good job of that. There had been fun, days at the seaside, a fortnight in Devon, holidays in Scotland. On those occasions, Richard had not accompanied the family; his absence had made the holidays all the sweeter.

When her tears had spent their course, Jean applied herself to Sally's letter again. It was difficult to read and the reason for Sally's poor handwriting became plain as Jean managed to decipher it. These short paragraphs had been written by a woman in pain.

To Whom It May Concern via Mrs Jean Chandler or her executors.

I am Sally Foster of Chandlers Grange, Chandlers Green, Nr Bolton, Lancashire.

On the above date, I witnessed an attack on my employer, Mrs Jean Chandler of this same address. She was viciously assaulted by her husband, Mr Richard Chandler. He tried to strangle her. When I rescued her, he hit me very hard in my stomach and I feel unwell. Should anything happen to me as a result of his criminal behaviour, accept this as testimony.

Mrs Jean, I have written the above in case one or both of us might become ill or even be killed by him. He has done it once and may well do it again. My pain is bad, though it will probably pass, but, having witnessed your husband's total loss of control, I am keen to leave this dated message alongside my will. He is a bad man and should be dealt with.

I sign this document formally with my full name, Sally Margaret Foster.

Jean Chandler reread the message, her mouth set in a hard, straight line. It should be taken as soon as possible to her lawyer. The will would have to be read by a solicitor and this, too, should be handed over. Murder or manslaughter, the man should be dealt with. And yet . . . And yet what? Why was she holding back? For her children, for herself, for the good name of the family? Or was she taking control now, just as Sally had done? A plan was forming itself, its inception not a part of her conscious mind. It dwelt at a level where thought did not reside, was a component of a deeper seam that contained instincts whose nature was almost animal.

She would go to her bed now. As Anna Chandler had said several times this evening, Jean would be needing her strength.

'I am not doing it, Miss Chandler, so you might as well stop wasting your breath.'

'You have not listened properly.' Anna righted the wobbly hat and looked round the living room of Woodside Cottage. 'He isn't there,' she repeated yet again. 'He is in a hospital drying out, Mrs Fishwick.'

'And when he's dry, he comes home, right?'

'Yes. Well, I expect so. He was raving so loudly that he was certified unfit for society. That will need to be reversed – but yes, I have no doubt that we shall be enjoying the pleasure of Richard's company within weeks.' The hat was becoming a trouble, so Anna removed a hatpin whose length was remarkable and placed the headgear on Pol's dresser. 'This cottage belongs to my brother. We need to move you out while we render it fit for human habitation.'

Pol folded her arms. 'Then I shall go to town and find a job. I'm not living in that crazy house. What do you want me for, anyway?'

'For my brother, who has taken a liking to you. Also, for stewardship.'

'Eh?'

Anna sighed as she noticed a chip on one of her nails. How best to explain this woman's role in the future of Chandlers Grange? 'A couple of nights ago, I stood in your garden and watched you dealing with Henry. You did very well. He is a bruised soul who has just retrieved his own dignity. You helped him do that.'

In spite of her better judgement, Polly was flattered. Yes, she was good with old people. Perhaps she might get a job in an old people's home, one of those private places up at Heaton, though that might be hard work, she told herself. 'I like him,' she admitted with reluctance, 'but I can't stand Richard Chandler. I want to get as far away from him as I can. I'd sooner have a job emptying Hitler's chamber pot than live in the same house as that bloody man.'

'And stewardship is a responsible matter, you know. Collecting rents, making a note of anything that needs doing on the tenant farms. You would be given some smart clothes and a room next door to Henry's. Your food, heating and lighting would be free, very few expenses of your own.'

How many more members of this damned family were going to try to bribe her into compliance in one form or another? 'I've been offered a job already by that flaming nephew of yours and he can bugger off, too. He wanted me to spy on the folk who are moving into Miss Forrester's old house.'

'Claughton Cottage?'

'Aye. I were supposed to be nice to them.'

Anna knew the reason for that. She had discovered

the name of the man who had bought the cottage and had added two and two together. Martindale. Yes, there had been trouble during the war, and a Martindale had played a part in an early come-uppance of her nephew. Perhaps the imminent arrival of Mr Martindale had pushed Richard into his most spectacular binge so far. 'What did he ask you to do?' Anna kept her tone light, as if she were discussing the weather or a recipe for fish.

'Well, I had to pretend to be her friend. I would have kept this house and he would have paid money into the bank for me.' Pol sniffed loudly. 'He's sly.'

Anna marked the understatement and managed not to laugh. 'You know how he treated his wife the other day?'

'Yes.'

'And the housekeeper died.'

Clearly stunned by this information, Polly sat bolt upright. 'Did he kill her?'

The visitor waited a few seconds before replying. 'He was not completely without guilt. There was an accident during the fracas. She died last night in the infirmary. Her spleen was ruptured.'

Polly Fishwick shivered involuntarily. She hadn't liked Sally Foster, because the woman had been a bit stuck up and hadn't been one for acting friendly in the village shops, but– Dead? 'Bad bastard,' she cursed softly. Lifting her chin, she addressed Miss Anna Chandler. 'His wife knows I used to be his mistress. What would she want me there for? I've never heard of anybody as wanted their husband's bit of stuff hanging round the house.'

Anna squashed another grin. For a bit of stuff, Polly Fishwick was extraordinarily large. 'Henry wants you – he needs you. As for Jean, she is sweet-natured and forgiving–'

'She's not like you, then.'

Anna's mouth twitched. 'No. She married into my family, so she shares none of my blood. Polly, remember that Jean has just lost her housekeeper. She will need all kinds of help.'

'I'm no good at housework.'

Anna's gaze wandered round the cluttered room. 'I can see that. To be perfectly truthful, I am no great shakes at it myself, but we cannot be good at everything, can we? These are exciting times, Polly. Jean has told me that the youngsters are going to set up a business in Bolton. There will be much to do.'

Polly was wavering. For some stupid reason, she liked this daft old bat with her too-big clothes and strangely elegant nails. 'I could do a trial,' she offered hesitantly. 'But, Miss Chandler–'

'Anna. Call me Anna.'

'Well, whoever you are, I'm still saying the same thing. Once he gets out of the hospital and finds me up yon, there'll be bloody murder.'

There had already been bloody murder, mused the older woman. 'And there'll be three of us and one of him. Also, don't forget that Henry has taken back the reins – he is in charge now.'

'Aye, but the other bugger'll kill me.'

Anna glanced through the open door at the object hanging next to the window. 'Bring your trophy along,' she said mischievously, 'we can hit him with that.'

Polly looked at Anna. Anna looked at Polly. Then the laughter started. The mirth was the glue and, within ten minutes, Polly found herself agreeing to a

209

month's trial at the grange, though she refused to bring the battered pan.

Meredith arrived at 34 Emblem Street with her brother and a letter. The missive, addressed to Mrs Martindale, was from Jean. 'I still think it's a stupid idea,' muttered Meredith as she stepped out of the car. 'Marie's mother hasn't been well – that's the reason for the move.'

Peter shrugged. 'Marie's mother will be lonely up there. Look how they live.' He glanced up and down the street, wondered how many people were crammed into these tiny dwellings. They were on top of each other, never short of company.

'There's something going on,' Meredith said. 'I think Mother is out of her mind. Great-Aunt Anna has always been crazy, but Mother? Our father murders Nanny Foster and–'

'Keep your voice down,' Peter advised.

His sister grimaced. 'Plenty of people know about it. Marie knows, doesn't she? Or she will soon, because you told her what Father had done, and the death will be in the newspaper. And you won't keep anything from your precious Marie anyway, will you?'

Peter grabbed her arm. 'Merry, are you jealous?'

She shrugged him off. 'Of course not. It's just that you gave away your heart very quickly. Jeremy is clearly smitten with Josie, but you? You've been mooning around for days.'

Peter had not been mooning around, but he was in no mood for argument. He had been sad and angry about Sally Foster, but he had not been pining for

Marie – not really. 'Merry, behave yourself or go away. We are here with a message and let that be an end to the silliness.'

He knocked at the door and waited, knocked again and was surprised when the door of number 32 opened. 'Hello,' said Elsie. 'Nay, they're out, lad. Marie's at work, so's Alf, and Leena's down town looking at curtain material. Were it summat special, like? Only I can give them a message when they come home.'

Peter had been told about 'Auntie Elthie'. Auntie Elsie was wearing a broad smile and a multicoloured turban fashioned from a scarf, plastic rollers peeping out at the front. Marie was plainly fond of this neighbour, so he decided to invest his trust in the woman. 'Would you give this letter to Mrs Martindale, please? And pass on our regards to the family – we are Peter and Meredith Chandler.'

Elsie, always ready for a gossip, took the envelope and leaned on the door jamb. 'You courting Marie?' she asked. 'Only you won't meet a finer girl and I should know, because I've known her since she were a baby.' She righted herself and took a pace back. 'You can come in and wait if you want – Leena won't be long.'

But Peter, who had been warned of Elsie's wandering tongue, thanked her and returned to his car.

Meredith lingered for a moment. She didn't wish to appear curt or rude, so she thanked Elsie profusely before joining Peter. 'I still think Mother is mad,' she repeated as the Austin pulled away.

'She would have to testify against her own

husband,' replied Peter. 'And as it was never a happy marriage, her testimony could be viewed as prejudiced.'

'So he gets away with it?'

Peter pulled out onto Derby Street and drove towards the town. 'Do you want to be pointed out as the girl whose father is being tried for murder? Is that your goal?'

'No, but–'

'Then leave it as it is. Surely, we have enough with the funeral? And stop arguing with Mother. She has lost her very best friend – she needs support, not criticism.'

They completed the journey home in silence, though Meredith was scarcely able to remain still. It was as if every nerve in her body had become unsheathed, as if her skin had peeled away to leave her open to every available hurt. She was not used to feeling like this; perhaps she should return to the hotel; perhaps the grange was not the place for her.

When they reached the house, she jumped out of the car and ran all the way to her room. She needed something. Oh, what would help her through all this? Should she ask the doctor for nerve tablets or a tonic? It was all too much, because everyone insisted on carrying on as if the world had not been shaken on its axis. Was she the only one who felt anything?

Flat on her bed, she stared up at the ceiling. There were twelve points on the ceiling rose round the central light fitting, yet she could hardly count the familiar decorations, because even now, in this supine position, she felt like a marionette whose strings were being pulled sharply by a cruel puppeteer. Somewhere behind heavy cloud, the sun was beginning to set on yet another day. And Father was going to get away with murder, quite literally. Why would the room not stay still? She must steady herself, she really must.

After ten minutes of restlessness and torment, Meredith dashed downstairs, made sure that the coast was clear, then returned quickly to her room, a bottle held under her cardigan. She took a mug from the shelf above the washbasin and half filled it with sherry. The edge had to be taken off life's cruelties.

And it hit her as soon as she had downed the first gulp. She was warm, she was free and her room was suddenly more colourful. When the cup was drained, most of her worries had melted; why on earth had it taken so long to find an answer? With a tiny amount of help from time to time, she would be able to cope with almost anything.

For a split second, she thought about her father, remembered the Chandlers' curse. But the moment passed and she refilled her cup. She would be able to stop; she was not going to be an old soak like her father, was she?

EIGHT

Leena Martindale sat with her husband at the kitchen table, a cup in one hand, a letter in the other. Her mouth was slightly open, while her eyes scanned the message for the third time. 'What does she want us there for? She must know you can't stand him.'

Alf peered over the top of the *Bolton Evening News*. 'Are you going to drink that flaming treacle you call tea? It'll be stone cold. Anybody would think you'd had a summons from the palace, the road you're carrying on.'

'I'm not sure I'm up to this.'

With exaggerated patience, Alf folded his newspaper and placed it on the table. 'What's the matter with you? That cup's been stuck in mid-air for about a quarter of an hour. It's like living on the edge of a flipping volcano. I'm sat here trying to digest me food and I can feel it in the air.'

She awarded him a particularly steely stare. 'Feel what?'

'The tension. This must be what Chamberlain went through when he got back with his bit of paper.'

'Eh?'

'Oh, never mind. We are having what I'd call a pregnant pause. Mrs Chandler is going to be one of our neighbours, like it or not, and–'

'She isn't. She's got a garden the size of a bloody football field – back and front. There's no way of calling her a neighbour, not like we're used to here.'

Alf sighed. 'She's got a detached house and we've got a detached house. So far, we're equal.'

'Equal?' Leena's voice was travelling skyward. 'Equal? Except for about ten bedrooms and a load of antiques. They probably don't bother with folk from the village.' She swallowed. No way was she going to admit that she was afraid. Just because she came from the 'bottom end', the industrialized area – why should she feel inferior? She was as good as anybody and she knew it. If someone had asked her, she would have insisted that she was not fearful. But she felt – oh, she didn't know what she felt. And her own husband was looking at her as if she'd gone daft.

'You've a face like a month of wet Sundays,' complained Alf. 'I've seen better-looking ones in butchers' windows with apples stuck in their gobs.'

'What shall I wear?' was the next subject to rear its ugly head.

'Clothes,' answered Alf, helpful as ever. Oh, God, she wasn't going to do one of her full-blown shopping jaunts, was she? It wasn't that the clothes couldn't be afforded, it was the fact that she visited every shop in Bolton, Manchester, Bury and all surrounding villages. Even then, she nearly always came back to the first outfit she had seen. And she wouldn't do it on her own, oh, no – she had to have her husband with her for approval. Approval? He was yet to get a word in edgeways on one of these expeditions.

'I suppose you'd be satisfied if I wore me wedding dress.'

'It wouldn't go anywhere near you,' he quipped.

She picked up the newspaper and clouted him with it. Sometimes, he displayed all the sensitivity of set concrete. Clothes were important – they could make or break a woman. It was all right for men – they needed a couple of suits, half a dozen shirts and a tie – they didn't have to think about it.

'You can take our Marie shopping with you,' he said now. 'I'm not traipsing about all over the place for a frock and shoes.'

'Oh, I shall. I'll need somebody sensible with me, somebody with a bit of taste and an idea of class. Just read your paper.' She jumped up to make more tea.

The front door opened and closed. 'Hello.' Marie's voice floated up the narrow hallway. She arrived and stood near the dresser. 'Mam, Dad?'

'What?' Leena paused, teapot held out in front of her.

Marie swallowed audibly. 'The housekeeper died. Mr Chandler's still in that clinic, and the lady's dead. It's in the *Evening News*, Dad, in the deaths column. It looks like he killed her. Peter came and told me this afternoon. Mrs Chandler was the only witness.'

Leena sank back into her chair. 'Oh, my God,' she breathed.

'And,' Marie continued, 'I learned from my job how hard that can be. There's no love lost between Mr and Mrs Chandler, so I don't know what she can do – the jury might think she was acting out of spite. It's very hard for a wife to testify against her husband, especially if she can't stand the sight of him. Every-

216

body in the house knows what happened, but Peter's mother was the only one who actually saw it.'

Alf felt the blood draining from his face. Flaming jumped-up coward. Just like him to kill a woman. His hands balled themselves into tight fists and he suddenly wanted to hit somebody. But no, Alf was a real man, knew he was a real man, and real men didn't go about clouting folk.

Marie continued. 'And, as Mrs Chandler told Peter, somebody else might get accused of it if she can't prove it was her husband. So she's calling it an accident, blaming it on a fall and the stand where they hang their hats and coats. This is terrible.'

Confused, Leena picked up the letter. 'She wrote this yesterday. When did the woman die?'

'The day before,' replied Marie. 'And yes, Peter says she wants to meet you, welcome you. She's a nice woman, Mam.'

'Have you met her?' Leena asked.

'No, not yet, but—'

'Then we don't know what she is. When's the funeral?'

'After the inquest. I won't be going, because I didn't know the lady. But Mam, Mrs Chandler – she needs friends. That was her best pal, you know. Please go – please say you will.'

'I'll think about it.' Leena busied herself with food and plates. Alf had eaten, but he was always interested in seconds. 'Another plate of hash?' she asked him.

Alf's eyes were closed. Bullets flying, grenades exploding, the man next to him groaning, an arm bloodied inside its khaki sleeve. Left flank, officer down, pick him up, carry him, hand him over, go

217

back for the other one. Fenner, spine cracked, mouth set in a grim line in order to stop his screams, arms dangling, run, run. Then the glasshouse, a few days' rest. Chandler. Standing bold as brass, arm in a sling, accusing Alf. Fenner on his trolley, spine dead, voice a whisper, nominating Alfred Martindale as a hero.

'Alf?'

Jesus, Mary and Joseph, that Chandler was one bad swine.

'Alf? Do you want some more?'

He opened his eyes. 'No, love. But I'll tell you what I do want. I want you to go out with our Marie and buy yourself a twenty-pound suit and some nice shoes. We've got to go, Leena. I think we may well be needed.'

It was Leena's turn to gulp with astonishment. 'Thanks, Alf,' she said.

He looked at his daughter. 'You and all – get yourself something nice. It's a very short life.' He stood up and left the room.

Marie sat and stared at her plate. 'Dad's upset.'

Leena nodded. 'Your dad's a decent man, Marie. He can't stand violence, you know. God alone knows how he got through that war, because he wouldn't hurt a flea.'

'He came out decorated,' mused Marie aloud. 'And cowards don't get that, do they?'

'No, love, they don't.' Leena pondered for a few seconds. 'There's a difference between a coward and a man who tries to keep away from trouble. With the war, Alf knew his duty. So that answers my own question, I suppose. Your father's a very brave man, a solid man. Don't ever forget that.'

'I won't.'

Upstairs in the little front bedroom of a house that was soon to become a part of his history, Alf lay on the bed he had shared for many years with his much-loved wife. She wasn't just a wife – the woman was his best friend.

Jean Chandler had not enjoyed a proper marriage; she had probably invested herself in her children and in the lady who had just died. 'I'm going to have to sort him out again,' he told Germany-on-the-ceiling. Funny how the reverberations of that bomb had made a hole shaped like the country whose air force had dropped the missile. Bert Ramsden had filled it in, but the damage still showed through layers of distemper.

From the kitchen below, the voices of his wife and daughter drifted up and touched his ears and his soul. Aye, they would have nice clothes for their visit to Chandlers Grange. Alf, too, would be decently dressed, but he knew that the social call was going to be more than a little tea party. Jean Chandler was preparing for something. And Alf Martindale was probably a part of her recipe.

The coffin, closed and ready to be despatched, stood in the centre of the hall. The large round table onto which Richard Chandler had been wont to crash his cane was placed to one side; at the commencement of her final journey, Sally Foster was to have pride of place in the house where she had served for well over two decades. Doctors had cut her open. Doctors had agreed with Jean's statement about the accident and the hallstand. Dr Beddows had kept quiet, while the letter containing Sally's message to the world remained upstairs. Richard would not be prosecuted, but he would be dealt with.

Jean surveyed her sons, straightened ties that didn't need straightening, made sure their handkerchiefs showed a crisp point above their breast pockets. Sally liked ironing; no – Sally *had* liked ironing. Even when the village women came in to help, Sally had done her fair share. No more of that. No more chats in the kitchen with a cup of tea and a scone, no more shopping in town, no more evenings listening to *The Archers* on the kitchen wireless. Sally had always laughed at Walter Gabriel's creaky old voice. She had liked *ITMA, Billy Cotton's Band Show, Family Favourites* on a Sunday–

'Mother?'

'Yes, Jeremy?'

'We shall get through it.'

'Yes, of course we shall.' The coffin was covered in flowers. Inside that box lay the remains of almost twenty-four years of close friendship. It should have been him; Richard Chandler deserved to be dead. The rest of that man's life would not be comfortable; it was time to redress the balance.

'Where's Meredith?' Peter asked.

'Upstairs. I shall go and fetch her.' Jeremy took the stairs two at a time – the hearse was due to arrive at any second.

She was not quick enough. Her brother's head was in the room and the bottle was at her lips; she didn't bother with a glass or a cup any more.

Jeremy froze. 'No,' he whispered. 'How long?' He almost knew the answer – had noticed how she had been eating strong mints. Meredith had never liked mints . . .

'What?'

'When did you start drinking?'

220

'It's only sherry,' she replied, 'just to get me through the funeral.' Since the first taste, Meredith had been trying to achieve the wonderful feeling she had experienced that first time. Sometimes, she almost got there, but she had to drink a little more each time.

'The Chandler curse,' whispered Jeremy.

'Nonsense. That only happens to men.'

'Does it?' He entered the room and sat on the bed. 'Don't you dare upset Mother today,' he warned. 'She has enough on her plate without being offered an alcoholic daughter with her cheese and biscuits. It will be just a matter of time before she finds out, but not today, definitely not today.'

Meredith, whose brothers had already fetched her things from the Pack Horse, was resident at the grange again. She ought not to have come home, should have insisted on staying away. But no, she was here to support her mother at this terrible time and the drink was just a temporary crutch.

'It is ten past ten on a Thursday morning,' Jeremy said, 'and you are drinking, supposedly in secret. You are an alcoholic, Merry. Alcoholics are born, not made.'

'You drink,' she snapped. 'So does Peter.'

'A pint or two on occasions,' he answered, 'but never from bottles hidden in our rooms. We are all borne of the same father, but the tendency does not exist in all of us. You are the unfortunate one.' The discovery was more of a shock than Nanny Foster's death had been. This was how it began, a few drops to get through a funeral, an interview, then an ordinary day. 'There is no way to deal with this except to stop,' he said. 'You can never have just one

221

drink. And no-one can do this for you, Merry. The decision must come from yourself alone.'

He stood up and left the room.

Meredith Chandler shook her head. What did he know? She could stop any time she chose and she chose not to stop at present. However, she must cope with this day and with her mother, so she took another strong peppermint from a paper bag and placed it on her tongue. With that and a squirt of Chanel, she covered up the scent of her sin. She was not an alcoholic, and that was definite.

Anna Chandler was settling her brother in what had been the small drawing room, the room in which Jean and Sally had done their sewing and knitting. It now contained the master of the family's bed, a wardrobe, a pair of easy chairs, a bureau and some occasional tables.

'He's got through a small fortune.' The old man shook a bank statement in his sister's face. 'And all the time, I was locked away like a prisoner in my own house.'

'Stop it,' Anna chided. 'I have a funeral to attend – and what is the point of upsetting yourself? It would take just a heart attack or a stroke and Richard would be back at the helm.'

'Yes.' Henry placed the page on one of the occasional tables. 'Yes, I know. And he would steer this ship straight into an iceberg. He has to be contained. Also, why can't I go to the funeral? I knew that poor woman for many years and I ought to be able to pay my respects.'

She tutted her disapproval. 'Don't start that again. You have a cold, just as you deserve after running

222

round outside in a nightshirt. Rather than risk pneumonia, you will stay here and do exactly as you are told for once in your life.'

'And Polly?'

'She is waiting outside. She will come in when the cortège has left. Understandably, she does not want to upset anyone today.' Polly had promised to meet Jean again, but she was holding back until the initial period of mourning was over. 'Polly Fishwick has a bit of intelligence,' announced Anna. 'Which is more than can be said for some people who want to go out and risk catching their death.'

Henry grumbled under his breath. In a sense, he was still a prisoner, but his jailer this time was not a heavily muscled farm worker. No, he was locked up by the frailty of his body, by the toll taken by years of foolishness. And, in spite of everything, he missed his whisky. There were times when his very nerve endings screamed for the comfort they had once found in a decanter. But that was behind him and he must not think of it.

'Right. I have left you a jug of tea and some biscuits.'

'Yes, Nurse. Thank you, Nurse.'

She grinned at him.

'By the way,' he said, 'you look like a bag of rags. Have you nothing that fits you properly?'

'No.'

He stared at her. The coat she was wearing would have gone round her three times with plenty to spare. 'And that hat is daft,' he pronounced. 'It wobbles.'

'I shall stick a pin in it,' she replied tersely.

He wondered how different Anna's life might have been had she married her labourer. She had been a pretty girl, full of fun and life; now, she was just another eccentric old woman who didn't care about her appearance. 'You should have gone to Kent,' he said.

Anna sighed. 'Don't start all that again. We have both led lives of disappointment, but there is nothing to be gained from muddying our boots in old ground again. It's all in the past, and that is where we shall keep it.'

'And where shall we keep him?'

She knew who he meant. 'Jean is talking about painting and decorating your old room. Oh, she won't lock him in, but I think the plan may well be to make his life in the rest of the house unpleasant. There is more to Jean than meets the eye, methinks.'

Henry nodded his agreement. 'The worm turned in the end. I should not like to be on her wrong side while she's in her current frame of mind. Women can be like that, you know; all sweet and quiet on the outside, a raging inferno inside.'

No matter how hard she tried, Anna could not see Jean Chandler as a raging inferno. No. She was just a woman who had been driven to the edge, who had stared into the abyss, who had dragged herself back into the land of the living. 'She's deep and she's no lemming, thank God. A lesser woman might have taken that final leap, but Jean is solid.'

Henry nodded his agreement. Jean owned resources, and that was just as well, because she had discovered within herself layers that could now be mined, brought to the surface and used as armour against a man who would, no doubt, be returned to the grange within the foreseeable future. 'I wish they'd keep him where he is,' he mumbled.

224

Anna sighed. 'Wait until the bill comes, then see how you feel. It costs an arm and a leg for a few weeks in there – and your arms and legs pay the bills now.'

He grumbled about bossy women, then his head dropped forward and a gentle snore emerged from between slightly parted lips. She stood and looked at him, remembered summer days, cricket matches, dips in the shallow stream that ran through the grounds. Henry had been straight and tall, slender, but well muscled, and the girls had loved him.

'You going?' he asked, suddenly wide awake again.

And Anna did something she had not done in years – she kissed her brother on the top of his head. 'I'll say a prayer from you,' she whispered.

'Thank you.' When his sister had left the room, Henry Chandler wiped some wetness from his cheeks. That was the trouble with old age – the eyes began to leak . . .

It was wrong to feel such fury; a doctor was meant to be kind, trustworthy – even predictable – but Mike Beddows felt far from professional as he made his way along the neat corridors of the clinic. He did not see the statues, scarcely noticed nuns and lay nurses as they flitted about in the course of their duties. Mike was focused; he was focused on the person in room 3.

He threw open the door and stared at the room's occupant. The face was still florid and swollen, but the man was sober, at least. Mike knew that he ought to care, that his brief was to make life easier for the sick, but every ounce of charity seemed to have been drained from his soul. Again and again, he told himself that alcoholism was a disease, that the man was not responsible for his own condition, yet he could scarcely breathe, so hot was his anger.

'Dr Beddows?' Richard folded his copy of yesterday's newspaper.

The door swung closed and Mike stood at the foot of a neat bed. He took a deep breath. 'I had a long talk with your wife last night. Her neck is healing, by the way.' He nodded towards the newspaper. 'Do you ever look at the deaths column? Is that the local paper?'

'No and yes,' came the reply.

'Sally Foster died.' Mike approached the seated man, leaning over him in an attitude that was almost threatening. 'She tried to protect your wife, who was being strangled at the time. By you. Do you remember that? Do you?'

Richard offered no reply, though his face bleached slightly, and the broken veins stood out against a paler backcloth.

'And, when Sally scratched your face to make you release Jean, you punched her in the abdomen. That ruptured her spleen and the doctors at the infirmary failed to save her. I understand from your wife that the dying woman left a letter, a statement about what you had done. She felt ill, you see, ill enough to know that she might die, so she wrote down all that had happened. Statements furnished *in extremis* are often taken seriously.'

Chandler's face blanched even further, causing the bulbous nose to shine like a purple beacon in dirty snow.

'The letter is with lawyers, I believe.' He was lying, but he ploughed onward. 'So, although you are not being prosecuted at the moment, I suggest you tread softly from now on. Your wife will not testify against you. That must be a great relief to you.' For Jean's sake, Mike had agreed with post-mortem findings, and the inquest would state that death was accidental.

'They wouldn't listen to her–'

'Wouldn't they? And would they not heed a statement written by the hand of your victim? You killed her.' The doctor shook a finger. 'You killed Sally Foster. Today, she will be cremated. That damned good woman has been wiped out by a nasty, drunken oaf. Find yourself another doctor – you are off my list.'

'You can't do that.'

'I just did it. I shall treat your wife, your children, your father and your aunt. But you can go to hell. And, let me tell you, there are many people who would love to help you on your way to perdition.'

Richard leaned back in his chair. The slight amount of strength he owned was draining towards the floor; he could not have walked an inch for all the tea in China. Yes, he remembered some of it; yes, he knew that he had gone too far that night. But murder? The woman must have had a weakness, because he had hit her only once. 'Get out,' he snarled. 'If you aren't my doctor, you have no business here.'

'I was her doctor,' came the swift reply. 'And today, we dispose of her. When you eventually get home, you will find some changes, Mr Chandler – and none of those changes will be for your sake. During my life as a doctor, I have met many, many people – alcoholics included – and, in my experience, drink merely emphasizes characteristics that were already there. The Scotch has simply made you less inhibited in your behaviour, but your wickedness was there already.'

227

'You go to hell.' The voice raised itself.

'And I shall prepare a place for you.' Mike turned on his heel and left the room.

Alone, Richard Chandler picked up his newspaper and found the funeral announcement, hands shaking from shock and from alcohol deprivation. God, if ever a man needed a drink . . . And there it was, Sally Foster, beloved friend and companion, near-sister to Jean Chandler, sadly missed by all who knew her, blah, blah . . .

He threw the *Bolton Evening News* on the floor and shuddered involuntarily. They all knew about it. The police had not been brought in – if they had, the doctor would not have come – but the whole family knew what had happened. He was a killer.

Outside the window, Dr Michael Beddows pulled away in his car. Richard looked down at his own murdering hands, noticed how they trembled because their usual fuel had not been provided; he had become an engine without oil, without petrol, without direction. And he was a murderer. Something akin to remorse was edging its way into his inner self. She had been a miserable bag of bones, his wife's other half, the one who had encouraged Jean to stay away from him, to remain in the safety zone. How right she had been.

His face was wet and he found himself sobbing. Was he crying for the dead woman or was he weeping for himself? Unable to think straight, his mind and body corrupted by years soaked in whisky, he could not work out why he was in such a state of grief. One thing alone was clear – he had no future. The tunnel in which he found himself was blacker than perdition, colder than charity, hotter than hell.

Richard Chandler had done wrong and there was no way of eradicating this latest sin.

The church was packed. For as long as many could remember, Sally Foster had been an integral part of village life. She had not been a chatterer, much less a gossip, but she had woven herself into the tapestry of Chandlers Green, was one of them, one of their own. So they left their farms and their businesses, many taking half a day from work to come along and pay respects to this quiet and self-effacing soul.

At the front, Jean, Anna, Meredith, Peter and Jeremy sat in place of family. They *were* family, had been Sally's only family. Jean stared resolutely at the altar, unable to glance to her right, unwilling to focus on the coffin. It was the best coffin available, because Sally deserved the best. A heavy silence occupied the church, a quietness broken only by a clearing throat or by the soft sounds of pages being turned in the order of service booklets.

The vicar read from St John, led prayers and hymns, then raised a hand towards Peter. The shy one, the reticent twin, rose to his feet, left the pew and stood in the small pulpit. At last, Jean took notice. Peter? Surely this should have been Jeremy?

Without notes, Peter began to speak to the congregation. 'This is a life to be celebrated. Sally Foster was there when we children cut our first teeth, then our knees and our fingers. Never once did she lose patience with us, and we were not the easiest of children. Jeremy was an adventurous soul, I was a mouse and Meredith caused more trouble than the pair of us put together. Nanny Foster taught us to read, to dress ourselves, to count and write.'

He sniffed back a tear. 'She grew vegetables, cooked our meals and, above all, she was a good and faithful friend. I never heard her raise her voice in anger. She was a whizz at card games and a terrible opponent when we played Monopoly. I know you all saw her as shy and quiet, but she had humour enough to join in at birthday parties and she was a positive influence on us and a great support to our mother. She will be sorely missed.'

Jean finally found the strength to look at the coffin. If Peter could face it, so could she. Tears streamed down her face, though she made no sound, while the resolve in her mind strengthened; he would suffer for this.

At the back of the church, Mike Beddows slipped in and stood near the door. He had travelled straight from the murderer's cell to the victim's funeral and his fury was huge. Nothing legal would be done; Jean, as the only witness, would not testify, refused to drag her children through the mire, was fearful in case she might not be believed. But her fear stopped there. Richard Chandler had done his worst and his wife would no longer tolerate his crassness. Mike shivered. What would she do? How far was she prepared to go? Could he persuade her to hand over Sally's letter? Should he?

Peter was reading 'If–' by Kipling. This, apparently, had been the dead woman's favourite poem. The doctor wondered how many here had truly known Sally Foster. Apart from Jean Chandler and her children, very few had taken the trouble to pass the time of day with her. Neatly dressed and with her mind focusing on 'her' family, she had flitted through their lives, a pivotal part of the grange's routine. Who would take her place; who could possibly step into such well-worn shoes?

It was over. People rose in a single movement and Sally Foster's coffin was borne out on the shoulders of six men, two of whom were the twin boys she had helped to raise. Mike Beddows blinked away his tears. When Jean left her pew to lead out Anna and Meredith, he watched her face. She looked exhausted, beyond grief and beyond reach. Yet there was a set to the mouth, as if her teeth were clenched to form a barrier which might hold back words she dared not utter. In that moment, the doctor's eyes met hers and he knew that she was capable of killing her own husband. If and when she did, Mike would keep his counsel. Sometimes, the breaking of law was acceptable; occasionally, it might even be termed essential.

Aggie Turner had escaped from potato-peeling. She was in the Bodega Coffee Bar with Josie and Marie, neither of whom seemed to be in the best of moods. She scooped froth from the top of her coffee and licked the spoon. 'I'd have been better off sticking to cod,' she mused. 'You two are about as much fun as a murder trial.'

Immediately, two pairs of eyes were riveted to the speaker's face. 'What made you say that?' asked Josie after a short pause. 'Why did you mention murder?'

'Don't know,' replied Aggie, pushing a tight red curl from her forehead. 'Because you can't beat a good murder for entertainment value, I suppose.'

Josie's eyes drifted across and fixed themselves on Marie.

The latter wriggled in her chair before biting into her lunchtime ham sandwich. Did Josie know? Had Jeremy confided in her?

'It's difficult – we know we can trust you, Aggie,' said Josie, 'but the fact is—'

'Trust me with what?' Eyebrows raised on the freckled forehead. Josie and Marie had never kept secrets from her. In truth, these three girls knew each other's innermost thoughts, so what was happening here? She leaned across the small table. 'Tell me.'

Josie shrugged a shoulder. 'It's not our secret,' she said, a false nonchalance painted into the words. 'It's someone else's.'

Marie launched into a change of subject. 'I've done it,' she announced. 'He leaned over my desk this morning and was looking down my cleavage. So I told him. I said, "Mr Garswood, any nearer and I'll be wearing you." He never moved, so I told him again, only louder this time. He ran back into his office as fast as sugar off a new shovel.'

Josie smiled, though there was discomfort behind her expression. 'About time, too. He'll be rubbing against you in the stationery cupboard next news. That is one dirty old man.'

Aggie leaned back and folded her arms tightly, her mouth set in a stern line. As far as boys were concerned, she was used to being left out of the equation, but what was going on here? She had mentioned murder as a joke, and these two looked as if they were on the way to the gallows themselves. 'That won't work,' she told Marie. 'Don't be going on about Greasy Garswood just to take my mind off things. I didn't get landed with the last Fleetwood catch, you know. What's going on? And why am I being kept out of it?'

Marie and Josie studied each other for a few seconds. During that small silence, they shared information that needed no voice. Marie answered after the pause. 'Aggie, we trust you – you know we do. But sometimes, things are best left unsaid.' She lowered her gaze. Josie, Aggie and Marie, three inseparable souls, had been welded together since infant school. And yet now, faced with murder, embroiled in a pattern woven by hands other than their own, two had to keep a secret from the third.

Aggie sniffed in a way that expressed her disgust thoroughly, then she drained her cup, rose from her seat and picked up her handbag. 'I've just remembered,' she said, 'Mam asked me to get some curtain hooks from Woolworths. So I'll go now and you can talk all you like behind my back.'

Marie opened her mouth, but Aggie steamed ahead.

'I know I'm not much to look at, so you two beauties get all the boys while I get the curtain hooks in life. That's just an accident of nature. But for you to keep secrets from me – that's taking things a bit too far. You know I'd say nothing. But you–'

'We have to ask permission,' said Josie.

'But you leave me on the sidelines. I'm not wanted in the team any more, girls. I'm a reserve, a laughing stock, all right for frying the chips, but not good enough to be let in on the serious side of life.'

'Please, Aggie.' Marie stood up. 'Please, you have to understand that–'

'Well, I don't understand, so I'm going for curtain

hooks.' The little red-haired girl turned and dashed out into the street.

Marie sank into her chair again. 'Bugger,' she said softly.

Josie stirred her coffee. 'Run after her if you like.' She clattered the spoon into its saucer. 'I have to get back, because we're having a lecture about selling food. Just think, I could be out of stockings and into meat pies.'

'Did Jeremy tell you?' Marie asked.

'No, my supervisor told me.' Josie eyed her companion. 'Yes, he did, and no, it isn't something we should talk about in public. This isn't about copying each other's homework, is it? It's life and death. It's stopped being funny. And I don't see why Aggie should have to carry the weight of it. Also, muck spreads, Marie. We can't talk to anybody about the boys' father.'

'No.'

After Josie had left for her lecture on food hygiene, Marie Martindale found herself wishing with all her heart that Peter and Jeremy Chandler had kept their secret to themselves. Boys came and went, but Aggie Turner was precious.

Aggie stared into the shop window, but she did not see shoes, boots and sandals. No, all she could see was a picture of Marie and Josie; all she could feel was rejection, isolation and disappointment. Although she joked repeatedly about her situation, Agnes Turner was genuinely fed up with her way of life. She had abilities that went far beyond the management of marrowfat peas and battered cod; she was a home-maker, had been born to cook, to

234

organize, to chivvy people along in their daily lives.

What had that been about? Why were those two suddenly a pair, with her acting as the dummy hand? 'I've got to stop feeling sorry for myself,' she whispered. But that wasn't going to be easy. Apart from time spent in the company of her friends, Aggie enjoyed a limited social life. Like many plump girls, she was treated as a 'good egg', a female Humpty Dumpty, a strong one who would not break, who would pick herself up and remain intact no matter how many times she was toppled.

Perhaps rounded people were not supposed to have feelings, she told herself for the umpteenth time as she walked towards her bus. She was of a lesser species, a sub-group with limited aspirations, little appeal and a sense of humour that would carry her through the worst circumstances. Enough was enough. She would be leaving home, but she would not be taking up residence at 34 Emblem Street.

Was she making too much fuss about one small event? Should she accept life for what it was, just a package of fish and chips, sometimes with peas? Josie Maguire and Marie Martindale were cleverer than she was. They had done better at school, had been assigned good looks and manners that pleased the opposite sex. Aggie had been the tagger-on, the one who made everyone laugh, a clown in the big top. It was time to do something for herself; it was time to move on.

Polly was nervous. Her hands were sweaty and she could not get her hair to lie properly – no matter what she did, it stuck up all over the place, allotting her the appearance of a character from a children's comic, an over-coloured creature who was emerging from shock. 'Bugger it,' she said to the image in the mirror. 'She can take me or leave me.'

Polly could not manage to imagine herself acting as a steward. She was willing to look after old Henry – he was a sweetheart – but the thought of living up there at the grange with the wife of her ex-lover was awesome. Perhaps she would get her house back after the repairs had been completed, but she suspected that Jean Chandler wanted to keep an eye on her. No. 'Jean Chandler is on your side,' she informed her image. Yet her heart was heavy as she closed the front door. Once Richard Chandler came home from the drying-out clinic, would any of them be safe? She knew his temper, had used bottles of witch hazel on the fruits of his rough treatment – and Sally Foster had paid the ultimate price, or so it seemed. 'I should have been nicer to her,' she informed herself as she took the short cut via the woods. 'She couldn't help what she looked like any more than I can.'

She climbed the stile, dropped onto the path and glanced to her left. The gatehouse stood empty; another person had moved into the grange and Polly found herself drawn to the company of Aunt Anna. Anna Chandler took people at face value, didn't harp on about the past, was even amused by the famous frying-pan incident. 'I'll be all right,' became Polly's mantra as she forced herself to walk tall. 'I am as good as anybody.'

The door was opened by Meredith. Behind the daughter of the house, a couple of village girls were mopping the amazing mosaic floor. Polly swallowed. 'I've come to see your mam – I mean your mother.'

236

'Yes. Do come in.' Meredith held the door wide. 'And don't look so miserable.' She laughed. 'Most people who see Mother come out alive and she had a good breakfast.'

Polly stepped inside. Half of her – the half she thought of as sensible – wanted to run. But she would not run, because there was nowhere to go and Henry needed her. She didn't fancy collecting rents, but perhaps she could get out of that. And she certainly didn't want Sally Foster's job, because cooking was an art into which she had seldom delved. She could do egg and chips and–

'Come in.' Jean Chandler was standing in the door of what Pol would call the best room. She seemed friendly enough, yet Pol was tremulous. The last time she had been in the company of Jean Chandler had been the day after Richard's attack. She swallowed nervously. 'I hope your neck's better and I am sorry for your loss.'

'Thank you. Do sit down.'

Polly sat. 'You look different, Mrs Chandler.' She shouldn't have said that – she was going to be an employee, no more and no less.

Jean patted her hair. She had spent eight pounds on a good cut and she was pleased with the results. 'It was time for change.' The words were weighted. 'A lot of changes are going to take place, Mrs Fishwick.'

'Pol. Or Polly – I don't mind which.'

Jean glanced downward. 'Sally Foster was more than a housekeeper – much more.' She raised her head. 'She looked after me, Polly. Life in this house has not been happy.'

Polly wriggled like a schoolgirl in the headmaster's

office. What would her punishment be? No matter what a woman thought about her man, she still objected when he went elsewhere – that was only natural. But Jean's expression was neutral. Polly spoke up. 'I'm sorry about a lot of things, Mrs Chandler.'

'Well, don't be. We have to move forward now, Polly. You know he kept his own father locked upstairs and that we were all forced to stay away from him? Don't you realize how guilty I feel? We should have got help, but Henry ranted and raved like a madman – he was playing his part.'

'Yes.'

'That will not be repeated.'

'Good.'

'And I would like you to care for Pa. When your house has been modernized, you may use it whenever you wish and you need pay no rent. Looking after an old man can be trying, so you will require a retreat – and the village girls will step in when you go home for a day or two. Also, my father-in-law is keen to better your situation. Our land manager is about to retire and he will train you to do his job on a part-time basis. You will collect rents, have estate buildings inspected – Woodside Cottage is a case in point – and report on necessary repairs.'

Polly sighed heavily. 'I'm not clever.'

'Neither am I.'

But Polly knew that this woman had abilities and education. 'I hardly went to school,' she said, 'because I was always looking after somebody – usually my grandad. My mother died young, so I had brothers and sisters to see to. My dad was feckless, we never knew where he was, so–'

'So you cared for a family when you were a child. That *is* education. You can read and write, you can count and you can use your head.'

'I suppose so.'

'Do not suppose anything – *know* it.' Yes, she would say it all. She would say it to this woman and to the Martindales this afternoon. 'It is time for plain speaking,' she began.

Polly felt her heart picking up speed. Here it came, the head teacher's cane, the standing in the corner, the humiliation–

'Did he really ask you to spy on the Martindales?'

Relieved, Polly nodded mutely.

'The man is going to need some form of restraint, and control will not come from within himself. Later today, I shall be meeting Alfred and Leena Martindale.' She paused for a few seconds. 'My husband is capable of doing great damage.'

'I know.'

'And we shall need to be on our guard – all of us. I am tired of the shame, tired of trying to make this house look perfect – this is Richard's whited sepulchre and I have kept the exterior gleaming. I have been too ashamed to admit my fear. But facing up to what has happened is the first step towards healing. I need your help.'

'You'll have it.'

'Shall I?'

Polly Fishwick looked into a face that had opened up. The hurt showed at last. 'I promise you that I'll do my best and I hope my best will be good enough. If it isn't, you can always say so. And . . . you know . . . about me and your husband . . . I am sorry.'

'Your apology is accepted. You had nowhere to go

and he used you. I want you to have a fresh start – so does Pa. Look what you do for him, Polly. He says he can remember things when you are there. That is your gift. Stop thinking so ill of yourself, start knowing your own value. You are wonderful with that old man – he adores you.'

'I'm glad he came to me,' Polly replied, emotion thickening her words.

'God sent him to you, then God sent you to me. Now, go home and make your arrangements. My children will help you.'

Alone once again, Jean began to plan the afternoon session. Alfred, Leena and Marie Martindale were expected. Peter was very taken with the daughter of that family, so it was time for Jean to meet the girl. It was also time to get all the ducks in a row. She smiled, remembered Sally saying those very words whenever she had organized something or other. 'I have all my ducks in a row,' Sally had said when her mind and house had been set in order.

It was time for Jean to train her mind on those flying birds; it was time to get her house under firm control.

Although three people had set out from Emblem Street to meet Jean Chandler, four returned. Leena and Marie, elegant in new suits and shoes, led the way back into the house. Alfred followed, tie loosened to express relief, and bringing up the rear in a plain coat was Agnes Turner. Still rather red-faced, Aggie shuffled into number 34 and plonked herself onto the horsehair chaise under the stairs.

Marie found herself grinning. 'You've got guts,

240

girl.' She could not trim the admiration from her words. 'Whatever gave you the idea?'

Aggie raised a plump shoulder. 'I told you there was more to me than batter and chips. When I heard the housekeeper was dead, I went for the job.' She stretched short legs and clasped her hands behind her neck. 'I'm a housekeeper.' She had acted on a whim and had arrived during the Martindales' visit. 'Sorry, I should have waited, but I thought I'd strike while the iron was still hot. Mind, I'll have to learn to cook better – but I got the job.'

'And thank God for it,' muttered Leena, 'because I wouldn't have known what to say. She wanted me for the job – me, what's recovering from TB of the lungs.'

'I'm your boss,' Aggie giggled.

Alf shovelled some coal onto the fire. He saw beyond the job offers and the tea and scones with which they had been served; Alfred Martindale had not come down in the last shower of rain. He could see right through poor Jean Chandler. And what would be the outcome of this charade? he wondered inwardly. Her husband was in an alcohol recovery unit, her father-in-law had been reinstated as lord of the manor, she had made a friend of Polly Fishwick and, to top it all, she wanted Leena to help out in the house.

'Dad?' Marie's brow was furrowed. 'Are you all right?'

Was he all right? Was he heck as like. Suddenly, the move to Chandlers Green seemed rash. Richard Chandler hated Alf with a passion that was almost tangible. 'I'm all right,' he replied determinedly.

Aggie plucked absently at a cushion. 'He had

something to do with the death of that woman, didn't he?' She had no need to identify the subject of her statement. 'And that's what you and Josie didn't want to tell me.'

Marie made no reply, but the answer lay in her silence.

'So, I shall be living up yon,' continued the visitor, 'and you and Josie can have a room each here.'

Marie bit down on her lower lip. She would miss Aggie and had been worried by the impasse created in the Bodega Coffee Bar. 'Sorry,' she whispered. 'I just did what I thought was best.' Anyway, Aggie could look after Mam. 'It's a good move for you,' she said encouragingly. 'That'll get you away from chip fat and vinegar.'

Leena was sitting at the table, her head lowered, hands splayed palms down on the cloth. The house had been awesome, wood panels, paintings, posh clocks, wonderful furniture. 'Shall we belong?' she asked her husband.

'Of course we will.' The certainty in Alf's statement was borrowed from a strength he was fighting to maintain. He knew Chandler's temper, his so-called morals, his evil. 'We shall have a grand life.'

Leena heard the hollow timbre in her husband's voice, and fear travelled quickly through her veins. The madman would be out any day. She swallowed the terror. 'She thinks we'll manage him between us, Alf.'

He nodded. 'Aye, as Shakespeare might have said, the lass is girding her loins – and we are the chain mail, love. The more, the safer – that's how she sees it. I was supposed to be taking you into peace, not another bloody war.'

Aggie nodded. 'There'll be enough of us. Between us, we can keep her safe. What can one man do against so many?'

Alf leaned against the mantel. 'God knows,' he whispered. No-one heard him and he prayed alone.

NINE

December roared in, winds heralding the advent of true winter, the last leaves driven away by the sheer force of weather, snow held off by constant shifting of air – it was plain that the wind could not make up its mind, because it skittered about like a premature spring lamb, no focus, no sense of direction.

Chandlers Green, exposed to the elements, open fields all around, was chilled further by the force of the gales. Trees in the woods bent as if they might break, washing was ripped from lines, children at play grew noisier as they tried to communicate above the loudness of nature.

Into this cacophony ventured Alfred and Leena Martindale, all their worldly goods packed into two vans. Claughton Cottage, with its new roof and cement rendering, was opening its arms to its latest inhabitants. With the new arrivals was their daughter, Marie, who had come to help with the move. Neighbours Elsie and Bert Ramsden completed the party and all were busy turning the house into a home.

Uneasy about her elders' imminent involvement with the Chandler family, Marie steeled herself and got on with the practicalities, her mind fixed on dishes and the placement of furniture. Peter's father would be home soon and Marie feared for everyone's safety.

It was very posh, she decided as she gazed around at brand-new seating, decent carpets, a gleaming cooker, fresh paint and wallpaper. Yes, Mam and Dad had come up in the world, while she had chosen to remain behind in the old house amid much of the furniture that had accompanied Alf and Leena through their married life. Claughton Cottage was lovely, she admitted, but it was not for her.

Leena joined her daughter and both stared through the French windows, their eyes riveted to a jungle that would remain untouched until next spring. 'Like a bomb-site,' commented Leena.

Marie agreed. 'Armageddon. You'll need a tractor.'

'It's a farming community.' A nervous hand came up and grasped Marie's wrist. 'We'll be all right, won't we?'

'Course you will, Mam. And I'll be here a lot – there's no way I shall let a week pass without visiting you. Then, when we get the phones in, we can talk, can't we? Don't worry. We don't want you ill again.'

Leena's grip tightened. 'And there's the other business – the grange – Mrs Chandler–'

'And Mr Chandler when he gets home,' added Marie. 'If you don't want to be there, don't go. We can always explain to Peter.' Although reluctant to give voice to the concept, Marie was almost sure that she had fallen in love. The visit to Chandlers Grange had sobered her somewhat, as she had not realized the full extent of the family's estate, but Peter remained constant and he was all that mattered. He loved the town; eventually, he would probably move there.

Anyway, Marie had been raised to know that she was as good as anyone, though she realized that her own mother was not over-endowed with self-confidence. Leena protested frequently, was heard to aver that she could hold up her head anywhere, yet Marie knew that her mother was nervous about mixing with a family whose origins were traceable through the lengthy annals of time. Anna and annals, mused Marie. Anna Chandler was writing the history of this village and had begun in the fifteenth century – and a sobering concept that was, too–

'Penny for your thoughts?' Leena was well aware of the subject of her daughter's preoccupation, yet she needed to hear it. Marie was in love and was probably out of her depth.

'Just realizing what a big job that garden is,' Marie lied.

Leena was not fooled for a moment. She recalled her own young days, remembered waiting for Alf, knew that she had hung on his every word and that the hours spent away from him had dragged endlessly. 'Marie?'

'What?'

'You love him, don't you?'

Marie retrieved her hand. 'Mam, I don't know, not properly, anyway. If I do love him, then the first person I'll tell will be myself, but you will come in third, I promise you. I suppose he should be second.'

'Do you think about him first thing in the morning and last thing at night and most of the time in between?'

'Mother!'

Leena laughed – she knew she was in trouble when her daughter used the word 'Mother'. 'Well, I'm just asking about your symptoms, that's all. Some girls get spots and go off their food. Edna Chadwick in our class at school kept fainting. Mother Emmanuel had to take one of the nursery cots into her office for Edna and we used to carry her there at least three times a week. She hung off the end of the cot at the feet end, mind, but she spent a lot of time in Mother's office.'

'She must have been small to fit in a cot at all,' said Marie.

Leena shook her head. 'No, she was about the right size for her age.'

'Which was?' Marie tapped her fingernails against the window she was meant to be dressing in green velvet, proper curtains with weights in the hems.

'She was eight,' replied Leena, 'and he was ten. I never liked him myself, funny-looking lad with red hair and buck teeth, Ernest Hourigan was his name, but Edna used to come over all funny every time she saw him. Each playtime was like dicing with death, Edna plastered against the railings to the lads' playground, him showing off, sparking his clogs and doing handstands till she fainted.' She sighed dramatically. 'It was a hard life.'

Marie sat on the window sill, her laughter contained deliberately. 'What happened to them?'

'She went in for doffing in Swan Mills and he went in for the priesthood. They sacked him after twelve months and he came home and married Edna. They

247

had five children and they brought them all up in two rooms over a newspaper shop.'

Marie eyed her mother. 'Are you telling lies again?'

'Am I heck as like. Eeh, I can see him now, scraping his clog irons on the flags till blue sparks came off them. And Edna nearly fading away when he went into the seminary. It was awful. There was talk of her entering a convent till she heard they never had ice cream.'

Marie could no longer contain her laughter.

'It's not funny,' objected Leena. 'She was a dead weight when she was unconscious.'

Marie dried her eyes. 'Well, I'm not starting fainting and Peter isn't going to wear clogs. I've only known him for three months and you know we sing from different hymn books. Peter's not a Catholic, so that's that.'

'Is it?'

'It has to be. And I can't see him turning.'

Leena watched her husband as he carried in a tea chest full of dishes. 'It wouldn't have stopped me and your dad,' she said quietly.

'I know, Mam. Come on, let's have these curtains up, or it'll be Christmas and nothing ready. Do you know where the hooks are?' Hooks. Aggie had gone on about hooks in the Bodega that day, the day she had made her mind up to escape from a life filled with fish and chips. Aggie was now installed at the grange and nothing further had been said about Meredith and her proposed business. Funny how things turned out – a reply to an advert had brought Marie the last thing she had expected: a husband. She swallowed audibly.

'Marie?'

'What?' She *had* told herself; she must face up to it now, because she had finally announced the news internally.

'Have you got one of your sore throats?'

'No.'

'You sure?'

Marie nodded and began to root about in a box, settled her mind on discovering curtain hooks. He wasn't a Catholic. 'There are just buttons in this one, Mam.' He would not turn – he came from a family with a documented past. 'Pass me that blue tin,' she asked. His family had a history of Puritanism, had fought King and Cavalier, had helped to decapitate the Earl of Derby. 'They're not in this one, either. Look in the hall, Mam.'

Alone, she pondered her fate. Peter loved her – he had said so often enough. Was love all that was needed? Would love carry her and him through the maelstrom that was religious and social divide? Josie was struck by Jeremy, but it wasn't love, not as far as Marie could work out. Josie was deep and quite selfish and was not easily opened to emotion. Josie was not ready for marriage; she would jump out of her job and leave home if and when she was ready, but love? Not yet . . .

Marie discovered an Oxo tin, tore off its lid and found what she needed. 'They're here, Mam,' she shouted. Upstairs, voices were raised, Elsie and Bert arguing with Dad about the placement of beds and wardrobes. Nothing momentous was happening, nothing had changed. Except that Marie Martindale was definitely in love. Yes, taken all round, it was best to stick to curtains for now.

249

*　　*　　*

Peter and Jeremy Chandler were at a loss. 'We can't tell Mother,' said Jeremy for what seemed like the tenth time. 'She has had enough and some to spare. But we can't bring Meredith with us, either. I suppose we could try to lock her in Grandpa's old room, but—'

'But that would make us as bad as our father. Anyway, she's asleep.' Peter sank into a chair. They were on the landing outside their sister's room and were making no progress. 'Did you find all the bottles?'

Jeremy shrugged. 'All is an unknown quantity, isn't it? I found some, but how would I know if there were more? I removed all that were findable, plus seven empties. Still sherry. Glad she hasn't moved on to gin.'

'What are we supposed to do? Mother is downstairs with the picnic, Aggie has worked for days to get it ready, and—'

'Fetch Aggie,' Jeremy suggested. 'Go on, Peter. I'll stay with Meredith – we need help. We cannot cope on our own and that's a fact. Aggie is a coper, that's plain enough. And Meredith definitely, absolutely, cannot come with us to Claughton Cottage.'

'But Aggie is coming – and so she should,' Peter protested. 'Why should she miss a bit of fun? She's been Marie's friend for ever – she is an important part of the welcoming committee. And she may tell Mother.'

'She won't,' Jeremy declared, certainty in his words. 'Aggie is a good egg and can be trusted totally. Also, we have no choice, because she is our only hope.'

When Peter returned with the new housekeeper,

she was bundled without ceremony or preamble into Meredith's room. Standing between the boys, she stared at the vision before her. Clothes were scattered to all four corners and a sickly smell hung in the air. 'Hell's bells,' she whispered when her gaze reached the figure on the bed. 'What time is it?'

'Twelve-thirty,' Peter answered, 'and we leave in fifteen minutes.'

'Is she drunk?'

'This is the worst we have seen,' said Jeremy. 'She didn't have breakfast, so the sherry has hit her hard. She's a bloody mess.'

Aggie bit down on her lower lip. She had entertained her suspicions about Meredith, whose moods changed as often as the wind in these parts, but suspicion was one thing, while certainty was frightening. 'She's only twenty-three,' she said for no reason whatsoever. 'I know, I know, they're born, not cultivated. I had an uncle the same and he started young. What do you want me to do?'

'We don't know.' Peter's voice was low. 'If Mother sees her like this, havoc will follow. We have had generations of it, and—' He stopped when a hand was suddenly placed on his shoulder. Everyone except the unconscious Meredith turned to see Anna Chandler. 'Aunt Anna!' Peter stuttered. 'Erm . . . we seem to have a . . . situation.'

'Go,' ordered the old lady. 'I am not as blind as Jean prefers to be, so I do know what has been going on. The three of you must take Jean to the cottage. Tell her that Meredith has a blinding headache and has gone back to sleep. I shall look after her.'

'But Mother may come up to see her,' said Jeremy.

Aggie shot into action, scooping up clothes and

toiletries and stuffing them under the bed. She picked up a perfume spray and filled the air with droplets of Chanel. 'If Mrs Chandler does come to see Meredith, she will find her asleep. Well, unconscious. And she will have a headache when she comes round, I can promise that, so you are telling no lies.' Breathless, Aggie sank onto the dressing stool. This was terrible. Meredith was such a good and clever girl, yet here she lay as drunk as a lord. 'We have to put a stop to this,' she muttered, 'nip it in the bud.'

Jeremy sneezed when the perfume tickled his nose. 'Stinks like an Amsterdam whorehouse,' he moaned.

Anna smiled grimly. 'And how would you know?' She addressed her next remarks to Aggie. 'You know what has happened in this house, don't you? That my nephew caused the death of your predecessor and that he will be home soon? Have you been told the absolute truth?'

Aggie's eyes slid across to Jeremy. He had trusted her; he had told her the facts about which Josie and Marie had felt unable to speak. 'Yes, I know,' she replied eventually.

'That's important,' declared Anna. 'No-one should be asked to work here without being fully conversant with recent events. This family is cursed.' The ill-dressed old lady raised her chin in an attitude of defiance. 'But Meredith is female and therein lies hope. Leave her with me and look after your mother.' It was time someone looked after Jean. 'Pol is trust-worthy, too – she's on her way to town, so she won't need to witness this, either, but she will need to be told soon about Meredith's little problem. I am sure she suspects already. Get along now – off with you.'

When they had gone, Anna Chandler sat for a

while in the room that contained the latest victim of the family curse. She stuck a hand-rolled cigarette between her lips, struck a match and inhaled deeply. The stage was set for Richard's return. Henry was installed downstairs, as was Polly Fishwick. They had their own rooms and a brand-new bathroom between them. At Claughton Cottage, Alfred and Leena Martindale were setting up home this very day, while the new housekeeper was very much on the side of the righteous.

But in the wings lay Meredith, lines unprepared, her part not yet learnt. The girl needed prompting so that she would not stumble, needed straightening out before opening night. God. This was beyond mending, yet it must not be so, because Jean would be needing a supporting cast in fighting fettle. What could be done? The cure came from within a person, not from pressure applied by others. Henry had endured enforced withdrawal, but the hell he had managed to survive was hardly humane. Was it too late for Meredith?

Anna stubbed out her cigarette, then went to run a bath. Whether or not she co-operated, Meredith Chandler would be sobered very shortly. Outside the bathroom, Anna heard the sound of the others leaving. She thanked all guardian angels for protecting Jean thus far. Then she went to heave her great-niece from her bed. It was time for tough action.

No-one had visited him. That damned doctor had been a couple of times in the early days, but, no longer in charge of Richard Chandler, even he had stayed away in recent weeks. Soon it would be Christmas, and the powers had decreed that he would be fit to go home in time for the celebrations.

Celebrations? He tossed a magazine to the floor and stared unseeing through the window of room 3. Sometimes, he felt as if he had been here for ever. They had tried to get him to join in something called group therapy and he was meant to be a member of Alcoholics Anonymous, but he still resisted. No-one was going to tell him how to live, no-one would separate him from his whisky and soda . . .

According to Dr Beddows, Father was back in the driving seat. Well, that would not last five minutes, because the old man was as mad as a caged monkey. He had been caged, too, because he could not hold his drink. Richard swallowed. Yes, Sally Foster was dead, because on that single occasion the drink had got the better of Richard, too, but that would not happen again. Moderation was required. He would drink less, was absolutely sure that he could manage to ration himself. Oh, he would have given a fiver for a double—

The door opened, but it was several seconds before Richard raised his head. They flitted in and out all the time, nurses, bloody nuns, auxiliaries bearing cups of tea, meals, newspapers. The Catholic priest had been an intermittent visitor until Richard had planted several fleas in his over-sized ears.

When the latest intruder neither spoke nor moved, he was forced to look round. He froze momentarily, then managed one word. 'Pol?'

She took a deep breath before venturing right into the room. He looked dreadful, putty-coloured skin threaded with veins, his nose purpled by split capillaries. Why had she come? Oh, she knew why she had come. It had taken courage to overcome her

254

essential fear of this fellow and she had no intention of backing out now. 'Hello,' she said finally. So this had been his home, this cell with its plain walls, cold green flooring, hospital bed with a crucified Christ hanging over it. He was dressed in a kind of uniform – grey shirt, grey trousers, carpet slippers.

'You've altered,' was his reciprocal offering. She wore a blue coat, good shoes, carried a sensible bag. And her face was not painted. She looked . . . she gave the impression that she was almost decent, though he knew differently. 'What brings you here?' he asked. 'It took you long enough.'

Polly chose her words with care. 'I've come to warn you,' she told him. 'Nobody knows I'm here, but I shall tell your missus when I get back. They're all out. They're all at Claughton Cottage.'

His pulse picked up speed. 'What?' he roared.

'Watch your blood pressure,' advised the visitor calmly, 'else you'll be taking a stroke and I've enough on with your dad – I shan't be able to cope with two invalids, so bear that in mind before you have any bad turns.'

Richard's jaw swung loose and he closed his mouth abruptly, biting his tongue in the process. 'What?' he asked again.

She sat down in a straight-backed wooden chair. 'I live at the grange now. Fred Baxendale's given up as land manager, so I do the rents and see what's what on the farms.' She was proud of that. She had a big notebook into which she copied all the tenants' complaints and they trusted her, even after just a couple of weeks. 'I'm the steward,' she said, savouring each syllable before allowing it to escape. 'And I live in, because I look after your dad.'

He gasped. 'But you refused when I asked you.'

Polly stared straight into his eyes. 'Yes, I did, didn't I? Only it was this way, you see. The night you killed Sally Foster . . .' She paused for effect. 'The night you murdered your housekeeper, your dad ran to me. Right through the woods, he came, wearing nothing but a nightshirt and a load of goose pimples. He was frightened halfway to death, because you locked him up and made everybody stay away from him. And I found out for myself that there's nothing wrong with him.'

'He's a drunk,' sputtered Richard.

Pol squashed a grin. 'Is he? Takes one to know one, eh? What's this place, then? Is it a holiday hotel or is it a drying-out clinic?' She enjoyed the short silence that followed.

'He was mad.' Richard made no reply to the other accusation she had thrown at him. He hadn't killed anybody, but what was the point of trying to explain to someone as stupid as Polly Fishwick?

She nodded. 'Aye, he was mad, but not in the way you wanted people to think. He was angry-mad, furious, helpless. He fought his jailers like buggery – anybody would. But now he has me and Anna to see to him–'

'Anna?' His eyes were beginning to bulge from their sockets.

'Oh, yes, forgot to tell you – she moved back in and all. Then, what with your Peter courting that Marie Martindale, they've all gone down there with a picnic, because the family's moving in today. Done that house up something lovely, they have, new roof, window frames and doors all painted – there's only the garden wants doing.' She watched the words as

256

they cut deeper and deeper into him, knew that she was doing more damage here than might have been inflicted even with the heaviest implement. 'Anyway, I was passing on the bus, so I thought I'd get off and pay you a visit. I'm off to town to get some new pans for Aggie.'

Richard was at a complete loss and it showed in his tone. 'Aggie?'

She shook her head as if reminding herself of her own stupidity. 'See? I keep forgetting, don't I? You don't know any of it and I should remember that. Agnes Turner – your new housekeeper. She's just a kid, but she's learning to cook and she takes no nonsense.' Polly paused again for further effect. 'I shall make sure I get a good frying pan,' she announced clearly, 'because it can come in handy, can a good frying pan.' She patted her neat hair. 'She's a friend of that Marie's – I think they were at school together. We're one big happy family now, Mrs Chandler, your dad, Anna, Aggie, your kids and me. Yes, we shall have a lovely Christmas.'

He struggled to his feet. 'Over my dead body,' he yelled.

Polly stood up. 'That can be arranged,' she replied, her voice steady. 'One false move from you and we'll put you out with the bins, because we've all had enough. Eeh, I bet you never thought you'd see the day when your wife and your bit of stuff moved in together, eh? We get on great, too. And Anna's a scream when you get to know her. As for your dad – he may be old, but he's very good with money.'

'Is he now?'

She nodded. 'They're getting Woodside done up for me in the spring – that's so I'll have somewhere

257

to go when I need a break. Oh yes, nothing's too good for me.' She stroked the silk scarf at her throat.

She needed a break now, he decided, a nice, clean break right through her neck. God, she was staring straight at him, was acting like an equal. How dared she, how dared any of them? 'You'd be nothing without me,' he snarled.

'I was nothing because of you,' came the swift response.

'I looked after you, didn't I?'

'You kept me a prisoner just like your dad. Oh, there was no lock on the door, but I was in jail, all right. You had me exactly where you wanted me – then your dad and your wife got me out. I belong to me now, just to me.'

He stood as still as a rock, eyes riveted to her, mind fixed on a future that sounded far from promising. 'So my daughter came back home and the boys never left?'

'That's right.'

'Jean was buying a house,' he reminded himself aloud.

'She was. But she was buying a house with Sally Foster and now there is no Sally Foster. So, all your family will be there when you come home. Isn't that nice? They'll be looking forward to it, I'm sure.' She failed to conceal the sarcasm in her last statement.

'And is Meredith still bent on starting a business?'

Pol hesitated before replying. Unless she was very much mistaken, Meredith Chandler was bending in a different direction, one that was very familiar to the man in this room. 'I don't know,' came the honest answer, 'but your aunt's still working on the history of Chandlers Green. Oh, and Sally Foster left a tidy

258

sum, you know. She hardly spent a penny piece for years, so that's been passed on to your wife. Yes, we're quite cosy.'

We? he snarled inwardly. 'Why have you come?' he asked.

'I told you – to warn you that things have changed while you've been shut in here. I thought it was only fair to let you know.'

'Well, you can bugger off now.' He turned away from her and waited until the door swung shut in her wake. When he was alone, he threw himself onto his bed and ignored the complaints it made. The last bloody straw? God, there were enough last straws to build a haystack. The fragrant one was mixing openly with her own husband's sworn enemy, Peter was courting the man's daughter, a friend of the Martindales was installed as housekeeper, Father was back in the land of the living, Anna had quit the gatehouse and was installed at the grange and, to top it all, Polly Fishwick had been employed as steward.

How could he go home to that? Home? That place wasn't a home, hadn't been a home in years. Things had improved once he had tricked the old man into handing over the reins, but that had all been ended. Sergeant bloody Martindale would be living right on the doorstep, his upstart daughter aspiring to marry into an ancient family, the dynasty that had founded the village, a long line of Chandlers that was traceable right back to . . . when? To before the Flemish weavers had arrived to show Bolton how to make cloth, to the time when candles had been dipped, not moulded—

He sat bolt upright. If that Martindale girl married Peter, she would be his daughter-in-law. He would be related, albeit only by marriage, to a man who had earned his living by trudging through the streets with rubbish and donkey-stones, balloons for the children, sometimes goldfish, marbles or toffee apples. No! But how to stop it? He needed a drink – he needed several. How many more days? Could he get out early? Where had he left his bank book, that account with his personal savings totted up?

Sweat collected on his brow, poured down to sting his eyes. She had done all this. Jean, the fragrant one, she who hadn't the faintest idea about growing older with grace, she who could scarcely count past five, the only woman he knew who could lose at cards while holding four aces and three face cards. She had gathered forces around herself, had girded her undesired loins against the return of her own husband.

He balled a fist and crashed it into the opposite palm, pain making him flinch as flesh bruised flesh. 'Damnation,' he cursed. 'I have to get out of here.'

The door swung inward. 'Coffee, Mr Chandler?'

'Coffee?' he roared. 'Coffee? What do I want with coffee when I'm being ruined? What good is coffee going to be when my own wife is plotting against me?' He glared at Sister Mary Vincent, wished he could bite back his words. He had to be good, had to act his part, must avoid being certified again. 'I'm sorry,' he managed, though the lie almost choked him. 'Yes, thanks. And would you check the date when I can go home?'

'Of course.' She placed cup and saucer on a wheeled tray that straddled the bed. 'And I hope you manage to stay off the drink, Mr Chandler. Drink causes more trouble than enough, sure it does.'

He gritted his teeth into a false smile, kept the grimace in place until the Irishwoman had left.

Women, bloody women, he was drowning in them. And the queen of all these witches was a few miles away, living in his house with her coven as protection. Frying pans? They'd doubtless be sitting round a cauldron, making a little manikin into which they could stick their poisonous barbs. He would not have been surprised to learn that they had taken hair from his brushes, nail clippings, sweat from his brow if necessary. 'Witch-bitch,' he whispered before drinking his coffee.

There was no point in trying to make a break for it. He had been judged insane by two doctors and the certification had been extended. It was important that he remained calm on the exterior, because calm meant eventual freedom. For over six weeks he had curbed his temper and it had not been easy. They were worried about his liver, about his kidneys, about his heart. They had syphoned off enough blood to fill a gallon jar and he had swallowed sufficient pills to furnish a chemist's shop. He had been X-rayed from every possible angle – they should be worried about radiation poisoning, never mind the booze.

Time passed so slowly here. And, while time elapsed, Jean and her cronies were settling themselves in, were preparing for the return of their enemy. He needed to be clever and he was clever, had always walked one step ahead of the rest. He must think, think, think. They were women, that was all. A few women, one old man and two lily-livered boys who clung to their mother's skirts. There was nothing to fear, but he needed a plan, a sure-fire way of guaranteeing his safe return to his rightful throne. Well, he had several days and he would use them well. It was time to prepare his next move.

*   *   *

Jeremy envied Peter. Peter, the quiet one, he who had been overshadowed by his bolder twin, had taken strength from Marie Martindale, was suddenly more self-assured and relaxed. Josie, on the other hand, shored up no-one, was a pleasant, witty but rather distant girl. And she wasn't here, hadn't bothered to take the day off work to celebrate the Martindales' move.

Peter, plonked on a tea chest in the midst of organized chaos, looked completely at home, but Jeremy felt like an onlooker, a guest who would be treated with politeness rather than with interest. Everyone else seemed content. Aggie flitted about with plates and cups, Mother poured tea, the older Martindales, squashed with their neighbours from Emblem Street on a large couch, were arguing happily about damp-proof courses and new fireplaces. Colin, Marie's brother, who had only just arrived, was standing next to Peter, while the lovely Marie handed out paper napkins and forks.

Aggie looked . . . she looked different. Unable to work out what had changed about the girl, Jeremy gave his attention to a ham and tomato sandwich, though his mind was really elsewhere. Pol had gone out, Grandpa was in his room and that left just poor old Aunt Anna to deal with his delinquent sister. He should go home, but could think of no excuse that might sound valid. There had been sufficient explaining to do regarding Meredith's absence.

Jean rose to her feet and pointed to a stack of paintings in a corner next to the fireplace. 'Those look lovely,' she exclaimed.

Leena blushed, but her husband was up and away

262

before she could make any reply. He prised himself with difficulty from his too-small space and said clearly, 'She did them.' The pride was obvious as he held up two of the watercolours. 'And she gets them out of her head, not from photos or from sitting outside looking at stuff. It started when she was in the hospital, didn't it, love?' The last three words were directed at his wife.

Leena found her voice. 'Yes. It was called occupational therapy. With TB, you have to do something to pass the time, so I picked painting and sewing.'

'She was good at sewing before she ever went into the sanatorium,' he insisted, 'but the drawing and painting teacher said she's got natural talent.' His chest expanded as he spoke. 'My Leena's what they call a primitive genius. We don't know what it means, but she got hung in Manchester.'

'You'll get hung if you don't sit down, Dad,' laughed Marie. 'Look at Mam's face.'

'That's not hung, it's hanged,' replied Alf, 'if you mean she wants to execute me. Anyway, it's time she stopped hiding her light under the bushes.'

'That's a bushel,' Marie grinned. 'One hides one's light under one's bushel, Father.' She spoke in a fashion that might have been labelled by her parents as gob-full-of-marbles.

Alf pretended to take a swipe at her. 'You get your kids educated and they throw it back in your face. We should have put them in the mill, Leena.' He held out his hands for all to see. 'Look at them,' he ordered. 'Even me calluses have got calluses. Survivors of war, these hands, and that's nowt to do with Hitler, it's with piking about collecting folk's rubbish all these years just so my kids could have a better life.'

'You're a martyr,' his daughter told him.

'I am that and me wife's an artist.' He returned to the couch and sandwiched himself back into a space scarcely large enough to hold a child. 'It'll have to be synchronized tea-drinking,' he sighed. 'Aye, we shall need to work out a system.'

Jeremy finally saw what his brother had seen. Here was a family that was welded together thoroughly, each component essential to its fellows, the whole functioning like a well-oiled machine. This was happiness; this was what Peter wanted and Jeremy began to understand why. For endless years, Alf Martindale had worked to provide for his loved ones. Here was his reward, a comfortable home – well, it would be comfortable soon – a place to which he would retire, a legacy for Colin and Marie. Father, born into old money, had expressed no ambition beyond a wish to be left alone to drink himself to death. That was the difference.

'Another sandwich?'

He looked at Aggie. What had she done to herself? She was the same, but different. Perhaps she had made a journey of her own; perhaps her escape from fish and chip shops had been her own catalyst, because she was suddenly . . . altered. 'Thank you.' He took another sandwich and perched on a stool.

Jean was in the corner with the paintings. She picked up each one, studied it, then returned it to the company of its fellows. 'Lovely,' was her final pronouncement. 'My daughter should see these. Are you still going into business?' She addressed Jeremy. 'Because if you are intending to enter the area of home decor, you might give some thought to Leena's work – if Leena wants to sell it, that is.'

264

'Who'd buy it?' sputtered the reluctant artist.

'I would,' replied Jean. 'And many, many more would, too. Your husband is right, you have a rare talent and don't dare allow anyone to try to refine it. This is clean, honest portrayal and your use of colour is wonderful.'

Leena didn't know about the wonderful use of colour. In fact, she understood little when it came to the art of painting. It was just something she did when she was . . . oh, it was daft . . . when she was the other Leena. That first time she had picked up a brush in the hospital schoolroom, she had been lifted away from everything, herself included. Forced to leave her early work behind in case it carried germs, she had simply picked up at home where she had left off – a stick of charcoal, sometimes a soft pencil, then paint and water. 'It takes me out of myself,' she said quietly. 'It helped me when I was ill and it helps me now. I forget to worry.'

'I understand,' answered Jean.

Leena dared not voice the truth, because the truth was scary and silly. When she worked with watercolours, it was as if she changed souls. Hours would fly by, would seem like minutes. She went into a different dimension where time was measured by some invisible mechanism that bore no relationship to earthly time. Yes, it was daft.

'You should paint every day,' suggested Marie.

But Leena could not paint every day. If she did, nothing else would be achieved, and– And what? There would be just herself and Alf, no kids to cook for, no Elsie to chatter with. 'I might,' she replied. 'But I have to get my bearings first. And I shall be helping you, Aggie.'

265

Aggie smiled broadly. 'If you want to paint, you paint. We shall manage.' But Leena knew that she would have to be there. Come the day, they would all have to be there for Jean Chandler.

It was the hair, Jeremy decided. And he had never noticed how pretty Aggie's teeth were. Yes, she had done something with her hair.

Alf was the one who framed the words. 'What have you done with all them lovely curls?' he asked his daughter's friend.

Aggie flushed slightly. 'Lovely? You should try dragging a brush through cinders, Mr Martindale. It was getting so as I needed a gardener's rake – or a combine blinking harvester. I must have twice as much hair as everybody else. When God saw me in that queue, He must have thought, "Right, I've all this rusty old wire to get rid of" – and He gave it all to me.'

'It's a beautiful colour,' insisted Jean. 'It's Titian. There are women who would give an arm for hair like that.'

'Well, they can have it and welcome.'

Alf persisted. 'But what have you done?'

Aggie glared at him in pretended annoyance. 'I've had a perm.'

It was Leena's turn to be puzzled. 'Nay, I've had a few perms in my time, but I came out a damned sight curlier than when I went in.'

The new housekeeper took centre stage, cake slice in one hand, milk jug in the other. 'Right. Perms. I read this in a magazine, so bear with me.'

They bore with her.

'A perm breaks your hair. It bends it and breaks it.'

Leena, alarmed, patted her own neat coiffure. 'Did you know that, Elsie?'

Elsie hadn't known and she said so.

Aggie picked up her thread. 'It alters the molecular structure.' Determinedly, the small girl ignored a glance that passed between Elsie Ramsden and Leena Martindale – if they couldn't keep up, they could at least keep quiet. 'Then the neutralizer glues it back together again,'

'Eeh,' breathed Elsie, 'the things you learn when you're having your dinner, eh?'

'So, I had a perm,' concluded Aggie.

'A backwards perm,' added Marie.

'Yes.' Aggie touched her smoother thatch. 'We just missed out the curlers and plastered it flat against my head. Right? Any more questions? Only my cake is getting stale and I've made another pot of tea.'

'That's us told,' whispered Elsie.

'Aye,' replied Leena. But she was looking at Aggie and Aggie was not looking at anyone. She was especially not looking at Jeremy Chandler. For another thing, the girl had lost some weight. Leena smiled inwardly. Would it be a double wedding? And what about Josie . . . ?

It was a job and a half. Anna, whose energy level was remarkable for her age, sat exhausted on the bathroom stool. In the bath, her great-niece was looking at her with round, frightened eyes.

'It has to be done now,' said Anna. 'If you carry on like this, you will go the same way as your father. Remember what he did, Meredith. Remember how poor Sally died, know that drink did it, that your

267

father is lost beyond retrieval now. He will drink again.'

Meredith closed her eyes. Her head pounded as if it contained the bass drum from a military band. She wanted to scream, needed to tell Aunt Anna to shut up, but any more noise would kill her. Everyone was against her – Peter, Jeremy, Great-Aunt Anna – even Aggie had started to look at her sideways. It was just a bit of sherry, for goodness' sake, a drop here and there to help her get through the day.

'I could talk until the cows come home,' continued Anna, 'but the only person who can help you is you. Open your eyes, madam.'

Meredith obeyed, though she allowed her eyelids to rest at half mast, because the full picture of Aunt Anna in her over-sized tweeds was not exactly cheering.

'I believe that it is not too late. You have only been drinking for a couple of months, so you can stop. Look at me, girl!'

'Please don't shout.'

Anna nodded, causing several strands of grey hair to fall forward, and she swept them away with an impatient hand. 'That pain in your head is caused by dehydration. That's the ridiculous thing – the more you drink, the less moisture you contain. Your kidneys are screaming for water; your liver will dry and shrivel until it has the consistency of shoe leather. Even your brain will wither away like an old prune.'

Meredith decided to fight back, though the effort proved costly. 'And your lungs are black,' she snapped, her head aching anew when her own voice reverberated inside her skull. 'So don't lecture me about bad habits.'

268

Anna agreed wholeheartedly. 'Yes, I have an addiction and yes, it might kill me. But it does not cause me to act like a brain-dead fool. Just think about your father – he will never reach my age. He lives to drink and drinks to function. What about your business ideas? What happened to all that?'

'I'm still thinking,' sighed the girl in the bath.

'You'd think better and faster with a clear head.'

'And the funeral slowed things down.'

Anna pulled the remains of a cigarette from behind her right ear and lit it. 'The funeral is just another excuse – no, hear me out. The funeral was caused by your father's drunkenness. Now, he is coming home in a few days. We shall have two alcoholics in the house. I was reading some letters the other day – bills and accounts and so forth written by our ancestor, James Alexander Chandler. He had the curse. He could not add threepence to a shilling some days – I can tell when he had taken drink, and he's been dead for a couple of hundred years. And here we are with the same thing, your father, you–'

'I can stop.'

'Can you? Then why haven't you stopped? You should be at Claughton Cottage with your brothers and your friends, but no, you are in the bath with a terrible hangover and a mouth like blotting paper. Am I correct?'

Well, of course. Everyone was correct, was right, was sure.

'Am I correct, Meredith?'

'Yes.' That was the trouble – everyone else had the right idea and being the only one in the wrong was a lonely place to live. It had started with the first drink. She had felt wonderful that one time and she had

269

tried to achieve that state of euphoria ever since. And it didn't work that way. But how to stop?

'I didn't say it would be easy, sweetheart.'

The tears hurt, the sobbing almost killed her. Her whole body was sore because she had abused it. Where was God when she needed Him? And Great-Aunt Anna never called anyone sweetheart.

Anna brought the stool to the bath, sat down again and held the weeping girl in her arms. It was a wet business, but it was worth it. 'If you only knew how much I love you,' whispered the old lady. 'I always wanted a daughter or a granddaughter and you are the nearest I can come. Meredith, I would lay down my life this very day to save you.'

'Oh, Aunt Anna, I am so sorry.'

'No. You are not sorry, you are strong. This will never be easy. If you go to a pub with your friends, you cannot drink. You cannot take wine with meals. Remember how you always refused?'

'Yes. I was afraid of drinking.'

'Then God is on your side, because He tried to warn you. Look.' She pushed the girl away and stared into her eyes. 'We shall open that shop or whatever. We shall make candles again in the town and I shall be there for you and with you for as long as I am spared. Your mother needs you, I need you, your grandfather needs you.'

'I know.'

'This is the first day. You are born again today. Because you are a woman, you can do this. If you leave it any longer, you may be lost.'

The water was cooling. It was a cold world. 'Two months is nothing,' Meredith said softly. 'Two years, twenty years – yes – I can see my future.'

270

'Crossroads,' answered Anna. 'Don't look left or right, because you are the only traffic on that road.'

'Lonely.'

'Yes, lonely. Go straight on, Meredith. Prove what you are – a great girl with an even greater woman inside. Believe in you.'

'I shall try.'

Anna left her great-niece to begin that solitary journey. On the landing, she sank into a chair, because her legs would scarcely bear her weight. Could Meredith do it, could she break the new and dangerous habit?

'Aunt Anna?'

'Yes?'

'Go down now. Go to Grandpa. You know I have to do this all by myself.'

So Anna did as she had always done. She put one foot in front of the other and placed her faith in God.

TEN

It was D-Day. Richard Chandler was getting out and his sons had been summoned to collect him. Sister Mary Vincent handed him the clothes in which he had arrived ten weeks earlier. They were washed and ironed and only the straitjacket, which had topped the ensemble on that fateful night, was absent.

The little Irishwoman eyed him quizzically. Since his general practitioner had abandoned him, he had received no visits except one, when a doctor from another village had arrived, reluctance etched into every line of his young face. And the patient spoke so little–

Oh yes, there had been that woman, the one who had left him wild-eyed with agitation, though he had fought to conceal it. Mrs Fishwick, that had been her name. And she hadn't looked too pleased at the end of her brief stay. Although his wife was listed as next of kin, there had been no telephone enquiries, no messages from his family.

Richard Chandler seemed to be universally unwanted. He had a grand-sounding address, some children and a terrible problem with whisky. In spite of her close relationship with Christ and her devotion to all His teachings, Mary Vincent understood the attitude. Not once during his stay had this man uttered a word of thanks. Most drinkers had their bad times, but they also had their better side. It was clear that this man owned no better side.

'Did they give a time?' he asked her.

'About ten o'clock, I believe,' she replied.

He glanced at his watch. Fifteen more minutes and he would be out of here. But what awaited him on the outside? A welcome from his family, a stretch of red carpet, a brass band and a finger buffet? Not likely.

'You must not take a drink again,' she warned.

'I know.'

'And there's a list of the meetings and locations folded into your wallet. If you can get yourself along to AA a few times a month, it will help no end. And your fellows will support you on the telephone when the going becomes hard. Do not suffer alone, Mr Chandler.'

He intended not to suffer at all. The lectures had been many, his liver, his kidneys, his eyesight, nerve endings, stomach, on and on had gone the list of reasons why he should never indulge again. Life was hard with a drink; without, it was a sight worse.

'You do know it will be the death of you, don't you?'

'Yes.' Everybody died of something and he would sooner die drunk than sober. Also, he had a strong suspicion that life at home would be greatly changed and that none of the changes would be in his favour. He would need to drink to survive mentally. Why didn't she go away? She stood there like an over-sized and black-clad doll, rosary hanging from her waist, a large crucifix suspended from its end. She wasn't a bad looker, but the wimple did her little justice and he could not wait to escape her piercing eyes. The nun knew that he would drink again.

She sighed quietly and accepted that there was nothing she could do. After years spent caring for drunkards, she recognized defeat when she saw it. At least this one had paid his way, had handed over money that might save a few of those who could not contribute, the tramps and the poor who were crowded into shared wards. 'May God go with you,' she said.

He looked at her. God had nothing to do with any of it. No longer master in his own house, Richard suspected that he would be marginalized as soon as he got back to the grange. There would be just himself and a bottle, but he would tread carefully, as he must not lash out again. This bloody woman was so calm, so resigned – she was enough to drive a teetotaller towards the demon drink. If he lost control again, he would be back here with Sister Mary Vincent, Sister Mary Clare and the beatified mother of the order – Olivia. Well, bugger that, he was going to keep his nose clean. 'Say goodbye to Mother Olivia for me,' he said, sarcasm colouring the words.

Sister Mary Vincent swivelled on the heel of her sensible shoe and left the room. There was no more to be done; he would drink himself to death and she prayed that he took no-one with him. There was a look in his eyes, almost an absence of emotion. So she travelled on to room 4, because there was hope in there. In room 3, there was just emptiness, isolation and a man whose spirit had been drowned by years of self-abuse. It was time to forget him, because, despite the precepts of her faith, she knew in her heart that he was beyond prayer.

Richard Chandler waited for his sons. Although he had concentrated for days, he had come up with no plan for his future, because all at home had changed and, beyond the little Pol Fishwick had said, he was unable to quantify those changes. There was nothing to be done until he had spied the lie of the land. It was enough for now to know that he would soon be away from here and back in the land of the living.

Where were they? Damn them, they never got anything right. 'Patience,' he muttered. Yes, he had to play them at their own game until he could invent some rules of his own . . .

It had been hell. For the first time in her young life, Meredith Chandler was beginning to understand her own father. This fact did not mean that she loved him, but she had some insight into his suffering. She was an alcoholic. The quantity she had consumed thus far would not impinge on her life, yet she understood that the rest of her days would be spent in active abstinence.

For most people, a drink was just a drink, something to be taken before, during or after meals, a passport to social banter and camaraderie. But she could never be like that. She could never join in, would be forever unable to take just one drink. Because inside her there was a demon that had existed since the day of her birth, a monster-in-waiting, a prescription for doom.

Anna was holding her hand again. Confined to her room by 'influenza', Meredith had hidden herself from the world for many days. Her brothers visited her, as did her mother, but Anna was her mainstay. And what a strange-looking mainstay this was, mused Meredith as she clung to her lifeline. Wearing a cardigan the size of a one-man tent and with her skirt stapled into place by nappy pins, Miss Anna Chandler looked as if she had dressed herself from the contents of one of Mr Martindale's collections of rags. 'Buy some clothes,' she pleaded yet again.

Anna tutted. 'Why? When I am at home, I mess about with chickens, geese and bees. They never complain. Anyway, I have better things to do with my money.'

Meredith sighed. Great-Aunt Anna was a hopeless case, yet— Yet Meredith was thinking about someone else. Recent days had been spent in self-pity, but she was emerging from that state and it had to be a good sign. Now, at last, she was actually looking at Anna, was seeing beyond her own frailty. 'I think I am coming out of it,' she said.

Anna inclined her head. 'You will never be out of it, my dear. You will cope with it. With help from your brothers and your friends, you will take each day, each hour, as it comes. In time, you will be able to sit in a pub with a glass of lemonade, but the craving will never leave you.'

Meredith swallowed. 'Father comes out of it today,' she whispered.

'Out of it and back into it.' Anna's tone was one of resignation. 'There is no hope for him, just as there seemed to be none for my brother.'

'I have been trying to imagine what Grandpa went through,' said Meredith, 'because this was bad enough. To be locked away after fifty years of drinking must have been hell. And I expect Father has had a dreadful few weeks.' The living evidence was all around – she needed only to look at her father and her grandfather to see what lay ahead if she continued to drink. 'I am going out,' she declared.

'There is no point in avoiding Richard.'

'I know. I am going out just to be out. If there is no ice, I shall borrow a horse and get out onto the moors. Hiding in here isn't the answer, is it? I must get back into my stride. I shall be all right.'

'Yes, I dare say you will.'

Anna left her great-niece and walked down the stairs. The hall clock, which had witnessed the assaults on Jean and Sally, echoed gloomily, as if it, too, had dreaded this day. The comforting clatter of dishes emerged from the kitchen and Anna allowed herself a tight smile. Agnes Turner was the best thing to have happened in this house for some time. She was cheerful, industrious and possessed of that wry, dry Lancashire humour. Kitchen sounds were so ordinary, so comforting, were reminders of the day-to-day events that kept life going.

In the drawing room, Jean was busy knitting. Even from the doorway, Anna noticed the tension in the woman's shoulders, watched needles that flew too fast, a spine that refused to relax against the back of the chair.

Jean looked up. 'Is Meredith better?' she asked.

'Yes, I think she has overcome the germs. I got another telling off because I have not stepped into life via the pages of *Vogue*. She is dressing as we speak and I think she will go riding this morning – needs to get some fresh air into her lungs.'

277

Jean put down her knitting. 'I am making this sweater for you, dear. If I see that old grey cardigan just one more time, I shall scream. As for the rest of your clothes – we need to get a new coat, and a hat that actually fits, then Leena Martindale will take in your skirts.'

Anna sat down at the opposite side of the fireplace. People were always trying to improve her. Oh, she knew she was the subject of much discussion within the village, but that had never concerned her. Life was not about clothes, it was about being usefully occupied and occasionally amused. 'I shall stay until he is home, so the hens must wait.' She returned to the gatehouse several times a day to check on the livestock.

'Thank you.'

'He will not take kindly to your arrangements.'

Jean shrugged stiff shoulders. 'The rooms are pleasantly decorated. He returns on his father's terms, as this is his house.'

'Henry has been agitated all morning,' said Anna.

'Yes, I know, but he will cope. Is Polly with him?'

'Yes.' Polly, too, was in a state that might have been described as nervous, though terrified would have been a more appropriate adjective. 'The poor woman has been in something of a pickle since the day she visited Richard. She knows him, Jean.'

'Yes, she does. And that is why we need her here. I realize that we are just women, but Polly, you, Aggie and I are prepared.'

'So are the children,' said Anna, 'and the twins have to fetch him home. How happy we have been without him.'

Jean would not have described the past ten weeks

278

as happy, though there had been a wonderful absence of immediate tension. But Richard had hung over her like Damocles' sword, a threat, a weapon that could kill, that had killed already. Still affected by Sally's death, Jean was fighting depression. Her symptoms – early waking, absent-mindedness and lethargy – had to be fought, because the most depressing item in her life was on its way home. Richard. Had she ever loved him?

'Jean?'

'I'm all right.'

'Did you take your tablets?'

She had not taken the tablets, because they slowed her down and she needed to be alert. 'Yes,' she lied.

'Dr Beddows is concerned about you. We need you to be well and the best thing would be for you to stay away from him altogether. The house is big enough – let me deal with him.'

Jean smiled. Anna was in her late seventies and she had lost weight at an alarming rate in the last couple of years. Undoubtably tough, she was not tough enough to deal with a strong man in his cups. 'Thank you, but this will be a joint effort, with Pa at the helm. As long as Polly is with him, Pa will take no nonsense.' Her smile broadened. 'It will be a shock when he realizes that his former mistress is his greatest enemy.'

'She made that clear when she visited him.' Anna glanced at the clock. 'They will be almost there. Any minute now, the beast will be on the loose.' Poor Jeremy, poor Peter – they were the instruments that would bring back the man who had caused so much anguish. But it had to be done . . .

The two women sat and waited for their foe to

return, both staring into the fire, both wishing that he would never come home and knowing that he must.

They had brought Richard's Bentley. He would not have liked to travel in his sons' battered Austin, as it was not particularly large and its suspension left space for improvement, so a nervous Jeremy sat behind the wheel of a bigger and much more powerful car.

'Can't we lose him on the way home?' Peter let out a deep sigh.

'He'd find his route,' replied Jeremy. 'Bad pennies are famous for turning up when they are least wanted. No, we are stuck with him. I just hope I can keep my hands off him.'

'And that Aunt Anna doesn't find the guns. She is a good shot, you know. I'd bet she could wing a blue-bottle if she concentrated. She wouldn't want to kill it, though, whereas . . .' His words died a natural death.

Jeremy picked up the thread. 'Whereas she would kill Dad as soon as look at him. Yes, I know. If you think about it, poor old Auntie has had a rough trip. She picked up where Sally left off, comforted Mother, looked after Grandpa, smoothed the way for Pol Fishwick to move in, showed Aggie what to do, attended to Meredith – it's a lot for a woman of over seventy.'

Peter drew a hand across his brow. It was the middle of December, yet he was hot because of his level of agitation. Like his twin, he hoped that he would be able to stop short of beating up his father. 'I vote we order another twelve bottles of whisky and leave him to it. Two months of solid drinking and he will be needing a shroud.' It occurred to Peter that he was not afraid any more; he was anxious, but not terrified.

Jeremy turned a corner. 'Horrible, isn't it? Hating your own father and knowing that he is a killer. I don't know which is worse – wanting him dead or wanting him alive and suffering. But it isn't going to be easy at home, Peter.'

'It never was.'

'No.'

They pulled up in the forecourt of the convent nursing home. The legend *St William's Recuperation Centre* was cut into stone above the main lintel and a figure of Christ, hands held out towards the road, stood in the centre of the lawn. 'We have to go in,' said Peter after a pause of several seconds. 'We may need to sign something.'

'A death warrant, preferably,' muttered Jeremy. Then he pulled a comb from a pocket and dragged it through his tangled thatch. 'We have to give peace a chance,' he said when the comb was back in its rightful place. 'Perhaps there has been a miracle – these nuns pray all the time. We may find a completely changed man.'

Peter grimaced. 'Yes, and a pig just flew over the chimneys.'

'At least you have Marie.'

'And you have Josie.'

Jeremy shook his head slowly. 'No. No-one has Josie. I can't talk to her – everything's a joke. Oh, I know she's a stunner, but there's nothing underneath. She's . . . she's insulated.'

'And you feel isolated.'

Jeremy nodded. 'Aggie's the one who keeps me

sane. She went on strike yesterday – did you hear about it?'

'No. Why on earth would she do that?'

Jeremy grinned. 'Grandpa wanted chips. Egg and chips, if you please. So she marched into his room and told him that she was withdrawing her labour – he laughed so hard that he spilled his coffee. She said she has cut up about three tons of spuds in her time and that she's going cordon bleu.'

'Did he get his chips?' Peter asked.

'No, he got *pommes frites* with *deux oeufs.*'

Peter laughed out loud. Aggie was a card, had turned herself into a character because she felt there was no other option. Overshadowed by the prettiness of her two friends, Agnes Turner had become the clown, the ice-breaker, the jolly good sport who performed the tricks, who told the jokes and got the laughs. Josie was very funny, as was Marie, but there was little warmth in Josie. 'We are lucky to have Aggie up at the grange,' Peter said. 'If nothing else comes of Meredith's advertisement, we got a damned good housekeeper.'

'I am beginning to wonder whether Meredith will function at all.' Jeremy laid his head on the steering wheel, hands clasping the rim as if his life depended on it. 'And we can't leave Mother yet. If this is privilege, Peter, I would rather not have it.'

'I know.' Peter opened his door. 'Stay there – I'll get him.'

Peter walked into the reception area and waited for his father. A rather stern woman took his name and asked for proof of identity. It occurred to Peter that those who cared for alcoholics must need to stay several steps ahead – some patients might have got

282

out via friends posing as family. When his driving licence had been scrutinized and handed back to him, he sat and waited for Richard Chandler to be returned to the less-than-welcoming bosom of his family.

A small nun appeared. 'Mr Chandler? No, no, please remain seated. Your father is on his way.' Mary Vincent was not supposed to say anything; every rule in the book forbade her to pass on information unless it went to an inmate's doctor, but this was a special case. 'He isn't over it, he isn't even trying,' she said bluntly.

'I know.'

'Ah.' She folded her arms and studied Peter. 'I suppose he causes a fair amount of trouble in the house?'

'Some, yes.' Trouble? The woman didn't know the half of it. 'I was afraid of him until recently. Our sister is not afraid.' His sister was a drinker . . . 'And I have to say that we don't want him back.'

'God bless, I shall pray for you. It's a terrible thing when they take to the drink. My own father died of it, which is why I chose to work here for my sins.'

'We have a long history of alcoholism,' Peter told her. 'It crops up in every generation. My great-aunt is writing the history of our family, and many of the documents she works with are hard to read because the writer was drunk. It goes back centuries. We call it Chandlers' Curse, as if it is a disease all on its own, as if my ancestors invented it.'

'Terrible.' She loosened her hands and touched Peter's shoulders. 'You will have some hard days ahead, but I must warn you – his body is breaking down beneath the weight of it all. Usually, after a month or two, we manage to get a little sense into

283

them. That doesn't mean a cure, but there's a bit of effort, at least. Your father has had scarcely a word to say for himself since he arrived. His liver is in a mess. I heard him crying once, after Mrs Fishwick came to visit, but he recovered sure enough.'

'He would be crying for himself,' said Peter.

Richard arrived. He carried no case of clothes, as he had brought nothing with him and had been dressed during his stay in garments issued by the clinic. His face was expressionless, his colour poor.

For a brief beat of time, Peter was back to his old self, a boy who had been so afraid that he might have needed to stand behind his gun-toting twin in order to go against this old man. Because Richard, at forty-five, was certainly old. There was a greyness about him, a lack of colour that rendered him almost corpse-like, while sloping shoulders spoke of inner hopelessness – but he had brought that upon himself, Peter insisted inwardly.

'Can we get out of here?' Richard's tone was harsh.

Peter stood up. In a voice loud enough to be heard the length and breadth of the nursing home, he spoke to his father for the first time in over two months. 'Raise a hand to my mother and you will bear the consequences.' The words were separated for emphasis. 'We all know what you did and there is a letter from the deceased. One foot out of step and you will be dealt with.' With the ultimatum delivered, Peter, not caring about the opinion of his small audience, turned and marched outside.

Richard Chandler stood still for a few seconds. Although his heartbeat had quickened, his exterior registered no reaction to words that still seemed to bounce off the walls, even though their deliverer had absented himself. So, blackmail was to be a part of their campaign. Who would listen now, with Sally Foster gone to her Maker several weeks ago?

Looking neither left nor right, Richard followed his son into the crisp air of mid-December. He had to play the game – for now, at least.

'Eeh, well.' Leena Martindale pulled open her door until it was against the wall. 'I've seen some sights, but this beats them all. Come in, Meredith. Alf's out – he would have enjoyed this. He used to bring his ponies home when he had the carts, but we've never had a proper horse parked at our front door before. What's his name?'

'Pepper,' replied Meredith. 'And he's a mare.'

Leena laughed. 'Sorry, I only saw the front end. Can I give her a couple of carrots?'

'Of course.' Meredith gazed around the hall. 'You have done an excellent job. Miss Forrester was very frail – I used to visit her two or three times a week – and the village did what it could, but you have made such a difference. And I see some of the paintings Mother has been speaking about.'

Colour arrived in Leena's cheeks. It was Alf who insisted on covering the walls in her work. There was not one piece here that satisfied Leena – there was always something she could have done differently, better. 'I've not had any real lessons.'

Meredith was studying a portrait of Marie. 'Did she sit for you?'

'No. I did her from memory.'

'And put her on a mountainside.'

'Well – yes. That's how I like to think of her – on her way to the top of the world.'

285

Meredith remembered reading somewhere that one should never underestimate the gifted amateur, because he owned the enthusiasm often denied to a professional. 'You are good,' she stated.

Leena dashed off, found carrots and brought them out to Pepper. 'I love animals,' she told her visitor. 'We thought we might get some now that we're living out of the town. There's room in the back for a couple of horses.'

'Do you miss Bolton?'

Honesty was best. 'Yes, I do. It takes a fair amount of getting used to, does the quiet. I miss the neighbours, hanging me washing out when the weather was good enough. I miss a lot of things. But when you've been as ill as I have, you have to do as you're told.'

Meredith knew what she meant. Mrs Martindale had to stay away from dirt and Meredith had to stay away from drink. 'Is Marie living here?'

'Aye, she is for now. She says she'll stop till after Christmas and New Year – her dad drives her to work and brings her home every night. And with us still renting Emblem Street, he can go there when he likes, make himself a cuppa. Marie's friend's supposed to be moving in about the middle of January.' She stroked the horse's nose. 'This one has a nice, soft mouth. I bet she's easy to ride, placid nature.'

'Older children learn on her. Yes, Pepper's a treasure. Never a dirty look, let alone a kick.'

They walked into the kitchen and Leena busied herself with kettle and teapot.

'Has Marie told you how we met?' asked Meredith. 'About starting a business of some kind?'

Leena nodded. 'She said something about it, yes. But I think she's been too busy with other things – like your brother for a start. Then there was the move – we're still not straight and Christmas is just around the corner. Ooh, that reminds me – tell Aggie I've done a couple of extra puddings and a spare cake.'

'Thank you.'

While Leena made tea, Meredith looked around the large kitchen. There was a dining area with French windows and a new cooker. There were many cupboards and shelves, a refrigerator and a dozen cookery books. 'Cosy,' was her conclusion. 'You've made it very welcoming.'

Leena smiled and placed cups and saucers on the table. 'It is a welcoming house. It's as if she's here and she likes us. Does that sound daft?'

'Yes.'

After this blunt response, both women laughed.

'But there is another level,' Meredith said when the mirth had run its course. 'I don't know about God and all that stuff, but there's an energy in us that stays around after we are gone. After my grandmother died, I used to see her at the foot of my bed, smiling at me.'

'Your mother's mother?'

'Yes. I never knew whether I was asleep or awake, but she made me feel so much better. And . . . well . . . people like you, with talent – that's tied up in it. I don't know what I'm talking about.'

'Join the club.' Leena poured the tea. 'My Alf says I'm the only woman he knows who can talk for an hour solid without knowing a thing about the subject.'

Meredith stirred her tea. She realized that she had to get her mental teeth into something and that her brothers, too, needed a sense of direction. They had qualifications enough to enter university, but the time for that had passed – they were not academics and had grown beyond the student stage. Everyone was ready for a challenge. 'We used to make candles.'

'I know. There's what's left of the old factory not far from the grange – me and Alf walked up there last Saturday.'

'And our great-aunt is writing an account of our family and its business.' She grinned wryly. 'Knowing Aunt Anna, it will not make pretty reading. She has been working on a way of softening beeswax while retaining the natural pattern left in the hive, then curling the sheet into a candle. Anyway, we may start to manufacture again. And I should like to sell your paintings.'

Leena gulped audibly. 'Oh.'

'The boys will be in charge of the factory – if and when we get it going – and I shall run a retail outlet. I've had all sorts of ideas, but simple is best, I think. Candles are back in fashion, and I want to sell things that will make people happy – fabrics, cushions, paintings and ornaments.' Yes, this was the answer – if she became involved, if she became responsible for other people, surely she would stay away from the sherry? Wouldn't she?

Leena smiled. 'Well, I shall be busy – a paintbrush in one hand and a rolling pin in the other. Mrs Chandler wants me up yonder three mornings a week till Aggie gets into her stride.'

It was Meredith's turn to grin. 'Into her stride? She's overtaken all of us. It took her three days to master choux pastry and the whole house knew about it. Aggie wears her feelings on the outside. She

288

has Grandpa in pleats – and she can wrap him round her little finger. Mother calls her a gem. Yes, she even makes my mother laugh.'

Leena stirred her tea before going for a change of subject. 'Are your brother and my daughter serious?'

'You should ask Marie, surely?'

'I have. She says nothing much, though she did promise I'd be the third to know, because she hasn't told herself yet – which means she hasn't told him. He'd be the second.'

Meredith chewed on a digestive biscuit. 'He's serious.'

'Is he?'

'Yes. I'd say he's head over heels, but that's just my opinion. Peter never does anything by halves, though he has changed. We've all changed since Nanny Foster died. He was the quiet one, but there's an anger in him these days. And I don't mean to say that Marie is part of the anger, yet she's part of what he has become. I think they could both do a lot worse. Jeremy's a bit out of it – Josie isn't from the same batch as Marie. So they have to stop being twins and start being individuals. Sorry, I do go on, don't I?'

'Don't we all.' Leena glanced at the clock. 'He'll be nearly home.' There was no need for her to mention the name. 'You should be there, love. For your mam.'

'I know. When I've taken Pepper back, I shall go home. I have the distinct feeling that Father's life will be somewhat restricted from now on. We have been turned into an army – for defence purposes only, of course.'

Leena, whose name was on the list of reserves, dipped a ginger nut into her tea. Meredith, delighted, did the same. 'It's lovely to be able to dunk. I shall

289

know where to come to show off my manners, Mrs Martindale.'

'Manners is for dinner parties and Buckingham Palace.' It was strange how so many of the small pleasures in life were forbidden by gentry. 'Is she putting him in your grandad's old room?'

Meredith nodded. 'Yes, but without the lock. I'm hoping we won't need locks. It shouldn't take long for him to realize that he's in Coventry. There are two rooms, one with a small table and a single chair – Aunt Anna's idea. He will be served meals up there.'

'Aye, but who'll take them up to him? Have you got one of them old suits of armour hanging about? And what if he comes to the table?'

Meredith raised her shoulders in a slight shrug. 'I think he will soon learn that he is not welcome in the dining room. And there is no longer a tantalus in there – Mother intends to serve just water and coffee with meals.' Even the sherry had disappeared, which was just as well . . .

'So that will keep him upstairs?'

'We shall see.' Meredith rose to her feet and Leena noticed how graceful she was, how elegant. She wasn't as pretty as Marie – no-one was – but she was certainly noticeable. 'What about your own love life?'

'I haven't met anyone good enough.'

They moved into the hall. 'Come again,' said Leena.

'I shall. I know where I can soak my biscuits in tea now. Also, you don't appear to mind having a horse parked at the door.'

They went outside and Meredith mounted Pepper by standing on a crumbling brick wall. Marie's

290

mother didn't know it, but she had gone a long way towards helping Meredith this morning. There was somewhere to come, a place of refuge with tea and biscuits and just the right amount of sympathy.

'Come soon to the grange,' Meredith begged. 'Mother is going to need a friend.'

'I will.'

When the door was closed, Leena allowed herself to sag against it. She had deliberately kept her mind locked, had not even thought about what Marie had told her. Please God, this poor girl was coming out of her brief flirtation with alcohol. Peter had told Marie and Marie had told her mother. It was important that no-one should offer Meredith anything but tea and coffee. 'God guide her,' she whispered before returning to her kitchen. So far, the country had proved quiet, but far from boring . . .

The car hit the dog on a blind bend just over Turner Brew. Immediately, Jeremy slammed on the brakes and slewed the car almost onto the pavement, its nose half an inch from a postbox.

'Jesus,' cursed Richard. 'What do you think you're doing? This is a valuable car. Drive on. It's only a bloody dog.'

Peter leapt from the car. Bloody was the word. He ripped off his jacket and stretched it over the thin, twitching body. Jeremy, who had the foresight to bring the keys so that his father could not drive away, joined his brother. Together, they lifted the dog and carried it to the car.

Richard was on the pavement. 'You are not putting that thing into my Bentley.'

'Just watch us,' answered Jeremy. 'You can get

back in and shut up, or you can walk the rest of the way.' They were at least five miles from home. While Jeremy cradled the injured beast, Peter opened a rear door, climbed into the car, then held his arms out to receive the patient.

Jeremy closed the door, then addressed his father. 'Get into the passenger seat. Now. You know the alternative.'

Furious, Richard climbed into a car that had cost five times the yearly wage of most ordinary people. He had scarcely closed his door when Jeremy crashed into gear and lurched forward, one hand on the horn, which he sounded intermittently. At a speed that might have attracted the whole body of the Bolton Constabulary, Jeremy Chandler hurtled towards the vet at the junction of Tonge Moor Road and Crompton Way. 'You'll have us all dead,' cursed Richard, 'and all for some bloody mongrel.'

'Shut up,' yelled Jeremy. 'That dog is worth ten of you – and that is a gross underestimation of its value. You are no longer the driver – you are a mere passenger and don't ever forget it.' He slammed on the brakes, removed the key from the ignition and jumped out, rushing immediately to open the rear door for his brother.

Together, they carried the unconscious animal into the surgery.

Alone, Richard seethed. He remembered the occasions when he had taken the belt to his sons, when he had tried to whip some sense into their stupid backsides. Well, it hadn't worked, because they were both hell bent on saving some scrawny animal when they should have been taking their father home. And there wasn't a damned thing he could do.

He rooted about in a pocket, found his wallet, opened it. The list of Alcoholics Anonymous meeting places fell out and he allowed it to remain on the floor where it belonged. Ah, he had four pounds and ten shillings. After glancing towards the vet's surgery, he made a run for it and entered the off-licence next door, buying two half-bottles, as they were easier to conceal; he also picked up some strong mints and a bar of chocolate. The food in that bloody dump had been unfit for pigs.

The first dose dropped into his stomach like rain onto parched ground and he sighed contentedly before taking a second, then a third mouthful. That was better. Tonge Moor Road looked rosier – the whole world was brighter. Feeling more contentment than he had enjoyed in weeks, Richard leaned back and closed his eyes. They could take as long as they liked in the vet's place – all was well inside the Bentley.

Jeremy returned alone, recognizing the stench of whisky as soon as he opened the door. It had begun already.

Richard opened one eye. 'Where's your brother?'

'Doing his duty,' came the swift response. The dog was on the operating table already, internal bleeding diagnosed, no broken bones found thus far. And Peter had refused to abandon the needy creature.

'Stupid,' snapped Richard.

Peter's twin turned his head slowly and faced the evil man who had fathered him. 'I hate you.' There was no expression in these three words; they were delivered flatly, evenly, and were made all the more dreadful by the sheer absence of emotion. 'Already, you are drinking. That is fine by me. You will live

293

upstairs in the rooms where you kept my grandfather. You will take your meals there and will be provided with enough booze to kill you as quickly as possible. When your time comes, Peter will not pick you up and take you to a vet, will not carry you to a doctor or back to the place you left today.'

Richard swallowed audibly.

'There will be whisky upstairs, but nothing on the ground floor. Your confinement will be of your own choosing. If you do come downstairs, any nonsense and Peter and I will beat you as you beat us. Understood?' The man's lock would be the whisky. 'Touch Mother or anyone else and Sally Foster's letter goes to the police.'

'How dare you?'

Jeremy smiled broadly. 'How dare I? How dare we? Peter and I have suffered abuse from you since we were about twelve or thirteen. Meredith's gender saved her, though she still felt the edge of your tongue. But you have dulled the edge, have failed to keep it sharpened. It is our turn now. We become the abusers, but we focus on you, just you.'

Richard blinked rapidly as the car pulled into the traffic. If the wretched boy had not been driving, he would have taken a swipe at him. God, the future looked bleak – even the whisky could not dull the pain of realizing that the fragrant one had armed herself to the point where even his own sons might turn on him. Then there was Pol. And Anna was home. And the Martindales . . . God, he needed another whisky, but he would not drink while this stuffed shirt was at the wheel. 'Can't you go any faster?'

Jeremy glanced sideways. 'Don't worry about me,

294

Father dear – get the bottle from your pocket and let the final damage begin.' The dog deserved a chance; this fellow deserved nothing. 'We had a dozen Johnnie Walker Black Label delivered to your rooms as a welcoming gift. By the way, the less you eat, the better. Your demise is eagerly anticipated by many, so please feel free to achieve it as swiftly as possible.'

There was no answer, would never be an answer. They were giving him a free hand, their full permission to destroy himself. And Jean had put them up to it, of that Richard was certain. This was all because of one miserable mistake, one occasion on which he had taken a drop too many and had lost control. The woman who died had been of no real significance, just a servant. But, like the dog, Sally Foster had been unduly appreciated by those who should have seen themselves as her betters.

The car swept past the gatehouse and up the driveway of Chandlers Grange. The moment Richard Chandler had waited for was here at last. He was free. Wasn't he? Oh, she didn't wear a wimple and a long black dress, but Jean was every inch the nun. By her side would stand a reformed whore – he tried not to laugh. Whores never reformed. Anna was on hand, too, would be throwing in her own tenpenn'orth at every opportunity. As for his children – they were probably his biggest enemies.

He climbed out of the car and surveyed the domain that had stopped being his. Father was no longer contained; the mad old bugger would be having the life of Riley while Richard was expected to inhabit the old man's rooms. Why should he? Why wouldn't Henry die?

Pol, neat and thinner in a good grey suit, came out

to greet him. 'Hello, Mr Chandler.' Her voice was as tidy as she was, the rougher edges honed smooth. 'Follow me, please.' She turned and walked back into the house.

Too stunned to do otherwise, Richard pursued her at a leisurely rate. She led him into a small sitting room that now contained bedroom furniture and an extremely well-dressed Henry. The old man gazed steadily at the unwelcome arrival. 'You are bypassed,' he stated baldly. 'It is all settled – we have found written proof of your fraud and you will not inherit the grange. The house will go to my grand-children. There are rooms for you and food will be provided. That's all. You may go now.'

You may go? Richard opened his mouth to reply, closed it when he saw the expression in Pol's eyes, a mix of hatred and triumph whose proportions seemed almost equal. She stood behind Henry's chair, a proprietary hand resting on one of his shoulders.

Richard heard a sound and swivelled. Jean hovered in the doorway, hair nicely done, face almost free of make-up, hands clasped at her waist. 'Ah, you are home,' she said.

'Of course,' he managed. 'That is obvious, even to you.'

Jean's eyes met Polly's as she reached out to gather strength from the other woman. She inhaled deeply before continuing. 'Jeremy is on the telephone enquiring after the dog you wanted him to abandon. You tried to kill me and you managed to kill Sally. I survived and I hope the dog thrives, too. You are here because your father allows you to be here. I should rather see you in prison, but I have my children to consider.' She nodded curtly and left the room.

Richard stared at his father and the whore. Anna was absent and for that small benefit he thanked fate. They had prepared themselves thoroughly, it would seem. With the will changed, with Anna back, with his sons and daughter poisoned against him, Jean would be very well pleased.

'Ah, Richard.'

Damn and blast, the whole coven was here. 'Aunt Anna,' he answered curtly.

She descended upon him, steel in her eyes, a false smile widening thin lips. 'Welcome home,' she trilled, sarcasm plain in the words. 'Jeremy says the dog has a chance – Peter rang to tell him. Isn't that wonderful, Richard?' She paused, moved her head to one side. 'After all, every dog has his day – isn't that right, Henry?' She looked at her brother. He was frail and old, yet misfortune had strengthened him, while Polly Fishwick was like a dose of magic medicine.

She repeated the words slowly, directing them at the room in general. 'Remember that, Richard. Every dog, every single dog, has his day. I believe you have had yours.' Then she left the room.

ELEVEN

Peter was suddenly an unwilling assistant to a veterinary surgeon; there was no-one else, so, clad in a green cotton smock and a white cap, he was forced to watch while the dog was shaved and opened up. 'My wife should be back soon,' the vet said repeatedly, but nobody came to relieve Peter. The operation had to be done immediately, as the animal was inches from death.

The vet, a middle-aged man named Donald Baines, was impressed by Peter's ability to remain alert and helpful while vessels were clamped, while blood was sucked out of the abdominal cavity, while stitching was completed. 'Now it's in the lap of the dogs,' announced Donald when he had done his best.

'Don't you mean gods?' Peter scrubbed his hands at a sink.

'No, I don't,' smiled the surgeon, 'I mean dogs. Strange creatures. They arrive fit as fiddles with just a small job to be done and they pass on without so much as a by-your-leave. Then some like your chap

298

here,' he nodded towards the operating table, 'come in at death's door and leave at about ninety miles an hour with the owner hanging on like billy-o to the lead. If it's his time, he'll stay asleep; if he chooses to torment us for a while longer, he will wake up starving in a matter of hours.' He took his place at the sink. 'Lap of the dogs,' he repeated as he picked up a nail brush.

Peter stood by the anaesthetized animal, towel in one hand, cap in the other. His eyes strayed to the latter item and the reality of what he had just done hit him like a bolt from the heavens. 'Mr Baines?' His voice was just slightly above whisper level.

'Call me Don.'

Peter swallowed. 'What would I need?'

'Pardon?'

'To be a vet – what does it take?'

Donald Baines awarded his companion a huge grin. 'Guts, determination, love of animals, years of study and sheer bloody-mindedness. And languages. You would need to speak dog, cat and, on occasion, rabbit.'

'Where do I go?' He still could not leave Mother, could not abandon Meredith, would not be separated from Marie. 'Does Manchester do it?'

'Yes, but you can't just walk in. Good results at school?'

Peter nodded. This was utterly ridiculous. A vet? Just because he had managed to stand through an operation without gagging? The dog lay with its tongue hanging from the side of its mouth, the rhythmic movement of its chest advertising that life was still present. He had helped to save the life of a . . . what was it? Part Alsatian, that was certain,

299

possibly part retriever, probably a Heinz fifty-seven varieties in every shop. 'Is he a stray?'

'Underfed,' replied the vet. 'Probably not wanted.'

'I shall call him Hero if he pulls through.'

'Talk to him,' Don Baines suggested. 'Let him know he's needed – that may help him when decision time comes. When you've had a word with him, come through to the house. Later, I shall put him in a recovery cage, but I would rather leave him here for now.' He pulled up some cot sides on the edge of the operating table, then left Peter and the dog together.

Peter stroked Hero's bony head, told him about the fields of Chandlers Green, about rabbits and hares, about Marie, Mother and Anna. 'You can sit with my grandfather – he will spoil you and you will become enormously fat. My mother will like you and Aggie will feed you. It isn't time, Hero. Not yet.'

Outside the door, Don Baines listened. Despite the need to steel himself, a vet also required the ability to appreciate and value animals. Although the decision had been lightning fast, the lad seemed a sensible type, one who would not panic when a cat needed to be destroyed, when a dog was beyond saving. Yes, he was talking to the unconscious hound, was probably going to keep him, might well go on to study veterinary medicine.

Peter joined his new acquaintance in a living room behind the surgery. 'Follow me,' Don said. They walked through the kitchen and into a single-storey lean-to. 'These are my dogs,' the vet announced proudly. Peter found himself on the receiving end of a St Bernard's tongue, while two small terriers circled him like racers on a track.

'Wonderful,' he laughed when he finally managed to talk. 'You saved them?'

'Yes. The two small ones are the only survivors from a bag in the Manchester Ship Canal and the Bernard outgrew his owners' pockets. They still visit and take him for walks. It's difficult to stay detached and, occasionally, emotion overcomes sense. These are my three failures or successes – that depends on their behaviour, of course. My son and my daughter are both vets. Susan does farm work, Alan looks after the pampered pets of Kensington. He is rich, she is poor, but they both serve.'

'And you are proud of them.'

'I am. Faced with a sick human, a physician usually gets some information, but a ten-foot python comes just as he is and, even if I could ask questions, I would prefer to stick him in a cold place to calm him down before I treat him. Parrots can be buggers, too. Are you prepared to be bitten?'

'I suppose so.'

The vet stood back and watched as Peter played with two insane terriers and a dog the size of a small house. Yes, the lad had 'it'. 'It' was not definable. Like the 'it' that belongs to great actors and painters, the factor was something extra and there were no words for this particular quality. 'I shall lend you some books,' he decided aloud. 'Some are quite contemporary, because study never ends. Yes.' He nodded thoughtfully. 'You should try for a place.'

'May I phone my brother?' Poor Jeremy, stuck at home with Richard the Terrible, was probably as concerned about Hero as was his twin. Permission granted, Peter made the call, then returned to sit with

301

Hero. This was his first patient and, if Peter worked hard, there would be many more to come.

He seethed. From his window, he had a clear view of the gatehouse, the place to which Anna Chandler had retired as a mark of defiance when her brother had been put away to dry out. God, if they wanted to see a real alcoholic, they should put Henry back to the bottle.

This was a fine pickle. He turned his head to the right and stared at a field that spread all the way down to Claughton Cottage. He could not see Alfred Martindale's place of residence, but he had passed it earlier, new roof, new paint job, new curtains, a horse tethered outside. Some people were getting above themselves, it seemed.

The door opened and he swivelled, lost his balance, righted himself and found Meredith standing with a tray in her hands. She placed it on the table and walked to his side. 'I'm an alcoholic,' she stated baldly. 'And I have got hold of it now. I just want you to know that it can be done. Grandfather was forced into it and I stopped living for a week so that I could rid myself of the sherry. I thought I should tell you that. So, would you like me to remove the whisky? I promise to sit with you if you need me.'

Richard dropped into an armchair. He blinked as he processed the information presented to him by his daughter. She had Chandlers' Curse. She was his daughter and he should care, but there was something missing inside him, an element which had arrived stillborn. 'I'll manage,' he said. 'No need for a babysitter.'

Meredith sat opposite him. 'I know how it feels,'

she told him. 'I know what it is to live from one drink to the next. It's horrible and I am very lucky, but it will always be a problem. Even after just a few weeks of drinking, it hurts. Aunt Anna got me through. Father, look at me.'

He obeyed.

'You killed someone. You almost killed your wife, my mother. The inquest on Nanny Foster agreed with the lie Mother told – the coroner was prepared to believe that the huge knob on the hall-stand was the culprit. You are lucky, because, if she *had* fallen downstairs, the umbrella part of the stand could have given her a blow harsh enough to split her spleen.'

No longer able to look at Meredith, he rose and positioned himself by the window once more. Why was she bothering? She hated him; they all hated him. His own fury simmered and was directed else-where. Had he been capable of bringing animation to his projected thoughts, Claughton Cottage might have been razed to the ground within seconds.

'Father?'

Oh, yes, she was still here. 'What?'

'Will you not try, at least? You have been dry for weeks now.' Already, the stench of whisky hung in the air – he had probably taken a drink as soon as the opportunity had presented itself. 'It is possible,' she said. 'Grandfather did it – you made him stop. Then I had to do it.'

If it took him the rest of his days, he would get Alf Martindale. What was the girl talking about? 'I shall eat now,' he announced. 'You'd better go.'

His mind was affected, Meredith decided. In spite of that possibility and in spite of the fact that she had

303

some insight into alcoholism, she felt her hackles rising. He didn't want to try. Was this the creature she might have become had she not been stopped by Anna, by Jeremy, by Peter?

Her head shook slightly. No, she had done it herself. There had been days when her instinct to run had been strong, yet that small piece of self had made her stay. No matter what anyone had said or done, the sherry might have won had she not wanted to gain ground.

'You are still here,' he said.

'But you are not.' Resignation dampened her tone. With her own fight to continue, she had nothing to offer a man who did not want to listen, a murderer whose total self-absorption carried him beyond the reach of his fellows. 'I walked out of this house many weeks ago, Father. I left because of you and your bullish behaviour towards my mother, my brothers and myself. But it was not really connected with alcohol, was it?'

'Go away,' he snapped.

'A good man could be destroyed by drink, but he would still be decent inside. You are not decent and you never were.'

Richard shrugged his shoulders. Her opinion did not matter; nothing mattered beyond . . . His head turned once more and he was thinking again about the man who now lived beyond that field, Martindale, his enemy, his target. How? What might be done?

Meredith walked out of the room and slammed the door. She had done her best and he would continue to do his worst. No matter. There were enough people about to make sure that the grange was safe.

Anna looked up from her newspaper when her great-niece entered the drawing room. 'No joy?'

'None.'

'Then consider yourself and only yourself. We must talk. It is time for you to pull together some sort of business plan – your mother and I shall be with you. We cannot sit here and wait to see what happens next. Your father's behaviour will continue to be erratic, but we have to move on. Polly will look after Henry – she is eminently capable of dealing with Richard–'

'Sorry.' Aggie threw in the word before entering the room in its wake. 'Does anybody here understand yeast? Only I think I've used too much and it's spreading everywhere.'

Meredith looked at Anna. 'Everywhere?'

Aggie raised her shoulders helplessly. 'When I say everywhere, I don't think it's hit Birmingham yet, but the kitchen table's a bit of a mess – looks as if it's eaten my wooden spoons. I must have read the recipe wrong.'

'Another Aggie disaster.' Anna laughed. 'Shall we need to call the army out?'

'Only if they're hungry.' Aggie led the other two women back into the kitchen and they surveyed the damage. She had brought life and fun back into a sad house; she was above and beyond value. She had enthusiasm enough for several and a tendency to exaggerate each one of her many disasters. Rising dough spilled out of two blue-rimmed enamel bowls.

'Only one thing for it.' Anna's face was grim. 'Meredith, fetch a gun. We must deal with the beast before it makes a break for it. If this reaches the village, the whole balance of nature could be affected.'

'And it could have babies,' said Aggie. 'If it breeds, the whole country could be in danger.'

Three women sat round a kitchen table, their laughter uncertain and edged by an element that might have bordered on hysteria. Like a hasty dressing, hilarity was a salve applied to a wound that simply would not close.

Polly and Jean arrived and the disease spread like wildfire. Handkerchiefs were employed, the three seated females rendered helpless by the knowledge that neither Polly nor Jean had the slightest idea why they were laughing.

On the stairs, a man stood and listened. They were amused by him, by the fact that he was now supposedly contained in the very rooms that had once confined his own father. He sat down. Something had to be done. But to get his hands on the estate, he would need to kill all of them – father, wife, aunt, children. Then there was the letter left by – what was her name? Foster – yes – she had damned her master on the very eve of her own death. God. There was also Martindale, bloody Martindale right on the doorstep . . .

Bank book. Where had he left that? It now represented all that remained within his own control, just a few measly thousand – and he could not stay here. Christmas alone upstairs? A tray, a cracker, a paper hat? He should march in there now and tell those cackling crones that he intended to return to table for his meals, that this was his house, not theirs. But there were too many of them. Pol, the whore who had served him to keep the roof over her head, was in the kitchen with them; her laughter, the most raucous, raised itself above the noise of others. Christ, he should break her neck–

The front doorbell sounded and he shrank back, watched as Polly Fishwick answered the door. Ah, the set was now complete.

'Hello, Mrs Martindale – come in – no – I'm not crying. I've laughed fit to burst me grandma's corsets.'

'I've brought you a couple of Christmas puds,' announced the visitor before entering the house. And it simply happened. The wife of Alf Martindale stepped into the hallway of Chandlers Grange. Richard's chest tightened and a red-hot knife shot through his upper body, tendrils of pain attacking his left arm. He had been warned about his heart – and about various other bodily organs – and he slipped a small pill under his tongue. No, this would not be made easy for them. Richard Chandler had no intention of dropping dead just yet. Calm, calm, he urged his inner self.

Leena handed the puddings to Polly, glanced upwards, saw a figure crouched where the stairs curved. Aye, he was here, the lord and bloody master, as Alf called him. She shivered, the involuntary shudder causing Pol to guide her towards the warmth of the kitchen.

Leena looked at the dough and rolled up her sleeves. 'Put that kettle on, Aggie,' she ordered. 'Let's see what we can do to save some of this.'

The front door slammed and all the occupants of the room jumped. Leena smiled grimly – she wasn't the only one on tenterhooks, it seemed. 'If this is the sort of mess Aggie's making, you'd all be safer coming to me for Christmas.'

307

Yes, they would be safer out of the grange. But it wasn't Christmas yet, and Leena wondered what the man might perpetrate before the holidays arrived. She dealt with the dough and kept her thoughts to herself.

'She doesn't want me.' Jeremy's tone was grim. 'I know she's a looker and I know she's good fun, but Josie's not interested in me.'

Peter, who was wondering about veterinary science, about Hero, about Marie, about his father's being back in the house for the first time in weeks, came to a halt at the Crompton Way traffic lights. 'Sorry?'

'Josie,' replied Jeremy. 'She's a no-go area. She's never unpleasant, but I get the feeling that she's not exactly head over heels with me.'

Peter put the car into gear and edged forward as the amber light showed. 'She treats everyone the same, Jer. I don't know what it is about her, but it's as if she's complete in herself.'

'Like a hermaphrodite?'

'No. Like a selfish person.'

Jeremy nodded. It wasn't that she was impolite, and she showed a degree of concern for those around her, yet there was something missing, something vital that seemed to have been excluded from her genes. 'She wants to get away from her family, just as Aggie did, yet there's very little enthusiasm for anything at all. She seemed keen when we first talked about a business, but she's gone off the boil.'

'She may warm up when things start moving.'

'Whole thing went off the boil,' grumbled Jeremy. 'Poor old Nanny Foster, Father, then Meredith and

308

her little problem. The whole world seems to have conspired against us. There's no fun any more.'

Peter did not agree. Things were bad at home, but Aggie and Polly had brought life into the house, Mother was looking a little better, Meredith was on the mend. If only Father were off the scene, life would be wonderful. Then there was Marie. He found himself smiling and he rearranged his features as quickly as he could manage. 'We have a dog,' he announced. 'I said we would keep him. And I am considering university after all – veterinary science.'

Jeremy shifted in the passenger seat. So, Peter was sorting out his life, was he? It had always been the other way round – Jeremy at the front, Peter bringing up the rear. Marie had made this happen. Before Marie, Peter had been less confident. 'Well, I hope you get whatever you want,' he replied eventually. This was all the result of the love of a good woman.

'Josie is focused,' announced Peter after giving the matter further consideration. 'I don't know what she's focused on, but she is going somewhere. And until she gets there, she won't be ready. And she won't get there until she decides what it is and where it is. So selfish is wrong. I think she's ambitious.'

Jeremy was having difficulty in understanding his newborn twin. It was almost as if the old Peter had disappeared, to be replaced by the quiet yet confident young man in the driving seat. Yes, Peter was behind the wheel now and the love of Marie had equipped him for the position.

The car swung through the gates and past Aunt Anna's abandoned house. They were home. Home? Home was where the heart should be; home was where Father would be taking up residence again.

Never mind, Jeremy told his inner self. There was always Aggie to cheer him and take his mind off the worst of things.

One of those strange moments of telepathy happened as Peter slewed to a halt on the gravel path. 'You could do a lot worse.'

'What?'

Peter turned off the engine and handed the keys to Jeremy. 'Your turn to drive the old man's jalopy next time, old thing.' He got out of the car and waited for his brother. 'Yes, a lot worse,' he repeated to himself.

Jeremy emerged on the opposite side of the car. 'Worse than what?' He knew the answer, knew full well what was coming. There was a special contact between himself and Peter—

'Than Aggie. She has dressed herself up for you, Jer. She has straightened her hair and straightened your life at the same time. And she is the one who is head over heels with you. Also, when you look at her properly, she is quite pretty.'

Jeremy lingered at the bottom of the steps. What a preposterous idea. Aggie, the also-ran, the clown, the little butterball who made everyone laugh, who had culinary disasters on a regular basis. Little Aggie, thinner now, looking taller, looking . . . looking like fun.

'She worships you,' said Peter softly. 'She tries to hide it, but when you come into the kitchen, she changes, stands straighter. There is more to Aggie than beauty, Jer, because she has a heart of solid gold, twenty-four full carats and all the softer for it. Josie – Josie is just Josie. I don't know who will get through to her – I wonder if anyone ever will. Aggie's the one, believe me.'

Richard Chandler appeared, his face purple with anger as he slammed closed the front door of the grange. 'Keys,' he snapped.

Jeremy looked his father up and down. 'You are not fit to drive.'

The man stumbled three steps past them and righted himself next to his car. 'I know what I'm doing,' he slurred.

Peter shook his head slowly. 'No,' he announced firmly. 'If you want to kill yourself all well and good, but you are taking no-one with you.'

'There are spare keys.' Richard turned to go back inside, lost his footing and collapsed in a heap. 'Damn and blast,' he cursed.

The twins stared at each other. 'We could take a chance,' Peter suggested, 'let him loose and hope the village is deserted. Close contact with a dry stone wall could be the answer for him.'

'And for us.' Jeremy pushed the keys further into the pocket of his jacket. 'Drag him in.'

They led their father up the stone steps and deposited him in the hall. With no further comment, they abandoned him and went to find their mother. Richard Chandler was of no particular importance, so they left him where he fell.

'So, you're going, then? Have you told your mother?'

Josie pushed a strand of hair from her eyes and studied her best friend. 'Yes and no. Yes, I'm going and no, I haven't told my mother. You are the only one who knows – apart from the agency.'

Marie glanced through the window and watched Bolton as it walked past the café, mothers with prams, men in suits, a ragman and his cart, the latter fully

311

laden, probably on its way to a refuse yard. There were still one or two rag-and-bone men who used ponies, she mused. 'You'll have to tell them, Josie. You can't just disappear off the face of the earth – your mother would go into a decline and your auntie would have the army out looking for you.'

'I know.'

'And what about Jeremy?' Marie awarded her full attention to the beautiful girl in the opposite seat. 'He's crazy about you.'

'He has no particular reason to be. I've never given him cause.'

'Love has nothing to do with reason.'

Josie took a sip of hot chocolate.

Marie folded her arms and leaned back in a chair that was rather less than comfortable. 'London, though. Are you not frightened? Big city, bad men and all that?'

Josie considered the question; it had never occurred to her that she should fear the man who had recruited her. She raised her shoulders slightly. 'I have phoned the office and it's a real agency. Anyway, there are plenty of jobs in London – I could temp for a while if this doesn't come off.'

'It'll come off if they've any sense,' said the loyal Marie. 'You're a walking coat hanger, Josie, and that's what they're looking for. We'll be seeing you in all the Max Factor adverts, next news. I shall be able to say, "I knew her when the only leg she had to stand on was fifteen denier Sandalwood or American Tan."'

'They're doing Mink now. A sort of greyish-brown for the older lady. Disgusting colour.'

Marie sighed and stirred her coffee. She didn't

fancy living on her own in Emblem Street, but with Josie and Aggie both gone, it was beginning to seem that she wasn't going to have a choice in the matter. And anyway, Claughton Cottage was nearer to Chandlers Grange, nearer to Peter—

'You're blushing,' laughed Josie. She reached a hand across the table and grabbed Marie's wrist. 'I have to do it. If I don't, I shall look back all my life and wonder why I didn't take the chance. Sorry about letting you down, love, but it's something I'm forced to do. Forgive me?'

'Course I forgive you, you great lummox. But I shan't forgive you if you don't invite me when you're settled in your Kensington flat with a cheetah and a bath with gold taps. Did you see that model with her cheetah on a lead? God, I'd be terrified.'

Josie withdrew her hand. 'I'm not ready to settle, you see. And I never wanted the ordinary life with a nice Bolton lad and nice Bolton kids. Jeremy is all right – he's more than all right, he's a catch – but if he can't see what's under his nose . . . well . . .'

'What?'

'Aggie, you daft beggar. Have you never watched her? Every time he opens his mouth, she sits up and listens. There's a lot more to Aggie than fish and chips, Marie – she's got a Latin O level, you know.'

When the laughter had subsided, Marie considered Josie's statement. 'She's always been left out with boys, hasn't she? But look what she's managed to do with herself – out in the countryside, learning to cook properly, new clothes, some weight off, hair done—'

'And living with the man she loves.' There was finality in Josie's voice. 'It's not that I'm leaving her my crumbs, you know. I like him. I like him, but I've never wanted him, never needed him.'

Marie lowered her head in thought, raised it again after a few seconds. 'You don't need anybody, do you? You just need you. I understand that.'

Josie grinned. 'It was all mapped out for me by the family, Marie. The tallest tree they've ever seen is management at Marks and Spencer. I want to go into the forest and choose my own timber. My mother's the one who will be afraid. When she learns that I'm off to London to be a model, she'll probably order a couple of chastity belts.'

'Marks and Spencer, of course,' quipped Marie.

'No doubt.' Josie inhaled deeply. 'Tonight, I tell them. Tomorrow, I give in my notice. The day after, my mother will be walking the streets in sackcloth and ashes. We shall be a house in mourning. She'll have Masses said and the priest will have to wear his purple vestments.'

Marie nodded absently. The easiest thing would be to throw in her hat with Mam and Dad, move permanently to Claughton Cottage, see as much as she liked of Peter . . . But a part of her wanted something different. It wasn't freedom, because her wings had never been clipped by her parents – she wanted independence and a degree of adulthood, bills to pay, meals to cook and . . . and Peter. She swallowed.

'Tell me what you're thinking,' urged Josie. She could see that her friend's brain had kicked into overdrive.

But Marie had promised already that she would tell herself first, Peter second, Mam third. 'There's a queue,' she replied after a short hesitation. 'Get in that orderly line, Josie Maguire, and I'll give you a shout when your number comes up.'

'It's your number that's up.' Josie laughed.

'What do you mean by that? I've never won a raffle in my life.'

Josie simply picked up her purse and pushed it deep into her handbag. If she wasn't mistaken, she would be a bridesmaid before she left for London.

'I ordered a bodyce peece for my wyfe.' Anna mumbled these words, then threw down her pen. The spelling of her ancestors showed innovation, to say the least. Nathaniel Chandler, 1785–1856, had been forced to order many 'bodyce peeces' for his 'wyfe', who had borne fourteen children, three of whom had survived. With every pregnancy, material was bought to let into that good woman's clothing so that her increasing girth might be contained and concealed.

This was hardly a labour of affection; Anna was falling further and further out of love with her own antecedents. Almost to a man, they had been drunken ne'er-do-wells who had impregnated their 'wyves' with monotonous frequency. 'A testament to their persistence,' she mumbled as she rolled yet another cigarette. As far as she understood, men in their cups were often unable to fulfil their husbandly duties.

The accounts were tedious and all the more diffi- cult to follow after a 'barrelle of mulberrye wyne' or a 'vat of mead' entered the table of calculation. Funerals were amusing. 'Fathere's coffine, beinge a lined caskette wyth sylke, 7 shillinges and 4 pense'; 'clothes to mourne, 3 shillinges and 5 pense'. All these things were accounted for, right down to a set of new buttons for a servant and a dark 'hand-kercheefe for my wyfe'.

The candle part was interesting: the history, the methods, the materials. And another factor was that each of the early Chandlers had been involved directly with the land, some managing to run a farm as well as a 'chandelrye', many even accounting for their mistakes – 'I planted too close in the rowes and did not yeeld as well as hytherto' and 'the feelds must wante to be fallowe for the seeson next'.

She tried to conjure up pictures of her brother ploughing, of her nephew sowing the furrows, but even her fertile imagination was not sufficiently elastic to encompass such impossibilities. Richard was in the house; this was his first night home after the clinic. There had been a bit of business between him and his sons on the front steps, but Anna had kept out of that, as had the rest of the household. Jeremy and Peter – the latter particularly – could handle him. She nodded. Peter had matured in one huge leap and Jeremy had long been an adult, because he had protected his brother and sister during the worst of Richard's rages.

It was two a.m. Anna, who had sat up with her documents, knew that it was time for sleep. She was in a small study next to her brother's room; she could hear his snores as they floated under the adjoining door and she hoped that Polly, who was ensconced in a room on the other side of Henry's, was able to sleep through such a noise.

After tidying a pile of ancient manuscripts, Anna rolled herself one last cigarette before bed. There was tension in her spine and she deliberately stretched herself out, placing her feet on a stool. Richard was here, and there was no getting rid of him. Henry had taken back his power, had disinherited his son in favour of his grandchildren, but the grange remained Richard's home. And he was drinking . . .

The snoring stopped. Relieved, Anna grinned to herself. Had snoring been a sport, her brother might have competed with the best. She took a drag of Virginia, blew a smoke ring, satisfied with her expertise. The blue-grey circle rose lazily upward, breaking only when it reached the unlit central chandelier. Anna reached across to switch off the desk lamp, then the noise began again.

But there was a different quality to the sound that emerged from her brother's bedroom. Frozen for a split second by pure fear, she managed to jump up when Henry screamed feebly. She hurled herself across the room and threw the door open. But she need not have worried.

At the other side of the bed was an awesome sight – Polly Fishwick in full sail, a white cotton nightdress billowing about her as she raised Henry's walking stick. 'Bastard!' she screamed at the top of lungs whose power was admirable. 'He tried to smother-cate him,' she yelled at Anna. 'He'd yon bloody cushion over his face – out, out!' Like a mad shepherd, Polly drove Richard through another door and into the vast drawing room. 'Go on, you fat ugly bugger, get out of me road before I fetch you one with this here stick.'

Anna looked at her brother. He was not injured, but his weary, lined face seemed even older. 'Follow her, Anna,' he begged, 'because I swear she'll kill him.' He sank back onto his pillow. 'And if I had the strength, I would help her.'

Anna shot out and pursued Polly into the hallway. Polly, her dark hair caught up in multicoloured curlers, had cornered Richard. Meanwhile, the rest of the household began to appear. Meredith, followed by Jean, then the twins and finally Aggie, wandered onto the stairs, each claiming a place from which the show could be watched.

Polly towered over the cowering figure. 'You are nowt a pound, you. I wouldn't even expect a bloody goldfish or a slab of donkey-stone off Alf Martindale's cart if I handed you in. You are less than rubbish, because rubbish gets weighed in and made into paper.' The diatribe stopped, but only for a second. 'Mind, if Miss Anna and young Miss Meredith are thinking of setting up in candles again, I reckon they'd get a fair amount of tallow out of you, you great fat lump.'

He looked up at her. 'You were grateful enough at one time,' he whispered.

'Grateful? Grateful? Bloody desperate more like.' The large woman swung round, her nightgown standing out like a small tent before settling against ample curves. 'He tried to kill his dad,' she told the audience. 'Tried to smothercate him with a cushion, he did. But I am a light sleeper these days, so I stopped him.'

Jean blinked, decided that smothercate was a good word, decided further that this was not the time to be considering vocabulary. 'You had better leave this house,' she told her husband.

He grunted, broke wind, then sagged against the wall. 'I was not killing anyone,' he achieved eventually. 'I was merely making sure that he was comfortable.'

318

Polly waded in again. 'Comfortable? I'll give you comfortable, you lying toad. Comfortable six feet under is where you wanted that poor old man. Pick on somebody your own size. Try Winston flaming Churchill – his belly's somewhere about the same size as yours and he finished bloody Hitler.'

A strange sound added to the untidy equation. Jean, who had sunk onto one of the stairs, began to laugh; but this was not ordinary laughter. The noise she made bore all the hallmarks of hysteria and it prompted Polly to indulge in further abuse of the lord and master. 'See her? That's your wife, the one you tried to strangle. She's on tablets. We could all do with blinking tablets at this rate. Now, sod off before I clout you. And you stink. A whisky drinker's farts always stink.'

This was hilarious, thought Jean. Her husband, who had killed Sally, who had just tried to kill his own father, was at the mercy of his own former mistress, who was now a firm friend to his wife. Everyone else remained motionless, because the scene being played out on the black-and-white tiling was compulsive viewing. She wiped her eyes. 'Good theatre,' she mumbled to herself. Yes, she had better start taking the pills again, because this wasn't right – she should not be laughing.

Richard staggered to his feet. 'I am going to bed,' he announced, the words slightly slurred.

Jean stopped giggling. 'Not in my house,' she stated.

'Your house?' His voice thickened and he coughed to clear a thirsty throat.

'Your father's house, then,' answered Jean. 'You will be given time to pack a small case and, as there

319

is no traffic on the roads at this time of night, you may take the car.' She addressed Anna. 'Please sit with Pa. He will be wondering where everyone is. Jeremy, Peter, help your father to pack – and find the car keys. Meredith, go back to bed – you, too, Aggie. Tomorrow morning, we shall have all the locks changed.'

He was routed and he knew it. What the hell had come over him? He could not remember why he had tried to stop the old man breathing, could not remember much . . . Except for her, the fragrant one in her pink dressing gown, standing now, halfway up the stairs, ordering him out of a house that was right-fully his own. Oh, he remembered her, by hell he did. They all wanted killing–

'Move!' Polly prodded him with the walking stick. 'You heard her – now, get gone. And don't come back, either, because I need my sleep. I can't be doing with watching you all bloody night, I've an old man to see to and a job of work to do, a proper job.' She was gloating now. Polly was important at last. The man who had rendered her useless, stupid and dependent was the one laid low – and not before time.

Aggie, all five feet two inches of her, joined Polly in the hall. She looked hard at Jeremy's dad, decided he wasn't worth worrying about and went to make cocoa.

On the stairs, Jeremy grinned – if looks could kill, his father would have been impaled seconds earlier on the steel from Aggie's eyes. 'Come on,' he urged his brother. 'Let's sort him out.'

Thus it was that Richard Chandler found himself seated in his car outside his house on a December

320

night that was less than clement. He was in possession of some clothes, the vehicle, a bank book and a hangover. Was he going mad? If he was, the damage had been done by the fragrant one and her coven – and by his own sons – and by his daughter, whose tacit acquiescence had shown in her unwillingness to intervene on his behalf.

Where to go? It would soon be morning, said the part of his mind that remained reasonable. This was not the time to go searching for somewhere to stay, so he would remain here, on his own plot, his own part of England.

'Bugger,' he spat before drifting towards sleep. He pulled the crombie round his shoulders and waited for sleep and sobriety to arrive. Kill his own father? Had he really tried to do that? 'Putting an animal out of its misery is no offence,' he said as he yawned his way into stupor.

Aggie was rinsing out cocoa mugs when he entered the kitchen; she knew without looking up that this was Jeremy, because she recognized his footfalls. He walked more heavily than his brother and at a slightly faster pace. Her heart, too, was travelling quickly, rather like an express through Crewe station – make way for rolling stock, no brakes, no intention of stopping. But she carried on with her job.

'It's three o'clock,' he announced, pulling out a chair and placing himself at the large table. 'You should be in bed.'

'I can tell the time,' she replied, wishing that her voice had emerged at the proper level. She sounded squeaky, like a teenager with a crush. Very appropriate, she reminded herself as she stacked the beakers. In a moment, she would have to turn and look at him. This was the first time they had been alone together, but he wouldn't look twice at her, not when he had Josie Maguire to take out for fun evenings. She braced herself and swivelled. He was smiling. 'What are you grinning at?' she asked. Everyone found her funny, whereas Josie Maguire, tall, elegant, slender, was adored and stared at like a piece of fine art, an exquisite sculpture.

'Smudge of cocoa powder on your nose.'

'Ah.' She made no effort to remove the offending blemish. 'Oh, well, that's me all over, isn't it?'

'Is it? Do you have cocoa smudges where the sun never shines?'

'What?'

'All over?'

She produced a feeble imitation of a smile. 'I wouldn't know. I don't spend that much time looking at myself in mirrors. Did you want something?'

'No. Just to talk to you.'

She parked herself in the chair opposite his. He was smiling as he might have smiled upon a playing puppy, and she resented the fact. Was she less than human because she was a little shorter, a little rounder than might be judged perfect? Did red hair and freckles make her less human than a tall, thin, perfect person with beautiful skin and a job selling stockings?

'Am I in with a chance, then?' he asked.

'What?' she repeated.

He reached across and wiped her face with the ball of his thumb. 'That's the cocoa gone. A chance, Agnes. I don't want to call you Aggie. I like you. Is that allowed?'

Aggie closed her mouth with an audible snap. 'But . . . er . . .'

'But er what? Butter wouldn't melt?'

She shook her head. 'No. But er Josie is what I meant.'

He frowned. 'Josie who? Oh – her. Yes, lovely girl, an absolute stunner. But er you wouldn't want her to tag along, would you?'

Her mind was racing. This was her job, her home. She worked in his mother's house and she didn't want to leave, not yet, anyway. There was an idea lurking at the edge of her mind, a thought that she might want to go to night school and get some A levels, then, perhaps, on to teacher training, but she didn't want to be forced to leave the grange too early if things got awkward.

'Agnes?'

'I'm thinking.' He was gorgeous.

'Right, thanks for the warning – shall we need the fire extinguisher?'

'We will if your Aunt Anna doesn't stop leaving her ciggies in mad places. What makes you interested in me, anyway? Has Josie given you the push?'

'We were never close enough for the push,' he replied.

'Oh.' For once in her short life, Agnes Turner could think of no clever answer. 'Right, then.'

'Is the meeting closed?' he asked.

'I don't think we were a quorum,' she replied.

'Yes, we were.'

Aggie rose to her feet. 'Any other business, Mr Chairman?' It was a dream. She would wake at any minute and this would be just another of her imaginings. Chances like this didn't fall into the path of

323

short, plump females with chemically straightened hair and a history in chip-making.

'Just the vote,' said Jeremy, his tone serious. 'All those who fancy a game of darts in the Chandlers tomorrow night, show hands.'

They both raised a hand.

'Carried,' he said. 'The ayes have it. Good night, Miss Turner.' He stood up and left the room.

She didn't know whether to laugh or cry. At three in the morning, she could not run down to Claughton Cottage, could not tell Marie the news. And what about Josie? Oh, she was bursting and there was no-one to tell. So she walked to the mirror over the kitchen fireplace, stood on tiptoe and told herself.

The girl in the glass was not ugly; she owned symmetrical features and a very winning smile. 'I'm glad you looked after your teeth, Agnes Turner,' she whispered. 'Just take the chance, girl. For once in your life, take the chance.'

TWELVE

He was freezing to death and his throat felt like the Khyber Pass: narrow and almost impossible to negotiate. For one of the few times within memory, Richard Chandler longed for a cup of tea. All he had with him was a bottle of Johnnie Walker Black, so he took a swig from that and shuddered as it made its way into a cavernous stomach; he was starving. Food. He had to find something to eat.

His head turned, stiffened neck creaking like an old hinge as he stared at the firmly closed door of his own home. Snatches of last night's happenings flashed across his brain in the form of an old film on sticky reels: a cushion, fury, the desire to see the old man on his way to damnation. Pol Fishwick floating about like a barrage balloon, stick in hand, prodding him, pushing him. Jean laughing. He gulped noisily. Witches and warlocks, the lot of them, and they should all die. But he was powerless.

Although, in reality, what had he to lose? Not much, not if the medics had told the truth. The tightness in his chest, that pain in his arm – these were the symptoms foretold by the doctors. His heart was in bad shape – he was in bad shape – and he would not have survived the very surgery designed to improve him. The orders from above had been no drinking, no smoking, small, regular meals and gentle exercise. It was laughable.

The door opened and that short, red-haired girl emerged, she who had passed by last night while Pol had threatened him. He rolled down his window. 'Where are you going?' he asked.

Aggie stood on the bottom step and glared at him. This was Jeremy's dad; this was what happened to Chandlers – but no. Jeremy had backbone and character, so he would not be reduced to this, surely?

'I asked you a question,' he said.

'And I didn't answer,' came the swift response. It was not yet seven o'clock, but she needed to tell someone about last night – well, about the early hours of this morning – had to make it real. Marie would be out of bed soon and Aggie wanted to catch her friend before she left for work. Jeremy – yes – Jeremy was interested in her, in who and what she was – she could have walked on water today, but she managed to maintain her hostile expression.

'I want an answer,' he demanded.

'You can want all you like. I have nothing to say to you.'

Even against a servant, he was ineffectual. This was, he supposed, the replacement for the grim-faced Sally Foster, his wife's confidante. But she was not long out of nappies, so Pol, who could not organize to save her life, was possibly assisting this new house-keeper in embryo. He watched as she skipped off down the driveway, not a care in the world, her progress swift, light and confident.

Bank book. The pages fell open and he studied the sum, decided it was enough to get him lodgings, food and drink for a few years. Gloomily, Richard stared into a future that seemed rather less than promising. A room in a boarding house, no servants, a lifetime of eating in cafés and restaurants – was this a fitting way for a Chandler to live? This house – this land – these farms and their tenants – he owned them, lock, stock and body weight. Aunt Anna was writing the history, the glory of a family whose roots could be traced back to the Bolton Charter of 1253, for goodness' sake.

He turned the key, revved the engine and began the drive away from the only life he had ever known, his sole home, his empire, his birthright. As he made progress to the south side of the village, he caught sight of the red-haired girl; she was opening the brand-new gate that led to Claughton Cottage. Ah. So news of his disgrace was already spreading. Alf Martindale and his good lady wife would have plenty to smile about today; and he had only a life of relative squalor to anticipate . . .

Marie rubbed her eyes. 'What are you doing here at this time? Come in. Dad's got the kettle on – he always takes Mam a cup of tea in bed to start her day.' She led Aggie through to the large kitchen.

'Hello, flower,' said Alf. 'What are you doing out and about this early on a cold and frosty morning? Have you got bed bugs?'

'No,' giggled Aggie as she dropped into a chair,

'but the master of the house has a flea in his ear. Polly says he tried to kill his dad, so she went for him with a walking stick. It finished up like a Laurel and Hardy film – we couldn't take our eyes off it. Two o'clock in the morning and all hell broke loose – reminded me of the kids' Saturday matinee at the Odeon.'

Alf frowned. 'Where is he now?'

'No idea,' replied Aggie. 'He stayed outside in his car all night, too drunk to drive, then he passed me on the road outside here about a minute ago. The only reason we feel safe is because there are enough of us. They've thrown him out and hidden the guns in case he breaks in again. The locks get changed today, according to Mrs Chandler.'

Alf poured four cups of tea and passed two to the girls. So, the bad bugger was out and about, was he? From what Alf had heard in the local pub, Richard Chandler's drinking was well past the post and he needed containing. The thought of him being out there was not comfortable. He left the room with Leena's morning cuppa.

'So, plenty of excitement, then?' asked Marie.

'Enough. More than enough.' Aggie took a gulp of hot tea. 'I needed that. I was up till God knows what time making cocoa for everybody. They should tell the police, Marie, but Mrs Chandler doesn't want the disgrace for Meredith and the twins.'

'Understandable.' Marie stirred some sugar into her cup. 'So, are you going to give up the job? I hope you don't leave the village. Once Josie's gone to London, I might stay here with Mam and Dad, because I don't fancy sharing Emblem Street with a lodger I don't know from Eve.'

This information stopped Aggie in her tracks. 'Eh?'

she asked before she could stop herself. 'London?'

Marie nodded. 'She's off to train as a model. This bloke walked right up to the stocking counter and gave her his card. They do Playtex, Max Factor and all sorts. Then, once she's learned the deportment stuff, she might even do fashion shows. And, like she said to me yesterday, she has to take the chance or she'll always regret it. Can't blame her, really. She's had enough of Marks and Spencer. Aggie? What's wrong?'

'Nothing. I'm just tired. I . . . I had to get out of that house as soon as I woke up, Marie. It's frightening.' The most frightening thing was not Mr Chandler and the carryings-on, oh no. It was Jeremy, He had come to Aggie because he was desperate, because the woman of his dreams was leaving him. Aggie was there, was on the spot, was a darts player, an amusement, something to fill in the space until a better option came along. All he had needed was the void filling for a while.

'Yes, it must have been scary,' agreed Marie. She could not imagine Aggie being terrified enough to run away. Aggie Turner had shifted aggressive or maudlin drunks from chip shops, had shunted them away as easily as most people swatted troublesome bluebottles. Marie had witnessed grown men near to tears when Aggie had refused to serve them – what was wrong?

'Has she told Jeremy she's going?' Aggie asked.

'I don't know. She might have phoned him. Why?'

'I just wondered, that's all.' Like a balloon with a loose string, she felt energy draining out of her body. She had been living on excitement, on expectation and adrenalin, but now, after insufficient sleep, she

329

realized how exhausted she truly was. And the real reason for her tiredness was that Jeremy did not care for her after all.

'You look shattered,' Marie said now. 'If you've nowhere to go, I'm sure Mam and Dad will take you in. I mean, you don't want to go back home to the chippy, do you?'

'What?'

Marie sighed. 'If you're running away, I just thought—'

'I'm not running away,' Aggie answered. The real reason for visiting Marie had flown off like a migrating bird, so agility of mind was required. 'I wasn't coming here,' she said, determined to hang on to her pride, 'I was just following him. He's still that full of booze, I managed to keep up with him while he drove away. I wanted to make sure he'd gone, that's all. And he passed your house – probably on his way to town – so I thought I'd call in.'

'Right.' There was more to this than met the eye, Marie thought. In fact, quite a lot did meet the eye, because Aggie was definitely out of sorts. Still, a murder attempt would be enough to rock anybody, she supposed. 'Drink your tea. I'm going to get dressed for work.'

Alone, Aggie closed her eyes and forbade the tears to flow. If she wanted to indulge in a bout of weeping, she would do it in the privacy of her own room up at the grange. She had been a damned fool, allowing herself to believe that a man like Jeremy Chandler could be interested in a girl like her, rusty-haired, freckle-faced and too round to be pretty.

Alf re-entered the kitchen. 'You all right, love?'

She opened her eyes and nodded. 'Yes. Just lost a

330

lot of sleep, keeping an eye on him,' she lied. 'I didn't want him trying to get back into the house, you see.'

He saw, all right. 'Look, Aggie, if it gets too much for you up yon, get yourself down here to me and Leena. I've shortened his reins before now and I can do it again if necessary. He was never decent, but the drink's made him a damned sight worse. I won't have you frightened – do you hear me?'

'Yes. Thank you.' She rose to her feet. 'Say ta-ra to Marie for me, please. I'd best get back and start burning toast.'

Alf sat down in the chair recently vacated by his daughter's friend. Poor kid. Nobody should have to put up with a wicked devil like Richard Chandler. He thought about going up to the house to reason with Jean Chandler, to beg her to get the police in, but the constabulary would likely want to know why she had said nothing thus far. She could say she'd been too scared, but . . .

Oh, God. Alf had come a long way, had travelled the streets, roads and avenues of Bolton for more years than he cared to remember, had heaved and hauled rubbish, had watched his wife near to death with TB. And what had he achieved at the end of it? A house in a dangerous place, that was all.

Leena wandered in. 'Oh, has Aggie gone? Our Marie told me she was here. Did you give her a cuppa?'

He nodded. 'Aye. And I think you'd best start thinking about going up to the grange more often.' Yes, there was safety in numbers. 'From what I've heard, Aggie could burn water – she needs a helping hand, love. I could run you up there in the mornings if you like.'

'After Christmas,' she replied. 'I want a nice Christmas and everybody's coming.' She was looking forward to that. The family from the grange, old neighbours from Emblem Street, her own children – a real party and room to accommodate everyone.

'You're talking nigh on a dozen people,' he told her. 'Don't you think that'll be too much for you?'

'More like fourteen,' she replied happily. The dining room was big enough – they could carry the kitchen table through and shove it against the one in the dining room, and–

'All right.' He knew when he was beaten and had the sense to keep quiet. Once Leena fixed her mind on something, it was stuck as fast as a bayonet after the charge of the Light Brigade – there was no shifting her. 'Just . . . just make sure you lock yourself in and keep safe when I've gone.'

'Why? Is Jack the Ripper about?'

Sometimes, jokes hit rather too close for Alf's comfort. 'No, but there's been a few burglaries, so think on and shut your doors.'

She put the kettle back on the stove. 'It's him, isn't it? Is that why Aggie finished up here at the crack of dawn?'

'Yes.'

Leena nodded. 'He was on the stairs yesterday when I took the puddings round. He looked like an animal at the zoo, behind bars and on the hungry side.'

'Bloody predator,' growled Alf.

'Eh?'

'Nowt. Just keep yourself safe – the phone'll be here in a few weeks anyway.' He would feel safer when the GPO had been and done its job. Although

332

the kitchen was warm, a shiver travelled the length of his spine. They might have thrown him out of the grange, but Richard Chandler was out there, larger than life and twice as ugly as mortal sin.

'Eggs, love?' asked Leena.

'Scrambled, please.' He wanted scrambling, that Richard flaming Chandler – though from the sound of things, his brains were already well on the way to being fuddled.

Leena cooked the breakfast, one eye on her husband. Deep down, she knew the cause of his fear, but she didn't want to say the words, was unwilling to make the threat more real than it needed to be. She served his eggs. 'There you are, love. Now, straighten your face before the wind changes, or you'll finish up looking like a smacked bum for the rest of your life.'

He relaxed and ate his eggs. Chandler was gone, the phone would soon be in and it was nearly Christmas. Like everyone else on God's good earth, Alf Martindale placed his trust in the Lord and hoped for the best.

Outside Preston's jewellers, the very place where he had bought Jean's wedding and engagement rings, Richard Chandler was finally sober. With his stomach lined by a full English breakfast and several mugs of strong tea, he waited for a degree of clearer thought to visit his brain.

Bolton. His town. The Romans had been and gone, Flemish weavers had been and stayed, cotton was on the decline and nobody wanted candles unless there was a power cut. King Henry, son of King John, had enfranchised the growing town in January 1253, though its unsigned charter had existed for two years

333

before that momentous date. Free trade for all its burgesses, debts to be honoured, acreages to be allocated, taxes to be collected, the town to have its own identity for the rest of time. Bolton.

He turned and looked at the needle which marked the spot on which the seventh Earl of Derby had been beheaded, at the inn in which that man had spent his last few hours in this fiercely Parliamentarian stronghold. Deansgate, Bradshawgate, Churchgate – these roads marked barriers long gone, places at which an intruder might be challenged before walking among townsfolk in these parts.

'We were a part of that,' he said to himself. But life moved on and here stood the son and rightful heir to the legacy of men who had shed blood so that this, the largest town in England, might survive. Where was the pride now? He fingered the car keys in his pocket and considered his next move. His vehicle was recognized everywhere and he sought anonymity, so the car had to go.

He crossed the road and walked up Bradshawgate towards an estate agency. With no intention of living in a boarding house, he would be forced to rent a small place on the town's outskirts. Unable to see beyond the point of immediate needs, his goals were a roof, a cheaper car and a fire at which he might warm his bones. Once these necessities had been secured, he would be able to plan the rest. And the rest was revenge.

Aggie Turner had always battled against temper. There was probably a grain of truth in the myth about red-haired people, because most of her mother's family, especially the redheads, were short-fused.

Pride straightened her spine as she made lunch for the family – steak and kidney pie, one of her safer options. A natural housekeeper, she still had a degree of catching up to do in the fine-tuning of her culinary abilities.

Village women came and went, the harder jobs completed by noon, and Aggie was left alone in the vast kitchen – just herself, some suet pastry and the smell of simmering meat for company. Until Polly arrived. Aggie looked up. 'Are you off out?'

'Later on,' replied Polly. 'The old man's asleep, God love him. Last night took a lot out of him, more than he wants to admit. Are you all right, love? You look a bit peaky to me.'

Aggie tackled her pastry. 'I'm fine – just tired.'

'I've come for the meeting,' said Polly.

'In here?' The kitchen was fast becoming the centre of this household. 'I've cooking to do.' Would Jeremy be at the meeting? 'What's it about?'

Polly lifted her shoulders. 'Eeh, don't ask me. But I was told to come here at twelve o'clock for a conflab and I'm here, but the conflab's not. Henry was supposed to come, too, but he's best left where he is.'

Aggie bridled. 'I wish somebody'd tell me when my table's going to be met round. If I'd known, I wouldn't have started this pie.'

Polly sat down. 'They won't mind.'

'Well, I will,' snapped Aggie. 'I'm swimming against the tide here. And I've the locksmith coming.' She busied herself with the task in hand, not even looking up when the rest of the household began to collect round her table.

'How's Agnes this morning?' asked Jeremy as he took his place at the end nearest the door.

'Fine.' She brought the meat across and began to throw it into her pie dish. When the container was full, she fixed on the lid of pastry and carried it to the oven, leaving it to sit until the time came when it would be pushed inside to finish. Quickly, she cleaned up her mess before finally looking at the assembled group. 'That's me done,' she announced. 'I'll carry on with the lunch after your meeting.'

Jeremy raised an eyebrow. 'Aren't you staying?'

'I wasn't invited,' she answered.

Jean cleared her throat. 'But you are a part of the household, Aggie. We want you to stay.'

Aggie faltered for a moment, but held on to her shredded dignity as best she could. She wanted to hit Jeremy with the rolling pin, but she managed to overcome the desire to do him grievous bodily harm – she would leave the grange when she was ready, not before, and she would not be leaving under a cloud. 'I need rest, Mrs Chandler, so, if you don't mind, I'll go and sit down until the locksmith comes.'

'Go to bed if you want,' suggested Polly. 'I'll put your pie in the oven in half an hour, and I'll sort the locksmith out.' She grinned. 'I'm good at sorting men out.'

'Yes,' agreed Aggie, 'I noticed.' But the sorting out of Jeremy Chandler would be subtle and would not require a walking stick. She walked to the door, turned, saw him staring at her. Yes, she would deal with him later.

In her room, she picked up a cushion and began to beat it with her fists – this was what her mother would term 'knocking seven shades of excreta out of life', a method often employed by the red-headed amongst the clan. When the tears flowed, she did not fight them, although she knew that she would live to regret the outpouring, because another downside for redheads was the fine skin and the way it advertised recent tears. Well, he could play bloody darts on his bloody own, because Aggie Turner was going bloody nowhere.

'So, there we have it.' Anna Chandler spread her hand-drawn plans across the table. 'Factory, shop, offices. The rent is dirt cheap and I've found a firm selling the necessary equipment at a reasonable price.' She took a cigarette from behind an ear and lit it. 'We are going into business.'

'And I shall sell more than just candles?' Meredith asked.

Anna nodded. 'You and Marie – if she wishes to join in – can sell whatever you like, but the main product will be ornamental candles. Look at the trends.' She tossed some magazines into the arena. 'There are tapers set in cast-iron holders, pillar candles with several colours, decorated stuff, too – studs and so forth pushed into the wax. It remains a volatile substance, of course, so your idea of allowing people to make their own candles is rather adventurous, Meredith. However, there are books now for those who want to take the risk at home – we can sell those, the wicks and the wax.'

'And there's the name,' laughed Meredith. 'Wicks and Wax.'

Jean smiled. 'No. We call it New Chandlers. I absolutely insist on that. At first, we shall hire just a few people, but as time goes on, who knows? We may expand.'

'My book will be for sale,' said Anna. 'That's the

337

only chance I have of selling it, I imagine. Did you know that I must pay to be published? And after struggling to translate the ramblings of my inebriated ancestors.'

Peter spoke. 'If I get into vet college, I shan't be helping.'

'We know.' Meredith pressed her brother's hand. 'But you'll put some of Grandmother's money in?'

'Of course. And Jeremy can take the wheel.'

Jeremy was not paying attention. There had been a change in Agnes and he needed to get to the bottom of it. 'What?'

'You will be in charge of the factory,' Jean told him.

'Fine.' He needed to get out of here, wanted to follow Agnes, but Great-Aunt Anna, hatless but with the hallmark cigarette in one hand, was holding forth on the subject of business plans and bank loans, investment and interest. And he was losing interest fast. It was strange how his affection for Agnes had developed so suddenly, but it was strong enough to make him worry about the shift of attitude.

'Jeremy?'

'What?' They were all staring at him.

Meredith shook her head. 'We were just saying that Polly and Aggie will take responsibility for the home front and we were wondering whether you might consider doing a course in management? Evening classes, of course.'

'Fine,' he repeated. 'Whatever needs doing, I'll do it.'

Meredith grinned. 'He's gone into a decline because Josie Maguire's off to London to seek her fortune.'

'Is she?' he asked. 'Well, good luck to her.'

They droned on about facts and figures while he studied the grain in the kitchen table. The clouds in his mind began to shift and were gathering a slight hint of silver at the edges – the light was dawning. He folded his arms and stretched out long legs.

'No need to kick,' grumbled Meredith.

'Sorry,' he said, 'but I have a call to make. About the dog.'

'Hero's fine,' said Peter. 'I rang earlier – he is going to make a full recovery.'

'Good.' With no further excuses on which to fall back, Jeremy remained throughout the rest of the meeting.

Polly pushed the pie into the oven at half past twelve, then lit rings under the vegetables. 'God help you,' she said cheerfully, 'but you're in for a funny dinner.'

At last, it was over. With fifteen minutes to go before lunch, Jeremy took the stairs two at a time. Grinning foolishly, he approached her door. He knew why she was sulking and had no intention of letting her off his hook . . .

The house was on Halliwell Road, just a two up and two down with a bathroom tacked on downstairs. The kitchen was about the same size as the pantry up at the grange, but it held a cooker, some cupboards and a couple of shelves. The other ground-floor room, whose front door led straight onto the pavement, was small, but furnished. It contained a sofa big enough to sleep on; that was vital, as he could not imagine running downstairs in the night every time he needed the bathroom. 'I'll take it,' he said.

The estate agent hesitated. 'It's only for six months. The owners have gone to stay with family for a while, but they will be coming back in June.'

'That is no problem.'

'And . . . er . . . I need a month up front, then a month extra in case of damages. If there are no damages, the money will be returned to you when you leave.'

'Fine.' Richard pulled his wallet from an inside pocket.

'And two forms of identification.'

He pushed his bank book and driving licence into the agent's hands, placing an extra five-pound note on top of these offerings. 'Keep your mouth shut,' he ordered. 'I am taking a rest from family problems and I don't wish to be traced. Do you understand?'

The young man relaxed. 'I do, indeed, sir. We all need to get away from time to time. Rest assured, your secret is safe with me.' He busied himself with plans for his five-pound bonus, and left Richard Chandler in his grim little house. If the landed gentry wanted to take a step down in the world, so be it – as long as there was the odd fiver in their calculations. But for the name and address on bank book and driving licence, Richard Chandler would not have been noticed, anyway – and what did it matter? Just another fat, middle-aged man in transit, but with a bit of money to spare.

Richard sat in his house and wondered what the hell he was doing. He had never boiled an egg in his life, had no idea of how to keep a place clean, would need help with laundry and ironing – could he run to a daily? Weekdays only, of course – on Saturdays he would eat out. Sundays, too – most pubs did meals.

340

He needed a woman. Not a Pan-Handle Pol, not a Fragrant Jean, just a decent body who would keep him fed and clean.

He left his little hovel and walked down to a newsagent, passing his newly acquired Morris van on the way. Parked outside his house, it was not a thing of beauty, but it possessed the anonymity with which he sought to cloak himself.

With the help of the proprietor, he made out a card and paid for it to be displayed in the window. Pushing a rolled newspaper under his arm, Richard then crossed the road and entered a seedy public house. Armed with a double whisky, some pork scratchings and a packet of crisps, he sat in a corner and watched how the other half lived.

Old men played a lunchtime game of dominoes, some hags in a window seat cackled; he noticed that one had not a single tooth in her head. The blowzy landlady screamed with laughter when a salesman type cracked a joke at the bar and, all the time, traffic roared past outside. He did not know whether or when he would get used to such noise. Had he made a mistake? Oh, what did it matter? Two or three more whiskies and he would be able to tolerate just about anything – or so he hoped.

Yes, Scotch had brought him this far and it would take him the rest of the way. As long as he took a few others with him, he did not fear the concept of death, since he was already in hell.

Aggie faced herself. As she had told Jeremy Chandler, she was not one to stand in front of mirrors, yet here she lingered, naked as the day of her birth, scrutinizing every curve, every fold, every

341

pocket of fat. 'You are not ugly,' she advised the mirror. 'There's a lot less of you than there used to be.' She cherished the theory that chip shop fat was absorbed by the system, that a person did not need to stuff her stomach with fried food in order to become its victim. 'I'm sweating it out,' she pronounced, referring to her daily walk on the moors.

Her clothes had been the first to announce her improvement – waistbands needing to be made smaller by a few hasty stitches, jeans that threatened to follow the law of gravity, undergarments too loose.

It was a good face, a nice face. Although 'nice' was insipid and a long way from perfect, it was a great deal preferable to buck teeth and receding chin. She was all right. She was healthy and bright and she was going somewhere; she was going to college and would become a teacher.

Tiredness forgotten, she dragged on underclothes, jeans and sweater, grabbed a duffel coat and a silly pom-pom tea-cosy hat, then left the house via the back stairs. Now she had to walk *him* off. There was more than just avoirdupois to lose today – there was *him*, a different kind of weight, not even a dead weight, because stillborn seemed a more appropriate adjective.

The side door swung behind her; let them have their meeting, because Agnes Turner had just resigned. She would keep the job for a while, but on her own terms from this moment. Mam and Dad would help, of course, as these rather less than visionary people were good to the core; if their Aggie wanted to train as a teacher, they would get behind her. But it would be nice to have some money of her own, a few quid put by so that she might live in a flat rather than in the college hall – Catholic training colleges were notorious for imposing discipline on residents. Another decision made itself – bugger Catholic. She would go neutral, would be an adult rather than a shepherded child.

She walked through the stable yard, now just a storage dump, looked at buildings that had once housed Arab-Irish horseflesh. She strode through Chandler fields, climbed Chandler stiles, marched along Chandler footpaths. Angry little feet took angry little steps, her footfalls harder than usual. She was stamping on *his* face; more than that, so much more, she was treading none too softly on her own brief dream.

When he got no response to his knocking, Jeremy Chandler opened the door and pushed it inward, but no more than an inch. Agnes was a fun girl, but she was not cheap and the entering of her bedroom would have constituted several steps too far. 'Agnes?'

'Jeremy?'

He spun round and saw his sister behind him on the landing. 'Ah, Merry.'

'She'll be stamping about outside,' Meredith told him. 'She's been making herself pretty for you and now she is upset. Someone must have told her about Josie leaving and she has added two and two—'

'And made seven. I guessed. Where will she be?'

Meredith shrugged. 'I went with her just once. She may have short legs, but she moves at a pace. I think she usually goes along the lanes and through the woods. Polly Fishwick's cottage is empty and there's a key under a plant pot, so she has a breather in there, then she comes back.' She touched his arm. 'Go after her, Jer. She is, without question, one of the most valuable people I have met so far. Marie is brilliant, Josie is . . .' Once again, she raised her shoulders.

'Is Josie,' he finished for her. 'And, until about half an hour ago, I truly had no idea about London.'

'I know.'

He ran taut fingers through his hair. 'I don't understand myself, Merry. One minute, she was just Aggie, then the next, she was . . . she was everything.'

'Just Aggie is how she has always seen herself,' replied Meredith. 'At school, she was the Just Aggie who made everyone laugh; after school, she was the Just Aggie whose parents lived too close to the gem we see. Even a diamond can look cloudy if you don't give it some attention.'

'She's a ruby,' he said, his voice almost cracking. 'If she were a gem, there would be fire in it.'

Meredith laughed. 'A true diamond carries many prisms and every colour in the world. Our Just Aggie is multifaceted and that is what you saw, brother. Go after her.'

For the first time in years, Jeremy Chandler kissed his sister. 'Thanks,' he whispered, 'and well done, you – with the booze. It isn't easy, is it?'

'Nothing worthwhile is straightforward,' she answered, 'so go and get her. And tell her hello from me.' As her brother walked away, Meredith dashed a tear from a cheek. She was a lucky girl; she owned two wonderful brothers and the chance of two excellent sisters-in-law.

The hoar of early morning had not completely disappeared and Aggie found herself in a magical world of pale silver and white, branches stroked gently by

344

an undecided sun, its rays bringing an eerie life to vegetation that was supposedly at rest for the winter.

With her immediate anger almost dissipated, Aggie made her way towards Woodside Cottage. There she would rest for a while; there, she would try to deal with the deeper fury, the place inside that remained untended, her core, that central part of self where rationale was more effective than emotion. She was the weak sun; she had to shine uncertain light into her own soul, and she would – yes, she *would* survive. 'His loss,' she stated as she negotiated a path across some visible roots.

She found the plant pot, raised it, felt for the key. When her fingers made no contact, she lifted the pot off the ground and used her eyes. Nothing. Polly had her own key and she did not come here often, so this was, indeed, a mystery. Then the noise began.

Tucking herself in as tightly against the wall as she could manage, Aggie made her cautious way towards the front corner of the cottage. In the unkempt clearing that was supposed to be the front garden, a man sat on a tree stump, his back towards her. He was chopping logs into finer kindling and Aggie breathed a sigh of involuntary relief; it was not Mr Chandler. The moment of ease was followed immediately by another emotion – if Chandler had been here, his family could have been made aware of his location. 'Knowledge is power,' she whispered to herself.

A hand touched her shoulder and she screamed automatically, but the brief sound coincided with the crack of axe on wood, so the man was not made aware of her presence. Slowly, Aggie turned her head. 'Oh, it's you,' she mouthed silently. 'Somebody's living here.'

Jeremy pulled his prize back into the woods. When they were beyond earshot, he asked the obvious question. 'Is it my father?'

'No. Somebody younger and thinner, though I never saw his face. We should tell your mother and Polly.'

'Why?'

'Because it's your house and Polly's home, isn't it?'

He nodded. 'Yes, of course it is. It's also nearly Christmas, so let the man stay – he is probably out of work and in need of shelter. He is doing no harm, is he?'

'I suppose not.' How could she mend herself now, with Jeremy in the way? She needed space, time, a few minutes to herself, but he had followed her. He had no right to follow her.

'Time enough to shift him when the repairs begin in the spring – leave him be, Agnes.'

'All right.' She didn't know where to look. 'Perhaps we should let him have his Christmas in the warmth, whoever he is. Season of goodwill, after all.'

They walked in silence for a minute or two, then he turned and pinned her against the breadth of an ancient oak. 'You've been crying.'

'I haven't,' she insisted. 'The cold makes my eyes water.'

He had wanted to make a game of this, but he found that he could not upset her any further. 'I didn't know,' he stated baldly.

'What?'

'About Josephine. Meredith announced it this morning at the meeting. Until then, I had absolutely no idea about her intentions. There was never anything between us.'

She could still hear the man chopping his wood. A flake of purest white wandered lazily through the air and landed on her nose. 'Snow,' she said. 'We had better get a move on. As for what you just said, I have no idea what you are talking about. Come on, hurry up before we get snowbound.' She dodged under his stretched arm and galloped ahead.

Jeremy blinked a couple of times, shook his head, then followed her. If Josie wasn't the cause of Aggie's mood change, what the hell was? He watched her skipping ahead, the pom-poms on her silly knitted hat bouncing as she moved. From a distance, she looked like a child at play – was she bringing out the paternal side in him? Did he have a paternal side? If he had, it had surely not been learnt from his own father.

He caught up with her at the gatehouse. 'For a short person, you move fast,' he panted.

She stopped. 'Do I? Well, remember that saying – good things arrive in small packages. I come from a family of short women on my mother's side. And there's another saying in my clan – poisons come in little packets, too.'

'I'll remember that.'

'Yes, make sure you do, Jeremy Chandler. I may be short, but I am lethal.'

He kissed her, suddenly finding her too irresistible, one little bundle of trouble in an over-sized duffel coat and a hideous hat.

Oh, God, she would die in a minute, she really would, and it wouldn't be from the cold. Her feet were off the floor and she was hanging from his neck, depending on him for support – and she shouldn't, mustn't.

347

He set her down. 'Hell's bells,' he exclaimed. 'That is one hungry small girl.' Then he kissed her again, because he had to.

Aggie was trembling. When he finally released her, she gasped for air and said, 'I thought I was her replacement.'

'Never in a million years, Agnes. You are one alone. I can say in all honesty, I have never met anyone like you – oh, and I am starving. Shall we take lunch, Miss Turner?'

She sniffed away her tears and answered, 'Yes, Mr Chandler.' And they walked home hand in hand.

It was a ghastly way to live – to pretend to be alive. The owners of the house had removed all personal items, so Richard was blessed with just the essentials – somewhere to sit, an electric fire and a small TV set. Halliwell Road was a busy route into Bolton and there was scarcely a gap in the traffic all day.

He poured yet more silver currency into a hungry electricity meter, found a glass, opened his Scotch and allowed himself a decent measure. Pork scratchings and crisps were all he had eaten since breakfast – he would have to find a fish and chip shop, he supposed. The rest of them – Father, Jean, her brats, Aunt Anna and the servants – would be enjoying true warmth, not this surface-scorching pair of elements whose heat never penetrated flesh and bone. He shivered and downed his drink in a single gulp.

The door knocker rattled. Was that the vibrations from constant traffic? No, there it went again. He rose and opened the door.

'Hello.' She was about forty, with pocked skin and far too much make-up.

'Yes?'

'I've come about the job in Weston's window. On the card. Daily help. I'm Freda.'

He held the door wide and she entered. He could smell cheap perfume over sweat. She reminded him of Pol – the old Pol, not the new one with her decent blouses, airs and graces. 'Come in.'

'I live next door,' she said, 'and I'm a widow with no ties. I used to be a carder at Swan Mills, only there's not as much work in cotton as there was. What would you want doing?'

'The usual,' he replied, huddling once more over the fire.

Uninvited, she sat opposite him. 'For a start, you want to lift that fire out – there's a proper fireplace behind and you can get coal delivered. They don't breathe, do they? Electric fires, I mean. I think there's still a back boiler, too, for your water. I can do plain meals and cleaning, your washing and ironing if you want – and I'll be handy if you're stuck, being next door and all.'

'When can you start?'

Momentarily nonplussed, she hesitated. 'Well, now if you want.'

'I moved in just today,' he said carefully. 'I shan't be here long, just until a bit of business is concluded. To save you cooking now, why don't you run out and find some fish and chips for both of us? I'll pay.'

'All right, whatever you want.' She took the money. 'Salt and vinegar?'

'Please.'

When she had left, he felt better. With a woman next door and a pub across the road, he would be all right for a few weeks – for however long it took. He

349

didn't even know what 'it' was, but he had some time now, time to think, to decide on their punishment. He poured another drink. 'Good health, Jean,' he mouthed, 'enjoy it while you can.'

The woman – Freda – would make his fire each morning, would wash his clothes and produce his meals. In every storm, there came a port, he told himself. But he would make damned sure that Jean's boat was shipwrecked; only then would he be able to rest in peace after the heart attack that now appeared inevitable.

She came back with a newspaper parcel and dashed into the kitchen. 'I shall want a key,' she called over her shoulder, 'you can't leave your door on the latch all the while. You could at one time. Oh, aye – back in the good old days we never locked up.' A bleached head appeared in the doorway. 'Have you got any bread and butter?'

'No.'

'I'll buy some in the morning. Don't worry, love, I'll look after you.'

She was a noisy eater, one who talked with her mouth full, who ate with it wide, dentures clicking as her jaw moved. Yes, she would do. Women like this asked few questions and were grateful for a few shillings. Unlike some . . .

THIRTEEN

Anna Chandler was up to her armpits in paperwork.

There was all the ancient stuff, ink-blotted copy-books filled with writing illegible enough for any medical consultant, accounts and journals produced by the drunk and the dastardly; there were line drawings of the old factory, architectural plans, recipes for wax components, instructions on the various methods for coating wicks; and, into all of the above, she was trying to weave the history of her village and of her family.

She threw down her pen. Why the hell was she bothering? The closer she looked, the more certain she became that she was the product of villains. And another villain was out there somewhere, mind addled by drink, murder in his heart – if he owned a heart, that was.

Then there was the modern stuff. The bank had expressed willingness to jump into bed with the Chandler family, but there remained much to be done. There were two units available at a very low rent, slightly off the beaten track near the bottom of

Chorley Old Road. She grinned mischievously. At least the candle factory would be practically on top of the fire station.

And Meredith had come up with the most brilliant idea for a miniature Tussaud's: famous people made from wax and displayed in the upper storey of the shop. The debate that currently raged was whether or not those figures would contain wicks, because it would seem eminently disrespectful to set fire to the Queen at the dinner table. Lighting up Jack the Ripper might be an acceptable activity, but the less notorious figures from British history would definitely be wick-free if Anna got her way. And Anna always got her way . . .

Aggie came in with morning coffee, plonked it on the desk and stood next to Anna. 'I can't cope,' she pronounced. 'It's had its stitches out now and it's all over the place. And it likes me. They always like me. I used to think it was because of the fish and chips, but—' The rest of her sentence was lost when Hero bounded in. 'Bugger,' cursed Aggie under her breath. This animal was a disaster on four legs and she was his repeated victim, a martyr to his whims and fancies.

The dog leapt on Aggie and she staggered back. 'It's eaten six sausages, best pork,' she said mournfully when the dog finally lost the keenest edge of its interest. 'And it's been trifling with my trifle when my back was turned.'

Anna loved Aggie. She recognized character when she saw it, felt that she was looking at a mirror image of herself. This was Jeremy's chosen one and Jeremy's taste was to be admired. 'Dogs love good people,' said Anna. 'If dogs like you, that proves your value.'

352

'I think I'd sooner be cut price in the January sale,' moaned the small girl. 'Can I not get revalued? Should we get a surveyor out? I might have radical faults in my foundations.' This sentence was directed at the dog. 'I'll have to be underpinned and it's all your fault, Hero,' she further advised him.

The dog panted in front of the fire. He was happy at last, history forgotten, future promising, an audience that participated in his lunacy and enough grub to satisfy even the most desperate hunger. Having just discovered double cream, he was begging for more, and Aggie, for all her protestations and tellings-off, loved him best of all. He did not belong to Peter or Jeremy, though he liked them well enough. No, this little girl was his, lock, stockpot and biscuit barrel.

'You love him,' laughed Anna, 'and he knows it. Look at him.'

'Hmmph,' snorted Aggie, 'he's wrong.' But she felt the twinkle in her own eye when she looked at the crazy creature. Hero was *all* wrong. He could not have been more wrong – thin legs, stringy tail and ears that seemed incapable of decision-making, one folded over like an envelope, the other a guardsman on parade, standing at full attention and never at ease. She, too, had been all wrong; she was losing weight and this unfortunate canine needed to gain some. They would both come good – she was determined on that score.

'He is devoted to you,' said Anna.

'Devoted to dinners, more like. I can't put anything down – if he thinks it's mine, he thinks it's his by default. Better keep an eye on Jeremy, make sure he's not disappearing bit by bit.' She cast an eye over the disordered desk. 'Have you had an accident?'

'Just an accident of birth,' replied Anna. 'I am up to Oliver Cromwell.'

'Which side were your lot on?'

'The side with the most barrels of barley wine, I should think.' Anna threw down yet another sheaf of papers and they slid stupidly all over the blotter. 'Leave them,' she advised. 'They'll find their own level, just as the Chandlers did.'

'On the floor?' Aggie bent and rescued an escaping page.

Anna laughed. 'Yes, on the floor, wrapped around a lamp-post – wherever they fell, they stayed. And we have to pick ourselves up, Aggie, before we, too, end up with nothing to show for all the years we have been here. Wasted lives,' she mused quietly, 'are a sin. Which is why you must answer your calling and go to college. Just don't go too far – Jeremy would fade away without you.'

Aggie felt colour rising in her cheeks. Jeremy was the consummate gentleman – she was the one who was having difficulty with the situation. The urge to travel in the night was strong – three doors down on the left, he slept, and she wanted, needed, to go to him. It was all right for Marie – she had a couple of fields between herself and Peter.

'When you look at these papers and see that we were original burgesses, we are an absolute disgrace.'

Aggie composed herself. 'So you were here in the thirteenth century?'

'We most certainly were – *anno regni regis Henrici filii regis Johannis, 14th of January, 1253*,' she read aloud. 'Yes, granted by William de Ferraris, Earl of Derby, and obtained from the king. Chandlers were

354

here before the charter, Aggie, but tracing beyond that gets hard.'

'It does,' giggled Aggie. 'I can trace our chippies back to Deane Road, 1947, but no further. I don't think we did chips in King Henry's day.'

The old lady had skipped into one of her pensive phases again. 'Make the most of your life and marry the man you love,' she instructed before picking up more papers.

Aggie heard the sadness. 'I will. And we'll always be here for you and for Jeremy's mam and grandad.'

But Anna had spotted something else on the desk, was rummaging and muttering. 'This reeve named Silas Morton was a pain in the side of the Chandlers – we kept being fined twelve pence for withholding rents. You see?' She waved the offending evidence. 'That is what drink does – fine upon fine upon fine – and let that be a lesson to you.'

Aggie was studying her own bit of paper. 'Hey, look at this. It wasn't just Hitler – it says "no burgess may sell his burgage to the Jewry". That's terrible.'

'But we could cut and burn our peat,' said Anna.

'What had Pete done?' Aggie placed the page with its fellows. 'Sorry, that was a bad one.'

'Yes, indeed, it was. Oh, here's a thing. "No burgess is to bake bread to sell except at our ovens." Never mind, no-one would have paid to eat your bread, Aggie.'

'I could get dragged into all this,' Aggie said. 'It's fascinating, isn't it? I mean, you are holding stuff in your hands – real stuff – that was held by your ancestors way back. My lot were digging up spuds in Ireland, I think. Never mind – we progressed to frying them.'

'You most certainly did.' Anna leaned back and watched the small girl leaving the room, spindly dog at her heels. Jeremy had claimed a real prize and Anna was glad for him. Marie, too, was promising, though Aggie was closer to home and easier to study. Yes, they would do well together, these two couples. What about Meredith?

Anna shook herself. 'Never mind the match-making, get on with your work.' She applied herself to the activities of reeves and courts, of landowners and tenants. In the kitchen, Aggie was murdering 'It's Only Make Believe', a song originally produced by someone with the name Conway Twitty. There were some stupid names around these days: Elvis, Buddy, the aforementioned Twitty. Aggie's singing was on a par with her bread, slightly overworked, assassinated by enthusiasm.

It was earplug time again. With the nonchalance of habit, Anna Chandler stuck two balls of cotton wool in her ears and rolled another cigarette. Yes, this was indeed a mad, mad world.

Polly was happier than she had ever been in her whole life. She was respected by tenants, who had begun to see her as one of them, by Jean, who admired her dogged efficiency, and, most importantly of all, by Polly Fishwick.

She stood in front of her mirror and adjusted her hat, a fake fur with a flat top and an upturned brim. It was warm and it suited her and she was ready to go off on her rounds. Eeh, if Derek could see her now, he wouldn't recognize her – good coat, decent boots, gloves. And she liked work. She hadn't expected to like it, but trudging along country lanes, visiting folk, writing lists of needs, collecting rents, drinking tea – she revelled in all these things. It was just a matter of confidence, and Henry Chandler had given her that, as had Jean, his daughter-in-law.

She popped next door to see the old man before setting off on her rounds. 'What the blazes are you doing now?'

He was standing on a chair and he did not flinch when she scolded him. 'I'm getting this book down off the top shelf,' he replied, 'and stop treating me like an infant, woman. I am having a good day, so let me be.'

She let him be. He was a funny old devil. Some days he was as weak as a kitten, then he would buck up and start his antics. When he was on terra firma, she spoke to him again. 'Anna's next door. If you need anything, shout for her, or pull the kitchen bell for Aggie.'

'Yes, Mother.' He stuck out his tongue.

'Keep that there,' she said, 'I've a stamp wants licking.' Then she set off on her journey.

She made her way through the village, watched children at play, noticed Christmas trees in windows. The schools had closed and the holidays had begun, excited voices raised in expectation, slides made in a thin layer of snow. It was wonderful to be alive.

She was halfway up the hill that led to Bankside Farm when she realized that she was being followed by a very shabby van. Thinking that she was impeding its progress on the narrow lane, she stepped aside to allow it to pass. But it stopped. She thought that her heart, too, would stop when she saw Richard Chandler stumbling from the driver's seat.

'What the hell are you up to?' she asked. 'You

shouldn't be driving, not in your condition.'

He managed to focus on her. She didn't look bad, but most people didn't look bad after a few whiskies. Even Freda Pilkington's skin looked almost decent after a couple of Johnnie Walkers. 'I want you to talk to her,' he said.

'Eh?'

'To Jean. Tell her I need some money. No, tell her I demand some money.'

Polly bridled. 'Tell her your bloody self.'

He thought about that, tried to remember why he was here, why he had followed this bloody woman in the first place. He was supposed to be anonymous, wasn't he? God, he was losing track of things – events were happening in the wrong order. It was not time to be here yet. To be where? Ah, yes, Chandlers Green – he wasn't supposed to arrive yet, because he didn't have a plan.

'I haven't got a plan,' he said.

'You haven't got a bloody brain, that's your problem,' she advised him. How on earth had she managed to fear such a man? One puff of wind and he would be laid out on the road – in spite of his weight, he was as weak as water. 'Get gone,' she ordered, her eyes fixed on the van's number plate. AWH 301, she noted in her head. 'I've work to do.'

He changed tack. 'I looked after you.'

'Aye, you did.' She knew that the edge of sarcasm would not cut through Chandler's drunken fog. 'And I looked after you. And you wanted me to spy. And your wife knows all that, so bugger off.' She swept past him and quickened her stride.

When she reached Bankside, the farmer and his good wife noticed that she was not quite with them, so they gave her extra tea with plenty of sugar. She wrote down her list in the usual fashion: point the north gable wall, replace a stable door, splice some good wood into the kitchen window frame. 'I'm not myself,' she explained before leaving.

The farmer's wife smiled. 'No, Pol, you're a damned sight better than your old self, God love you.'

She left the farm, hoping as she walked that God would, indeed, love her enough to get her home without meeting that bloody man again. He had disappeared as easily as this morning's fall of snow, had evaporated into the atmosphere, a ghost, not even a shadow. It was almost as if she had imagined the scene. But no. She wrote in the back of her note-book AWH 301 and made her way back to the grange.

Leena Martindale was preparing her table. There were still a few days to go, but she wanted to be on top of the job. Marie, who had taken a day off work, had helped her father to carry the kitchen table into the dining room and she was currently dressing a small tree on the sideboard. The main tree – a whopper – was positioned in the sitting room.

Leena counted up again. 'There's your dad and me, you and Peter, Aggie and Jeremy, Anna and old Henry, Jean, Bert and Elsie, Polly–'

'Our Colin and Meredith – that's fourteen.'

'I had it at thirteen at one point, Marie. But it's not going to be thirteen, because if Henry's too ill somebody will stay with him. I couldn't be doing with thirteen.' Leena did not walk under ladders, never put new shoes on a table, seldom left her house if the thirteenth of a month fell on a Friday. It was all rubbish, of course, but there was no point in tempting fate.

'Mam?'

'What?' Thank goodness the crockery had been easy to match – there was a lot to be said for plain white.

'There's a man in our back garden. He's just crouched himself down in the bushes over there, next to that old shed.' Marie pointed.

Leena joined her daughter. 'Where? I can't see anybody. Are you sure you weren't imagining things? With sun shining on frost, your eyes can play tricks.' Leena's heart had picked up pace, but she kept the fear from her voice.

'No, no, I'm sure. I wish that phone would come, Mam. What shall we do?'

'Nothing,' replied Leena. 'The doors are locked. We'll be all right.' There was movement out there – whoever was hiding seemed unsteady on his feet – or on his haunches – because the neglected vegetation was becoming agitated. 'Or shall we run up to the grange? Marie? Marie? Where do you think you're going?'

But Marie, poker in hand, was already out of the room.

'Marie!' Leena pursued her daughter into the jungle. 'Marie, stop where you are!' For once in her life, Leena regretted not having been tougher with her children. She had loved them, had reasoned with them, had tried to bring out their best. And the best of this one was currently striding along with a brass and iron poker. 'Don't hit anybody,' she screamed.

Marie pushed her way into the undergrowth. What

360

might have happened if she hadn't taken a day's holiday? Mam might have been burgled, attacked, hurt. Angrily, she parted the final curtain of bedraggled greenery, and there he was, bottle held in both hands, head tilted back as he poured the final dregs into his mouth.

Leena caught up with her daughter. 'Oh, it's you,' she said flatly. 'Mr Chandler. What can we do for you?'

He belched, then grinned. 'You can die,' he replied, the words slurred, 'and take your husband and your brats with you.'

Marie lowered her weapon. Peter's father. This filthy, drunken tramp was probably going to be her father-in-law. 'What is the matter with you?' she asked. Then she spoke to her mother. 'We should get the police.'

'Police?' he echoed. 'This is my land, my village, mine.' He struggled to his feet. 'All of it's mine. Handed down.' He waved his arms wildly. 'It's my right, my inheritance – not theirs.'

Marie turned to her mother. 'He looks like something that's fallen out of Yates's Wine Lodge on a Saturday night. Will you run to the phone box while I keep an eye on him?'

Leena shook her head. Jean Chandler had enough on her plate without the police coming to dig up this terrible man's past. He looked as if he had been living rough, too, clothes shabby, face covered in stubble, skin rather less than clean. She stepped forward. 'Right, you. I shall say this once and only once, so try and get a grip of it, will you? Bugger off.'

He blinked. 'What?'

'I said I'd say it just that once. My husband saved

361

your worthless life seventeen or eighteen years ago and what did you do? Tried to have him drummed out of the army, tried to ruin him. Well, you never shifted him then and you'll not shift him now. You'll shift none of us, because we are here to stay. This is our house. We haven't even got a mortgage. All right? So get lost. You are the one who deserves the dishonourable discharge, Mr Chandler.'

He carried on blinking slowly.

Marie knew that her mouth was wide open and she closed it quickly. So, her dad had saved Peter's dad's life. She had known for a while that the truth would be something of this nature, yet it was strangely hard to take in. Why would a man whose life had been saved turn on the one who had saved him? She framed the thought. 'Why do you hate my dad?'

Richard found his dry tongue. 'Cocky bastard.'

Marie nodded. 'Yes, but he has a wash and he doesn't run round drinking whisky in the middle of the day. You killed Nanny Foster.'

He reverted to his blinking.

'You killed her and you tried to kill your wife. We all know that. The whole village probably knows it,' she lied, 'so get gone while the going's good. Loads of people round here are after you – loads.' Lies were sometimes a necessity, she told herself determinedly.

Richard staggered back. There was a letter written by – what was her name? Foster – and she had left all her money to Jean . . .

'What are you waiting for?' asked Leena. 'The bus to town?'

He rallied. 'I have my own transport, thanks. You know . . .' He searched for words. 'I paid her. She was a servant, no more, and she never spent a penny piece of wages except on stockings and the like, then she left it all to . . . to whatsername.'

Leena whispered in her daughter's ear. 'He's on about Sally Foster. She left a packet to Jean, and he wants his money back.'

'There's no plan,' he wailed.

'Jesus,' snapped Marie. 'Look, just go away.' She pushed him towards a hole in the hedge. 'Go on, get out, and make sure you don't come back.'

He fixed his eyes on the two women, Martindale's women. Most of the troublesome creatures in his life were female. 'You will never know what hit you,' he said, before collapsing in a heap on the ground.

'Well, we all know what hit him,' muttered Leena. 'What must we do with him? He could die out here – it's mortallious cold.'

'I'm trying to worry about that,' replied Marie, 'but before we worry any more, let's go in and put some warm coats on – no use us getting as cold as he is.' They went inside, Leena muttering about alcohol dragging heat away from the skin and causing hypothermia.

When they returned to the garden, there was no sign of the intruder. Marie poked her head through the gap in the hedge and saw him staggering across the field towards the lane. She brought her head back into the garden. 'We must stop this gap,' she said. 'Now come on – we are going up to the grange.'

Leena shook her head in near disbelief. She had come to live up here for peace and quiet, but it was turning out to be a circus, what with comings and goings and folk falling over in other folk's back gardens. 'All right,' she agreed, 'I suppose we'd better tell Jean he's on the prowl.'

*   *   *

'Well, if it continues, we must get the police.' Jean
looked at all her companions and saw their concern.
Aggie and Marie, the girls chosen by her sons, sat
together at one side of the table with Leena; Anna,
Polly and Jean occupied the opposite side. 'I think it
may be time to tell the truth,' Jean concluded. 'We
cannot carry on feeling threatened in this way. If he
is going to follow Polly, if he is determined to damage
your family, Leena, we have to stop him. It is
happening not just at the grange now; he is spreading
his poison beyond this house. I could not forgive
myself if he hurt anyone else.'

Polly had related her tale about the van in the lane;
Marie and Leena had just finished giving an account
of the scene in the garden.

'But I must think about it first,' Jean went on.
'There are my children to consider, and now Aggie
and Marie–'

'Don't worry about us.' Aggie folded her arms.
'Marie and I can look after ourselves. You do what
you think is right. If they want to know why you
never said about the other things – Sally Foster and
all that – you can say you were afraid.'

'Sally left a letter.' Jean put her elbows on the table
and rested her chin on steepled fingers. 'She knew
she was badly hurt. Oh, God – can you imagine what
this will do to us? Newspapers and . . . I shall speak
to the children and Pa, too. But please, let us have
Christmas first. Life will be altered when we start the
business of getting him caught. Please, please, one
Christmas of peace – no Richard, no misery, no
police until the New Year.'

Leena nodded her agreement. 'And I don't want

Alf worried, either. We can do synchronized worrying after Christmas – how's that for a big word on a Monday, eh? And I shall come up here every day, if you don't mind, Jean. Until the phone's in, I shall feel safer.'

'Of course,' answered Jean. 'Aggie, put the kettle on, please. The twins and Meredith will be back shortly from their walk.'

'With Hero.' Aggie's voice was mournful. 'Hide everything that looks edible and don't talk to him – leave all that to me. He obeys me.' She rose to her feet. 'I'm a liar, but at least I make an effort.'

Not for the first time, Jean Chandler wondered why she had not fetched the police in the first place. There would be endless questions, Richard would be arrested, there would be press and neighbours and shame. But she had good friends. She looked at Polly. 'Go and tell Pa what has happened. And thank you – all of you – for your support.'

They drank tea, and when the boys and Meredith came back the whole tale was told once more. Hero, after performing two laps of honour around the room, collapsed in front of the fire while the stories got their second airing.

Anna, who had been unusually quiet so far, joined the discussion, leaving Polly to look after Henry. She agreed wholeheartedly with Jean's decision – her nephew had taken several steps too far and he needed to be stopped. Yes, they would have their Christmas first, but as soon as the holiday season was over, Richard would be dealt with.

To Anna, her sadness seemed bottomless, as did Richard's capacity to do harm. Yes, she was a Chandler, and yes, she took a strange pride in the fact that she could trace her ancestry – however tainted – back to the thirteenth century. Now, however, no matter what the outcome, this ancient family had to face the courts once more; and this time it would not be a simple matter of a twelve-pence fine instigated by Reeve Silas Morton in a local assizes. This time, it might involve twelve good men and true, because the charge could well be murder.

The world was in a constant state of flux. There were trees where there had been none, bends in roads had honed their sharpness, lamp-posts had been breeding in the night.

Richard Chandler narrowed his eyes against a low-hanging winter sun. Driving at under twenty miles per hour, he made his unsure way back to Halliwell Road. If all the other dozy beggars on the road would shape up, he could be home in a few minutes. Home? He sneered. He had just been home, hadn't he?

Chronology was becoming a problem; days melded together, the events of one period slipping backwards or forwards in an order that seemed random. Often, he set off for one place and ended up somewhere else – hadn't he followed that big woman today? Pol? Strangely, the only place in which he felt tidy and safe was the grubby little house towards which he now drove. Plan. He had to make a plan. She would be there – the one whose presence made him feel better . . .

Freda. Yes, that was her name. Freda had become a necessity. She asked very few questions and she liked a drink in the evenings. He got breakfast, dinner and tea – as she termed his meals – and he was seldom alone. Freda was there when he woke, cup of tea,

366

boiled egg, slice of toast and the daily newspaper; she was there with his other meals and she was cheerful enough. He paid for all the food, she cooked it, they both ate it, so for four pounds a week she tidied up a bit and cleaned his clothes.

She did Saturdays, Sundays, high days, holy days and midnights if required. Richard had met his match, because, once dusk fell, she drank almost as much as he did – and he paid for that, too. Still, at least he had company, someone who sat with him; the fragrant one with her ponytails and make-up was a thing of the past.

He parked in a more or less parallel fashion outside the house, opened the van's door, cursed when a bus almost removed it. Climbing from the driver's seat, he steadied himself against the bonnet before making his way into the house. She was there – he could smell some sort of stew cooking.

Freda, more content than she had been in ages, put her head round the kitchen door. 'Get yourself a drink, love. I've left the bottle and a glass on the fireplace.' She was not a daytime drinker, but she accepted that men were different, that they drank whenever they wanted to.

He sat down. At least she understood him. Freda didn't go flapping about every time he looked at her wrong; with Jean, a man would have needed to tread on eggshells in order not to upset her. She was too frail for a real man, a proper man.

Freda appeared again. 'I've stewed a bit of steak, Richard, and I'll just bob down to the chippy for some mushy peas. The spuds are nearly done. I could open a tin of marrowfats, but that new chippy does a grand job with peas. I won't be long – you have a little rest.'

That was the other thing about Freda – she knew her place. Although she used his Christian name, she treated him with respect and she talked about matters mundane, chattering away for hours about the price of fish on Ashburner Street market, about nylon stockings and boiled ham on the bone. She was what Richard's father might term a 'witterer', but Freda wittered in a way that was strangely comforting.

She let herself out onto the pavement, cardigan gathered against her puny chest. The wind was bitter today, a harbinger of Christmas. Christmas, yes. She would bring her little silver tree into Richard's house and would eat with him on Christmas Day. They could have wine. She had a couple of wineglasses somewhere in a cupboard at home.

Turners' was not too bad – just four people in the queue. 'I only want peas,' she announced, 'if nobody minds – two lots, please.'

Mag Turner doled out the peas. She and her husband were new to Halliwell Road, having opened this, their third shop, only weeks earlier. The other two shops were in the capable hands of staff, but Mag and Jim wanted to nurse this one through its first few weeks. 'There you go.' She passed the package to Freda, then rooted for change in the till. 'You still working for that man – him four doors up from here?'

'I am,' replied Freda.

'He's just come home in a terrible state.' Mag had dropped her voice, and with a sideways movement of her head she beckoned Freda to the quiet end of the counter. 'A double-decker had to swerve – I've never seen a man drive so badly,' she whispered. 'He'll be causing accidents, next news, I'm sure. Any road, the police'll be catching up with him if he doesn't shape. Is he a heavy drinker?'

Freda pulled herself to full height. Strangely, she felt bound to defend her employer. 'No more than most,' she replied. 'I treat people the way they treat me, and he's all right. I mean, he likes a drop, but most of them do, don't they? My Eric, rest him, used to come home in some states when Bolton lost a game.'

'Who is he?' asked Mag. 'Only I'm told he's new round here – a bit like us, really. We've not long taken this shop.'

'And thank God you did,' replied Freda, 'because them there Arkwrights used rancid fat. His name's Richard Chandler, the bloke I look after.'

Mag tried to conceal her reaction. 'From Chandlers Green?' she asked, her voice as controlled as was possible. 'Up the moors? Them that used to make candles in the olden days?'

'I think so, yes.'

'Well, fancy that.' Mag shook her head. 'Bit of a comedown for him, isn't it? Round here, I mean. They own farms and all sorts, that family – from what I've heard, like.'

Freda caught the edge of a memory and she clapped a hand to her forehead. 'Ooh,' she exclaimed. 'Don't tell anybody, will you? See, he only told me a couple of days ago – he's what they call in dispute over land.' She mouthed the rest. 'He wants to be incognito till all the legal bits get sorted out with this here dispute.'

He was in dispute, all right. According to Mag Turner's daughter, Aggie, the chap was in dispute right up to his eyeballs, much of it 70 per cent proof. As soon as Freda and the peas were off the premises,

Mag went through to the back of the shop. It was time to phone their Aggie, so she could inform Chandler's wife of his whereabouts.

As she picked up the phone, Mag shook her head in near despair. Aggie would have been safer in fish and chips – you knew where you were with fish and chips. You cooked them, wrapped them, sold them, paid your bills and slept the sleep of the just at the end of the day. Their Aggie, God help her, was housekeeper in what sounded like a madhouse – and she was talking about getting engaged to Chandler's son.

Jim put his head round the door. 'I need more fish, love.'

'Give me a minute.' Yes, she had fish bigger than cod to fry first. Aggie had said something about Mrs Chandler's not knowing where her husband was. Well, she would know any minute now, that was certain sure.

Jim was back. 'What's up, love?'

She beckoned him. 'That woman's just told me – our Aggie's boyfriend's dad is that drunken bugger four doors up. I'm phoning her.'

Jim picked up the fish. 'She should have stopped at home. She knew where she was with us, our Aggie. Fetch some more vinegar when you're done, Mag.'

Mag clutched the phone. She didn't know why, but she suddenly felt uncomfortable about this new shop, as if the whole thing had been spoilt. Oh, she was being stupid, wasn't she? He was just another drunk and she would tell his wife to come and sort him out.

Aggie replaced the receiver, then stood where she was, head down, deep in thought. Well, she knew where he was, and soon Anna would know too. It was funny how she always ran to the old woman when she had a problem or something important to say. Anna was . . . she was what Aggie termed dead ordinary – no side to her, none of that landed gentry rubbish. The whole family was like that, she supposed, but Anna's eccentricity and quirky brain appealed greatly to Aggie.

Polly joined her. 'You all right, girl? Not bad news, I hope.'

'No, no, I'm fine. It's just . . . where's Anna?'

'Writing her book.' There was a gloomy edge to Polly's tone. 'She's lost somebody called Richard Cromwell, so the room's in a worse state than ever. Last time I looked in, she was muttering under her breath, summat about Parliamentarians never being trustworthy. And her stockings are laddered again.'

'I'll go and help her,' said Aggie.

Anna was seated centre stage, piles of manuscripts around her feet. 'Don't bring your dog in here,' she ordered, 'I have mislaid–'

'–Richard Cromwell – I know. Is he in the bottom drawer where you keep your notes?' Aggie closed the door.

'I've looked.' Anna sat back and lit a cigarette. 'Anyway, he isn't a note, he's a small book. Very sneaky, these Cromwells. I prefer the monarchy – easier to keep up with. What's troubling you?'

Aggie imparted her news. 'And Mam says he is going to kill somebody when he drives drunk. Anyway, that's where he is, and this Freda woman is looking after him. She drinks, too, according to my mother. She's an amazing woman, is Mam – she can find out all about a person in about ten seconds flat.

So, if you think Mrs Chandler should know, I'll tell her – or you can, if you like.'

Anna drew hard on her cigarette and sat back in her chair. 'Safer to know where he is, I suppose. I'll do it. Aren't you going out today?'

'Yes.' The younger woman felt the heat in her cheeks. 'We're all going – all four of us. Meredith may come, and we might meet Josie in town afterwards.'

'Quite a party, then.'

'Yes.' Aggie sat down. 'You don't think we're being a bit previous, do you? I mean, what does Mrs Chandler really think?'

Anna smiled. 'If her children are happy, she is happy. Enjoy yourself, Agnes. Jeremy says you are to be Agnes from now on.'

'I know. Mind, he calls me Trouble.'

'A trouble he is delighted to endure. Agnes, go and enjoy yourselves, all of you. Life is terribly short – I know that sounds trite now, but it is only too true. He adores you and Peter loves Marie. Make the most of each other.'

'And you will tell Mrs Chandler for me? About him, I mean.'

'Of course. Go and prepare yourself for an important day. The rest of us will celebrate with you at Christmas.'

When Aggie had left, Anna spotted something lurking beneath the bureau. Ah, there he was. On hands and knees, she went forth to drag Richard Cromwell back into the land of the not-quite-living. 'You're not getting away as easily as that,' she informed the slim volume. 'Bloody Puritans. All the same; all wind and water.' Then she set about the business of accounting for the movements of her

372

family in the year of Our Lord 1658, when the afore-mentioned Roundhead had become Protector of this green and pleasant land.

She would talk to Jean in a few minutes . . .

Meredith was not finding her journey easy. The decision to stop drinking had not been hard, because common sense had dictated it; but keeping a promise made to herself was a different matter altogether. A promise made to others was easily honoured, because others became one's conscience, and while she had sworn to family and friends that she would never take another drop, the difficulty lay within herself and the vow she had made to Meredith Elaine Chandler. She was the scene of a huge conflict; she was also both armies. Sometimes, it felt as if the Battle of Hastings was taking place within her belly, lances, horses, arrows and all.

She became very active, almost manic in her preparations for Christmas, in the planning of New Chandlers, for the imminent engagements of her two brothers. The faster she ran, the more desperate became her need for a drink, so life became a circle, a running away from and towards all at the same time. And everything had to be kept away from Mother; Mother had enough on her plate. And now Meredith knew where her father was.

She walked away from the bright blue door, looked back, saw flaking paint and brickwork in dire need of pointing, accepted that there was no-one at home. The van described by Polly Fishwick was not parked outside; this meant that Richard Chandler, possibly in his cups, was out and about with a killer weapon at his disposal. A car was not just a means of transport; in the wrong hands, a petrol-driven vehicle was an unexploded bomb, a guided missile which, if its master failed to hold rein on its path, was capable of killing many.

What to do? She tapped a foot on the pavement, looked at her watch, decided that it was time for her to leave this place. Perhaps Mother was right; perhaps this should all wait until after Christmas. And what might she have said to him – what new aspect had arisen? None. It would have been the same old ground – 'I am an alcoholic and I know how you feel' – and what use was that?

In times such as this, times of indecision and defeat, the urge to run to the sherry bottle was gargantuan. 'One day at a time,' she whispered as she walked away. She would conquer this. One day at a time, she would get there.

'Are you sure?' Marie clung to Peter's arm. 'It's such a big change for you. Look what you've been used to.'

He tutted. 'Yes, look what I have been used to. I am the son of a loveless marriage, my mother is damaged to the point of nerve tablets, my sister is fighting the demon drink, Grandfather has been down the same road, my father is rampaging about in a rusting van – why should I not move? Jeremy will be up there, as will Meredith – I am not needed. And, if I get a place at Manchester, your house is so much nearer to the station.'

'And everyone will think we had to get married.' She blushed.

'They can think what they wish to think. Your priest knows the truth, anyway, so to hell with them all.' He looked at his watch. 'Come on, let's go inside

374

– Jeremy and Aggie should be here soon. And I must ask you the same question – are you sure?'

Marie Martindale had never been more sure of anything in her short life. This was the man for whom she would have travelled to the moon and back. They were going to have a joint engagement and a joint party to celebrate the same. Weddings would be separate – she and Peter were to be married in March, Aggie and Jeremy had yet to fix the date. 'Of course I am sure. I love you. I can't imagine a world without you in it and I don't want to.'

He kissed her nose and led her into Preston's jeweller's. The rings, which were being sized, would be ready today. Aggie was to have a ruby to reflect what Jeremy called her fire; Marie had chosen a Ceylon sapphire of palest blue ringed by ten tiny diamonds. Later, Meredith and Josie were supposed to join them at the coffee bar. For the sake of the twins' sister, the four had decided to postpone the usual champagne celebration.

Aggie and Jeremy came into the shop. The little girl sighed with delight when she tried on the ring, an oval ruby flanked by two white diamonds. 'I'm going to cry,' she moaned.

'God help us,' quipped her fiancé, 'we need to get out of here before the flood.'

Two happy couples walked the length of Deansgate, laughing, talking, enjoying their day.

Across the road, a man watched them, his vision blurred by drink. He still recognized the Martindale girl – he could almost smell the enemy. She was with one of his sons and they had just come out of Preston's jewellery shop. Fury rose in his gorge and he retched unproductively into the gutter. 'Over my dead body,' he muttered when he had righted himself.

Unaware of their witness, Peter, Marie, Jeremy and Aggie moved on towards the coffee bar. Nothing could touch them today, because they were outright owners of this island of happiness.

FOURTEEN

'We can just leave it outside the house,' argued Aggie. 'It's Christmas, for goodness' sake. And it's only a tin of ham and a few bits.'

Jeremy looked at the few bits. 'Have you been talking to Jesus on the quiet, Agnes? Because this looks like the feeding of the five thousand all over again. We don't even know who he is – and I'm sure we should have told Mother and Polly that he's living in Woodside Cottage.'

'It's Christmas,' she repeated.

Jeremy accounted for Aggie's 'few bits'. 'Ham, mince pies, a Christmas pudding, nuts, cakes, pasties, home-made biscuits – I hope he has good teeth – sausage rolls, bacon, eggs, bread, butter, marmalade, milk, tea, scones, jam, chocolate, whipped cream, sugar – what on earth are you up to?'

But Aggie had romantic notions about the tramp in Woodside Cottage. On the day of his discovery, she and Jeremy had found each other. It was all a part of that great panorama known as karma. 'What do you mean by good teeth? There's nothing wrong with my biscuits.'

'Try telling that to the dentist.'

It was as if the tramp had been a part of the magic, but Aggie couldn't work out how, or why. All she knew was that her life had changed minutes after the chap had appeared in that untidy front garden. 'He's a catalyst,' she said.

'I thought he looked English,' replied Jeremy, though he was silenced when a tea cloth was whipped across his head. 'All right, you win. But you're encouraging him – and don't tell me again about Christmas. What if he isn't there? That basket of yours might attract rats.'

She sighed dramatically. 'Yes, I do tend to be a magnet for rodents, don't I?' It was her turn to duck the mock blows.

Leena Martindale wandered in, her face a picture of concentration. So deep was her reverie that she walked right past the young couple and picked up one of Sally Foster's recipe books from the mantelpiece. She flicked a few pages, found the right one, announced to the room, 'Well, mine didn't turn out like that,' then walked out again.

Jeremy shook his head. 'Do you ever wonder about the fourth dimension, Agnes? I mean, are we really here, or are we a circle within a circle? Are they on a different plane with an alternative timescale?'

'I'll just put a few after-dinner mints in,' replied Agnes.

Jeremy, realizing that he occupied a dimension all his own, laughed out loud, then went to fetch coats. He was in serious danger of becoming contented, because Agnes matched him joke for joke, blow for

378

blow – she was the ideal companion. Josie he scarcely thought about. She had drifted into the small engagement party, had looked elegant, distant and totally uninterested. She was leaving her heartbroken family and a Marks and Spencer that would probably manage without her, was due in London by mid-January. Josie would make someone an excellent display wife, something to put on a shelf alongside golfing trophies. He brought the coats, picked up the basket and followed his fiancée into the woods. Aggie was certainly too real to be a trophy . . .

Anna stared at them through her window. She had made good progress and was almost ready for the Hanoverians. As far as she knew, George the First had spoken scarcely a word of English, so Walpole must have had his work cut out when it came to explaining the system – it was a bit like Anna trying to decipher the scribblings of a long line of alcoholics. What were those two doing?

She pulled the curtain aside, watched Jeremy struggling with an enormous basket, Aggie skipping along next to him. A picnic a couple of days before Christmas? Fair enough. As long as people did not mind frozen extremities, let them get on with it was Anna Chandler's motto.

Henry entered, pen in one hand, crossword in the other. 'Four down,' he announced, 'the discussion's salvation, twelve letters.'

'Conservation,' she answered automatically. 'It's an anagram of conversation.'

He filled in the word, looked over Anna's shoulder and through the window. 'Good to see those boys happy,' he remarked, 'and as for that young madam, well, I like her. What is she up to now? A picnic in the snow? I hope they're wearing woolly vests.'

'I find myself at odds with George the First.'

'What do you expect?' Henry laughed. 'He was a bloody Kraut.' He ambled back into his own quarters, was replaced by Polly.

'She's gone looking for him,' said the new arrival. There was no need for her to identify the 'she' or the 'him'. 'She can't settle. Peter's taken her. Sometimes, you know, people meet trouble halfway and—' She stopped in her tracks. 'Is that Aggie and your Jeremy?' She pointed towards the figures in the distance.

'It is indeed, Polly.'

'In December? With a picnic basket?'

'They march to their own drummer,' mused Anna.

'They march to their own bloody deaths in this weather.' Polly left; it was time to cajole the old man into his purpose-built ground-floor bathroom.

Anna returned to the commencement of the Hanoverian dynasty and Katherine Chandler, whose husband had died in a riding accident shortly after the birth of her one and only son. Katherine had grabbed the reins, had kept the accounts in good order and was easy to transcribe. So the Hanoverians had made Anna's life slightly easier after all, and, for that, she was inordinately grateful.

Jean Chandler recognized that the path through depression was not an easy one and that there were no maps to help her on her way. The pills took the edge off life, but she needed to climb back into reality, wanted to face her demons. Like a novel, life was something to be written by one person, and it was time for her to make her own marks. 'Next

380

chapter,' she muttered as she stared through the windscreen.

'Denouement,' agreed her son. Like his mother, he needed to see in order to believe. 'I just cannot imagine him living here.'

'You plan to live somewhere very similar.'

'Yes, but I shall come home for a bath,' came the reply. 'I believe he does have a bathroom, though – Aggie's mother says there is one tacked on at the back of the house.'

Jean placed a hand on the arm of her beloved son. He was so precious and now, at last, so sure of himself. One student's application had been withdrawn and Peter had been awarded the place in the veterinary department at Manchester; at the beginning of October next, Peter would be an undergraduate. 'He wanted you both to go to university,' she said, 'but he will not be with us when you go. At least, I hope he won't.'

'I have no need to become the feather in his cap,' said Peter. He fixed his gaze on the tawdry front door, bright blue and with the number hand-painted in black. 'There's that woman again.' Two pairs of eyes marked the progress of Freda Pilkington as she walked, basket on arm, towards the shops. 'She isn't exactly a sight for sore eyes, is she?'

Jean laughed. 'No, but neither was poor Polly. She will be dependent on him – that is the only qualification she needs. Your father wrote his own set of commandments, Peter, and "Thou shalt obey thy lord and master at all times" is the first. Do you hate your father? Does Jeremy?'

Peter considered the question before answering. 'Hatred is, perhaps, too strong a word. We certainly

381

feared him. Jeremy was stronger than I was, and Meredith was the strongest of all.' But even Meredith was paying the price. Sometimes, Peter looked at her and saw the pain when she refused a glass of wine. He crossed his fingers – Meredith *had* to be all right.

'I feared him,' said Jean now. 'Sally did not and she was the one who paid the highest price. My conscience has pricked, but we shall have him arrested after Christmas. It has to be done. I just hope it will not be detrimental to anyone's progress. Jeremy will be going into the business, you will be married soon . . . oh, God. What is the right thing?'

'The eternal question, Mother. The answer is that there is no answer. But he should pay for what he has done – and for what he continues to do. Marie's mother is lucky to be alive, because the TB was bad in both lungs. Now she lives at our house for much of the time – and why? Because of him. If prison is the only way, it must be the solution.'

Jean sighed. 'Yes – prison, or one of us becomes a murderer. Not a great deal of choice, what?'

'Very true. As I just said, the answer is no answer.'

The blue door moved inward and Jean crouched down in her seat as her husband stepped out of his house. Unsteady on his feet, he waited to cross the road.

'Going to that pub, I imagine,' said Peter.

'And she will have gone for their lunch,' answered Jean. 'I expect even your father will be eating in on Christmas Day – she will probably provide for him. Look at him, Peter. He can scarcely walk. According to Dr Beddows, Richard's nerve endings are no longer as sensitive as they should be. He is destroying himself.'

Peter agreed. 'Yes, but he must not be allowed to

382

take others with him, Mother. So. What now? Shall we go home?'

Jean pulled a piece of paper from a pocket. 'Belt and braces, Peter,' she said. 'I don't know how much this is going to cost, but I should feel a great deal safer if he were watched. Damned nuisance, as we need every penny for the business, but this has to be done. I cannot have Leena Martindale becoming ill again. She is terrified, you know. And he hates that family with an extraordinary passion.'

'Because Marie's father saved his life. We know all about it now. I agree. He cannot be allowed to do any further damage. So, where do we go?'

'Great Moor Street,' she replied. 'Let's see what can be done to clip his wings.'

Jeremy was glad to be rid of his burden. After depositing it on the step outside Woodside Cottage, he straightened, a hand pushed into the small of his back. 'You are making an old man of me,' he moaned.

Aggie put a finger to her lips and beckoned. Together, the pair dashed off and hid behind a clump of bushes. They saw the door opening, watched the man as he stooped to pick up his bounty. 'He's smiling,' Aggie whispered.

'So he should,' came the reply. 'He has enough food there to see him through several weeks. I wonder where he came from?'

Aggie shrugged. 'Well, Jesus was homeless at Christmas, wasn't he? And the three wise men came bearing gifts on Twelfth Night. We are wise men.'

'And he is no baby in a manger.'

She glared at him. 'We are all babies inside. Stop

383

your nit-picking. We have done a good deed. He might be in for a lonely Christmas, but at least he'll have a full stomach.'

The man carried his basket into the cottage and closed the door. Aggie sighed contentedly. 'That's a few weeks less in Purgatory.'

Jeremy shook his head in mock despair. 'Peter's taking instruction – any children of theirs will be raised as Catholics. Will you want the same?'

She clouted his arm none too gently. 'This is a hard world, Jer, but let's not make it any more difficult. No child of mine is going to be disgraced because he went for a walk instead of to church. I'm not joking.'

'I can see that.' He rubbed his arm. 'So, what do we do?'

'Register office,' was the swift response. 'My Irish ancestors will spin so fast in their graves that the earth's orbit could change. No. I'm not having my kids kneeling for hours on end at the feet of the Immaculate Conception just because they've eaten a sweet during religious education. Nuns and priests are cruel. People turn out paranoid.'

'You've made your decision,' he said.

'I have,' she agreed. 'I am a marked woman because I was an injured child. I've already worn out two missals and a rosary. It's not for me and it's not for my kids. Come on, let's get back. I am freezing.'

'I can warm you up,' he offered.

Her cheeks, already coloured by the cold, became brighter. 'You're a good hot-water bottle,' she answered, 'so save it for tonight.' Temptation had got the better of her, and she felt no guilt at all. The more she thought about things, the clearer it became that she was no Catholic.

The man stood back in the cottage kitchen, far enough from the window to be sure that he was not seen. There they went, the bringers of gifts. He had never spoken to them, but he was grateful for them today. At something of a hiatus in his own life, he was pleased that the young couple had thought of him. But he had plans of his own; today, he was to start in a new job.

He let himself out, locked the back door and pocketed the key. From behind a hedge, he grabbed his moped and wheeled it well out of earshot before mounting it and kicking the mechanism to life. If things went to plan, he would soon be able to pay rent on a place of his own. All the same, he was thankful for that box of goodies and he would not forget the kind donors.

Meredith lingered in the middle of a cold and empty space. Her life was rather cold and empty, but she had no intention of filling it from a sherry bottle. This was her future. Spider webs decorated corners, and an old desk, one injured leg shorter than the other three, leaned for support against a window sill.

This was to be the shop. Next door, in a larger building, the factory would be installed. New fire regulations meant some extra expenditure, but, as Anna had pointed out, the fire station was just doors away. God forbid that the place should go up in smoke . . . She shivered. Would he? Could he? Fearing one's own father was a terrible thing . . .

She went upstairs and tried to imagine how it would look, a series of glass cases, some fastened to walls, others on pedestals, a chamber of horrors in a deliberately dark corner. These wax figures would be moulded, but their exteriors would need to be hand finished. From the ceilings of both storeys, real chandeliers would be suspended, pulleys allowing height adjustment and easy access so that spent candles could be replaced. 'We shall be employing people,' she told the emptiness, 'and that has to be a good thing.'

Downstairs once more, she sat on the window ledge and rested a sketchbook on the wonky desk. She pencilled in a craft area, a huge candle-display counter, bookshelves and an area where paintings would be displayed, many of them produced by her younger brother's mother-in-law. Would Meredith marry? Did it matter? Did she want to pass along the faulty gene that carried alcoholism?

Oh, she would meet somebody and all that would be forgotten; both her twin brothers had run head-long into love and it would happen to her eventually, of course it would. Aggie and Jeremy were going to remain at the grange, before and after marriage. Peter would be leaving soon; there was no reason on earth why Meredith should continue to live at home. Yet a terrible foreboding sat deep in her core, a feeling that all was not yet resolved. Meredith would stay with Mother until Mother no longer needed her.

Right. She required carpenters, painters, a glazier to replace some broken panes. Floors wanted rubbing down and staining – plain boards would be best, she thought. Walls should be green, but a dullish colour, possibly moss, but paler than moss. Or pale blue – that was a good background, a greyish sort of blue. The chandeliers would be bold and plain, possibly in wrought iron. And, of course, the shop must carry candlesticks in all shapes, sizes and materials from silver plate to glass.

Anna's book should be centre stage. As always, Meredith found herself smiling when she thought of Anna. What a character she was. When Father had shut Grandfather upstairs, Anna had clattered about the house for days on end, then, when her delinquency had borne no fruit, the old lady had shifted herself to the gatehouse. According to Anna, one got a great deal more sense out of bees, hens and geese than was obtainable from the human animal.

Peter and Mother had gone up Halliwell Road to make sure that Father was still there. 'Then, she will have him watched,' she mused aloud. How could anyone watch anyone properly? Who would be there during the hours of darkness? Would a private detective work through Christmas and New Year?

Meredith closed the sketchbook, looked at her watch and decided it was time to go home. Christmas was to be spent at Claughton Cottage, but there were things to be done, gifts to wrap, cards to prepare. This was a time for rejoicing, a time when Anna and her swivelling hat would be very much present at church services, when choirs would sing and children would shout with joy.

However, while she locked the door of her new business, she felt the chill of winter as it whipped through layers of clothing to touch her very bones. Deeper than that, an extra coldness bruised her soul. He was still out there somewhere. And while her own father was at large, Meredith Chandler could never feel settled.

He gazed into his third double Scotch, wondered how the hell he was going to make sure that his son did not become involved with the Martindale girl. Which son? He had always had difficulty separating the two, and both had come out of Preston's. Another swig helped him to concentrate. Preston's, the best jeweller's in the north – what had he bought there all those years ago? Ah, yes, the fragrant one's engagement and wedding rings. 'Three diamonds on a twist and a plain gold band,' he muttered.

'What?' asked an old man who was passing Richard's table. Richard glared at him. 'There's no talking to some folk,' spat the grey-haired drinker as he staggered onwards. 'Don't know why they bother coming in if they don't want to speak to other people . . .' His voice faded as he crossed the room.

Richard watched the stumbling figure; he was looking at himself as he would be in a few years. Did he have a few years? Those little white tablets were becoming increasingly important; the pain in chest and arm was now a frequent visitor, a companion, almost.

He could remember things from years ago – like the plain gold band, the very band that had tightened around his own throat – but yesterday, today, last week – these were all melding together like a blob of mixed Plasticine, colours gone, faded and combined to a dirty brown. Forty-five was not old, yet his mind was playing tricks on him. Sometimes he had difficulty remembering where he had parked his own van. But he always managed to get home, that was the main thing. Freda was his home; Freda and her stupid, monotonous chatter, the wittering that had become a lullaby, now represented his one and only anchor, his safe mooring when storms brewed.

He would have to ration the drink for a while,

because he had things to do, plans to make. There was stuff in the grange – stuff he had bought and paid for, much of which was valuable. There was madam's jewellery for a start, and a few paintings small enough to be portable and of a worth sufficient to double his bank balance. He would be taking things that already belonged to him, so it would be no crime.

'Richard?'

He looked up. She was a decent, warm-hearted woman and he was probably late for a meal again. 'A drink?' he asked.

'Too early for me, love. You finish that and come home. I only nipped across to tell you the dinner's ready – I've done a nice Lancashire hotpot and a treacle tart for afters. Come when you're ready.' She left him where he was. Now, that was a woman who knew her place. She catered, cleaned and wittered. He should have chosen better in the first place. When his glass was empty, he made his way back to a coal fire, a decent meal and the company of a good woman.

It was in the *Bolton Evening News*, a middle-page spread, the whole caboodle, photographs, interviews, a lengthy editorial piece about the proposed New Chandlers.

Richard Chandler, who felt as if all air had left his lungs, knew that the pain would begin any second. He slipped a tiny white tablet under his tongue in an effort to nip the episode in the bud, but the agony won. He leaned back in his chair and waited for the terror to pass. It was too late and he knew it; he could not change his lifestyle and the required operation would not work unless he did. So he lived with it and waited for the living to end. And, by Christ, his family worked hard at bringing that end closer.

When he was relatively composed, he returned to his reading. There was a large photograph taken in the hall at the grange, Henry in the centre, Jean standing behind him, a caring hand resting on his shoulder. She was flanked by the rest of them – Jeremy and the housekeeper, who was now announced as his fiancée, Peter with the Martindale girl – their engagement, too, was declared here. Polly was in the photograph, as were Anna and Meredith, and they looked so contented, so happy about their own cleverness. 'I *am* Chandler,' he declared to the empty room. How dared they do this? Did they expect him to sit here and accept it with good grace?

The factory-cum-shop would be behind the fire station, on the corner where St Edmund Street met St Helena Road. There was a picture of ruins, remnants of the old factory in the village, then underneath a smaller headline – THE CHANDLERS ARE COMING TO TOWN – were interviews. Anna had much to say about her book and about the family's founders who could be traced right back to Bolton's original charter.

The fragrant one had spoken. *My son, Jeremy, will be at the helm of the factory and Meredith, Anna and I will run the shop. Peter, Jeremy's twin, will be studying veterinary science at Manchester University, but he is to be married in March and his wife, now Marie Martindale, will help to run the business.*

So, one of them would have a degree. No Chandler thus far had enjoyed higher education and Richard's single goal had been to see his sons graduate – that would have been testament to him, to his achievements. But no. Only after he had left did one of them announce his intention to attend university.

When questioned about her husband, Jean Chandler's answer had been simple. *He will not be involved.* Five words. 'He will not be involved?' He tossed the paper to the floor, and there they sat, all in a row, staring up at him from the rug. There was no escape. He picked up the damned thing and read more about the new business, what it would manufacture, what it would sell.

There followed a chatty little piece about Christmas and about Marie Martindale's family, who would be hosting this year's event at Claughton Cottage. *This will be a pleasant way of marking the engagements of my sons,* the fragrant one had told the reporter, *and we can take this opportunity to rejoice at the arrival in the village of the Martindale family.* She looked good, too, hair done, clothes smart, make-up toned down.

'He will not be involved,' he repeated, more quietly now.

Thus he had been dismissed by the woman who had married him, by the father who had sired him and by the daughter and sons who offered him no respect. He would not be dismissed. He refused to be a mere bystander while his family plotted against him. Oh, Jean had hidden her cleverness so well; here she was now in black and white for all the world to see, the mother of three Chandlers and the wife of no-one. This was to be his punishment.

He must not rage. Rage brought the pain and the pain would be the death of him. How could a man so weakened defend himself? As a cheap clock marked

391

the passing seconds, its sounds hollow and without purpose, he tried to pull together the remnants of his resolve. There was one last job to be done before he died: he would burgle his own home. He knew the old place's weaknesses and its strengths and he would need no keys to gain entry. Was burglary enough?

Paraffin was stored in the old stable block; the fabric of Chandlers Grange, most of it completed by the middle of the eighteenth century, was dry enough to burn like a November bonfire.

Oh, yes, Richard Chandler would celebrate this Christmas in his own special way. He gazed around his small living room, looked at the tawdry little tinsel tree, so carefully and gaudily dressed by Freda. Next to it stood two Christmas cards, one from her to him, one from him to her. The paltry show hurt, because he remembered Christmas at the grange: a massive tree in the hall, log fires, mulled wine, carol singers at the door. Damn them, that was his home, his Christmas, his right.

Freda would be disappointed. Lonely for many years, she was like an excited child, but it could not be helped. She would be here soon and he would tell her that he had received an invitation from old friends. He turned the newspaper over, hoped that she would not read it. Because from this moment, he would need to be extraordinarily careful. The whisky – well, he would manage on half a bottle a day for the time being. The clock ticked and he dozed while waiting for her to come. He would give her a bonus, an extra fiver for her trouble. His conscience salved, he slept the sleep of a man whose anger was just, whose rights would soon be asserted in one final coup.

*   *   *

Christmas Day dawned bright and cold, just a thin frost reflecting the sun's rays from lawn and evergreen foliage. Meredith yawned, stretched, pulled on her hooded dressing gown. She was beginning to feel clean and in charge of herself, was even managing not to worry about wines at the table, because she accepted the fact that she could never partake.

A child again, she prepared to go downstairs for the opening of the presents. This always took place in the hall; gifts were stacked under the huge tree, a fire would burn bright in the grate. As she was probably the first up, she would have the privilege of lighting that fire; she had helped Aggie prepare it the night before.

For a few moments, she lingered at her window and breathed in the beauty of this special day. She remembered last Christmas, overshadowed by Father and his excesses, Mother cowed and quiet, Sally holding together the remains of this family. Great-Aunt Anna had come for Christmas lunch and Grandfather had been locked upstairs. 'Evil,' she reminded herself. 'Remember, he is evil.' There was still a small corner of her soul that felt sympathy for her alcoholic parent, but she urged herself to stop thinking about him. He was gone and Mother was all the better for it.

He was with a woman, or so Aggie had said. In his house, just four along from Turners' Fish and Chips, he would be eating his festive meal with a peroxide blonde. 'Why couldn't you have been different?' She dashed a disobedient tear from her cheek. 'Why couldn't you fight this? For the sake of your children, you should have overcome the demons.'

A robin twittered and fussed in a nearby tree.

Fierce little creatures, robins. They fought and died or they fought and survived – it was inbuilt, it was what they were. 'Father is what he is.' Should she have visited him with a gift and a kind word? No, it would not have done the slightest amount of good.

She opened her door, closed it again quietly when she saw Aggie leaving Jeremy's room. The whole household knew what was going on, of that Meredith was certain, but no-one seemed to mind. Mother had never seemed so relaxed, yet sometimes, when Meredith caught her off guard, she saw suffering in Jean Chandler's eyes. The suffering must be remembered. There was a sense of waiting, as if the wonderful world now occupied by the Chandler family was temporary and precious, because he was still out there . . .

Mother was already up and the hall fire was blazing healthily when Meredith greeted her. Aggie, yawning and happy, slid down the banisters. 'Sorry,' she said to Jean, 'but I promised myself I would do that on Christmas Day.' She went off to start breakfast, which would be served at the central table in the hall. 'Happy Christmas,' she threw over her shoulder as she disappeared into the kitchen.

The family gathered, Aggie brought in steaming dishes containing eggs and bacon, the dog followed the food and got in everyone's way. Meredith's eyes peered over the rim of her coffee cup and took in the happy scene. It would be all right, wouldn't it? He was on Halliwell Road; he would not walk in and spoil everything. Would he?

Elsie Ramsden was in her element; she had spent her first ever Christmas Eve in the countryside and she was overawed by its beauty. 'You know what, Leena, you never know what you're missing in town, do you? Eeh, I know you've earned it, love, but you are so lucky. What a house, eh? We were cosy in that bedroom, me and Bert. Yes, it's great.'

Leena, struggling with a fifteen-pound turkey, basted the breast then placed it back in the oven. She had prepared the vegetables, and now all she had to do was make sure that everything was ready at the same time. 'Synchronize,' she muttered to herself.

Elsie had rambled off and was exclaiming all over again at everything she saw in every room. 'Leena?' she called.

'What?'

'There's a man stood across from your front gate.'

Leena Martindale's heart skipped a beat. She dashed through to the room where Elsie stood, joined her at the window. It wasn't him. 'He's messing with his motorbike, that's all. Happen he's broke down. Come on, Elsie, let's have a cuppa before the gang arrives.' God, when would they be free of Richard Chandler? Why did she think that every man seen in Chandlers Green was going to be him?

She went back for another look and the man had gone. But Leena remained uneasy and she didn't know why. Had the man outside been sent by Chandler? Was the motorbike chap a spy for Chandler? Oh, it was Christmas Day, time to forget all the mithering. Once the holiday was over, Jean would get him sorted out. She stood for a while, saw no-one, then went back to prepare a pot of tea for her guests.

Outside Claughton Cottage, the man stepped further back into the trees. He had a nice hamper back at the cottage; he would go now and have something to eat. As far as he could make out, everyone and everything was as it should be. Nevertheless, he lingered awhile before returning to his borrowed cottage. It was Christmas Day and he deserved a rest.

A compromise had been achieved. As Richard could not function in Chandlers Green during daylight hours, he and Freda had lunch together, then watched the Queen's broadcast. They drank a toast to the monarch, Freda feeling worried when she saw how little Scotch Richard allowed in his glass.

'I'm driving,' was his explanation.

Freda offered no answer; she had seen him driving in some terrible states, had even been a passenger while he had careered all over the road. Perhaps the friends he was going to visit disapproved of drink. 'Where did you say you were going?'

He hadn't said. 'Friends up Wigan Road,' he replied, 'people who have been helping me with the land disputes.'

There was more to this than land disputes. Freda had read the *Bolton Evening News* article and she, too, had noted the words *He will not be involved*. She suspected that his so-called dispute was of a marital nature, which was why she had started to take slightly better care of her appearance. She and he got along well, so, if he was going to be on the market in the foreseeable future, Freda would be putting in a bid.

'I must go soon,' he said, 'but feel free to stay. At least this television set is working.' For the first time in years, he actually had feelings for another person. Freda mattered. She was virtually his sole contact with the human race and he felt comfortable in her

396

company. Freda was no raving beauty, but she accepted with equanimity her role in his life. She knew her place; she was one of his kind of people.

'I'll miss you,' she said as he pulled on his greatcoat. She passed him his trilby and was thrilled to pieces when he kissed her on the cheek. Blushing beneath layers of panstick whose purpose was to fill the indentations on her cheeks, she giggled like a girl. 'Go on with you, you'll be having my head turned.'

'Happy Christmas, Freda,' he said. 'You stay here for as long as you like.'

She watched him as he drove away, then closed the door and skipped along to her own house next door. Having been invited to stay for as long as she liked, she was determined to make the most of the opportunity. The long-awaited chance having finally arrived, she was glad of her own foresight. Days earlier, she had bought a nice nylon nightie in pink with a matching peignoir. She would use his bathroom, would prepare herself for his return.

Armed with talcum powder, soft towels and her new ensemble, Freda Pilkington returned to Richard's house, poured herself another glass of wine and watched television for a while. She stoked the fire, made sure that there would be plenty of hot water, then enjoyed a leisurely soak in a proper bath.

The man of her dreams would return in a few hours and she would be ready for him, as would his whisky. And she had every intention of keeping the home fire burning until he was back where he belonged.

FIFTEEN

He circled the village and came in from the north, avoiding Claughton Cottage completely. Although it was dark, he feared being seen and, on Christmas Day, few cars were out on the road, so the sound of his noisy engine might have attracted unwanted attention. It was half past four. If Chandler tradition held, albeit in a different location, the main Christmas meal would be served at about five, so he had plenty of time.

When the car was tucked away in a small lay-by, he walked quietly through the place in which he had been born, the village created by his forebears, the very seat of the Chandlers. With the digits of one hand curled round the bottle of life-saving tablets in his pocket, he made deliberately slow progress round the edge of the Chandler estate, pausing occasionally for a much-needed rest. The threatened heart attack, the event his family probably awaited, must not happen tonight.

He arrived at the back of Alf Martindale's house. Through a small gap in the neglected hedge, he could watch two rooms, the kitchen and the dining room. In the former, he saw Peter, knew that it was Peter because the Martindale girl was hanging round his neck like a medal on a chain. Jeremy entered, a silly paper hat on his head; in hot pursuit was the little red-haired housekeeper. She was blowing a whistle from which a tube of paper emerged, a coloured feather on its end. 'And a good time was had by all,' he muttered.

The rest of them were in the dining room, his father dozing in a wheelchair, the rest laughing, drinking, preparing to eat. Anna and Jean were pulling a cracker; Martindale sat at the head of the party, a bright green crêpe-paper hat crammed onto his thick skull. 'Softly,' Richard murmured. The white tablets could do so much and no more; there was a limit to the number he could take in one day. 'Easy, now.' He remembered his horses and how he had talked to them – 'Easy, now,' he would say to a wayward stallion.

It was time to go. And he must take with him this mind-picture, this memory of his family's final betrayal. They were breaking bread with the man he loathed most; one of his sons was about to marry the daughter of that same man. They had plotted and planned, had probably worked for months to make his life as miserable as possible. He had been tidied away into a clinic so that these traitors would have time to plot his demise.

Had his resolve required any underpinning, it would have received it now, in this moment. He was on the outside looking in; where Richard had once sat as master, Alf Martindale luxuriated in happy company, in a warm house, surrounded by good food. This very house had been built three or four generations ago, a manager's home produced by Chandler money for the Chandler business. 'Damn and blast them all.'

He kept to the edge of the field and backtracked in the direction from which he had approached. There were ruts in the land, dips and rises hardened by frost, so his progress had to be slow. With no torch to light his path, he was forced quite literally to follow his nose across land on which he had played as a child, land of which he had been master. And he must remain calm.

They had finished the main course and Alf had called for half-time. 'They have it at Burnden Park, forty-five minutes each way and a rest between,' he said, moving his belt buckle by an inch or two to allow for expansion. 'So we should have a break and all. But let's raise a glass to my wife and to Elsie, because that was a marvellous turkey.'

They toasted Elsie and Leena, Meredith using the orange juice to which she had managed to confine herself. It had, indeed, been a lovely dinner and the company was excellent. It was all so cheerful. Peter had been right – Marie's family did know how to express affection, how to have fun. It was nothing to do with money and privilege – it was tied up in respect and in making room for each other. Colin, Marie's brother, kept staring at Meredith and Meredith did not object to his attentions . . .

Bert volunteered to be the half-time entertainment, drawing from his pocket a harmonica. 'I've fetched me mouth organ,' he said, 'as well as me wife. So, she will lead the singing, because she's a walking mouth organ, is my Elsie. Any requests?'

400

Aggie wanted 'Teenager in Love', Meredith shouted for 'Maybe Tomorrow', Peter asked for 'Apache'.

Bert nodded gravely, as if considering the requests. 'All right,' he announced, 'you can sing any words you like as long as you can make them fit "The White Cliffs of Dover".' He launched into a medley of war songs.

Meredith and Marie noticed a tear on Elsie's cheek when she sang 'It's a Long Way to Tipperary'. She was thinking of Brian, her lad who had never returned from the Battle of Britain.

Groans and moans came from every throat when Bert's *pièce de résistance* turned out to be 'Knees Up Mother Brown'. Marie said she was so full that she couldn't lift her feet off the floor, Jeremy declared that he had no knees because Aggie was sitting on them and she was a dead weight, Polly announced that she wasn't showing her knickers for anyone, let alone Mother Brown, whom she had never met.

A great cheer went up when Leena brought in the flaming pudding. This was followed by laughter when Alf appeared at her side with a small fire extinguisher, its nozzle poised over the dish. Peter whispered to his sister, 'You can have pudding – the fire burns the alcohol off.' Meredith squeezed his arm and was grateful for his love. But she stuck to cheese and biscuits, as there was brandy butter and the rule could never be relaxed.

Coffee and after-dinner mints completed the feast, then everyone adjourned to the front living room where the tree and an open fire were the only sources of light. There followed a quiet time while the company digested food and breathed in the

401

contented atmosphere, some coming dangerously close to sleep as the minutes ticked by.

They were shocked into full awareness when someone hammered at the door. Leena rubbed her eyes. 'Who the heck can that be at this time on a Christmas night? Is anybody expecting anybody?'

Nobody was. Alf went to admit the caller and was followed into the room by a tall man in an old army greatcoat and with a leather hood – the sort worn by motorbike riders – pulled over his ears. He removed the latter item and apologized for the disturbance. 'Mrs Chandler?'

Jean recognized him, yet could not quite place him. 'Yes?'

'Sorry to disturb your dinner, madam, but I have been keeping an eye on a certain party. That party is on his way to the grange now. I followed him up from Halliwell Road about an hour ago. Normally, I would have reported back to the office, but with it being Christmas, the boss won't be there. I thought it was best to come here. Sorry,' he said again. 'But I read in the *Evening News* that you were all spending the day here.'

Aggie leapt up. 'My dog!' she screamed. 'My dog's up there.' She pushed past the man and went to fetch her coat, Jeremy hot on her heels.

Bert, Alf and the stranger walked to the door, 'Stay here,' Alf said to Peter and Colin. 'You look after the ladies while we find out what's going on.' He paused, stared at Polly. 'Are you all right?'

Polly looked as if she had seen a ghost. Her mouth opened and closed, but no sound emerged.

Leena rushed to her side. 'Nay, love, don't be

402

frightened of him – my Alf's sorted him out before now and he'll do it again.'

Polly broke free of Leena's restraining arm. 'Derek? Is that you?'

'It is,' replied the newcomer. 'And I would like to thank the young man and woman who brought Christmas to my door.' The young man and woman in question were halfway out of the house, as were Alf and Bert. 'I must go, love,' he told his wife, a half-smile decorating his homely face. 'And I can't get the police, can I? Because at the end of the day, the grange is his home.' He disappreared as suddenly as he had arrived.

Polly sank back into her chair.

'I knew him right away,' declared Anna. 'He was a woodsman for quite a few years. Then a frying pan entered the equation, didn't it, Polly?'

Polly nodded. 'He might get hurt.'

'Richard would not know where to find a frying pan,' answered Anna. 'Meredith? Meredith, are you weeping?'

Jean ran to her daughter's side. 'Sweetheart, don't cry. Whatever he intends, he will be stopped.'

Polly, too, had begun to sob, but for a different reason. Seeing him again and remembering how she had treated him made her ashamed. Derek was a nice man. She should have been content with a nice man.

Elsie did what Elsie always did in such situations – she went off to make copious amounts of strong tea. Then they sat and waited for the men to come home. 'Just like the war,' Elsie said mournfully after her second cup. 'We waited then and all.'

403

Henry snorted and opened his eyes. 'Did I miss anything?' he asked.

'He could sleep through an invasion,' whispered Anna. 'Now, come on, everyone – do buck up. We have to hope for the best.'

'What?' asked Henry.

'Nothing,' she replied. Her brother had suffered enough.

Colin moved across the room and sat on the arm of Meredith's chair. 'You'll be all right,' he said. 'My dad will straighten things out.'

She dried her tears. Like his father, this young man had strength. She smiled at him, and the older women looked at each other. Even now, in the darkest of hours, the matchmaking went on.

'Any more tea in that pot?' Henry asked.

The women got on with the business of clearing and washing dishes, Henry drank tea, was told that the men had gone to walk off their dinner and that Aggie had accompanied them. Minutes dragged, became an hour, and still they lingered quietly in the firelight while Christmas tree lights flickered.

When dishes were cleared and cleaned, the real business of waiting began. Meredith leaned against the arm of Marie's brother and took solace from his nearness. Christmas was over; Father had ended it.

Every single downstairs window was closed and locked.

He placed the two cans of paraffin on the pathway and, using the hammer he had taken from a stable, smashed a pane. It was easy to release the catch and raise the sash. Then he placed his booty on a small table to the left of the window and climbed inside. A

404

dog barked, the sound coming from the kitchen, but the grange was beyond earshot of the village, so the noise was no cause for concern. 'Breaking into my own bloody house,' he mumbled softly. The frantic barking was getting on his nerves. Steeling himself, he picked up the containers of paraffin and walked towards the hall.

The lights were out, but he could see the tree twinkling in a corner. His eyes, already adjusted to the blackness outside, marked items of familiar furniture as he made his way across the space towards the stairs. He knew every creak of every board, breathed in the scents of a home that had been his since birth; it remained his and no-one could deny the fact. This was his to own, his to enjoy, his to destroy. With a paraffin container in each hand, he made his way to the fragrant one's room. In her little jewel case sat several thousand pounds' worth of items, some handed down and carefully reset after centuries of wear. They were his heritage and he would reclaim them.

Larger items he would leave outside on the steps to be carried to the van when he had finished here. He must be careful not to take too much, as he was not capable of carting a great deal of weight to the place where he had been forced to park his van. There were few regrets when he thought about the extent of his proposed actions. Chandlers Green was no longer in the hands of the family; all that would be lost was this meaningless pile of sandstone and even that was well insured.

Jean's room was at the back of the house; the view from her windows was countryside only, so he switched on the light before drawing tight the curtains. She had left her knitting on an ottoman and he dragged the work from its needle, tearing away until the whole item was destroyed. As he ripped at it, he envisaged her face bloody and battered, eyes gouged from their sockets. 'Easy, easy,' he ordered softly. The dog continued to bark.

He opened the jewellery case, saw diamonds, pearls, emeralds, opals. Swiftly, he crammed the lot into his pockets; he was not stealing, because everything here was the property of the Chandler family, of which line he remained the moral heir. Henry might have deleted him from his will, but Richard had every right to line his own pockets. The engagement ring was missing – she was probably sporting that at Martindale's table. Let her keep it; let her enjoy that one piece, because it would remind her of the man she had betrayed.

The girl had some pieces. He made his way to Meredith's room and emptied her jewellery case, too. Paintings and ornaments he would forget. 'Let them all burn,' he said as he sprinkled paraffin all over the landing. Jewellery he could sell in Manchester; larger items might be more difficult to liquidate, so he simply dismissed them from his agenda.

Dripping the rest of the paraffin onto the stairs, he returned to the hallway, tossing the empty cans onto the floor. From a trouser pocket, he took a box of matches and was preparing to scrape one of its members along the sandpaper edge when the front door was thrown open.

'Chandler!' yelled Alfred Martindale.

Others followed him in; the little red-haired girl flew across to the kitchen. 'Hero!' she screamed.

Derek Fishwick and Bert Ramsden stood one at each side of the rag-and-bone man. The word 'hero' seemed to echo around the walls, bouncing back to plague Richard Chandler's senses. Yes, here came the hero, Victoria Cross and Bar.

Alf inhaled the fumes and placed his arms across his companions' chests, urging them nearer to the door. 'Stay where you are.' These words were squeezed from a corner of tightened lips. He opened his mouth fully. 'Strike that match, Chandler, and I shall make bloody sure you burn with the house. You will not get out alive.'

Richard laughed mirthlessly. 'Neither will you. There's no court martial here, Martindale. I'll take you with me if it's the last thing I do.'

Jeremy stepped in. 'Take me, too,' he said. Then he wandered casually across the hall and switched on the central chandelier. He folded his arms. 'Get on with it, then – we have a party waiting for us. Standing where you are, you'll be the first to catch fire. A fitting end for a man whose fortune came from naked flame, don't you think?'

The man at the bottom of the stairs blinked. This was becoming complicated. Alf Martindale was a great one for complications.

Alf walked towards his enemy. He was truly terrified, but he knew what had to be done.

The match rasped against the box, but did not catch light. Alf took one massive swing and knocked Chandler to the floor. 'If it hadn't been for Fenner, you would have ruined me, you miserable, heartless bastard.' He kicked away the match-box and Derek Fishwick retrieved it. 'Go away,' snapped Alf at Polly's estranged husband. 'This

407

bugger is mine.' The woodsman-turned-detective returned to his place by the open door.

Richard struggled to his feet and reached blindly for a weapon. His hands made contact with a vase on the ornate hall stand and he threw this item into Alf's face. Strength returned to him – he was young again – proud again – and he launched himself at Alf.

Alf floored him once more. 'I'm hard-faced, you see, Chandler. I'm not officer material, so your pretty vase just bounced off. There's a lot to be said for time spent out in all weathers.' He could taste blood in his mouth, but he would not let this fellow see the pain.

'Leave them,' urged Bert when Derek tried to step forward again. 'This is personal. Let Alf get his tenpenn'orth out of him. He's waited long enough for the chance.'

Alf, who was plainly getting the better of Chandler, stood back while the man ran upstairs. 'Run, run,' he yelled. 'Go on, you lily-livered freak – go while you can.' He turned to Jeremy. 'Get the police – now. We've got him for attempted arson and possible insurance fraud, at least.'

Jeremy picked up the phone. Before dialling the number, he called to his father, 'One last chance. Get out of here now and we shall forget that this ever happened.'

Alf was ready to forget nothing. His anger burned bright as he launched himself up the stairs. 'No more chances,' he shouted. He wasn't having his Leena hiding and spending all her time with other people just to be safe; he could not bear the thought of Jean Chandler and her family waiting for this man to come back. He had come back. He was here now and he had soaked the stairs in paraffin. 'Get the fire

408

brigade, too,' he shouted to Jeremy. 'This place will have to be made safe before you and your mother can come back.'

Jeremy dialled. He knew that Alf was right, that allowing Father to leave now would just postpone the inevitable. It had to be done, had to be finished here and now.

When the two men were struggling at the top of the stairs, the kitchen door opened and Hero dashed out, Aggie hot on his heels. 'Stop him,' she screamed. 'I don't want him hurt.'

But it was too late. One of Hero's ancestors came to the fore and the mongrel was suddenly 100 per cent greyhound. In less than two seconds, he was at the top of the stairs. Alf took a swing at Chandler, missed, saved himself from falling down the stairs, and, in that split second, Hero leapt forward.

The rest happened in slow motion. As Richard moved a step to push Alf downstairs, the dog passed between the two opponents, his thin body making harsh contact with Richard Chandler's legs. The man swayed and hovered for what seemed like minutes, his body apparently suspended over the drop. He lurched, turned and tumbled, his body bouncing all the way down to the bottom. Once there, his head made sharp contact with a solid knob on the huge Victorian hallstand, then he rolled, twitched, and foamed slightly at the mouth before becoming completely still.

Alf, suddenly breathless, sank onto the top step. He could hear Jeremy speaking to the operator, heard Bert's voice saying, 'Looks like yon man's a goner.'

Once the call was completed, Jeremy slid down the

wall and sat on the hall floor, his face devoid of all colour. Aggie ran to him, knelt beside him and drew him into her arms. She had never seen a dead body before, and she turned her back on the scene. Chandler's eyes were wide open and bulging. The clock struck, but she could not count the time.

'Is he really dead?' Jeremy asked.

'Yes, I think so, love.'

'He banged his head on the knob of the hallstand.' Jeremy closed his eyes. 'Mother pretended that Nanny Foster had died in that way. Fate is strange.' He swallowed a sob. It was hard to know how to feel. The dead man was his father; the dead man had been hated by all who knew him. Guilt and shock combined to make Jeremy too weak to stand.

Derek Fishwick bent over the body, felt for a pulse, proclaimed life extinct, then dragged the dog back into the kitchen.

'It was my fault,' Aggie said softly. 'I opened the kitchen door and Hero just shot out like a bullet from a gun. I should have kept him in there. He thought they were play-fighting and he joined in – he does that with me and Jeremy.'

'It was an accident,' said Bert, 'an accident that was waiting to happen.' He gazed upstairs at his best pal. 'Alf?'

'What?'

'Are you all right?'

'No. No, I'm not. Just leave me where I am till they come.' How often lately had he prayed for Chandler to be dead? And how many men had he, Alfred Martindale, killed in the course of a dozen battles? This was different, because this had been personal.

Police and firemen arrived. The latter party set

410

about the business of distributing foam to make the carpets safe.

The group was split, each member taken away and questioned separately; a female constable went off with the sergeant to visit Jean at Claughton Cottage. It was midnight before the torture ended.

The body of Richard Chandler was removed from the grange to be taken for post-mortem. Police seemed satisfied with the explanations of witnesses. They retrieved from Richard's pockets a large amount of jewellery, which they recorded, bagged and took to one of their cars.

The same cars carried Alf, Bert, Jeremy and Aggie back to the cottage, while Derek made his own way to the little house in the woods. He went inside, made a fire, drank a bottle of beer. It was over. The man who had destroyed so many lives no longer existed. And his Polly was all right.

It was almost the middle of January before the funeral could be arranged. Richard Chandler was laid to rest in the family vault, a chamber created beneath the church built by his ancestors. According to the post-mortem report, he had been dead seconds before reaching the hall stand, had suffered a coronary occlusion during his fall down the stairs. All the twitching and foaming had been produced by the relaxing muscles of a corpse.

A large party left the church after the service, each of its members there to support Jean and her children. Outside, in the rays of a weak sun, stood a little woman with dyed blond hair peeping out beneath the brim of a borrowed black hat. Jean went to her. 'Did you look after my husband during his last few weeks?'

411

Freda Pilkington nodded. 'He were good to me.'

'I am pleased,' answered Jean. 'Take your flowers in – he is in the crypt below. Thank you for coming.'

Freda entered the church and descended to the underground chamber. The vicar was there, as were the undertakers. She placed her flowers with the rest and stood back, wondered how to pray. A lapsed Catholic, she muddled her way through a half-forgotten Hail Mary, then left Richard to his Maker. How long had she sat in that pink nylon nightie? 'Stay as long as you like,' he had said. And he had never come home.

This one true mourner left the churchyard and watched as his family and friends walked away. It had been in all the newspapers, including the nationals. Richard had gone on Christmas Day to burn down his own house, had stolen his estranged wife's jewels, had fallen to his death down the stairs. With him had disappeared Freda's chance of happiness and she missed him sorely. Whatever he had been to his family, he had treated her well.

Polly Fishwick clung to the arm of her newly discovered husband. He had never forgotten her, had never stopped loving her, had returned to try to win her all over again. They had buried the bent frying pan together; now, they had buried her former lover. Aware now of how fragile life was, Polly was determined to hang on to it and on to Derek for as long as she could.

Back at the grange over tea and sandwiches, the young ones sat together in a quiet group. It had been hard for all the Chandlers; Richard had been a bad man, but he had also been their father. Yet there was strength in the group. Colin had added his weight to the equation and these six had stuck together through every spare moment of every day during recent weeks.

Peter bit into a salmon and cucumber sandwich. 'Hero was the hero,' he remarked thoughtfully. 'Father had only weeks to live. According to the coroner, he must have been in great discomfort. Hero probably put him out of his misery.'

Everyone made the right noises, each showing agreement with the speaker.

The dog in question arrived on cue, tail wagging hopefully when he saw the food. Peter stroked the bony head. 'Remember Mr Baines?'

The dog whined.

'He saved your life and I assisted,' Peter informed the animal. He stood up. 'I am going for a short walk,' he told Marie. 'I won't be long.'

Outside, Peter Chandler wandered across the lawn, hands deep in pockets, mind deep in contemplation. Turning, he looked on the façade of a house that had remained standing in spite of his father's plans. It was a thing of beauty, a testament to builders long dead, to craftsmen of many trades who had laboured hard in days long before the invention of cement mixers and electrically powered tools. 'My home,' he said aloud. 'Our home.'

Soon, he would move to Bolton with Marie, would start his journey towards a new life and a career as a vet. But Chandlers Grange would remain his and Jeremy's and Meredith's. It was the very core of a family that would rise again phoenix-like from ashes that had remained metaphorical – no thanks to Father.

All three young Chandlers were struggling with

413

the ambivalence of thought and feeling. Guilty, they remembered wishing their father dead; angry, they recalled how he had treated their poor mother. Achieving some sort of equilibrium was going to take time and affection and loyalty. Jean, bruised and battered, would be comforted by her friends, people who had replaced Sally, that dear companion whose life had been terminated by Richard. Jeremy had Aggie, Meredith leaned on Colin, Peter depended on his Marie.

In the end, it all came down to love and to chance, because the former arrived by means of the latter, a meeting in an hotel room, an idea spawned by Meredith, chance, love and faith. And the cement was Anna, the one whose tenacity had encouraged the family to go forward into New Chandlers.

Peter sat on a stone seat, his eyes widening to take in the landscape that was his own. They would survive, all of them, because they had to.

A scuttering of feet on gravel announced the approach of Hero. Peter turned to greet the animal who had adopted Aggie, who had captured the heart of Don Baines and his makeshift assistant weeks ago. This was the dog whose actions had terminated the life of Richard Chandler.

In his mind's eye, Peter saw the vet's kindly face, heard his voice as he spoke about the innate intelligence of dogs. They owned an extra sense, or so it seemed; they knew when to persevere and when to give up. Hero had persevered, had lived, had acted in accordance with his own wisdom.

Peter stood up and turned to walk back to the house, Hero at his heels. As he climbed the steps, he heard Don Baines speaking after the operation was over, listened all over again to the words of his mentor. And in that moment, he accepted his father's fate.

Richard Chandler had been killed by an act of dog. And that fact was strangely easy to accept.

THE END

A SELECTED LIST OF FINE NOVELS AVAILABLE FROM CORGI BOOKS

THE PRICES SHOWN BELOW WERE CORRECT AT THE TIME OF GOING TO PRESS. HOWEVER TRANSWORLD PUBLISHERS RESERVE THE RIGHT TO SHOW NEW RETAIL PRICES ON COVERS WHICH MAY DIFFER FROM THOSE PREVIOUSLY ADVERTISED IN THE TEXT OR ELSEWHERE.